The Moon & His Tides

USA TODAY & WSJ BESTSELLING AUTHOR

giana darling

The Impossible Universe Series. Book One.

Published by Giana Darling
Edited by Erica Russikoff of Erica Edits & Jenny Sims of Editing4indies
Proofed by Sarah Plocher and Sarah Kleehammer @booksbatsandbrushes
Cover by Cat at TRC Designs
Formatted by Cat at TRC Designs

"The sun watches what I do, but the moon knows all my secrets."

— J.M. Wonderland

To the men who feel too much and were never taught the unspoken vocabulary of their hearts. And to the women who give them reason to learn that language.

Playlist

"Moonlight" — Grace VanderWaal
"Secret" — The Pierces
"Such A Simple Thing" — Ray LaMontagne
"Cello Suite No.1 in G Major" — Johann Sebastian Bach, Yo-Yo Ma
"Turn Me On" — Norah Jones
"You Make Me Feel So Young" — Frank Sinatra
"La Lune" — Billie Marten
"I'd Have To Think About It" — Leith Ross
"Come Away with Me" — Norah Jones
"Harvest Moon" — Neil Young
"Sunset Lover" — Petit Biscuit
"Don't Matter To Me" — Drake, Michael Jackson
"That Moon Song" — Gregory Alan Isakov
"Prelude in D Minor" — Johann Sebastian Bach
"Thinking 'Bout Love" — Wild Rivers
"My Universe" — Coldplay, BTS
"Movement" — Hozier
"Paradise" — Coldplay
"Skinny Love" — Bon Iver
"Moonlight Sonata" — Beethoven
"Sometimes Things Just Fall Apart" — Rence
"Nocturne No.1" — Chopin

Chapter One

Sebastian

She was the most beautiful woman I'd ever seen.

I knew a lot of beautiful women. Not only because I was Italian and my country was a great producer of three things—carbs, cars, and gorgeous people—but because my mother and three sisters were, biased or not, the most beautiful women I'd ever met.

Until I saw her.

I shouldn't have been able to discern the curve of her delicate features in the murky light that illuminated the car from the passing streetlights, but she sat behind my seat, wearing a shade of white that picked up the light like a beacon and made her shine like an angel.

She looked like one.

My hands clenched reflexively on the steering wheel as I thought about peeling her slim form out of the fancy silk dress she wore. I knew she'd be slight and pale all over, pure like freshly fallen snow.

I wanted to mark all that fine, classy skin with my workingman's hands, debase those delicate ears with foreign-accented filth as I described to her all the ways I was going to make her come for me.

She was beautiful, but she looked like a woman who hadn't had a good orgasm in a long time. Of course, some women showed the promise of beauty, finely shaped and gorgeous like an ornate vase but filled, alas, with nothing.

I didn't believe this beauty was that.

No.

Not when her wide pale eyes, fixed on a mark outside the moving vehicle, slid just a hair toward me whenever she thought I was preoccupied with the road. When her breath puffed softly from her moistened, parted lips, and her small hands—hands I wanted to *fill up*—curled and uncurled restlessly in her lap.

And that was only the first time I drove her.

The second was midday two days later, and the light was bright but grey under London's habitual low ceiling of clouds. My palms sweat inside the supple leather driving gloves the luxury car service provided all their drivers with, but I affected a casual pose of legs braced and arms crossed loosely while I waited for her outside Harrods.

She was wearing white again, this time a neat little suit under an undone coat that would have been demure to the point of dowdiness but for the fact that she paired the low-cut blazer with a sheer white camisole as thin and clingy as condensation against the slight swell of her breasts.

My mouth went dry, but I managed to take the heavy shopping bags from her and open the door to the Rolls Royce smoothly.

"Good afternoon, Mrs. Meyers," I'd said because it was the policy at Luxury Regent Car Service to do so.

I had a dossier provided by the company with all of her details.

Savannah Meyers, wife of Adam Meyers, the very famous British actor. Preference for classical music, heated interiors even on warm days, bottled Evian, and unsalted Marcona almonds.

So she was married.

It didn't matter. She was so out of my league it felt blasphemous just standing too close to her. Even then, I wasn't the sort of man who thought marriage was sacrosanct, at least not to most.

My father had cheated on my mother every day of my life. If not with other women, certainly with booze, cards, and shady backroom deals with Made Men.

But Savannah was married to Adam Meyers, a man I'd admired from afar since I was fourteen and fluent enough in English to watch every movie I could get my hands on. He was my idol, and his *wife*, his gorgeous wife, was in a car with me. There was something disturbingly sexy about that, about knowing his hands had been on her. I imagined I could see the marks they'd made on her skin like a highlighter, emphasizing all her feminine curves to lewd heights.

I got a whiff of her scent when I opened the door for her. Lilac or something sweetly floral, something clean and classy that probably cost hundreds of pounds because it came in an upmarket bottle.

My dick hardened.

I watched her as I pulled out into the street and began the journey to her home in Chelsea. Her eyes were once again fixed out the window, but her lips, painted a deep raspberry that I wanted to trace with my tongue, were tipped up at the corners in an enigmatic smile. One hand played at the low edge of her flimsy camisole, thumbing the lace border between her fingers.

A growl worked low in my throat as I thought about taking that lace in my teeth and tearing it in two. My animal brain wondered what kind of sound she would make as I exposed her, and it settled on a soft gasp, the noise of a damsel in distress.

Only I wouldn't save her.

I'd ruin her.

Right there in the back of the Rolls, her berry lipstick smeared across the window as I held her face against the glass and worked myself into her tight pussy, her cum dripping onto the smooth leather seats as she convulsed around my driving cock.

The low edge of my growl worked its way up my throat before I could contain it. I flashed my gaze up to the rearview mirror and caught her wide, almost childlike blue eyes. I felt that gasp like a hot grip around my cock.

She tore her eyes away as a flush the same color as her lipstick warmed her pale skin.

I'd never been so turned on in my life, yet I'd seen next to nothing of her sweet body and knew even less about her life.

Che cavolo! She didn't even know my name.

Someone honked at me when I waited too long at a green light, and I cursed under my breath.

If I wasn't careful, I'd run us off the road, and I needed this shitty job like Catholics needed the Pope. It was my lifeline. If I lost it, I couldn't afford the rent in the one-bedroom apartment I leased with four other flatmates in Shoreditch. I wouldn't be able to pursue the acting gig that had brought me to London in the first place, a leading role in a theatre company on the outskirts of the city.

If nothing came of it after the play's run ended before Christmas, I'd have to slink back to Naples, back to my mother and sisters without the money to support them or the out to take them away from our stinking homeland. I knew exactly what would happen if I went back. I'd be railroaded into joining Tossi and his crew in our local Camorra affiliate.

I'd spent my entire youth working to stay away from the Mafia, and there was no way in hell, even for a woman as beautiful as Savannah Meyers, that I was going there now.

Despite my conviction, when she spoke, ten minutes into what would be a thirty-minute drive thanks to the late Monday afternoon traffic clogging London proper, I almost crashed the car.

"I'd prefer classical, Chopin or Bach if you have it."

I didn't hear a word.

My mind locked on the crystalline lilt of her words, the way they softly clicked together like chimes in a breeze.

"Excuse me?"

She asked again while I just stared at her like a *stronzo*.

"Sorry," I said, flashing her a wide grin because even though I was probably younger than her and definitely not good enough for her, I couldn't help but flirt. It was instinctual. "Your speaking voice is *dolcissima*."

A frown folded the skin between her eyebrows. It made her look both haughty and adorable. I bit back my grin.

"You're Italian," she guessed.

"*Parla italiano?*"

There was humor in her voice but not in her carefully schooled face as she said, "No, not at all. I'm afraid English is it for me."

I shrugged. "Lucky you. It's a difficult one to learn."

She shifted just slightly forward, but it thrilled me like it had when I was a boy and I'd caught a fish on the line, reeling it in, playing it slow but steady toward me.

"You seem to speak it very well," she said, and I realized belatedly that she was American.

I grinned at her in the rearview as I flipped on the indicator and turned left into Chelsea. "My father was Irish."

She raised her eyebrows, her mouth a perfect deep pink circle of shock. "Interesting combination. Hot-blooded, I suppose?"

I winked at her. "Passionate is my definition of choice."

She smiled slightly. "I'm sure. And what brings a passionate Irish-Italian to dreary, proper London?"

"The women," I said with a smirk. "I didn't have enough money to make it to America, so I figured England was the next best thing."

Her laugh was delighted. "My accent betrays me."

I shrugged. "It's charming."

"Not more so than you," she returned, those big blue eyes sparkling with humor.

"Ah, such a compliment from *la duchessa*, I will treasure it," I teased her.

"Oh please, do stop speaking in Italian before I disgrace myself by going from 'duchess' to 'pile of mush on the floor.'"

"I can't say I haven't turned a woman into a 'pile of mush on the floor' before, but usually, it involved more than just my voice," I teased.

We smiled at each other in the rearview mirror for a moment before she seemed to remember herself, and I returned my eyes to the road. I could feel the air shift as she closed herself off again, tugging the mantle of class and poise around her shoulders like a mink coat.

"Classical," Mrs. Meyers reminded me softly, primly. "Bach, if you have it."

She didn't speak or look at me for the rest of the trip.

But it didn't matter; the damage was done. I was hooked on her brand of class, on the idea of stealing that wealth for myself and dirtying it up.

I went home that night and fisted my cock to an intense orgasm, picturing all the ways I'd do just that.

Chapter Two

Sebastian

"I can manage it," my sister repeated, a steel edge of determination in her tone. "You focus on what you need to do."

I drummed my fingers on the steering wheel as I sat outside The Ivy restaurant waiting to pick up Mrs. Savannah Meyers the following Friday afternoon. I'd driven her six times in the past week, but the rapport we'd established hadn't been revisited. If anything, she was even more careful around me, a portrait drawn against the back seat in oils and old-school ideals.

"You don't *have* to manage it, Cosi," I said between my clenched teeth. "You think if we move to England, we completely abandon our values? I'm the man of this family. It kills me that you're the one supporting la *mia famiglia,* but I understand that you need to do it for our mother and sisters. That doesn't mean I'm not pitching in with what I can to lessen your responsibility, *capisci*?"

"Sebastian, money is not an issue. Please, save what you make to get an apartment without four other males sharing the one bedroom," Cosima insisted.

I didn't want to dwell too long on how it was exactly that my twin sister was making enough money to support a family of five, including tuition at one of the top art schools in the world for our older sister, Giselle. I didn't want to think about it because those dark, troubling thoughts that carved me up like a butcher with a cleaver were reserved for the dark hours I lay sleepless in bed, when the good little Catholic boy in me reared its naive head to worry about our eternal souls.

It disgusted my pride, as both a man and an Italian, two separate but entirely too arrogant sides of me, to rely on my sister to support my family. However, I was also disgustingly grateful because I had a plan. I just needed time.

I was a good actor. It could be argued that there were innumerable good actors out there.

I was also, it had been said by many, *many* women, unaccountably attractive. Of course, it was easy to see that there were many, *many* attractive people in this world, and it wouldn't be wrong to assume that many of them wanted to be actors.

So what set me aside from the rest?

Well, I doubted very few people had grown up using their acting skills to survive as I had. When lying became a matter of violence or absolution, food or starvation, their safety or ruination. Everything in my life thus far had boiled down to being a good actor. If the Mafia came calling for my father, I had to be prepared to spin a good tale, convince them that he *was* coming back from wherever he'd disappeared to, and that *of course,* he would have their money for them on his return.

The safety of my mother and three sisters depended on me acting as the man of the house from the time I was eight years old. Now, eleven years later, I was still honing my craft, but even though the life-and-death circumstances had passed, I practiced with the same intensity. My tool of survival had become my passion.

I'd also been writing stories since I was a boy, stealing papers and articles from my father's desk so I could pen my own words on the back using one of Giselle's pencil crayons. They weren't grand tales of dragons and princesses because I was a poor boy in the Italian countryside; we didn't have the scope or sensibilities to waste time on other worlds. No, my stories were about desolation and small joys, the intricacies of life made so real on the page that I imagined I could feel the grit between my fingers when I held them. I reached out to the stack of papers that comprised the screenplay I had been working on for the past three years and fingered a page just to feel the texture of it.

Cosima knew these stories, these talents, and she called them "my gifts." She spoke about them with the same reverence as a disciple of her religion, and I knew in a way that twisted my insides that she would do anything to ensure my gifts were brought into the light.

"I'll send Mama and Elena what I can," I finally responded. "I don't care if you have it covered, Cosi, at least they'll know I'm thinking of them and working for them too. They can use the pitiful cash to buy better groceries or save it toward Elena's computer fund."

There was a silence and then softly, "*Va bene, fratello mio.*"

I closed my eyes and pounded my head back against the seat rest as pain radiated around my sensitive heart. "One day soon, *bella mia Cosima*, we will be together again."

"One day sooner, not later," she stated authoritatively, and I again wondered what she was doing in order to secure that promise. "*Insieme.*"

"Together," I repeated in English, feeling the ache where my twin sister, my best friend, should be in my life like the loss of a limb.

The opening of the back door jarred me out of my thoughts, and I raised shocked eyes to the rearview to see Savannah Meyers sliding inside.

"*Cazzo*," I cursed, knocking my script off the console between the front and back seats in my haste to disconnect my call with Cosima and apologize to Savannah for my lack of professionalism.

"Sebastian?" Cosima called before I could cut the call.

"What a lovely name," Savannah said, her eyes creased at the corners with suppressed mirth even as the rest of her face lay perfectly still.

"You'll be hard-pressed to find an Italian name that isn't," I told her with a wry grin as I quickly picked up the papers that had spilled into the back. I tried to distract her with my charm so she wouldn't look at them too closely and wonder. "You'll also be hard-pressed to find an Italian who wouldn't curse like a sailor after being startled the way you did me just now."

Her lips pressed, but there was amusement there too. "Is that your way of apologizing for cursing in front of a lady?"

My grin turned wicked. "I believe actions speak louder than words… If we weren't the definition of lady and the tramp, I would apologize in my usual way."

Her pressed lips curled. "Let me guess, with a kiss?"

I winked at her. "Exactly, though not on the mouth. Surest way to get any woman outside of the family to forgive you. Trust me, nothing says 'I'm sorry' like an orgasm."

This time, she let herself laugh and the wind chime sound peeled beautifully between us.

"You are outrageous," she said with a shake of her head.

The movement dislodged a curl, tumbling it across the smooth peaches and cream of her cheek. My fingers twitched to tuck it behind her diamond-studded ear, and the papers I had successfully collected tumbled back to the floorboards.

I quickly ducked back over the console, twisting awkwardly to pick them up, but Savannah was already there with a sheaf of papers in her hand. I watched her eyes snap to the words like the collision of two magnets.

"You write," she whispered, holding the discarded papers in her hand reverently.

"Uh," I swallowed harshly. "Yes."

"Screenplays?"

"Mostly."

"Hmm," she hummed lightly, then shifted the papers she held into her lap and held out her manicured hand to me. "Give me the rest."

I barked out a surprised laugh. "*Scusi*?"

"Pardon," she corrected me primly. "Now, Sebastian, hand me the rest."

"It's private." I tried even though I recognized the determination in her eyes because I'd grown up with women, and I learned their capacity for stubbornness from an early age.

Her response was a sharply arched brow.

I sighed, feeling all few of my eighteen years as I petulantly passed her the screenplay I'd been working on for the past twelve months.

"Eyes on the road," she reminded me as she settled back against the creamy upholstery with her eyes already trained on my words.

It was a seventeen-minute drive to Savannah's beige brick and white paneled townhome on Halsey, but it felt infinitely longer with my story in her small hands, her big eyes eating up every word with an avidness that disturbed me.

I tried at one point to intervene after she let out a small gasp, but she merely held up a hand when I spoke her name, silencing me immediately.

My gloved fingers thrummed mutely against the wheel as I speculated what classy wife-of-the-amazing-Adam-Meyers Savannah might think of my story. It was about a poor immigrant boy in 1920s New York who ends up selling his soul to a variety of shady characters in order to pay for the safe arrival and setup of his big Italian family.

It was allegorical, obviously, but set in a period of time I'd always found awesomely mysterious, shadowed by backroom deals, Mafia corruption, and scandals that never saw the light of day, thanks to a few well-greased palms.

Corruption, greed, and a ruthless need to survive.

These were the things I knew.

These were things I had been taught growing up poor in Napoli, desperate to free my family from the shackles we'd been born into.

So I knew somewhere deep in the marrow of my bones that my story was good because it was *true*. It was so gritty I imagined I could feel the sand between my fingers as I touched the pages, smell the acrid scent of urine in the dank, muddy alleys of New York City before asphalt was poured. I loved it. It was good. In fact, I was banking my future *and* my family's on it being fucking brilliant.

Yet my heart barely beat in the tight grip of fear that had hold of it at the thought that this woman—my sort of boss and total stranger—might not like it.

When I pulled up to the tall, gold-tipped iron gates of her townhome, I had to clear my throat twice before I could say, "Mrs. Meyers, we're here."

She ignored me.

I swallowed past the gargantuan lump in my throat and tried again. "Mrs. Meyers?"

Nothing.

"Savannah," I finally barked, my nerves breaking under the stress of her silence.

Immediately, her head jerked up, her lips parted and eyes widened as though I had caught her doing something she shouldn't.

"We're here," I repeated.

"Oh," she said, surprised. "Do you have someone else to drive after me?"

"No…"

She nodded curtly. "Excellent. Then, as I am assuming you won't want to part with these papers, you can either sit quietly or go for a walk while I continue reading."

Before I could formulate a response, she pushed the button for the partition to rise between us and simultaneously sat back comfortably in her seat.

I was dismissed.

Not knowing whether to curse at her or do as she said, I chose the latter because it meant keeping my job. But I muttered filthy, derisive Italian words about the rich taking liberties as I shoved out of the Rolls and made my way away from the Thames toward Hyde Park.

I tried to let the clean, classic lines of Chelsea's mostly Georgian architecture distract me from the strange power the woman in the Rolls held over me. Mostly, it worked. I loved the meticulousness of the neighborhood; how clean the streets were right down to the flowers trimmed perfectly in their window boxes and the acute angles of the hedgerows. It was the antithesis of Naples with its sloping buildings, cracked and painted sun-dried colors that hurt the eyes under the yellow afternoon glare. The people too, wrapped up neatly like presents in expensive scarves and layers of thickly knit weaves. They nodded or smiled demurely at me as I passed, their conversations muted, contained just to the pocket of air between them. In Naples, on any given day, the streets were teeming with families, markets, or traffic, the people sweating, yelling because they were aggravated by the heat and the noise and their small, small lives.

I inhaled a deep, cleansing lungful of damp, cold air and held it tight in my lungs. It helped anchor me to this place, which was so special to me because it was *nothing* like home.

Yet it was also empty to me in a way that home never had been.

Simply, I had no one to love in London.

And I was Italian enough, man enough, and romantic enough to believe that life wasn't worth living unless you were loving.

I'd had brief flings with a handful of women in the few months I'd been there and countless nights with others just to slake my unquenchable thirst for sex, but none of that was intimate, and intimacy was something entirely different from sex. It was the way a body knew another, lusted after its uniqueness so much that only that single form could satisfy it. The way one human could anticipate another, the way they could strip you down to the bolts and build you back up again with their mouths when used to form kisses or words.

I craved that intimacy and found the promise of that in Savannah Meyers.

So even though I was terrified to have someone of her caliber read my words, I was also oddly touched and fiercely aroused because it was a part of me she held between her hands and scrutinized with her eyes. I felt the phantom touch of her even then as I walked down the streets away from her, trying to purge my mind of her.

I couldn't.

Something about this woman echoed in me, and I knew I'd explore it if I was given the slightest opportunity.

Explore her until I knew her tight curves and satin edges as intimately as a tailor with his custom creations. I wanted to run my fingers over her seams and into her silk-lined depths, pin down her hands, and sew her mouth to mine with unyielding kisses.

My mind reeled with the imagery, loops of grainy black-and-white film clips on repeat behind the screens of my eyes. I tried to calm down, bit the inside of my cheek until it bled, and thought of Neapolitan grandmothers sweating and sagging in the sun, but still, by the time I reached the pink awning of Peggy Porschen Cakes on my way back from the park, my cock was so hard it was an actual miracle it hadn't punched a hole through my trousers.

I figured, eyeing the explosion of pink and girly that was the bakery, that going inside to buy an outrageously priced cupcake was a good distraction. But the delicately frosted, pale pink frothed cakes seemed like something *la duchessa* would enjoy, so I bought one for us both.

I ate mine on the way back to the car, unable to stop the impulse to stick my thumb in the sweet icing and suck it off with a curl of my tongue and hard suction with my lips. I knew without knowing that Savannah Meyers's nipples would taste just as sweet. And when the chocolatey cake melted on my tongue, I knew her pussy would melt between my lips just the same.

When I finally arrived back at the car, I was as agitated as a caged animal. I slammed the door closed behind me after I got in the front seat and immediately twisted to look at Savannah. Sometime while I'd been walking, she had lowered the partition and the papers in her hands, so when I found her, she was utterly demure. Her hands crossed primly in her lap, and her face was held in perfect repose.

Porca miseria, the need to fuck her wet, rough, and messy until she was ruined with orgasms, and I'd laid waste to her perfection, thrummed through me nearly too powerfully to ignore.

"Well?" I barked out.

She smiled only slightly, but it was smug, nonetheless. "I see that the ever-charming Sebastian succumbs to grumpiness when he's nervous."

My teeth ground together until a muscle in my jaw spasmed. "Hardly. If I'm grumpy, it's because I should have been off the clock an hour ago."

"We both know you can count this as overtime. Don't be mean and spoil my fun, Sebastian. I was just about to tell you what I thought of your screenplay. Aren't you at all curious?"

I glared at her faux innocent expression even as I loved her playfulness. "Of course, Mrs. Meyers, it's not as though you practically *forced* me to give you my words. Why wouldn't I want your very solicited opinion?"

She bit her lip in mock apology, but I knew it was to hide her smile. "Excellent. Well then, quite simply, I loved it."

My eyebrows shot into my hairline. "Do not play with me, Savannah."

"I'm not playing, not about this," she said, all teasing gone. "Tell me, you're meant to play the lead, aren't you?"

I shrugged churlishly but lifted my chin in confirmation.

"I see it," she said softly, her gaze pressed like soothing hands to my cheeks. "The intensity and the passion and the faux swagger all undercut by a soft heart."

"What do you know of my heart?" I retorted.

Her lashes fluttered over her eyes like curtains caught in a breeze, and I realized that she was showing me everything in that gaze, a panoramic view of her soul. "Sebastian, you're an artist." She gently rustled the papers as she picked them up. "I just spent the past ninety minutes reading it, and now, I'm holding it in my hands."

I swallowed thickly and rubbed at the back of my neck.

"Do you have work as an actor?"

"*Sì*," I answered, forgetting myself for a moment. "I'm over at Finborough Theatre doing *Bury the Dead*."

She pursed her lips in thought for a moment before she straightened her shoulders. "I'm sure you know that my husband is a very well-regarded actor here in England."

I snorted. To say that her husband was "very well-regarded" was such a typically British understatement. After I'd learned I would be driving his wife, I'd done my research. I'd watched him through the silver screen for years, but finding out more about his life had been a revelation.

Adam Meyers's story had been open to public consumption since he was a boy. He'd been born to a family of nobility that had long ago lost their estate but not their brand of wealth or elegance. He'd been a top student at Eton, which is where he met and became best friends with the princes of England, Arthur and Alasdair Whitley-Fairfax, and hobnobbed with the crème de la crème of British society before he'd gone on to study business at Oxford University. When Arthur enlisted in the navy, Adam had too. After four years in the service, they had both emerged as men, but surprisingly, while Arthur had resumed his princely duties, Adam had turned to acting. Unsurprisingly, his fame was assured before he took his first step on the London stage as the youngest ever Hamlet to be cast in the West End, but it was secured the moment after the curtains closed and he received the first of many standing ovations.

If Cosima thought I was gifted, Adam Meyers was a messiah.

So, yeah, I understood that Adam Meyers was "very well-regarded."

"I may be Italian, but I haven't been living under a rock for the last decade," I told her.

"So dramatic, it's a wonder I didn't guess you were an actor from our first meeting," she scolded me. "Well, what most people don't know is that Adam's secret weapon is me."

"You?"

"Yes," she said, sitting up straight like a straight-A student preening under attention from her teacher. "Me. We met when he was working on his first film, and ever since then, I've scouted his projects for him. You see, I have an eye."

"An eye," I repeated, amusement washing away my anger.

"Yes." She pouted. "You don't believe me, but you see, I'm a modern-day muse."

"Oh, I don't doubt that," I said, my eyes moving over her loveliness. "You certainly inspire me."

She rolled her eyes, and I loved that I'd broken through her porcelain doll shell to see the spirited woman beneath it. "Focus, Sebastian. I'm trying to tell you that not only do I love this screenplay but I'm also in a position to do something about it."

My heart stopped, then restarted with a painful, stuttering thud.

"I'm serious," she stated before I could doubt her again. "Please, let me make a copy of this quickly. I'll run up and photocopy it and then give you back the original. I won't make any promises, but I think I can get this into the right hands."

I peered at her and swallowed four times before I found my voice. "Why would you do that?" When her face softened, I sharpened my tone. "And don't give me some *cazzate* about you just doing something nice for a fellow human being. Everyone has a reason tied to greed for doing *anything*, and you? The classy wife of a celebrated actor, what reason could you possibly have to help an Irish-Italian immigrant chauffeur wannabe writer and actor?"

Suddenly, Mrs. Savannah Meyers looked as I imagined she had as a child, a little lost but edgy with restless need and impossible hope.

She licked her lips nervously and looked up at me through her lashes. "You're right. I'm not altruistic by nature. I'm selfish and savage in my pursuit of what I want… You don't get to where I am by being generous."

"A society wife?" I asked, hiding my vulnerability behind cruelty.

"Yes," she sniffed. "And a muse. It might not seem like such an accomplishment to you, but I was born in hell on earth, and now I live in heaven. I can do that for you. Just let me copy these papers, Sebastian. Trust me even though you have no real reason to besides the fact that it feels *right*."

I hated her for knowing how right it felt. If she remained impervious and perfect, hidden behind the partition meant to separate us, I would have said no. But she'd let down her guard enough to show me her flaws, and it was those, her selfishness, and ruthless ambition that made her tangible to me. The intimacy germinating between us took root and began to flourish.

I held her wide blue eyes solemnly as I said, "Make the copies, but if nothing comes of it, I don't want to know about it, *capisci*?"

Savannah pressed my screenplay to her chest, and I imagined that through those pages, pure extensions of myself, I could feel the thrum of her heartbeat against my own.

"*Capisco*," she said with a bad accent and the most beautiful grin I'd ever seen.

And I decided even if she trampled all over my dreams, it was worth it to see a woman like Savannah Meyers gift me with her smile.

Chapter Three

Sebastian

Bach was on.

"Cello Suite No. 1 in G Major."

I'd done my homework and listened to everything I could find by him, and then, wanting to impress, I'd borrowed a book about him from the London Public Library. Interestingly, Johann Bach's middle name was Sebastian.

Savannah was *la duchessa.* If I wanted on the right side of the partition (*her side*), I needed to step up my game in a way I'd never had to before.

So I read the book and listened to his compositions every night after work for a week.

I was ready to impress her.

It had been nearly a week since she'd photocopied my screenplay, but we hadn't spoken of it. Instead, she had distracted me each time I drove her with tidbits about London society, and I learned that she had her fingers in many, many pies. Savannah may have been a socialite, but she worked hard to network for her husband, and it seemed that she knew anyone who was anyone in town, up to and including most of the Royal family. After eating the cupcake I'd bought her from Peggy Porschen's, we'd been back four times, and I'd discovered Savannah had a weakness for all things vanilla. So being the utter *stronzo* I was, that is falling in love with her over the lowered partition in her town car, I made sure to pick her up bearing ridiculous confections like iced vanilla pound cake and vanilla frosted cupcakes topped with salted caramel. Each time, she reacted as though I'd pulled down the moon and had it faceted like the world's biggest diamond for her and her alone to wear.

It made me feel fucking ten feet tall, and after a lifetime of feeling small and poor, always striving for more, it was ridiculously heady. Her beauty was magnified by the knowledge that I had the power to amplify it. I was the one who gave her reason to smile that smile and laugh that musical laugh. So it was no surprise my fierce attraction to her had escalated to a near sexual obsession.

My fingers drummed on the steering wheel as I waited for her that evening, the sound muted by the thickness of my leather driving gloves. I wanted to finger that classy pussy while wearing those gloves, see the smear of her wetness on the fine finish, and smell her fragrance embedded in the seams whenever I brought them to my nose.

I adjusted my hardening cock in my uniform and took a deep breath as I spotted Savannah gliding out the doors of The Goring Dining Room. My breath caught, then held in my throat at the sight of her slim curves tucked away in a silk dress the same shade as the inside of an oyster. Her pale blond hair curled around her heart-shaped face, catching the light like a halo, her deep red lips the same shape as Cupid's bow.

She was made for me—by the hands of God or the devil, I didn't care.

I had to have her.

The cold air felt good against my burning skin as I stepped out of the car. My pulse was hammering erratically as though I had a heart murmur, and my collar felt too tight as I watched her walk down the few steps in ridiculously sexy spiked heels.

She smiled at me as she drew closer, and it was a smile I'd yet to see.

A wide parting of her red lips, pearly teeth on full display, and a tiny dimple tacked neatly high into her left cheek. Her eyes shone with uninhibited joy at seeing me.

"*Mozzafiato*," I said without deciding to, so enchanted by the beguiling childlike wonder in her eyes as she stared up at me that I could have been mugged at that moment and not noticed or cared.

She laughed and then, distracted, lost her footing so that her body collided softly with mine. I caught her easily and pressed her hand over the lapel of my suit, over the rapid *tap* of my heart against its cage. I watched with male satisfaction as her mouth fell open like a blooming rose.

"What does that mean?" she questioned softly.

"Breathtaking."

"Oh," she muttered adorably.

I grinned down at her, noting the fluttering, pale blue vein in her neck. I wanted to bite it and feel the pulse between my teeth.

"I think you are the most beautiful person I've ever seen," she whispered, my arms her confessional, and I, her priest.

It wasn't the first time I'd heard that; there was a reason my twin sister and I were in the entertainment business, our beauty had rocketed us out of the mire we'd been born into. Still, her words wrapped a bow around my pounding heart, and I wondered vaguely if it was a gift someone like her would accept.

The heart of a poor Italian man with no formal education and very little money.

She blinked up at me owlishly, and I didn't bother to beat back my deep chuckle even as unease tightened my chest. I gave her a squeeze before releasing her to open the back door. "As much as I like holding you, I would hate to see you embarrassed if anyone saw the lady cavorting with the tramp."

She rolled her eyes at me as she slid into the back seat, and then shocked by her less-than-perfect demeanor, she covered her eyes with a hand. "Oh Lord, I must have had more champagne than was prudent. That was incredibly rude of me."

I shook my head as I closed her in, then moved to the front seat to get behind the wheel. When I looked in the rearview mirror at her, a blush stained the skin above the collar of her dress like a wine spill.

"I'm inebriated," she told me soberly.

"I'm assuming that isn't something you do a lot of," I teased her as I pulled into traffic.

"I don't like to be inebriated. It's… uncouth."

Our eyes caught in the reflection of the mirror and fused as though attached by electric cables. I felt the currents race along my skin, and my voice was deeper, dangerously dark, when I said, "Well, *duchessa*, I prefer you like this."

"Drunk?"

"Intoxicating," I corrected as the swell of Bach's movement undulated throughout the Rolls. "As intoxicated as I feel, being near you."

"You are either the cheesiest man I've ever met or…" She laughed softly, an edge to the musicality of it.

"Or?" I asked over the snap, crackle, and electric pop of chemistry between us.

Her wide eyes found mine in the mirror, utterly guileless and slightly confused. "Or you're too good to be true."

"Trust me, I'm not that." I barked with laughter at the very thought of it.

She scowled at me, adorable in her irritation. Not for the first time, I wondered how old she could be. Something was wonderfully childlike about her, yet she was clearly mature, refined, and elegant in the way of money and years spent living idly.

"You look like something out of Michelangelo's studio," she retorted with a haughty tip of her chin.

I winced. "Have you seen the size of the dicks on his statues? No, *duchessa*, I can assure you, I'm built much more proportionally than that."

She covered her sharp exclamation of laughter with her hand and then reclined in her seat with a little contented sigh. "I like spending time with you."

"Most women do." I laughed at her immediate frown and shrugged one shoulder. "It's the truth."

"Oh, I have no doubt," she sniffed. "I'm sure you're a very popular chauffeur."

It was my turn to frown. "What exactly are you implying?"

"Oh, I know the women in my sect, all bored housewives or stressed financiers and CEOs. Faced with the temptation of you in that spiffy uniform, I'm certain they are only too thrilled to tip you *generously* for your services."

"*Cazzo*, I am not a gigolo," I cursed, surprised at how much her insinuation stung.

She pursed her lips and cocked her head. "No?"

"*No*."

"I've offended you."

"I'm sure a lady such as yourself hasn't had reason to fraternize with poor boys much, but not all of us succumb to turning tricks to earn a few pounds," I educated her between clenched teeth.

"Believe it or not, I used to be poor," she said softly, apology threaded through her words like a pretty ribbon as she offered her gift up to me. The gift of insight into her true self, a gift I was eager to tear into with my fingers and teeth.

"You don't smell like it," I told her, peering into the rearview as we waited at yet another backed-up traffic light.

She was quiet for a minute, and I wondered what she was thinking. If she had been poor, there was no way she could misinterpret my statement. Everyone who'd experienced it knew that true poverty had an odor. It was hot like scorched pavement and sharply sweet like overripe fruit burst open and left exposed too long in the tropical heat. The heat was flavored with shame, with the anger that would crop up and hit you over the side of the head when you dared to question, *how was this fair, why me, will it ever end?* It was the sweetness that invaded the senses, though. Close to putrid, it denoted the stink of hope gone rotten.

Sometimes, I showered twice a day to rid myself of the stench I still imagined lingered deep in my pores.

"I have some keepsakes," she murmured finally. "I don't know why I keep them when the memories haunt me, but sometimes when I get stuck in the mud of my past, I smell them." Her eyes tipped up beneath painted lashes to latch onto mine. "They still smell the same, even buried deep in the heart of my walk-in closet in my multimillion-pound Chelsea townhome."

"Stink like that never goes away," I told her even though, after what she had just shared, I knew she understood that already.

"No," she said, even quieter, her gaze straying out the window.

We were quiet then, only the emotional swell of Chopin's third movement sweeping through the cavernous Rolls Royce. I was disappointed that her sweet, flirty mood had sunk into post-tipsy contemplation, yet I was also weirdly grateful to know that beneath the silken class and studied manners, Savannah Meyers was just as human as me.

"Sometimes I miss it."

"The stench?" I clarified.

"Maybe. I grew up in the poor South, in a small town like a wet spot on a map in Alabama. Sometimes I miss the wet heat, how it stuck my clothes to my body and made everyone smell ripe in a way that was base and somehow intimate. The weather made everything bare and sultry. People passed the time fucking in long, damp grass and dunking naked and entwined in cool ponds. They escaped the heat by getting drunk on cheap clear booze and stomped out their crazy on wooden floors in dirty bars listening to George Strait. Most of my friends got pregnant too young or dropped out of high school before the ninth grade."

She paused to drag a deep breath into her lungs and blink dazedly at whatever past she pictured that played out the window.

"We were animals, basically. We didn't think about the consequences. We just lived and acted on all our impulses… That's it. That's what I miss."

My mind whirred with images of Savannah on her back in green Southern grass, her pale skin slick with our sweat as I beat into her clutching pussy like a beast. Savannah in my arms, hefted up against the inside of the bar bathroom door, my hand over her shouting mouth as I fucked her drunk, driven to come. The idea of this lady stripped of her varnish and bare beneath me had my dick hard as a fucking rock in my pants.

Impulsively, I flicked the indicator and pulled over onto the darkened curb beside Regent's Park. Savannah watched me under hooded lids but didn't protest.

"Lift your skirt," I told her, confident enough to be convincing without ordering.

If she didn't want to play this game with me, now was the time to say so.

She bit the edge of her perfectly shaped lower lip, then sucked it into her mouth as she deliberated. I groaned at the sight, and she jerked her eyes to me, her wet lip popping out into a shiny, tempting pout.

"Lift your skirt and spread your legs for me," I repeated, and it was an order this time.

A delicate shiver rattled her slim shoulders, and for a minute, I thought she wouldn't do it. I was basically a stranger to her. More than that, she was technically my *boss*, years older than me, and fucking *married*.

It wasn't my first time seducing a taken woman or an older one, but something about Savannah's class was so fucking pure that my fingers on her skin seemed wrong like an oily handprint on a pristine pane of glass.

I held my breath as achingly slowly Savannah's sweet thighs parted beneath the rippling silk of her dress. The fluid material rode up her thighs until the shadowed apex of her thighs was visible to me.

"Wider," I said, and it came out harshly, whipping against her exposed flesh so hard she flinched, then blushed brightly.

Without hesitation, she pushed her thighs farther apart with her palms on the inside of her knees. She wore nude thigh highs trimmed in a thick edge of lace and attached to flimsy-looking white garters.

My mouth was dry when I commanded, "Show me your breasts."

Savannah's throat worked rapidly as she swallowed back her unease and slowly exposed each milky breast, the fabric beneath propping them up so they were beautifully plump and high.

The desert in my mouth flooded at the thought of taking those sweet pink nipples between my teeth.

"Play with your nipples."

Her eyes widened, and she chewed almost viciously on her lip, but she still did as she was told.

My blood hummed with power, throbbing through my body in time with the string quartet in "Bach's Piano Concerto in D Minor."

"You like doing what I tell you to, *farfallina*? A little butterfly caught in my net," I hummed. "Would you like to make yourself come for me?"

She licked her lips, and the pulse in her pale throat throbbed.

"No thinking," I reminded her, my voice thick with the music of my homeland. "Just do as I say, Savannah."

I waited, staring into those wet velvet blue eyes and hoping beyond hope she'd let me play with her mind while she played with her pussy.

With a gusty sigh, she tipped her head back against the leather seats, closed her eyes, and brought one of her hands from her breasts down to her sex.

"Perfect," I purred. "Are you wet for me?"

A low whimper was her response as she dunked two elegant fingers into her wet center. I could hear the liquid sounds of her arousal as she dipped in and out, but I couldn't get the right visual.

"Take off your underwear."

Her eyes flew open. "Sebastian… I'm, well, I'm not as young as—"

"Take. Off. Your. Underwear."

With her lower lip tucked between her teeth she carefully peeled her white satin panties down her legs. I held my hand out for them.

"Seb," she breathed, part protest and part plea.

I flexed my fingers. "Give them to me."

She leaned closer to put them in my hand, the intoxicating scent of her expensive floral perfume mingling with the heady fragrance of her pussy. I brought the wet scrap of fabric to my nose and inhaled deeply as I locked eyes with her.

Savannah's breath stuttered through her open lips as she watched me.

"Lean back, spread those gorgeous legs, and play with yourself for me."

"You aren't going to play with me yourself?" she questioned softly, an edge of neediness to her words that thrilled me.

"No." I crossed my wrists over the steering wheel and relaxed back in the seat so I could watch her through the rearview mirror. "You want to be dirty again, Savvy? A woman like you, a lady with pearls and silk dresses and a chauffeur to drive you around?"

"Yes," she hissed softly as she parted her legs wide and exposed the pink folds of her golden-haired cunt to my gaze.

My voice was in my throat when I said, "I don't need to put my hands on you to show you what a dirty slut you can be, *duchessa*. Doing all the filthy things I tell you to do with your own classy hands is even better. You're going to come all over that leather seat with only my words and your fingers taking you there."

"*Oh*," she breathed, her legs spasming at my words. "Yes."

I didn't tell her there was also no way I was risking my job further, a job I desperately needed, by actually touching her. At least this way, once the drink wore off and the passion faded, I could hide behind the fact that she'd technically done everything herself.

"Say my name when you come," I told her. "Rub that clit for me and add another finger to your pussy. I want to hear how wet I make you."

Even in the dark, I could see how her perfect pale skin was pebbled with goose bumps. I wanted to count each mogul with my tongue, taste the bitterness of her perfume at her pulse points and feel them pound viciously with her heartbeat.

I wanted to grip my cock too, jerk off violently to the erotic perfection in the back seat but I wouldn't.

I'd lived a life that taught me early. All acts were expressions of power, denoting either an abundance or lack of clout. In this situation, *la duchessa* in all her ladylike faultlessness sitting in a car I was the driver of but didn't even own, I needed to accrue all the power I could scrape together. Savannah may have been higher than me on the social scale, but between us, especially when her cunt was bared, *I* was the one in control.

"I've been wondering what you taste like," I told her conversationally, only my words were more bass and persuasion than treble and volume. "Do you taste like sugar, sweet Savvy? Melted caramel spilled between your thighs for me to lick up?" I received a panting gasp in response as her fingers slid through the wet mess of her pussy. "Or are you salty and fresh like ocean water, like a mermaid dredged up from the sea?"

"Sebastian," she said and the whole world seemed handed to me in that one word.

It was an offering that no man however disciplined could refuse. And I wasn't disciplined; I was a hedonist and Savannah Meyers was quickly becoming a buffet of pleasure.

"Taste yourself," I told her. "Take those fingers out of your sucking pussy and sink them deep between those pretty red lips."

When she hesitated, I growled low and watched her shudder

almost violently at the sound of it.

"Do it."

She did. Her fingers trembled, slick with moisture that glowed silver in the moonlight spilling in through the tinted car windows. I held her eyes as she brought them to her parted lips, then slowly slid them over her tongue and straight to the back of her mouth before closing her lips in a tight seal. I could hear the noise of her sucking, licking, and swirling. My cock was so hard it felt bruised and beaten, throbbing painfully in my unforgiving trousers. I squeezed a big hand hard around it for a long beat as I watched Savannah lick her fingers clean.

"What a good little slut you are, Mrs. Meyers," I praised her, my voice warm because I wasn't sure how she would respond to the degradation and I wanted her to know I meant it as the most perverted kind of compliment.

Her eyes, closed to focus on her oral skills, opened to half-mast and she purred with pleasure when she said, "Thank you, Sebastian."

"You're welcome. Now, add another finger to that tight pussy. If you ever want to replace it with my cock, you'll need to get used to feeling filled up."

She moaned softly, immediately returning her saliva-slick fingers to her cunt. I could see her wetness glimmer on the insides of her thighs above her stockings, on the rich leather under her ass, and a dark part of me, the part born in dark alleys and seedy backrooms, wanted to force her to lick up her cum from the seat when I was finished with her.

"Would you do anything to please me, Savvy? To be my perfect, gorgeous slut?"

"Yes," she whispered.

I studied her. She was still too lovely, too untouched by sin. I wanted her dirty, corrupted by my words until she spilled over, ugly but frank like garbage from a split bag.

"Has anyone ever played with your ass before?" I asked her.

"Oh, my goodness," she panted, her fingers pumping faster.

I grinned darkly. "Tilt your hips and place one of your legs up on the seat beside you so I can see all of you. Then suck on your left index finger and trace it slowly over that tight asshole."

She did as I bid immediately, so far gone that her flush was a permanent red stain under her normally flawless white skin, and her eyes were open to mere slits. I groaned loudly at the sight of her dusky rosebud as she opened herself up to me and then cursed viciously in Italian when, without hesitation, she sucked on a finger, traced it over her rim and then plunged it inside with a rumbling moan.

Her head thrust back against the seat and she squeezed her eyes tight, her features twisted into a grotesque but completely compelling look of pain-edged pleasure.

"You're going to come for me, aren't you?" I taunted her softly. "You're allowed to, Savvy. Show me what a dirty woman you can be. Imagine it's me in that pussy, and your husband in that tight ass."

"*Fuck*," she shouted, her fingers beating into her flesh loudly, brutally.

I imagined it too, my cock inside her, rubbing against Adam Meyers, snug deep in her ass, our big bodies sandwiching her between us.

Ruthlessly, I squeezed my balls through my pants so that I wouldn't embarrass myself by coming in them.

"Imagine us sawing back and forth inside you, filling you up until you don't even have room to breathe. Would you come for us like that, dirty *duchessa*? Show me how you'd come for us."

With a hoarse shout, she came. I watched her wetness seep out over her pounding fingers, how her thighs shook and her breasts heaved. She was sweating, out of breath, her hair tangled into golden ropes, her clothes all in disarray, and I'd never seen Savannah Meyers so goddamn gorgeous.

"Good girl," I muttered softly as she came down.

I gave her privacy to recover without my searing gaze even though I wanted to share that time with her, pull her soft, slaked body into my arms and fit her warmed curves to my granite edges. Instead, I started the Rolls and pulled back onto the road to take her home. By the time we reached her flat, my dirty Savvy was gone and proper Mrs. Savannah Meyers was back in her place, ankles crossed, hands loosely clasped. Only a few tangles marred her perfection, but my belly heated again knowing I'd been the one to muss her.

We made eye contact and I watched as her flush reappeared, a flash like a warning sign, before she reined in her reaction.

"I suppose we'll do as the British do and pretend this never happened?" I said with a small wink, even though something in my chest was curling up with decay.

She opened her mouth, her brow furrowed in protest but then she closed it again and sighed heavily. After looking out the window for a moment, she looked back at me and smiled sadly.

"Thank you, Sebastian," she murmured.

I fought the urge to laugh just as hard as I fought the urge to shout in misery. Who was I to think that a man like me could steal a woman like her from an international icon like Adam fucking Meyers?

"Any time, Savvy," I told her, my face a firm mask of charm.

She bit her lip then nodded and got out of the car. I cursed under my breath as soon as she was gone then steadied my still pounding heart with three deep breaths. I cursed again when there was a soft *tap tap* against my window and I looked up to see Savannah peering through.

I lowered the pane, but she was already speaking before it was even open an inch.

"I've already told you I'm a selfish creature and a greedy one. I take what I want when I want it and I won't let anything stand in my way on the path to acquiring it. Well, I think you should know, I want you now, Sebastian. I want you now so badly I feel it in my blood like a dangerous drug. So I'm warning you, I'll find a way to have you."

I blinked at her, completely blindsided by her speech, so it was incredibly easy for her to lean forward and press a chaste kiss to my slack lips. A kiss that seared itself like a brand into my skin so that even a minute later when she disappeared into the house, and an hour after that when I finally arrived home, and then the next morning when I woke up already on the edge of ejaculation, I felt that kiss tattooed on my mouth.

Chapter Four

Sebastian

It was difficult to see through the bright lights on the stage that fell away as sheer as a cliff drop to inky blackness over the audience, but he sat in the front row, so he was impossible to miss even in the shadows.

Adam Meyers. Six-time nominee for an Oscar, two-time winner, with literally dozens of other accolades under his belt. Best friend to British royalty and husband to Savannah fucking Meyers.

And he sat in Finborough Theatre on the closing night of a revival production of *Bury the Dead,* watching me act.

For a brief, uncharacteristic moment of panic, I thought I literally couldn't go on. My idol was sitting not ten feet from me, so close I could imagine the feel of his eyes on me, hotter than the blazing theatre lights. If there was ever a time that the show could not go on, it was absolutely now.

But then I remembered myself. I'd grown up in Mafia country, hounded from the age of twelve to join the Camorra so that by the time I was a teenager, avoidance was no longer a viable option, and I'd had to use my fists and wits to escape their clutches. If I could face down a mean, money-eyed Italian in an alleyway, I could face down a gentile, money-backed Adam Meyers in a clean but slightly decrepit theatre in Kensington, London.

Not only could I withstand it, I could own it. I'd been gorging myself on adversity since I was a child, so this panic, this fear of failure, was nothing but premium fuel to me. I used it. And I bloody well killed it.

In fact, there was no doubt in my mind that I gave the performance of my life, just as there seemed to be no doubt from the audience, given the standing ovation I received at the end of the play.

Afterward, I lingered in our communal changeroom, drinking from a bottle of grappa an overeager, too-interested stagehand bought me opening night because I'd mentioned it was the only liquor I had a taste for. I did not doubt that Adam was out there, mingling with the others at the closing night party with patrons from all over London. Finborough was a smaller theatre, outside the theatre district in the West End, but it was still relatively influential. I'd known it would be a night to hobnob, and I was dressed accordingly, in the only nice suit I owned, one that Cosima had sent me the money to buy. It was all black, from the tip of my tie to the soles of my Santoni leather loafers, and it made the gold of my eyes fucking glow. My hair was tousled, but I wasn't the type of man to care, and I hadn't shaved in a few days, so my jaw was defined by the dark shadow of a coming beard. I looked dark and dangerous. Women would flutter around me like butterflies, ready and willing to be trapped in my net, and even some men would circle, tempted like moths to my flame. I was confident in this because I was lucky enough to be born beautiful and loved enough to realize it. Yet there I was, cowering backstage after everyone had joined the party because I was scared of one man.

To be fair, I'd essentially cuckholded him, *and* he'd been a hero of mine since I was fifteen. If that wasn't a landmine to be avoided at all costs, I didn't know what was.

"Seb?"

I turned to see the overeager stagehand, Maggie, popping her head around the door with a frown.

"You coming? People are asking to see the star of the show," she told me with a beatific smile.

She was cute, with one of the nicest pair of breasts I'd had the pleasure of seeing half spill out of a top, but I didn't fuck people I worked with.

I thought of Savannah and amended that thought.

Apparently, I only fucked people I worked *for.*

"Are you hiding in here?" she asked me, head cocked and eyes wide because she knew me. She knew Sebastian Lombardi didn't hide from anything, let alone people. I was a natural-born charmer. Normally, I'd already be out there performing like it was my second show.

"Of course not." I smiled at her, straightened my shoulders, and made my way toward her where I slung a comfortable arm over her shoulders as I walked us both into the front reception hall. "I was just giving the other actors a chance to shine before I upstaged them."

She laughed. "I think it's a bit too late for that. Now, I've been tasked to take you straight to Michael so he can introduce his star to investors."

I allowed myself to be swept up in the meet and greet of theatre politics, wooing my director and producer Michael Horton's friends as easily as breathing. The familiar routine of hook, reel, and netting conquests lulled me into a false sense of security, so over an hour later, when I finally felt the electric touch of a heavy hand on my shoulder,

I wasn't prepared to turn around into the face of the man I'd been avoiding all night.

I was surprised by Adam Meyers even though I knew enough to be prepared.

No, it was more than that. I was *wowed* by him.

He was older, of course, though not as old as his wife. There was no silver in his flaxen gold hair, almost brown where it was cut close to his skull at the sides but pure gold in the length on top, a perfect lock falling over his forehead. His face was all steep planes, his jaw so square it made acute angles, his nose a strong bridge and a sharp edge, only a perfectly pressed divot in the middle of his stern chin softened the cut of his haughty, perfect features. He was a tall man, his muscles firm curves under the pressed points of his suit. I wondered if we stood hip to hip if he would be eye level with me. A strange part of me hoped so because Adam's eyes called someone to sin, bright as Eden's green grass or Eve's seductive apple and surrounded by a thicket of brown lashes so long they tangled together.

I blinked and realized I'd been staring too hard, too long at a man I should know very little about.

Then I blinked again, a hard closing of the eyes to erase the attraction I'd sketched out in his form.

He did the same.

I frowned at him, wondering madly if he'd been checking me out too.

When he winked, I knew for sure he had been, and desire shot like Cupid's arrow straight through my chest to my groin, where it burst into flames.

For the first time in my life, I was attracted to a man.

"Sebastian Lombardi," he said in a strong, low voice. "Good to meet you."

I froze like a little boy caught red-handed with his fingers in the cookie jar. How did Savannah's husband know me? Could he have hired a private investigator to follow us?

Adam Meyers's hearty laugh cut through my panic, and when I finally focused on him, it was to see him shaking his head and collecting a lone tear from the corner of his fresh grass-green eye.

"Sebastian, good God, man, you should have seen your face. You looked practically apoplectic!" he said through his low laughter and stepped forward with his hand extended. "Adam Meyers, though obviously, you know that."

I took his proffered hand, surprised by the electric current that spasmed between our joint palms and skittered up my arm.

"Obviously," I managed to say dryly, which wrung another startlingly sexy chuckle from him. "And you obviously know who I am. May I ask how?"

He frowned and tilted his head to the side mockingly. "Why, you think I'm a bad husband? Because, Sebastian, let me tell you something, a good husband knows *everyone* who works for his wife, least of all to ensure her safety, most of all to curtail any jealousy. Normally," he added the last with a slight shrug.

I had the feeling he was laughing at me, delighting in the sweat he could feel slicked to my palm, a palm he still held clasped in his own, loving the way I pressed my lips together and not just because he found it funny but because he liked the way my lips looked doing it.

My heart thundered like the old failing engine of my family's 1965 Fiat 500. For the second time in my life, I felt drunk nearly to sickness with a combination of alarm and arousal.

"Normally?" I muttered.

His smirk widened, drawing my notice to his slightly fuller upper lip. I wondered how it would feel if I tested it between my teeth.

"Normally," he repeated with a blasé shrug. "Of course, what we have here isn't exactly society's definition of normal, is it, Sebastian?"

It unnerved me that he kept saying my name, but it completely nonplussed me that he said it with *meaning* as though he'd looked up the definition of Sebastian and was moved to express it. And the way he conveyed it made me feel just as venerable and revered as the name denoted.

"You aren't exactly acting normally right now, Mr. Meyers," I said diplomatically because, in truth, I wanted to punch him in the gut.

Who was that forward yet convoluted during a first meeting?

I'd been speaking to him for ninety seconds, and he already had me twisted deftly into complex sailor's knots.

He chuckled again and stepped even closer, nearly too close to be acceptable. "Ah, excuse me if this is the incorrect way to greet my wife's lover. You see, I've never had such a meeting before. I don't know the correct form of address."

I blinked so hard I saw spots.

His grip on my hand tightened painfully, and his grin turned sly, wolfish. "You look shocked, Sebastian. Why is that? 'Thou shalt not commit adultery' in thought or in deed. You think my wife knowingly went behind my back and cavorted with her chauffeur?"

My mouth flapped open and closed like wet laundry hung to dry in the wind. The sheer force of my shock seized my system and made it impossible for me to even think, let alone respond.

Adam's eyes glittered illicitly, stolen gems I coveted even in my current state. "Yes, Sebastian, my wife told me all about your little game together. How you made her spread those slim thighs and touch her pink cunt."

I loved the way his dirty words sounded in his posh British accent, the way the word *cunt* was decadently round, a juicy morsel I wanted to eat off his tongue.

"She came home stinking of drink and sex, and when I made her bend over to show me her pussy, it was still so swollen and slick. I had to get on my knees, press that sweet arse higher, and lick her clean with my tongue."

My stuttering breath wafted across his lips as he leaned, just for a second, into my face. "I half expected to find the salt taste of you inside her sweetness. And you know what, Sebastian?" He pulled away to an acceptable distance, but he pulled the air between us with him so it stretched taught and vibrating. "I wish I had."

Unbidden, a groan rumbled through my chest. *Cazzo* but the image of the strong, powerfully built man on his knees behind delicate Savannah, holding her down, the span of his hand the entire width of her small waist, as he ate her and imagined eating me out of her… was enough to make a man weak in the knees. And I was not a man who succumbed to weakness of any sort.

Anger followed swiftly on the heels of my arousal, throwing kindling on the fire blazing in my belly until it raged inferno bright.

I bared my teeth at the Brit and watched his eyes flash. "You think you can cage me in a corner with your bullshit dirty talk? Take me by surprise by knowing how much your gorgeous wife melted at my words, her hand manipulated by *me* between her slim thighs in that pretty pink cunt?" I asked, spewing his words back at him. "You should be thanking me, Meyers. If she'd actually had my hands on her, my cock in her, she wouldn't have come back to you at all."

Gauntlet thrown, I breathed like a stuck bull, glaring at him with the full weight of my confused, aroused fury, and Adam Meyers only stood there. He stood there looking me in the eye for a good minute, reading something written in the gold there that I wasn't sure I wanted him to see. Then his gaze swept thoroughly, carefully over every inch of me, an archeologist discovering bones buried beneath the earth. I gritted my teeth at the invasive scrutiny, but I allowed it.

I didn't want to think about *why* I allowed it because I had the feeling it had something to do with the loss of that intimacy I craved and how, in only minutes, Adam had established that between us.

"You look good angry," he finally said, pushing his hands in the pockets of his expensive suit and rocking back on his designer loafers.

"Are you seriously flirting with me?"

His grin deepened the dimple in his chin. I wanted to place my thumb there, hard, and force his mouth open for my kiss.

"Why should my wife have all the fun?" he asked me.

"I…" I cleared my throat and looked around at the party in full swing around us. "What exactly do you want from me here, Mr. Meyers? You want to take me in the back alley and fight for her honor? You want to warn me off so I never touch her again or report me to my boss so I lose my job?"

My gut cramped at the thought of being fired. It was a well-paying job and relatively easy despite the calamity of driving in London proper. I didn't know how long it would take me to find another or if I even could find one as good with my lack of education and skills.

"Relax," Adam's deep, British-clipped voice interrupted my misery. "I don't want any of those things. Though, taking you into the alley, pressing you up tight against the wall, and forcing you to jack off for me as I tell you all the dirty ways I want to exploit your body, well, that does have some serious merit."

So it was official: my longtime idol, famous acting heartthrob Adam Meyers was hitting on me.

Madonna mia! What was happening?

I glared at him. "Are you fucking with me?"

Adam's eyes creased heavily at the corners as he laughed, and even that little detail was hot enough to be made illegal. "Unfortunately, no. Though that's an option I'm trying to put on the table."

"Stop fucking around with me," I growled, stepping closer and, in doing so, realizing that we were, give or take half an inch, the same height.

Why did that make my dick so hard?

"Fine." He leaned forward again. I could feel his breath on my face and smell his aftershave, something rich that smelled like money. The good ole boy playfulness fell from his features, revealing the starkness of his desire. "My wife told me about you after the first time you drove her. 'I have a gorgeous Italian man driving my car,' she said in that breathy voice she uses when she's aroused. Then she told me about your screenplay. In fact, she practically skipped into the house one day with it in her hands and shoved it in my face, spouting nonsense about how I just *had* to find someone to produce it. Only it wasn't nonsense; I read it and bloody well loved it. So I came here to see you act, to see if you had the chops to pull off the role of Roberto, and somehow, God saw fit to bless you with the gift of prose *and* performing, as well as a level of sexiness no man or woman could possibly be immune to. I wanted to kiss the writer behind the words the moment I read the screenplay. I wanted to place the man who made my wife come with only his filthy words on his knees before me so I could fuck his throat the minute my wife told me about it. And I wanted to fuck *you* the moment I saw you glorious as hell on that stage for all to see."

By the end of his tirade, we were both breathing too heavily, as though we'd run a race over his hot-as-coal words.

"Is that plain enough for you, Sebastian?" he taunted me.

I swallowed the tangled mess of words in my throat and tried to speak. "You know this is fucked up, right?"

Adam's solemnity broke free with a grin and a shrug. "You've never fucked a man before? You should feel how hard I am thinking about being the one to break your cherry ass."

I shuddered and tried to clench my teeth to stymie it but failed.

Adam laughed loudly. "We'll start slow. You, me, and my wife."

Unbidden, my mind conjured an image of pretty little Savannah on her hands and knees, her little Cupid's bow mouth stretched grotesquely by my wide cock, and her satin pussy clenched tight around Adam's driving dick.

My cock was leaking in my suit.

"Oh yes," Adam rumbled, seeing the lust play out over my face. "I promise it'll be just that hot, sexier actually. Have you ever had a threesome before, Sebastian?"

"With women."

"Ah." He nodded, looked around the room, and then leaned over to pluck two glasses of champagne from a passing server. He handed one to me, watched as I threw the entire glass back, and then laughed as he handed me the one he'd grabbed for himself. "You'll find sex with another man satisfying, I think. That animal inside you? The one desperate to rut and fuck without concern for your partner's comfort and gratification? That beast can come out with a man, and if we're both lucky, there will be a fight for the top that will satisfy the savage in ways you can't even imagine."

Again, my mind summoned an image of Adam and me grappling—hot, sweaty muscles slick under our hands as we pushed and shoved for supremacy.

"When?" I asked.

Adam's pine-green eyes flashed with predatory heat. "Now. Drink up, say your goodbyes, and meet me out back in that alley you're so eager to take me to."

He smirked at me, ducked his head, and turned on his heel to power through the crowd. People attempted to stop him, but he was on a mission. A mission to get to the alley where I was fairly certain I was going to have my first threesome with a man.

"Was that Adam Meyers you were just talking to?" one of my co-leads, Jasper Hartley, asked me. "I've been wondering all night what a man of his caliber is doing here. Do you know him? Looked like it."

"No," I said even though I knew I would know him *intimately* imminently.

"Well, what did he want?"

I shook off my stupor, clapped a hand on Jasper's shoulder, and winked. "To congratulate me on stealing the show, of course."

Jasper laughed as I moved away even as he called, "Yeah, yeah, fuck you and your talent, Lombardi."

I flicked my fingers back at him and ducked into the back room to grab my shit before I powered out the exit door.

A car was waiting.

Specifically, a Rolls Royce identical to the one I drove for Luxury Regent Car Service.

I barked out a laugh as I shook my head and made my way to the back door. Before I could open it myself, it swung wide, and Savannah herself peeked out to beam at me.

"I knew he'd convince you."

Despite my vague discomfort, Savannah's arrogant charm soothed me. I knew her. After countless car rides and conversations and our little tryst beside Regent's Park, I knew this woman intimately. Enough to know that I wanted her no matter what stood in my way. The fact that Adam Meyers was the roadblock didn't hurt, of course. In fact, it was quite the contrary.

Savannah tugged my hand so that I practically fell into the car, and I laughed when she immediately straddled my lap, the skirt of her pale pink dress riding up to expose the lace top of her nude stockings. I groaned and passed my hands over the silken fabric and up over her even silkier thighs.

"I told you," she whispered against my lips, her forehead tight to mine. "I'd find a way to have you."

I groaned as her tongue flicked out to trace my lips. Fisting a hand in the back of her short curls, I tugged her closer and plundered her mouth.

Cazzo, she tasted like heaven on my tongue. Fire erupted between us, ravaging my system so that all I could feel was the heat of her like flickering flames in my hands. So I was startled when I felt her shift in my lap, tipping her hips back and her ass up.

I forced my heavy lids open as she ducked her head to work her lips over my left ear and neck, her fingers working open the buttons of my shirt until it fell limply open at my sides. Adam was behind her on his knees in the vast well between the L-shaped seats. He held my eyes as he flipped over her skirt, then ruthlessly tore off her panties, wrenching a gasp from her.

His green eyes then lowered to the sight between her spread thighs, and he groaned, "She's already drenched for you."

I tipped my head back as I moaned at his words, at the feeling of Savvy's teeth digging into the apex of my shoulder and neck.

"Still, based on the size of the bulge you've got straining against your trousers, I'd better get her stretched and ready for your big cock," Adam muttered, distracted by the sight of him sinking what he showed me was three fingers deep into Savvy.

She moaned loudly and shuddered in my arms. I lifted her under her armpits so I could suck at her braless breasts under the silk of her dress and felt her next moan vibrate against my mouth.

I jerked again when I felt a big hand palm my straining erection, but Adam's words, muffled by Savvy's wet folds, kept me still. "Let me get this cock inside her pussy."

My balls were already drawn tight, the base of my spine tingling with pins and needles. I wanted to come *now,* and I wasn't even inside her. I hissed as Adam undid my belt and trousers, then reached under the fabric to wrap hot, thick fingers tight around my shaft.

"Yeah," he rumbled against the inside of Savvy's thigh, and I knew he was staring at my cock in his hand as he gave it a few hard, twisting, *perfect* pulls. "Savannah, sweetheart, you're going to love him filling up your little pussy."

"Yes," Savvy whimpered against my neck as I felt him run my flared head up and down her soaking wet slit. Her juices ran down my length, leveling a trail that cooled quickly, then was replaced, shockingly, with the wide, wet press of a tongue licking up the spillage.

Adam groaned against my shaft, then tipped it farther back under Savvy so he could loudly slurp up her wetness and my precum from the tip. "Bloody delicious."

"*Merda*," I groaned at the searing heat of his mouth on me, of knowing Adam fucking Meyers was on his knees with his tongue on my cock and his hand on my shaft, ready to sink his wife onto my cock so she could fuck me and he could watch. I strained to keep from thrusting in his hands as he deftly rolled a condom down my shaft, but his deep chuckle made me aware he knew how much I was enjoying his touch.

"Be a good girl and take him all, Savvy," he ordered, and a second later, he placed my tip at her entrance, grasped her hips, and forced her down until I was balls deep in her clutching heat.

Both Savannah and I groaned into each other's mouths as we kissed. She sat on my dick, adjusting to the stretch and burn for a long moment before she started to roll her hips.

I held her hair away from both sides of her face and ran my nose down hers before I looked into her eyes and said, "*Mozzafiato.*"

"Too good to be true," she repeated back the words we'd spoken when we'd first played that night in the car.

My eyes went to Adam, who came up on the seat beside us, his trousers undone and pushed down so that his cock was exposed and framed by his pumping fist. I couldn't help the near fucking whimper that squeezed from my suddenly tight throat as I took in the sheer length and width of him. He was so big, bigger even than me, that I couldn't comprehend that massive cock in Savvy's tiny, clutching cunt.

Adam chuckled that deep, smoky laugh and responded to the wild surprise in my gaze. "She struggles, Sebastian, just like she's doing now on your nice, thick cock. But that's half the fun, isn't it?" He cocked his head, shuffled closer on his knees, and jutted his cock through his fist up at me. "Do you like it?"

I'd never thought about a man like that.

I grew up deep in the heart of machoism territory, a place where homophobia was as glorified as its Lamborghinis and Ferragamo. A place where a man was only a man if he had a wife and at least two other women on the side, probably with a brood by each.

There were many good things about my homeland, but open-mindedness was not one of them.

So, obviously, I'd never thought of a man like that.

But Savvy's pussy a wet velvet clasp around my cock, her sweet tits bouncing beneath thin silk as she used me to get off, the sight of that thick, swollen cock with its smear of precum at the tip made my mouth water.

All I had to do was lean forward an inch closer to her husband jerking off beside us, and I could taste that cum on my tongue.

Adam spread his legs farther apart and thrust his hips into his tight fist, fucking himself hard. I wondered errantly, shockingly, what it might feel like to have him fuck *me* that hard.

"So hungry for it," Adam rasped out as he stared at the arousal starkly written on my face.

I groaned painfully as he swiped his thumb over that wet pearl at his tip and then raised it in offering for my lips. My gaze cut to his and found his green eyes blazing neon bright.

"Taste it," he ordered.

And even though I hadn't obeyed an order from a man in any capacity outside of the theatre since before I could remember, because I couldn't trust my father or any of the Made Men who invaded my life as a youth, I wanted to obey Adam. In fact, I felt an answering softness at the base of my normally titanium spine that whispered I would submit to most anything he willed me to do.

So it was easy to lean forward, eyes fused to his, to take that cum-coated thumb in my mouth and swirl my tongue hard over the ocean-brine taste of him. We groaned simultaneously, me at the shockingly delicious flavor of him, and he at the sight of me with Savvy bouncing on my cock and me sucking away salaciously at his flesh.

"So bloody hot," he praised me, pulling his wet thumb out of my mouth and tracing it over my lips before he brought his hand down to cup and squeeze his balls.

He stared at me, not his wife, as he pumped his hips, and he didn't close his eyes as he muttered, "Going to finish on you."

Savannah panted in agreement as she ground down hard on my cock, and I knew that she was close to coming all over me.

So, apparently, was her husband. Because thirty seconds later, his drives grew erratic, and he fell forward, one hand searing hot on my shoulder so he could brace himself as he pumped his cum all over my chest.

Savvy gasped loudly, smeared her pebbled nipples in his semen coating my torso, and came hard, sloshing wetly up and down my rock-hard dick.

My orgasm came last, but it was brutal. It ripped my breath from the fabric of my lungs and rattled my spine like a rabid dog, so that I was lunging manically into Savvy's still clutching pussy and panting hotly *this* close to Adam's hovering mouth as he stared down at his handiwork drying on my chest.

I closed my eyes and collapsed against the back seat with a low groan of completion that had Savvy laughing lightly in my ear and Adam chuckling.

"Good, isn't it?" she purred, arching into my hand as I ran it down her damp spine.

"*Magnifico,*" I murmured because I didn't have the strength to do anything else.

Adam chuckled again, and I felt the sound in my groin. "We agree. So, Sebastian, we have a bit of a proposition for you."

My fog of sexual satisfaction parted as anxiety cut through it. "Mm-hmm?"

"Don't look so frightened," Savannah said, pressing a hand to my cheek so that I would look into her soft blue eyes. "When I told you I wanted you, I didn't just mean your gorgeous body. I want to know you."

My eyes darted over to her husband, who had tucked his softening cock back into his pants. I found myself oddly disappointed by it.

He smiled reassuringly. "As you're aware, I have a certain degree of notoriety. I'm happily married, but I'm also seriously bisexual. Savannah and I have been looking for someone like you for a long time."

"Someone like me?"

"Someone to join us, covertly," Savannah clarified.

"In bed," I confirmed.

"In our lives," Adam corrected. "We want to have an exclusive sexual relationship with you, Sebastian. Preferably, you'd move in with us to cut down on the messiness of matching schedules and sneaking around. We'd say you were our new chauffeur, but really, you'd share our bed and our lives. And we want to find the right people to produce your screenplay. It's brilliant, and we believe in it, in you."

I swallowed thickly, staring back and forth between them. The ground beneath me was quaking, tectonic plates perched on the edge of each other, about to change the shape of my future forever.

"Why me?"

Surprisingly, Adam answered, and he did after leaning in to take my other cheek in his palm so that they both framed me. "Because sometimes you meet someone, and the magnetic force at the heart of them connects with the force at the center of yours. Inexplicably, irreversibly. We aren't stupid enough to let a man like you fall through our fingers. I promise this isn't some ruse or game, Sebastian. We want to take care of you and make you happy because we know in a way that's elemental that you're going to do the same for us." He paused, then moved closer until his full lips skimmed my own with each movement of his mouth. "Say yes."

These two beautiful, wealthy people were asking me to exchange my hovel for a mansion, my lack of job security for a life of luxury, and my deep horrifying loneliness for the highest caliber of company I ever could have dreamed of. It seemed too good to be true. But looking at Savannah, her soft, childlike blue eyes wide with sincerity, feeling the connection to her I'd felt since the beginning, I trusted her to take care with me.

Turning my gaze, I blinked at Adam, noted the gorgeous tangle of his long, thick eyelashes over those forest-floor green eyes, and I was both surprised and not surprised that the answer that bubbled up my throat to irrevocably change the course of my life was, "Yes."

Chapter Five

Sebastian

My four roommates didn't ask me where I was moving so abruptly, and I almost wished they had. Maybe then I would have hesitated over my answer enough to second-guess my impulsive decision to move in with an incredibly high-profile *married* couple I knew next to nothing about in order to be their driver and boy toy. But they didn't.

In fact, the only two in residence as I crossed the living room with my leather duffel bag of meager belongings barely glanced up as I passed through. It reminded me of the deeper reason I'd agreed to Adam and Savannah's indecent proposal.

Obviously, it was about the money and the chance to see my dreams come true.

But honestly, I would have agreed without any of that.

I would have agreed just for the intimacy I so lacked in London.

For someone(s) to care about where I went and when I would

come home. For shared space that went beyond five adult men struggling to share a dingy toilet in Shoreditch because the rent was dirt cheap. These desperate men did not have the desire or means to indulge in the intimacy I'd grown up with, the kind I couldn't shake the desire for.

They struggled merely to exist, while I yearned to be moved as the tides by the moon, by a power and feeling greater than myself.

I craved the familiarity of truly knowing a person; of understanding instinctively when to speak and when to listen, of reacting to a subtle cue a loved one didn't even know they were projecting, and you didn't even consciously know you were reacting to.

Of a person's very fragrance feeling like home and a pair of arms to hold you tight whenever you had need of it.

I had my family, the four women who tethered me to the earth like gravity, but they were so far away. Italy might as well have been a different planet, and I didn't have the means to draw it closer with frequent visits.

Still, I had them, and they made sure I knew it. Even my eldest sister Elena, who was not prone to wasting time and was not effusive, made a point to talk to me once a week on my calls home.

Christmas in London had been a lonely affair, but we'd all video conferenced for most of the morning, and on New Year's Eve, when I went out with the lads, I'd found someone pretty to kiss at midnight without any hassle just as I never had to work hard for female attention.

So why was I so desperate for more?

And not just the body and mind of Savannah Meyers, beautiful, whimsical waif though she was.

But for *him*.

The dangerous temptation of a *man* with eyes greener than a verdant forest canopy and hands I couldn't stop from imagining moving firm and domineering over my flesh like a horse breeder checking the quality of his livestock.

I wanted him physically in a way that made me sweat, but what shocked me most was the fact that I wanted his mind too. Just as I wanted Savvy's.

I'd spent the past ten years of my life wishing for a life exactly like Adam's. He was my idol, the light at the end of the dark tunnel of my adolescence. The fact that he was actually there now, a tangible figure who wanted a very prurient part of my life was too surreal, too tremendous to truly comprehend.

How was I supposed to resist the draw of that?

Maybe a different man could have, but I was too hot-blooded to scorn a chance at sex and intimacy even though I knew in my bones it would all end in tragedy.

How could it not?

"I'm out, lads," I called to Johnny and Ben, who sat on our sunken, creaky green couch playing *Call of Duty* on the television.

"See ya, mate," they said in unison without looking away from the set.

"Won't be back," I reminded them as my hand closed around the doorknob. "I told you last week I was moving out."

"Right-o." Ben nodded, his tongue tucked between his teeth as he jammed his thumb repeatedly at the controller. "Break a leg!"

They weren't listening, but then they never did when they were fixed on a video game. I gave up, knowing that Russ would probably have a roommate in to take my place within a fortnight. He was the only semi-organized lad of the lot of them, an administrator at Finborough Theatre who collected strays like an old lady with cats. He'd taken one look at me the day I pulled up to the theatre to begin rehearsals for *Bury the Dead* after being scouted for it at a theatre house in Rome and asked me if I needed a place to crash. He was the one true friend I'd take away from my days in this flat.

"All right," I said to no one as I opened the door and stepped into the hall. From outside the apartment, I peered in one last time, breathing deep the stale scent of ramen that permeated the walls from the take-out place downstairs, counting the discarded beer bottles on the kitchen table from last night's gaff about town. "Goodbye," I whispered, allowing myself to feel nostalgic and oddly bereft that this chapter of my life was drawing to such an unceremonious close.

When I closed the door on the apartment, though, I didn't look back.

I walked down the four stories to the street, dodging a biking deliveryman outside the ramen place, and set off along the wind-swept, sleeting streets toward the other side of the train tracks.

IF I HAD ANY DOUBTS BEFORE, they were multiplied tenfold when I arrived at the Meyers's elite address in Chelsea. Their gorgeous yellow stone mansion was a hive of frenetic activity, the top door and basement entrance open to admit streams of people going in and out. A smartly dressed man with shoulders like a linebacker checked me in before he let me through the gate, but I was surprised he was able to keep track of everyone in the chaos.

"*Scusi*," I said when a small ginger-haired woman carrying a truly enormous display of flowers bumped into me on our way to the stairs. "Can I give you a hand with that?"

Her smile was weak with relief. "I promise I go to the gym, but these flowers must weigh about forty pounds."

I laughed as I slung my duffel crosswise over my shoulder and assumed her load. It wasn't bad, but then, I was six foot four and built like a giant compared to her tiny form.

She glared at me, fisting her hands on her hips. "Well, you don't have to make it look too easy."

I shot her a wink. "Lead the way. I'd be helpless without you."

She shook her head at me, and I had the sense she was used to men much more handsome and charming than myself.

"I'm Chaucer Williams," she offered as she pushed the open door even wider to allow me entry. "And before you start, yes, it's a tragic name for a girl, and yes, my mother is a literature professor at Oxford, and she wrote her dissertation on Chaucer when she was pregnant with me. Let's just call her cruel error a result of crazy pregnancy brain, shall we?"

"'The greatest scholars are not usually the wisest people,'" I quoted.

She blinked wide brown eyes at me as we paused in the foyer. "I'm sorry, did you actually just quote Chaucer to me?"

"Overdone?"

"No, not at all. I mean, not with this crowd." She waved her hand around the chaos happening in the Meyers's home, the beautiful clutch of people collected around a coffee table through the open archway to the right and a striking man wearing a muscle shirt and pink stiletto heels even though it was winter assembling what looked like a champagne tower in a room to the left. "They can quote anything from the silver screen, but most wouldn't read a book, even if they were the lead in its adaptation."

"Ooof, I sense you don't have a lot of love for actors."

Chaucer shrugged, but her grin was impish as she moved again to lead me deeper into the house. "You work for them long enough, the fascination tarnishes."

"Mmm," I hummed, noncommittal, as we moved down a panelled cream hall with towering ceilings into a large kitchen at the back right of the house.

It was all done in variations of white, but everything was textured and complicated, from the pink veins in the massive marble island to the paint strokes on the plaster walls that saved it from being austere and instead became warm and vibrant. A man and woman bustled in the space, the clear directors for the three young people diligently assembling a collection of finger foods for platters laid out on a palatial wood dining table at the back of the room near a wall of windows.

"What's going on?" I asked my guide as she directed me to leave the flowers on a credenza already filled with them.

"Oh, honey, clearly you're new to the team. Adam and Savannah host parties the way some people attend church. It's a monthly occurrence, if not biweekly." She frowned at me. "Who did you say you were again?"

"I didn't," I started to introduce myself when a heavy hand dropped to my shoulder, startling me so badly I stepped back into the person who'd touched me.

This resulted in my back pressed tight to the torso of a man tall enough to lean forward and whisper, "Careful," in my ear as he steadied me with another hand at my hip.

Adam gave me a subtle squeeze before releasing me and stepping up in line with me to address Chaucer. "This, Chaucey, is our new driver, Sebastian Lombardi."

"What happened to Albert?" she asked, suddenly glaring at me. "He was my favorite! Much better than that nitwit, Oscar."

"Not that it's any of your business," a familiar American voice spoke coolly from behind me, and a moment later, Savannah appeared beside Adam in all her refined beauty. "But Albert decided to retire. Happily, I was more than satisfied with my service at Luxury Regent Car Services, and we were able to steal young Mr. Lombardi away from them."

She turned her back on Chaucer in a deliberate way that illustrated her irritation with the young woman and offered her delicate hand to me as though she were a queen at court with peasants. I raised it to my mouth and brushed a barely-there kiss over her knuckles. Chaucer couldn't see the red stain that bloomed in Savannah's cheeks, but Adam and I could. I looked at her husband for signs of jealousy, but he only shot me a satisfied sidelong look and squeezed me where he still clasped my shoulder.

"Sebastian's more than that," he offered Chaucer warmly, flashing his movie star grin. For a moment, the bottom dropped out of my stomach, and I wondered, horrified, if Adam was going to tell her I was their new boy toy.

Instead, he smoothly continued, "He's a very talented screenwriter and actor."

Chaucer cocked an eyebrow at me. "Is that so? An *actor*."

I shrugged at her helplessly. "When God gives you good looks like mine, it's practically blasphemous not to take advantage of them."

She blinked at me, then gave in to a reluctant giggle. "I can see why Savannah was taken with you."

"Can you see that I'm currently rather vexed that nothing seems ready for the soiree tonight?" Savannah asked as she fingered the petals on a massive peony in one of the arrangements on the sideboard.

I still couldn't believe I knew a woman who said things like "vexed" and "soiree" or that I was so attracted to her for exactly her haughtiness and sleek grandeur. She wore a tidy little skirt suit in some kind of tweed material in pinks and pale lavenders. With her hair gathered into a loose twist at the nape of her neck and a pair of ridiculous yet sexy schoolgirl shoes with heels on her feet, she was almost impossibly alluring. A prim, proper little miss in need of educating from someone with more experience.

The irony of our significant age difference compared to our burgeoning sexual dynamic wasn't lost on me, but it wasn't important either. It was exactly the contrast between Savvy's maturity and grace, and her almost childlike wonder and vulnerability that hooked me through the gut and dragged me inexorably toward her.

Sensing my gaze, she smiled just slightly without looking at me.

Adam's tight grip on my shoulder drew me back into his conversation with Chaucer.

"He's got the run of Albert's carriage house," he explained. "You'll be happy to show him the place? I'm afraid I have to run to a meeting, and Savannah has to finish setting up for tonight."

"I'm happy to make myself useful," I offered. "If there is anything I can do to help."

Savannah's eyes sparkled, but her mouth remained unsmiling as she studied me critically. "Well, you do look like you can carry a heavy load."

I resisted the childish urge to flex for her, but just barely. Instead, my smile stretched wider between my cheeks, and I had the satisfaction of watching her blush as my eyes traced her small figure. "I could throw you over my shoulder to demonstrate."

"Caveman," Chaucer shot back, not flirtatiously, not really. She was a woman numb to the glory of the limelight, but she was a woman all the same, and she enjoyed repartee as much as the rest of them.

I pouted, pressing a hand to my heart. "You're objectifying me, and we've only just met. I'm wounded."

She laughed, a high, yipping hiccough of a giggle that suited her diminutive stature and round curves.

"Enough," Savannah said, and her voice was the west wind bringing winter to the sun-drenched kitchen. Now, her eyes sparkled like ice. "We are simply too busy for idle chitchat. Sebastian, do settle in and then find me to discuss my schedule for this week."

"Yes, ma'am," I said somberly even though laughter lodged in my throat.

Her little nose wrinkled slightly with distaste at the moniker. I knew without having to be told that "ma'am" made her feel old.

Adam coughed to hide his own laughter and clapped me on the back. "Good man, I'll see you shortly. This is your new home, so make yourself comfortable. Chaucer," he said by way of goodbye before he brushed a swift, light kiss on Savannah's cheek. "Sweetheart, I'll see you tonight."

"Don't be late," she reprimanded as though she could see into the future and knew he would disappoint.

Adam's smile was a slow, closed-lip smirk that spoke of mussed bedsheets and late-night debauchery. I had the feeling he was often late, for very good and very wicked reasons.

After he swept from the room, the air seemed to flatten as though Adam had stripped the atoms of their current. It was so strange and wonderful to be in the presence of one of the greatest men in cinema, a man I'd admired for so long, that I doubted I'd ever become used to it.

A soft touch on my arm drew my attention to Savannah. Her wide eyes were so clear that staring into them was like looking into the bottom of a depthless lake.

"The enchantment fades," she murmured, leaning close so that the words were a secret kept from Chaucer. "Remember, Sebastian, you're here because *I* want you here. My husband… he is as transient as the tides."

I studied the gorgeous, carefully cultivated woman before me, surprised by her transparent attempt to manipulate me. Not because I thought she was incapable of manipulation but because her words reeked of insecurity. For a woman with so much, I wondered how she could still feel so small. It awakened a tenderness in me I'd previously only ever felt with my mother and sisters. A tenderness based on the heart-aching idea that I could make this wealthy woman's life a little richer in ways unique only to me.

The lasso around my heart caught in Savannah's small hand tightened inexorably.

I traced the line of one of her fingers on my forearm out of sight of Chaucer. "Well, consider me the shore, hmm?"

Her nostrils flared delicately, and I knew she understood what I was implying.

In this fledgling liaison between Savannah, Adam, and myself, I understood that I was the only one who would remain steadfast. Of course, I was. I had little to offer the likes of the Meyerses, and they had everything to offer me.

If I wasn't so in lust with Savannah (and frankly curious about Adam), the unbalanced nature of our agreement might have been enough to give me pause. Instead, I assured my traitorous, overly passionate heart that I was entering into the dynamic with eyes wide open and emotions warily closed off.

This was sex and power.

An exchange as old as time.

If it made me seem like a prostitute, well, gigolos weren't ill-regarded in my home country, and now, I understood why.

"*I'm glad you're here,*" Savannah mouthed, raspberry-painted lips cutting the air into words I could read with my eyes.

Behind her, Chaucer shifted on her feet and delicately cleared her throat.

It was enough to stir Savannah into remembering herself. She stepped away and glanced with studied boredom at her glittering diamond Cartier watch.

"Chaucer, hurry along with Sebastian and then see what is taking the caterers so long to set up the platters." Without waiting for confirmation of her orders, she sailed out of the kitchen on elegant high heels.

I watched her go, noting the roundness of her pert ass beneath the skirt. When I turned back to Chaucer, she regarded me with a vaguely worried expression.

"I'm a hedonist," I explained unabashedly as I adjusted the weight of my bag over my shoulder. "I enjoy beauty wherever I find it."

She snorted indelicately, red curls shivering as she shook her head like a disappointed Italian mama at me. "You're trouble is what you are."

I shrugged because there was no use in refuting it.

She shook her head again and, without another word, turned to lead me through the open French doors at the back of the kitchen beside the breakfast nook. The flagstone patio extended from the house in an organic oval shape, then broke off into a pathway leading through surprisingly dense greenery.

"This is quite a garden," I murmured as I took in the traditional English garden design and the antique-looking wrought iron furniture that made it feel like a fairy-tale kind of place. "Not what I would have imagined for the Meyerses."

"Oh, Savannah wanted something a little ritzier. Trust me. But this was Adam's mother's house, and he refuses to live anywhere else while in town."

Curiosity gripped me by the throat. "Oh? I think I read Adam's mother was a countess?"

"The daughter of an earl who married a marquis," she corrected automatically just as we burst through the garden into a small clearing where the flagstones encircled a beautiful oval swimming pool that was being decorated by three women with floating lanterns and bouquets of white flowers. "You needn't worry about the titles or his parents, really. His mother passed away ages ago, and he doesn't speak to his father and his new wife."

I wanted to ask more. Pump Chaucer for information until all of Adam's secrets spilled between us for me to dissect and pick at. I told myself my curiosity was purely professional, but that didn't explain why my heart picked up into a gallop at the thought of the darkly golden-haired actor with the slight cleft in his chin.

She stopped mid-step, Converse sneaker posed in the air, to suddenly turn and shoot me a glance. "Don't hope for it, okay? I like you so far, and I don't want you to ruin that."

"Don't hope for what?" I echoed innocently even though her words found purchase in my chest.

I barely resisted the urge to rub the pain there.

Chaucer was smart, and she wasn't having any of it. "Adam is a movie star. He doesn't have time for friends, not even his lifelong ones or his wife most of the time. So you can get it out of your head right this minute that he'll want to become chums with the likes of you. You're his driver, end stop."

"You've read me all wrong," I promised as I stopped beside her. "If I was interested in a Meyers, it wouldn't be the Oscar winner."

"If you think Savannah didn't have a part in getting him that Oscar, you need to think again," she countered, suddenly angrier than she should have been.

I watched, bemused, as she stomped through the manicured shrubbery at the left of the pool and disappeared.

"I thought Brits were reserved," I muttered as I tromped off after her.

The path was too narrow for my shoulders, the branches clutching at me like greedy lovers. I cursed as one scratched the vintage leather jacket I'd found in Camden Market for fifty pounds.

"*Cazzo!* Where the hell are we going?" I demanded, but I didn't need Chaucer to answer because I'd finally stumbled into the small clearing at the back right of the property.

Nestled like a fairy tale in some magical forest sat a white-shingled cottage with a deep green gabled roof and ivy climbing across its face. The windows were mullioned and steepled like something from one of the many Italian churches from my childhood. Those flagstones that led from the main house to the pool were almost haphazardly placed in a skipping pattern that led to the red-painted door.

It was fucking beautiful.

"Your house," Chaucer offered unnecessarily, but she wasn't looking at me so she couldn't see how the small structure had affected me. "Albert thought it was just fine, so I won't hear anything about how cramped or old-fashioned it is, you hear me? The chauffeur we had before old Albert was some young fop who thought he was too good…" She turned to face me and witnessed my wide eyes. "You like it?"

I swallowed the surge of emotion in my throat. It wasn't what I would have picked for myself if I had a million pounds, no, but then, I'd never been much of an unrealistic dreamer. Growing up in Napoli's slums meant I knew too much about the hard knocks of life to let my mind soar in the clouds.

But it wasn't about what the house looked like.

It was the fact that I'd never had space to myself, and I was an eighteen-year-old man.

Cosima and I had shared a bedroom for most of our youth, and then I'd moved to London into an apartment with four other blokes.

This was paradise.

Better than a dream, just like Savannah.

"Yeah," I said, my voice heavy with emotion. "Yeah, I like it just fine."

Chaucer squinted at me as though she couldn't quite understand me, and it irritated her. "Well, come on, then. You can put your bag down, and I'll help you with the rest."

"This is it."

Her red brow carved lines into her forehead. "One bag?"

I shrugged a shoulder. "I like to travel light."

She peered at me again, and I wondered if she'd missed her calling as a schoolmarm. Done with her scrutiny, I moved past her toward the house. A small gnome with a green hat and rosy cheeks peeked out from behind a copse of lavender.

I couldn't believe such a place existed, let alone in Adam and Savannah's backyard.

The unlocked door swung open soundlessly to reveal an open-concept interior consisting of a farmhouse kitchen, a tiny living room with a round, stone fireplace, and a desk set up toward the back wall of windows I could already picture myself writing at.

"*Bellissima*," I declared softly.

"The bedroom and bath are upstairs."

I ignored her as I moved into the house. A framed photo of a family was left on the mantel of an older gentleman I thought must have been Albert. It seemed like something he would have taken, and I wondered about the circumstances of his leaving.

But not enough to change anything.

Mama used to say to us all "take luck when it comes and know it is a rare gift. If you look too long at where it came from, it might pass you by."

I was old enough to wonder how my mother had gained such wisdom and was seasoned enough to know what it meant. If you looked a gift horse in the mouth, you were bound to find motivations you didn't like.

So I plucked the frame from the mantel and handed it over to Chaucer. "Make sure that finds its way back to Albert."

She gave me another look, but I turned my back on her before she could examine me too hard. The stairs creaked under my feet, and the narrow walls were almost claustrophobic around my big body. However, I was used to being oversized in Europe, and it didn't bother me. The ceiling upstairs was only seven and a half feet at best, even shorter where the gabled roof cut into the room, but I loved it instantly.

It was all done in heavy wood furniture with a quilt that had to have been handmade over the big bed. The bathroom was tiny, the shower so narrow I wondered how I would make it work, but I didn't care.

It was all *mine*.

"Savannah won't like what you're wearing." Chaucer had followed me up the stairs and perched on the edge of the bed while I explored. "She expects the help to dress well, or it reflects poorly on the family."

I arched a brow and looked down at my white tee, dark jeans, and leather jacket. They were all cheap, of course, but I'd never been accused of being poorly dressed. Even if I'd wanted to change, there wasn't much else in my closet better than this except for the suit I'd worn at the closing of *Bury the Dead,* and I wasn't going to wear that to a house party. No matter that it was being held by a *duchessa.*

Chaucer laughed. "You look mortally offended."

"I've been called beautiful one too many times," I admitted with a good-natured shrug. "I'm not afraid to admit it's gone to my head."

She shook her head, red curls tumbling pleasantly over her shoulders. "You're an interesting man. Actors usually have big egos."

"I just told you I was beautiful."

"No, you told me people say that. You don't have the right bearing. You seem almost…" She tucked her tongue between her teeth. "Almost like you don't want people to look at you for too long."

My hands fisted spasmodically at my sides as her words hit just a little too close to the mark. I felt the vibration from the impact in my teeth. She had no idea what she was saying, just a shot in the dark. I was moving into this quaint house to begin a relationship with Savannah and her husband; if I had real intimacy issues, why would I seek out such a complicated emotional situation?

Because you know it's going to fail, a little voice whispered in the back of my mind.

Because you know a poor boy from Napoli won't succeed under the glittering spotlight of civilized pop culture for long.

Because your father didn't love you and your best friend and twin left you, and you have no one left because you aren't worthy.

I shoved the thoughts away through sheer force of will, fixed a grin to my features, and turned to change the topic and remind Chaucer why people in my hometown called me "*l'incantatore*," the charmer.

Chapter Six

Adam

Another party.

If I had a nickel for every party I'd been to in my twenty-eight years, I'd be a very rich man.

Although I'd been born very rich, and in those twenty-eight years, I'd only succeeded in making myself obscenely richer.

The truth was, the parties, the money, it all bored me to tears.

Being famous was a side effect of my lifelong addiction to dramaturgy. I wasn't gauche enough to complain to anyone about the trials of being an international movie star. Not when I had scads of money, the pick of any script I deemed worthy, and more connections than the Prime Minister himself.

No, I was a lucky man.

Lucky *and* skilled.

I'd earned my place at the top of the heap, so why did it feel so wrong looking down at the masses?

Maybe because I'd never been an ordinary man.

As a member of one of the oldest peerages in England, one that had somehow managed to retain the colossal wealth of their ancestors despite the death tax and perils of modernization, son to Marquis Peter Andrew Yardley, who was known throughout the United Kingdom as one of the most civilized and criminally *dull* men of our time, I was born under the magnified lens of public scrutiny.

Hell, Arthur Whitley-Fairfax, Crown Prince of England, was my best mate at Eton, and I was a regular at Buckingham Palace.

So why did this embarrassingly privileged sense of *ennui* and vague disgust with society persist within me?

As if summoned by my thoughts, the rich, rumbling sound of masculine laughter drew my attention from a sleep-inducing discussion of Academy Award politics to the tall, dark, rough-around-the-edges man my wife and I had invited into our home.

Sebastian stood in the center of the room as though he had been born into this life instead of wedged into it by the sheer force of Savannah's desires and my inability to say no to them. He was holding court with a Russian prima ballerina known for her resting bitch face who was currently laughing so hard, one delicate hand was pressed to her stomach, and a British director, Sir Ronald Rothschild, a known introvert who was snorting expensive whiskey through his nose as he clapped Sebastian on the shoulder.

It was obvious from the moment I'd seen the handsome Italian on the stage of Finborough Theatre that he was born to be an actor. Too many people believed they could make it on the best international stages and silver screens because they were beautiful, but the truth was, beauty was a hindrance as much as it was a boon. Beauty got you in the door, but talent and an almost manic work ethic bought you a lasting stay.

Sebastian Lombardi was talented, no doubt about it. The way he transformed himself into a war-torn soldier who refused to be buried and laid to rest as one of the many who died for a supposedly "glorious cause" was absolutely staggering. I found my heart palpitating oddly, erratic pounding against my breastbone, followed by weak tremors as though my pulse was being manipulated by Sebastian like an orchestra by its conductor. At one point, tucked in the front row in the dark of an indie theatre, I felt transported to the battlefield, as scared and alone as Sebastian's character had been minutes before his death.

So talented.

But God, it was more than his beauty and his talent.

He positively oozed passion.

On stage and off when I'd confronted him. How glorious he had been in the face of my sudden appearance. Not cowed by my reputation or accolades, not awed by my own good looks, nothing so reactive, so simple and shy.

Whatever game I had hoped to play—something sly and mean because he was handsome enough to tempt me, but I was irritated he had caught the eye of my wife, that she had pushed me to once again take on a lover in our already tense marriage—evaporated in the steam that rose between us.

He had been confused, furious, indignant, and undoubtedly *aroused* by our repartee. It had taken nearly everything in me not to reach between our bodies—already too close for propriety—and cup the hardening length I'd glimpsed pressing against his inner left thigh through his trousers.

He was totally unlike the male lovers I had taken in my youth before meeting Savannah and then, again with her. We both seemed to prefer pretty men with slight frames, narrow faces, pouting mouths, wide eyes, and stylish hair. It was a risk to associate with such men, men who harnessed their sexuality and were not afraid of their own fluidity. I had built a career on being a man's man of actors. I played Hamlet and Macbeth in the theatre, Jonathon Cross in the series of gritty spy thrillers that had first launched me to cinematic fame, and then Lord Byron, the ultimate womanizer, in a biopic that had secured my first Oscar.

No one would accept that Lord Adam Meyers was bisexual.

They wouldn't understand that loving both men and women was not *all* I was, like a two-dimensional sketch stuffed into a labeled envelope, but merely a facet of who I was and what I enjoyed.

And how could I blame them when I had spent nearly my entire life struggling with my sexual identity and how it should or should not impact my personality?

Which made my attraction to the utterly masculine specimen of Sebastian Lombardi entirely nonsensical. He was too big, too wide in the shoulders, and quilted with dense muscle from wrists to ankles. His beauty wasn't gentle or pretty. It was a slap in the face, a hand to the throat, a tight vise suddenly wrapped around my balls. I was as attracted to him as I was terrified by him, and the combination was heady.

Heady enough to make me forget my pledge to myself and my wife that we would not take any more lovers after Oscar Hampton, a local burgeoning set designer who left our bed rather acrimoniously last year. That we would focus on the failing love between the two of us, strengthen it and each other.

An open sexual predilection was all well and good when the main relationship was strong, an iron pole on which to hang all the rest, but somewhere in the last two years Savannah and I had grown tarnished and dull.

She bored me now, almost as much as the rest of the poor sods under my roof that night, and I knew she found me frustrating. Why didn't I do as she wished the same way I had as a young twenty-five-year-old with a thirst for fame and success?

We were going through the motions of our life, two business associates living under the same roof.

But then… Sebastian.

I'd never been so in lust with my wife as I was watching her struggle to take the thick length of his cock in her snug little cunt. She was small and pale, prim and elegant. Against Sebastian's glaring virility and rough, Italian-soaked curses, his big, tanned hands consuming her slight frame, his full mouth devouring her little cries, I'd been nearly torn apart with desire.

The contrast of them together was too much.

I hadn't intended to involve myself in that first tryst.

I knew he had never had relations with a man before and I told myself it was foolish even as I unzipped my trousers, knelt on the seat beside him, and released my throbbing length into my hand to present to him like a gift.

My dick hardened dangerously in the middle of my drawing room as I remembered the way he'd gazed at me, like I was both the most dangerous creature he'd ever beheld and the most beguiling.

And then, when he'd tasted my cum, instinctively sucking it from my thumb, I knew.

No matter my pledge to Savannah, to myself, I had to have him.

"Adam, you look flushed," Miranda Hildebrand cooed, running her lacquered red nails down my arm as she leaned close in a cloud of floral perfume. "Are you all right?"

"I think you could use some air, Adam."

The voice came from over my shoulder, but I knew it was Sebastian immediately. There was only one other Italian man at the party, Gianni Valentino himself, and the older man's voice didn't have the same effect on my libido as Sebastian's did.

I shifted to allow him into our loose semicircle. His scent assaulted me instantly, something with heat and spice that made my mouth water.

"Miranda, Bobbi, I'd like you to meet Sebastian Lombardi," I introduced, pausing as Sebastian flashed them his wicked grin and bent over each lady's hand to deliver a kiss to her knuckles. By the time he was done, both scarlets were beaming at him from under their curled lashes.

"How quaint," Miranda purred in her signature breathy voice. She was a dead ringer for Marilyn Monroe and she took every opportunity to showcase it. "How do you know our Adam?"

Our Adam.

My teeth clenched at the moniker.

What was it about celebrity that made public figures possessable?

Though, my father had called me "my son" whenever the opportunity arose, and it had irritated me since I could cogitate. In my opinion, no human being could be wholly owned by any other. Not even Savannah was allowed to get away with calling me "her" Adam.

Sebastian seemed to sense my tension and placed a chummy arm around my back to squeeze my shoulder. "He was kind enough to give me a job."

"Oh?" Miranda's interest noticeably cooled. She wasn't the type of woman to associate with those lower on the totem pole than herself.

"He's being modest," I said, finally remembering my social graces. "Seb is a screenwriter. A rather fabulous one if I do say so myself. I merely offered to help him find financial backing for the project."

Bobbi fluffed her orange hair and leaned forward to place a greedy hand on Seb's exposed forearm. Irrational irritation sparked through me. I wanted to reprimand him for being overly casual with his rolled cuffs when the rest of the men were wearing dinner jackets.

I wanted to tear Bobbi's manicured hand right off her limp wrist.

"You know, I am a very wealthy woman," Bobbi offered. "Why don't you tell me about this little project of yours?"

"I would love nothing more, *bella*," Sebastian replied, placing his hand over hers in a familiar move that made fifty-five-year-old Bobbi Gerkan blush like a schoolgirl. "But Adam really does look in need of some air, and he promised me a Cuban cigar I'm itching to get my hands on."

Bobbi laughed. "Men and their cigars."

Sebastian shrugged charmingly. "I'll hold you to your interest, though. By the time I'm through with you, you'll barely be able to stand from boredom."

Miranda and Bobbi both tittered because they were absolutely *not* picturing being bored boneless by the Italian but they had no doubt they'd be weak-kneed nonetheless.

Fury ate at my heels and a headache settled between my temples. I went to sip from my Scotch only to discover melting ice in its place.

Sebastian clapped me on the back and pushed me none too gently between the shoulder blades to propel me away from the women. I moved, but I did it with a scowl on my face, my ill-humor fitted so closely around me it threatened to choke.

People spoke to us as Sebastian followed close at my heels, forcing me forward unless I wanted to be stepped on. When I looked over my shoulder to snarl at him, his strong features were fixed into an affable grin as he nodded at the partygoers who acknowledged me.

It was only when we made it into the relative peace of the kitchen, the door swinging closed behind us on the din of the party, that Sebastian stepped up beside me. For some reason, it made me feel better to see him there, within easy reach, hovering close like a bodyguard.

Like he cared that I was ill-tempered, and he wanted to protect me from anyone who might want a piece of me until I could sort myself out.

I'd known the man less than a week, and he was already under my skin.

The sensation was unpleasant but also not entirely unwelcome.

A good character often did the same, crawling under my flesh until it became a part of me. Even after I'd finished a film or play, they stayed with me, eternally stitched into my soul.

The idea of such intimacy with a near stranger should have repelled me, but as Sebastian ushered me out the back door to the softly lit patio, I found myself pressing closer to him. Our shoulders knocked once, twice, then settled together as we stopped by a gurgling water feature at the edge of the shadows. It was too cold out for the partygoers to linger outdoors and despite the vastness of the gardens around us, it felt oddly intimate to be in the yard alone with everyone else in the house.

He surprised me by staying quiet while I discarded my empty glass on the patio table and pulled a crumpled pack of Dunhill cigarettes from my trousers. Most people reprimanded me for my smoking habit, but I only indulged when my restlessness threatened to strangle me.

When I wordlessly offered them to him, he plucked one from the package and tucked it into the corner of his mouth, pouty lips parted around the slim column.

My throat went dry.

Eyes to that sinful mouth, I struck the gold lighter Savannah had given me one Christmas and held it aloft for him. I nearly jumped out of my skin when he casually reached out to cup his hand around the wavering flame, propping his pinky on top of my knuckles to do so. Electric heat burned through the connection straight through to my gut.

Our eyes connected over the flickering red-blue fire, and I noticed how dashing he was in the low light. Only the steep angles of his face were cast in dull gold, the harsh cut of his cheekbones, the slanted line of his strong jaw and brow, and the ridge of that Roman nose. He tipped his chin then, and light spilled over his eyes, spotlighting those uniquely colored yellow irises.

I wasn't sure I'd ever seen such a masculine example of beauty, but it stirred me through to my soul.

One of his brows rose slowly, questioning my thoughts maybe or my intensity. When I didn't move, he sucked on the cigarette and gently, almost playfully, blew the smoke in my face.

Despite my irascible mood, a smile tugged at my mouth.

"Who knew Adam Meyers could be such a bear," Sebastian mused idly, looking out at the garden instead of at me.

Perversely, I wanted his attention back on me as much as I relished being spared his scrutiny.

"Well, you try being the host of a party full of high-society Brits and tell me what kind of mood you find yourself in." I sounded as ill-tempered as a child, but I couldn't help myself.

Ever since Savannah had come home smelling of heat and spice, of Italian man and sex, I'd been on edge.

"If you don't want me here, I'll leave," he offered, as if reading my mind. When I looked at him, faintly struck by his perceptiveness, he shrugged casually. "Sex and intimacy are two very different things. You didn't just invite me into your marital bed. You invited me into your home. I was raised without two pounds to rub together in the rubbish of Naples. I won't hold it against you if you've reconsidered the invitation."

It took me a moment to comprehend exactly what he was

suggesting. "You think I'm acting like a right arse because I've realized I invited a heathen into my civilized house?"

Sebastian looked slightly over his shoulder at me, smoke curling from his mouth over his left ear in a caress I wanted to mimic. "I wouldn't blame you."

A short bark of laughter erupted from my chest. It shouldn't have felt good, but it did. The tension I'd been gathering inside my chest all night loosened, one knot of many untangled. Freed, I sucked in the clean night air and then took a long drag from my cigarette.

"The first memory I have is throwing an absolute fit as a lad because my nanny forced me to wear a cravat to one of my father's business events. Have you ever worn one? Well, it's like being strangled by a starched bit of fabric wrapped too tight around your throat. To this day, when I'm too long in polite company, I get that feeling like a vise across my neck." I angled my head to shoot him an indolent look. "It isn't the heathen I take umbrage with, you understand? It's with the lot of *them*."

I tossed a hand at the house behind me the way one tossed garbage into a can.

Sebastian's eyes tracked the movement. They were darker than gold in the low light, something like amber, and just as sticky. When he looked back at me, I felt myself get trapped in them and gave up my struggle as easily as a fly.

"Why do you live like this then?" he questioned with quiet sincerity. "You're a rich, powerful man. Do as you want."

This time, my laughter hurt as it rattled through my chest like a caged thing struggling to get free. "Once an editor friend of mine suggested I write a memoir. Foolish man. I asked him why I would want to write about the memories that trap me to this day." I paused, sucked in the acrid smoke of nicotine, and let it travel to my head in a lovely rush. "Do your memories trap you?"

"Memories," he agreed. "Circumstances."

"My cage may look different than yours. Gilded, perhaps. But that doesn't mean I'm free."

"And you want to be free," he surmised, eyes bright with intelligence.

At some point, he'd flicked away his cigarette and moved closer to me, where I sat half inclined on the stone table. He loomed over me, hair dark as a night without stars, shoulders wide enough to hold up the world. I itched to trace the breadth of them with my palms. Test the strength of them with my teeth. Mark him up, mark him *mine*, with punishing lips.

"Freedom is an illusion," I said because my cynicism was a matter of my very Britishness and upbringing.

"Freedom is a choice," he countered, bearing down on me now, stepping up so his legs straddled either side of mine stretched out in front of me.

His scent was everywhere, in my nose, on my tongue. It was potent, almost animal, making me want to growl.

"You're a child for thinking so," I told him with all my aristocratic, haughty grandeur.

He had the gall to grin down at me. "And you're an old man so stuck in his ways you don't see how easy it is to correct them."

"I am only twenty-eight. What would you have me do?" I asked mildly even though something inside me seethed and boiled.

He was close enough to kiss.

So why wasn't I kissing him?

Why was I indulging in the mockery of a conversation and not bending him over the table?

I didn't get to know my lovers this way, in the way of quiet, oddly intimate silence spent smoking out of doors, in the way of invasive questions and raw answers.

I didn't do this, and I didn't *want* to do this now.

My black mood hovered on the horizon, but closer, something else beckoned as warm and enchanting as the sun.

A sun named Sebastian.

He touched me then, a hand on my shoulder, and his grasp seared through my blazer, button-up, and bone.

"I'd have you do exactly as you wished," Sebastian said softly, innocently, even though something was dark and eager in his eyes I felt mimicked in my gut.

"Society, career, and family be damned?" I countered harshly.

"*Castrarsi per far dispetto alla moglie*," he murmured in spiced Italian. "Do not cut off your balls to spite your wife. I think in English, it's do not cut off your nose to spite your face. Which is greater, what people think of you or what *you* think of you?"

"What do you think of me?" The question pooled on my tongue before I could swallow it down. How stupid it was to ask such a man what he thought of me.

We were as different as night and day.

The dark, raw masculinity and irreverence of Sebastian contrasted with my well-bred attractiveness and sharp, cultivated class.

Maybe that was why I liked him.

Because I didn't trust him not to rip me open at the seams like a savage looking to plunder.

"What do you wish to do to me right now?" he countered, hand tightening almost painfully on my shoulder. "Fuck the crowd inside. It's just you and me in the dark."

A shudder rippled through me at the lavish lasciviousness of my thoughts. This I was comfortable with.

This I could use.

The desire ate at me with voracious teeth, taking huge chunks out of my resolve. My rapidly diminishing veneer of civility.

Because the truth was, I was just as heathen as the man before me.

No, I thought as my lips pulled back over my teeth, and something like a snarl rose from my throat, *more*.

Before I could think, I was standing, forcing Sebastian back, unbalanced. I caught him around the forearm and tugged him harshly into my front, plastering our bodies together from toe to clavicles. When he was steady, we were close enough to share the same breath. He tasted of tobacco and something sweetly addictive like fortified wine.

I raised the smoldering end of my cigarette into the small gap between us and sucked too hard on the filter. It dropped from my fingers, and I crushed it beneath the toe of my shoe, holding the smoke in my mouth.

Sebastian watched me all the while with those huge golden irises as keen as a wild cat.

When I tipped my head to the side and leaned close, he understood what I wanted and mirrored the movement.

His lips parted, and carefully, I curled the smoke over my tongue and into his mouth. The silver mist swirled in that pink cavity and then disappeared down his throat. A groan worked up mine, and I fed that to him, too, this time with my lips sealed over his.

Chapter Seven

Adam

The moment our mouths met, it was over.

Sense.

Reason.

The world of glamour, power, and money at our backs blazing like a beacon.

There was nothing but two ill-suited men clutched together in the dark, taking from each other with silken thrusts of tongue and hot, seeking lips.

It might have started with feeding him smoke, feeding him my desire on a groan as angry as it was lusty, but it finished with what he gave me.

A head rush greater than the nicotine lingering on our breath, a freewheeling sense of calm like dropping from a plane before you pulled the chute.

Peace.

Amid the heat and ecstasy of our embrace, sank deep in the desire I felt boiling through every atom of my blood, I felt peace.

A clang from the kitchen had us both jumping apart like schoolboys caught looking at titty mags. Sebastian laughed softly, touching two long, strong fingers with furred knuckles to his swollen mouth. He looked at me with wonder and a kind of keen-edged intensity as though he wanted to take me apart and discover what made me tick.

I took an instinctive step back.

"I've never kissed a man," he mused, then laughed again. "What a strange thing."

"To kiss a man?" I croaked, voice ravaged with desire.

"To like it."

I closed my eyes as he offered those words so simply. How could he be so nonchalant in the face of his rapidly shifting sexuality?

I still remembered the acute terror that had stabbed me through the heart when I'd had my first kiss with a boy in the back of the rectory at my estate. He'd tasted like communion paper, and his lips were as thin and dry as Bible parchment.

I'd thought I would die the moment our lips met, and when I survived, I felt such staggering guilt that I thought it was only a matter of time before lightning struck me down.

Not because I was religious.

I'd never given a damn about it.

But because I'd been born the son of a marquis, and no matter how quickly the rest of the world marched on into modernity, the peerage of England still had decades to go.

"Light in the loafers," my father would say about Cousin Ernest. "A pansy little fag."

"Hey," Sebastian's voice cut through memories and anchored me in the present. He was holding my forearm, his hand big enough to grasp the muscled width of it. "Was I that bad?"

A joke.

Bloody hell, he *jokes*.

"You seem very unperturbed about kissing your first bloke," I said, and somehow, the words were accusing, which was preposterous because I liked kissing them too.

Something careful moved over his features, and his eyes pierced mine like golden pins. "You have a good mouth, and happily for me, you know how to use it."

"No gay meltdown," I prodded, feeling like I was coming out of my skin.

His head cocked slightly to the side, and a piece of inky hair curved over his head like a perfect comma. "I'd hate to steal your show."

"If you're so comfortable, why don't you do something about this?" I dared, crudely cupping the painful erection caught beneath my trousers.

Sebastian's brow spasmed as he looked down at me, then back into my scowling face. "You want to use me?"

I opened my mouth to say something, but I didn't know what. I didn't like the way he said those words, so coldly, or the way calculation entered his previously warm expression.

But he was already stepping closer, pushing my sternum with the heel of his palm until I once again sat on the edge of the table. Without waiting for permission, he straddled my legs, clamping them tightly together so I felt trapped by his powerful thighs and the large body curled over mine. Panic singed the edges of my dark mood, and regret began to seep through.

"Sebastian—"

"*Stai zitto*," he said and I knew enough Italian to heed his order to shut up.

His fingers were large, almost clumsy on the clasp of my belt. The sound of metal teeth unlocking was a loud rasp in the quiet night, but not as loud as my gasp when he tucked his tongue between his teeth and courageously reached into the placket of my pants to pull my cock into his hold.

"I wondered how heavy you would feel," he admitted, tongue sweeping over his full bottom lip as he stared at his hand uncovering my shaft through my boxers. "Like tempered steel."

Fuck.

How could he be so assured? I was the seasoned Dominant here, the one in control, the one with real goddamn experience.

But here I was, trapped on a table, nearly ruined by the simple clasp of his workingman's palm around my swollen flesh.

"Stroke it," I demanded, gathering the tattered remnants of my control to issue my imperious order.

The bastard grinned, shuffled closer to hide me from anyone potentially walking up the path back to the house, and gave me one strong stroke from root to tip. It wasn't private enough. Normally, I'd never mess around with something so potentially catastrophic to my career as a public handjob from a man, but something about Sebastian scrambled my senses. I tipped my head back as I succumbed to the pleasure searing through me.

"Like that?" he asked, but it wasn't innocent.

No, this bastard knew what it was like to be played with because he'd had countless women play with him and countless women to play with himself. Just because I was his first man didn't mean he'd lost all his sexual confidence.

Yet something ached in me to know he was doing this with me, for me, even though I was being a surly cad. Something that went soft inside my chest knowing he trusted me to take him over to this unexplored side of his sexuality.

I'd never had a virgin before, and the honor of it was hard to ignore.

"Tighter," I ground out through my teeth, then hissed as he obeyed.

It was difficult to know what to watch, his tanned grip on my straining cock and the way he smeared my precum over the tip or that ridiculously handsome face with the dark brows knitted together in concentration over molten yellow eyes.

"I'm going to make you come for me," he told me in a low rumble I felt strike my bones like a tuning fork.

I was already close, almost unmanned by the simple grasp of his hand.

"It'll be messy," I warned because I'd always come copiously.

"Mmm, *va bene*. I remember," he murmured, adding his other hand to the game he was playing with my dick.

He twisted one this way and the other that on the up stroke.

My brain whited out at the edges.

"Yeah," he encouraged, watching my face with stark hunger. "I never knew pleasuring a man could be so powerful. To hold you in my hand and watch you quake… I have a wet spot on my trousers."

My eyes darted to his black pants. He shifted, angling his hips forward so the strain of his erection and the wet spread of his leaking precum caught the light from the lanterns hanging in the tree overhead.

"Fuck," I cursed, undone by the sight. My head fell forward onto his hard chest and the scent of him scorched through my nose down to my gut. "I'm going to come."

"Do it," he urged, moving fast, panting almost as hard as I was. "Come all over my hand. I want to see you make a mess of yourself."

That was it.

That filthy order uttered in hot, lightly Italian-accented English set me off like a rocket.

My spine tightened, and I exploded in pleasure so acute it was almost agonizing. I clamped a hand on Sebastian's shoulder as I shook and came and came all over his hand, all over my shirt and open trousers.

The only sound in the aftermath was the ragged rasp of my breath, the faint pound of Sebastian's heart beneath his breastbone where my cheek was pressed, and the din of the party in the house behind us. As I slowly came back to myself, the closeness of our positions and the odd sanctity of the silence induced that old panic to take hold. Just as I tensed to move away, Sebastian shocked me.

His free hand moved up to run fingers through my rumpled locks, smoothing them back from my damp forehead.

Such a simple act, a sweet one especially from such a big, bold man.

It eviscerated me nearly as much as the orgasm.

I tore myself from his hold, noting he let me go easily, and stepped out from between his body and the table. I needed space like I needed air.

When I saw Sebastian dominate the stage at Finborough Theatre, I knew I had to have him. I would have done it for Savannah anyway, maybe, despite our vow to stop for a time. My wife and I liked to play, and it had been too long since our last dalliance. But sitting at the front of the theatre, enraptured by the way the great, big Italian man with expressive hands and seemingly 24-karat-gold eyes moved across the space and owned it, I'd felt viciously compelled to own him for myself. I'd never been the kind of Dominant who liked to collar his subs or mark them with spit, cum, or teeth, but my brain conjured images of that black hair caught tight in my fist as I craned his head back to bite at his neck, paint the skin above a thick leather collar with bruises as plum-purple as his lips.

I should have known then that the ferocity of my lust wasn't safe.

But I'd never reacted to a man the way I did to him in these last few furtive moments caught together like fish tangled and flapping in the net of our shared desire.

An orgasm was supposed to be a release, not an undoing, so why did I feel so completely exposed?

My hands were almost too tense to do up my ruined suit pants, and I had to button my blazer to hide the stain of my ignoble orgasm.

Whatever moisture remained in my mouth was lost to the sight of Sebastian untucking his white shirt to use the tails as a towel for his cum-soaked hand. The bottom row of his abs stood in stark relief beneath his olive skin and the thick trail of black hair arrowing down into his groin where his erection strained against the zipper of his suit pants.

"Not bad for your first time," I congratulated churlishly.

Fuck, I was being a right prick, but I couldn't help it.

Those perceptive eyes were steady on me as I shoved my hands in my pockets and began to walk away with forced casualness.

"Practice makes perfect," he said with a modest shrug before rooting his clean hand through all that thick black hair. It curled artlessly over his forehead, and I knew why Savannah liked him. I knew why Bobbi and Miranda had puffed up under his attention.

He was a star, and it had nothing to do with his celebrity or lack thereof.

It was because a man like Sebastian gave off so much light and energy, he was magnetic. Combined with his invasive gaze and curious mind, it made him a dangerous creature.

One who would eat me alive if I wasn't careful.

"I prefer to play with my wife present," I lied coolly. "But this was… nice. Enjoy the rest of your evening. Try not to let Miranda corner you in the kitchen. She's been known to climb unsuspecting men like a jungle gym."

Shadows coated Sebastian like a velvet cloak he wore too well. He stared after me implacably as I raised my chin in farewell and finally turned on my heel to walk around the side of the house to an unused entrance. As I took the stairs to the primary bedroom to change clothes, I resolved to make sure Sebastian Lombardi and I were not caught alone again.

Chapter Eight

Sebastian

My cock was a weaponized thing with a hair trigger that threatened to go off at the barest hint of movement. I held still for long moments after Adam fled from me, drinking in the cool air, the dark night, and the heady sensation that little old me had frightened such a legend.

In truth, he had frightened me too.

Simply because holding his heavy cock in my hand had felt as right as sitting Savannah's pretty pussy on my dick in that town car.

I was a romantic man, an Italian and a writer, so probably more romantic than most. Therefore, I believed in things like fate and kismet, in energies colliding and quantum entanglement.

It was too soon to say I felt those things with these two carefully cultivated people with pretty veneers housing seriously fucked-up demons, but something of it was there. A kind of magic in the touch of flesh to flesh, the sense that I'd spoken to Adam like this before, known him and her in an elemental way that spoke of previous lives or two halves of a whole meeting after a long separation.

I stared down at the hand that had held Adam and had played with Savannah. Such a plain hand, wide palmed and ridged with calluses, long fingers with strong, blunt nails. A workingman's hand, a peasant's touch on such precious skin.

The contrast made me feel both powerful and strangely vulnerable.

Could a man like me be allowed to love and keep two people like them?

What happened in the fairy tale when the pauper fell in love with both the prince and the princess?

"I wouldn't expect much from my husband."

Savannah's voice drifted like the scent of English roses through the garden, and a moment later, she appeared through the bushes on the flagstone tiles. She was dressed in white, a color I was gathering was her signature. It was a high-necked dress with overlong, tapered sleeves constructed of a lace so fragile looking I wondered if it would rend under one touch from my strong fingers. Her short, curled blonde hair made a corona of light around her beautiful face, backlit by the house lights spilling into the yard.

She was exquisite, of course.

I felt the primal urge surge through me the way it had when I'd gazed at all of Adam's unrumpled perfection to muss her up. To put my filthy mark on her and remind her we were both just humans in different packaging.

"I don't expect anything," I responded honestly.

My shoulder brushed the swell of an evergreen bush at my side, releasing the pungent piney fragrance. I plucked a little branch of soft pines and twirled it between my fingers as I approached her.

"I've been married to him for five years," she continued as though

I hadn't spoken. Her eyes tracked the movement of the stem around and around in my hand warily, as though the delicate needles were lethal. "He's the kind of man who is like an iceberg. The ten percent he shows on the surface is dynamic enough to make people think that's everything that he is. But beneath the water, he is as complicated as they come, and he does *not* enjoy being known."

"And you do?" I countered mildly, close enough to sweep the soft, scented pine bough across the curve of her jaw and down her throat. Gooseflesh blossomed under my caress, but she was otherwise unmoved.

"To a certain extent," she allowed with a haughty tip of her chin. "If the person is worthy."

"And how does one prove their worth?" I asked, curling over her, crowding her with my body in a way I sensed she would like.

I wondered if there was a theme linking these two married lovers. If they yearned for intimacy just as much as they feared it. If all the celebrity and accolades in the world truly meant nothing in the face of their own self-criticism.

Mama had told me once that people without family were like bottomless wells. No matter how much you tried to fill them up, they remained empty because their foundation was cracked.

I wanted to ask Savvy about her family and upbringing, about that soft Southern grass and the stench of poverty she had spoken of briefly in the town car. My heart wanted to excavate everything she had hidden in the layers of her being, but my head told me it would only lead to rejection, so I focused instead on swirling the pine needles over the shell of her ear.

She shivered slightly, then lashed out to grab my wrist, stalling my movements. When her eyes met mine, they were slate blue with cold resolve.

"You prove it by being loyal to *me*." Her other hand reached up to my cheek, her thumb nail scraping along the stubble already sprouting along the edge of my jaw. "I found you, Sebastian. I will be the one to show you love and care. I will be the one to bring you fame and success."

A vague sense of alarm trilled through me, but I was distracted by the way she curled her fingers around my ear and yanked me closer to her glistening, raspberry-painted mouth.

When she spoke next, I tasted champagne on my tongue as she breathed the words into my mouth. The way this encounter mimicked my prior one with Adam was slightly eerie, but again, I was too lulled by Savannah's utterly feminine sensuality to take proper note.

"You're mine," she whispered before sliding her small tongue over my bottom lip. "For as long as you are in this home, you're mine more than anyone else's. Not your mother's, not your father's, not your friends'. Not Adam's. But mine." Her sharp, straight teeth bit into my lip and tugged so pain burst brightly through me. "Can you do that for me, handsome? Can you give yourself to me like that?"

The teenage boy in me wanted to howl *yes* to the moon swollen and fertile in the sky above us, but the small part of me who had earned my manhood young defending and providing for my family as the sole responsible man of the house took pause.

"Can you give me you in return?" I asked, collaring her throat gently in my hand, the pine needles crushed between our skin so their fragrance permeated the air.

"What I offer isn't enough?" she asked, her eyes low-lidded with lust but her voice still crisply superior.

"Nothing is free," I said, even though the words reminded me of Adam, of the hypocrisy of me saying that when I'd just argued with him that freedom was a choice.

"If you work hard," she purred, tracing her free hand from mid-chest to the curve of her hip and over her belly. "I'll see what I can do."

"Well…" My voice was in my gut as I moved us back, back until her shoulders met the wall in the shadows at the side of the house, obscured from the door by the evergreen hedge. I followed the path her touch had just carved on her body until I found her hand at her hip, then clasped our fingers. Together, I used them to gather the hem of her knee-length dress up and up until it was clenched in her palm, and her sheer nude panties with a slight frill were exposed to my gaze. A wicked grin flexed between my cheeks as I slowly lowered myself to the hard flagstones to take care of my second Meyer of the evening. "I better get busy then."

Savannah's hands sank into my hair on a soft sigh, and her head hit the house siding with a gentle *thwack* as she gave herself over to me.

It always confounded me how a man could dislike going down on a woman. The power of being the one allowed to pleasure her most vulnerable place, the taste of her sweet arousal as it started to leak out of her soft folds onto your tongue like so much honey. It was heady, addictive.

I could have spent hours on my knees on the uncomfortable flagstone servicing my *duchessa.*

My nose pressed into the mound of her clit as I breathed in her intoxicating scent, and when she squirmed, I rubbed it back and forth over the bundle of nerves.

"You have to be quiet for me, Savvy," I said. "Can you be good for me and swallow your cries?"

She gasped as I opened my lips over her through the mesh fabric and sucked her clit into my mouth, laving it with my tongue. The abrasion of the wet panties over her sensitive flesh made her hips jerk against me.

"Do you think I can make you come without even taking these off?" I taunted her, snapping a finger in the elastic at her thigh so she gasped again. "Yes, I think that's what I'll do. Make you drench these with your cum and send you back into the party smelling like sex."

"Sebastian," she moaned, half scandalized and half aroused.

I loved that about her. That smooth transition from lady to wanton and knowing it was all because of me.

The angle wasn't good enough to feast on her properly, so I tugged her hips into my grasp, and her legs automatically locked over my shoulders so her sex was tipped up into my mouth. I growled my approval into her sweet pussy and renewed my efforts to make her come apart for me.

Laughter from inside drifted out the open French doors onto the patio, but I liked the risk of discovery, knowing anyone could find us locked together in the dark. The game of playing the Meyers's chauffeur but being their secret lover was salacious and sexier than I could have ever imagined.

They knew they shouldn't have me, yet they couldn't help themselves.

My cock kicked in the confines of my trousers, but I focused all my attention on the pretty pussy in front of me. I curled the fingers of one hand beneath the soaked edge of her underwear and slowly pressed two into the snug heat of her cunt. The wet sounds of my pumping fingers were lewdly loud in the quiet dark.

"*Una figa così graziosa*," I murmured against the inside of her thigh. "Such a pretty pussy, Savvy. And so wet for me. Do you want to come already? Are you that eager to come apart on my tongue?"

I twisted my fingers inside her and rubbed at her front wall until her legs spasmed around my head and her face clenched with sharp-edged arousal. She was so fucking gorgeous like that, wrecked for me, only my shoulders and my fingers wedged inside her tight heat keeping her aloft.

"They might hear you inside," I whispered because there was no insecurity with Savannah, not like this. She was no longer the British lady but that Southern teenage girl lying in the grass, touching herself and wishing for filthy, desperate fantasies. "Some of the guests might touch themselves to the sound of your gasps later tonight. Would you like that?"

She did. Her breath coming fast and heavy, a furious pink blush spilling down from her neck to her chest in the cowl-neck of her dress. She wanted to be desired by everyone almost as much as she wanted to be respected and admired by them. It was a delicate balance to strike, but I thought she thoroughly succeeded.

I smiled before running my tongue over the place my fingers fucked and then up to her swollen clit to give it a long suck.

Her fingers in my hair turned to claws, and her hips gave little aborted jerks as she fought to get closer and squirm away from the intense feeling unfurling between her legs. I didn't let her move an inch. She was mine at this moment, even if she couldn't truly be mine in any other.

Her underwear was saturated with my spit and her leaking juices, the combination all over my chin as I ate at her regardless of the mess. When she came with a wail she muffled in the crook of her elbow, I licked up every inch of her dripping pussy until she was done shaking.

"Sebastian," she whispered the way a disciple might murmur the name of a deity at temple. "Sebastian."

I memorized her tone and the exact way her mouth formed the letters of my name so I would never forget what it felt like to be revered by a woman I admired so much.

"Savannah," I praised her lavishly in the single word then pressed a kiss to the inside of each pale, smooth thigh, in love with the vulnerability of those thin-skinned curves. "My gorgeous *duchessa*."

I rested back on my heels to gently lower her to the ground, keeping my hands on her hips to steady her as she wobbled slightly.

"You did so well for me," I told her as I gently rubbed a finger over the drenched placket of her panties and adjusted them slightly so they sat better over her swollen pussy. When I looked up at her from my knees while I adjusted the folds of her skirt back down over her thighs, her gaze was black, pupils blown wide, mouth a lax oval of shock and tenderness.

She looked in that second almost… scared of me. And when she stepped back slightly out of my grasp, her spine was pressed flat to the wall like she couldn't bear to be close to me any longer.

"Savvy," I breathed, opening my hand between us like a gentleman before a lady in the British court, a strangely polite gesture given what we'd just done but my dirty girl was gone and in her place that buttoned-up lady.

She shook her head slightly then stopped suddenly like she'd given too much away.

"The party," she told me with an abstract wave of her hand, already shuffling to the side to reenter the house. "I must get back."

I put my hands in my pockets to keep from reaching for her. "Okay, *duchessa*, have a good time."

She nodded, but didn't look at me as she turned and walked delicately around the barren bushes back into the house where the noise and glamor swallowed her whole.

And I remained alone in the dark wondering why the two people who had invited me into their home to be their lover had both just run away from me like the devil was chasing them.

Chapter Nine

Sebastian

It was late by the time I dragged myself back to the carriage house.

My carriage house.

At least, temporarily.

It felt good to toe my shoes off and move through the cool, shadowed space, but I wasn't in the headspace to be alone and enclosed. The animal within me was restless, prowling, and growling. It wanted something more than Adam's cum on my fingers and Savannah's orgasm on my tongue. It wanted… It *wanted.*

It was as simple and overwhelming as that.

I had a home. I had lovers. I had the promise of success.

Yet I was still alone.

Without Cosima, without Mama and Elena and Giselle.

Without the comforts, however rank, of my home country.

A foreigner in a foreign land.

Called like a wolf by the moon, I moved to the mullioned window overlooking the corner of the pool and fought the urge to howl.

I scrubbed my hands over my face, then checked the time on the clock over the microwave. Three in the morning. The guests had left, save for Savannah's good friend, Ramona Waters, and Miranda Hildebrand, who had been put to bed after too much liquor hours before. Adam had locked himself in his office with a well-known producer and director soon after our tryst in the garden.

The pool was empty, and I desperately needed to purge myself of this energy.

It would have been easier to come. I'd given two orgasms that night and had none of my own. But the idea of crawling into bed and touching myself until I came on my stomach, seed cooling, body spent but mind ringing, was its own kind of torture.

So I shucked off my clothes right there beside the front door, leaving only black boxer briefs because I didn't own swim trunks, and pushed back through the door.

It was cold, the kind of damp chill special to England that gnawed hungrily at your bones, but I'd always run hot, and I enjoyed how it sharpened my tired senses. The pavers were slightly slick with dew, and the lush grass crunched underfoot as I cut across to the pool. Without hesitating, I dove into the deep end, body knifing with minimal splash into the heated depths.

When I emerged, shaking water from my hair like a dog as I treaded water, a cool, American accented voice said, "Eight out of ten from the American judge, a six out of ten from the Russian, and ten out of ten from the Brit."

It was a husky voice, yet oddly lyrical and feminine. When I turned, it surprised me to see a young woman, a few years younger than myself, sprawled across a chaise lounge. Even in the dim pool lights, her riot of overly thick, wavy hair was honeyed blonde. Her features were in shadows, but it was clear from the coltish length of her thin limbs that she was still a teen.

"I expected higher from the American," I countered, pushing my slicked-back hair off my face to smile at her.

She shrugged one bony shoulder. "Americans like star power, and you're an unknown."

A true laugh startled up my throat. "Touché. Why don't we rectify that? I'm Sebastian."

She gave an unladylike snort as she leaned forward, legs straddling the chaise, elbows falling between her thighs so she could curl over and prop her chin on her hands. The movement brought her out from the shadows and showcased a face crowded with large features. A wide mouth, full, lush lips that dominated, and large, catlike eyes a rich indigo blue. Thick light-brown eyebrows slashed across her forehead and though her nose was well formed, it was lost amid the drama of her other features.

She wasn't beautiful, not really. But I knew with the certainty of a man who'd been raised with beautiful women, who worked in an industry where beauty was currency, that she would be a knockout when she grew into her big-featured face and put some meat on those long bones.

"*Just* Sebastian?" she asked suspiciously.

I flipped on my back to float leisurely. "Just Seb, if you want the intimacy. Though, if we're going to be friends, I'd like to know what to call you."

But she wouldn't be deterred from cynicism. "You're supposed to introduce me by your full name so I can *ooh* and *aah*"—each exclamation was met with a hilarious expression of exaggerated amazement—"over what movies you've been in or directed or produced."

"Well, I haven't done any of that."

She waited, one thick eyebrow cocked, until I laughed and amended. "Yet."

"Ah," she said with all the gravitas of a much more mature woman. "There we have it. Give it a bit and you'll be introducing yourself by your last name first."

"Like Bond?"

"Yes, but honestly, he's probably the only one who deserves to do that," she allowed graciously.

She was a riot, the best conversation I'd had all night. Oh, I'd enjoyed Adam and Savannah, but they twisted me up until I couldn't breathe, and this slip of a bold thing was unspooling me with good humor one inch at a time.

"He's a fictional character," I pointed out as I started doing a lazy backstroke. "They're capable of pulling off things most people would never dream of."

"True. But if I had the choice, I'd live like that, too."

"Like Bond?"

"Like my life was a storybook."

"Why don't you, then?"

"It takes a lot of courage to go after what you want," she said the way my mama might have, scolding me for being naive. "I'm only sixteen, you know. One day, though. Even if I never do anything worthwhile, I'm going to introduce myself by my last name. It's easy to get away with stuff when you're that confident, and opportunities always seem to come to people who believe enough in themselves. Even when they shouldn't."

"You're very wise for a sixteen-year-old," I told her sincerely, as I hopped out of the pool and leaned back on my palms, smiling slightly as her eyes raked over my wet, muscular torso and then rolled in disdain. "I know we just met, and I still don't know your name, but

I'm halfway enchanted by you already."

"It's the confidence," she agreed, peering at me like an old woman through spectacles. Arriving at some decision, she abruptly flipped onto her belly, face still in her hands as she faced me, feet kicking an easy rhythm in the air behind her head. "My name is Linnea Kai."

"Lovely name for a lovely girl."

"Don't flirt with me," she scoffed. "Not when it's just pity flirting."

"Who says?" I demanded, kicking my feet through the water to splash in her direction without actually spraying her.

She waved a hand toward her body, the oversized *Caged* band tee swallowing up her scrawny figure and that glorious mane of rumpled hair. "C'mon. I'm young, but I'm not dumb."

My laugh felt good in my chest, loosening the tension I'd harbored there all night. I held my hands up in surrender. "If I'm feeling any pity tonight, Linnea, it's for me, not you."

"Now you sound more like an actor."

I laughed again and watched the way that wide mouth twitched as she fought a smile. This was a kid who'd had to grow up a little too fast and now resented her youth instead of embracing it. I knew the feeling because I'd been the very same.

Maybe I still was.

Eighteen going on eighty.

"What brings you to the Meyers' house?" I asked, swinging my legs through the backlit waters.

She moved again, quicksilver, to sit upright and hug her knees to her chest. I had the feeling she didn't often keep still.

"My mother," she said with a sniff. "She loves these things."

"Most people do, even if they've never been."

"Yeah," she agreed, looking into the distance at something I couldn't see in her memories. "I'd rather be back home."

"Home?"

"Maui."

"I've never been before."

"You wouldn't want to leave. It's so… alive. It's not just a paradise, you know? People think it's all sunshine and flowers, but there's an underbelly. A balance. Volcanic rock and fertile soil. Scorching days and storms that roll through, whipping up the ocean and ripping open the earth." A pause as she shivered, falling out of her reverie. "You wouldn't want to leave," she said again for emphasis. "I never have before now."

It was late after a long, tiring, and frankly confusing night. January in London was as damp and chill as any other month, and my skin was starting to numb. Yet I found myself leaning toward her, a flower tipped toward the sun. Her energy was a palpable thing I wanted to bask in.

"You sound like me when I speak about Italy." There was no reason to share with this girl. She was a stranger. Absolutely nothing linked us together but being in the same place at the same time in mostly the same mood. Somehow, there was a magic in that. A space for intimacy that was made sacred and safe by the fact I'd probably never see her again. "Everyone thinks it is the most beautiful country in the world, but it has its shadows, and I grew up in the darkest pit."

"But you loved it." She uncurled her legs to stand, tall and gangly, the points of her collarbones sharp through her shirt.

"I did."

"Why did you leave, then?"

"There was nothing there for me. No future, anyway."

"Because you wanted to be an actor?"

"Because I wanted more for my family and myself."

Why was I talking to this slip of a girl about any of this? I watched wearily as she stepped to the edge of the pool deck, toes curling over the tiles. All that hair rustled in the wind, softening her striking bone structure. She was a beauty, already, the signs barely buried beneath the surface ready to be unveiled, but she didn't have a clue. She was all awkwardness and young candor standing there in front of me with her head dipped to one side, eyes earnest even in the dark as they took me in.

I had the sudden revelation that she wasn't looking at my body, wasn't aware of my beauty, at least not in an impactful way. She was peering beyond that, into the shadowy depths I hadn't shared in so long.

It made me uncomfortable, but not as much as it made something long-neglected, deep inside my chest stir with warmth.

"Are they still back there?" she continued her line of questioning. "My dad and my uncles still live on the island."

"My twin sister moved to Milan on our eighteenth birthday. My older sister is in Paris studying art."

"Fancy."

I shrugged, the movement dislodging a piece of wet hair over my forehead into my eyes. "All Giselle ever wanted was to be an artist. Cosima and I have been working since we were kids to make it happen."

Linnea cocked her head. "Why would you put her dreams before your own?"

It was such a childish question that it threw me for a moment. There were only a handful of years between us, but I suddenly felt ancient, bones heavy and creaking beneath my skin.

"Many reasons," I murmured, looking into the glimmering blue of the pool, shining with lights in the dark night. "She had a bad time of it in Naples, too soft and young and pretty. Every place has its underbelly, but we lived in the one in Napoli, and she drew bad characters to her like moths to a flame. But she had talent. Talent enough to get into the school of her dreams and get a tidy little bursary so we could afford to dole out money for the rest. I'm still saving money for my eldest sister to attend graduate school in the States. She's whip smart," I confessed proudly. "She wants to be a lawyer."

"What about you, though?"

"I'm here, aren't I?"

She peered at me closely, twirling a lock of thick blonde hair around her finger like a cog working in a machine. "Following your dream now, I hope."

"I always was," I assured her, though for a moment that hadn't been true.

When I was fourteen, I'd almost capitulated under the weight of pressure from the local mafioso to join his ranks. We hadn't seen our gambling addict of a father, Seamus, for weeks, and Mama was down to making us pasta in olive oil and ground pepper for every meal, the portions getting smaller every day. A mafioso showed up at our house when Mama was out and the girls were all home with me. He'd threatened to take them as payment for Seamus's debts.

I'd never felt fear like that before or since, the bone-deep certainty that all that stood between my sisters and a truncated lifetime of misery was *me*.

I shivered, and it had nothing to do with the cool British air.

"So you want to be famous?" Linnea clarified, walking on her toes at the edge of the pool, all long lines and fluid grace, dragging a toe in the heated water from time to time and balancing with her arms held out at her sides.

I shrugged. "As a byproduct of acting and being good at what I love."

She shot me an unimpressed glare. "Are you just saying that to like… impress me?"

I arched a brow. "You're sixteen years old. Why would I want to impress you exactly?"

"Because you know my mum," she insisted, jutting her chin forward.

"Who is…?"

"Miranda Hildebrand," she said almost pugnaciously, and I wasn't sure if it was me she was taking umbrage with or the fact that Miranda was her mother.

Given that Miranda was currently sleeping off about six drinks too many in one of the Meyers' guest bedrooms, I assumed it was the latter.

Still, I didn't want to insult my new young friend by pointing out that Miranda was a B-list celebrity at best, known more for her failed marriages to famous men than for her own mostly soap-filled career.

Instead, I said, "I live in the same estate as Adam Meyers and his wife. Don't you think I've already got as much of a leg-up as I need?"

Her full mouth flatlined, and she fisted her hands on her hips. "So you *do* want to be famous."

"*Cazzo*," I muttered under my breath. "Of course, I do. Anyone who wants to be an actor wants to be famous because you cannot perform without an audience and it's better to perform for one who loves you than hates you. It's hardly something to judge someone over. Everyone wants validation of some kind, especially an artist."

I paused, noting the way she rolled her lips between her teeth.

"Don't you?" I asked softly.

She jerked a little as though I'd pushed her. "No."

I cocked my head. "It's not a weakness, you know?"

"I don't care what anyone thinks," she stated mulishly, and then, when I maintained steady eye contact with her, the line of her shoulders softened. "Unless they matter to me."

"That's fair. I want people to enjoy my work, but I don't care much about what people think of me as a person beyond my family. They mean everything to me."

"Families don't often survive this," she warned me, as though she was a sixty-year-old veteran of cinema and not a girl on the cusp of womanhood. "Fame and success and Hollywood."

"If you love something, you fight for it."

"But it comes down to the question of which you love more, fame or family? Sometimes, it's too much to fight for both."

She watched me shrug a little helplessly with those intense feline purple-blue eyes and brought her arms up to hug herself as though she was only just now noticing the cold. After a moment, she let out a soft, dramatic sigh Scarlett O'Hara would have been proud of and collapsed in on herself like a ribbon, falling seamlessly to the tiles beside the pool. Lying on her back, she trailed a hand in the water and looked up at the sky.

"You can hardly see the stars in London," she murmured. The words practically ached with homesickness.

I slipped back into the water to warm up, still unwilling to go to bed even though exhaustion tugged at my lids. Resting the back of my head on the lip of the pool, I looked up at the same sky, my gaze automatically finding the moon.

"When I miss home, I think about my loved ones looking up at the moon. It makes me feel better to know wherever we are in the world, we're under the same sky."

For the first time that night, Linnea looked over at me like I was someone worthy of looking at. Like I was beautiful.

"I like that," she whispered before looking up at the stars again. "Under the same sky."

We stayed like that for a long time, staring up at the dark night littered with dim stars and the fat swell of the moon. It was peaceful in a way that settled my restless spirit, and when I finally dragged myself to bed, I fell into a deep sleep the moment my head hit the pillow.

Chapter Ten

Sebastian

"Are you ready to go, darling?" Savannah asked me the moment I walked into their beautiful, light-filled kitchen the following morning.

She stood at the counter drinking coffee from a dainty cup and saucer with a gold rim while she looked over her tablet. The drinking and lateness of the night before had absolutely no bearing on her beauty. Her skin was unblemished and glowing as though she'd pulled down the moonbeams and swallowed them whole. In a pink tweed skirt suit that was no doubt designer and high heels, she looked ready to meet with *Vogue*.

I blinked at her a little owlishly.

She sighed, but a little smile played at the edges of her pink-painted mouth. "Late night?"

I grunted because, yes, it had been, and the guest house contained no coffee.

Her laughter roused me from my stupor. "I saw you in the pool with Miranda's unfortunate-looking daughter before I went to sleep."

"She's a kid," I corrected with a frown because that was ungenerous of her. "I'm sure she'll grow into herself. There are many ways for a woman to be beautiful, and very few of them have anything to do with her looks."

Something softened slightly in her face as she looked at me that made something soften within me too. "I'm surprised I didn't tire you out."

I was too tired to flirt well, but I managed a crooked grin as I stepped close to take the coffee from her slim fingers and swallow it all down in one gulp. Finished, I kissed her fragrant cheek. "You riled me up and left me wanting, and you know it."

The sound she made was practically a purr of satisfaction. "I know nothing of the sort, I'm sure."

"Mmm," I hummed as I noticed the fancy Italian espresso machine on the counter and set about making a fresh cup without asking for permission. "Do you want another?"

"Well, seeing as you stole mine, yes, I would."

"It was for your own good really," I teased. "If I'm driving precious cargo, I need to be alert."

Her coyness fell away like a veil, and a genuine little "O" of sweet shock formed between her lips. Unable to give up my mission for coffee, I sacrificed one hand to tug her closer and tuck her into my side. As I tamped the coffee, I pressed another kiss to her hair.

"Don't act so surprised, *duchessa mia*," I murmured. "You must know how precious you are already. It can't take a poor Italian driver to make you see sense."

But to my surprise, she shivered a little at my words and pushed just a little bit closer into the curve of my arm. "Not everyone can be as kind to themselves as I'm coming to find you are to yourself."

I shrugged a shoulder and pressed the button to start the percolation. The rich scent of expensive Italian coffee wafted between us like an aphrodisiac.

"If I am stuck living in my own head for the entirety of my life, it only makes sense to be kind to myself," I explained.

Savvy looked up at me, and even in heels, it was a long way to look. She seemed so small then, so much younger than I knew she was. It was a vulnerability that beckoned me closer, that tempted me to cut the line on my parachute and tumble into the depths of love with her.

What a complicated, wonderful creature she was.

"I want you," she said softly, intimately, her hand curling into my white dress shirt. "But I doubt we have time before my brunch meeting."

"I can be efficient," I said. A fast flash of wolfish teeth.

"Afraid there's no time for fun this morning, my beauties," Adam declared in that posh accent, sweeping into the room like a king in his court. The morning light glinted in his golden hair like a crown. "Sebastian and I must hurry if we're to make it to the lot in time."

Irritation crumpled Savannah's smooth brow. "Excuse me, but I believe I have priority over using Sebastian's services. I was the one to find him after all."

"Yes, and what a good eye you have," Adam agreed, sinking a proprietary hand into her carefully done hair and sealing her open mouth with a heated kiss. When he pulled away, her earlier annoyance was mingled with a little bit of awe.

I knew now what it was like to be kissed by Adam Meyers, so I understood completely. Unbidden, my fingers moved to my own mouth, pressing into the slight divot in my full lower lip as though I could feel the imprint of Adam's mouth still there.

He caught me then, eyes brightening as they swept over my face, and noticed the raw expression there.

"Sebastian," he murmured low, resting his hip against the island counter in mock casualness. "Come here and bid me good morning like my wife."

Savannah made a dainty little *hmph* noise that I would have called a scoff on someone less elegant. "It was you who kissed me, Adam."

"Yes," he agreed before raising a brow at me. "Sebastian?"

I hesitated, shame and eagerness warring inside me. It felt wrong to want this. To want to go to him when he called like I was some kind of trained dog. To go to him and worse, to kiss him. His mouth a hot claim on mine.

My hands curled into fists and sweat broke out lightly on my forehead.

"Go to him," Savannah cooed, and when I turned my gaze to her, she looked predatory and almost vaguely malicious. As though my discomfiture was a delight to her. As though it turned her on to know that I'd go against my grain just to pleasure her.

Fuck, these two would do my head in if I let them.

So why did I *want* to let them?

Before I could let caution eat into me too deeply, I took the five steps forward to Adam, watching the glint of deep satisfaction in his eyes as I obeyed him.

A shiver bit into my spine and left a permanent imprint.

"Good morning," Adam said, his tone and expression exceedingly helpful like he was assisting me rehearse my lines for a play.

"Good morning," I said, a little distracted by the way stubble dusted his square jawline like shards of pure gold. He had one of those divots in his chin, not a dimple exactly, but a depression that I thought my thumb might fit into perfectly.

A small hand found its way to the back of my neck, nails scratching at the short hairs there.

"Kiss him for me," Savannah encouraged, her thumb stroking over my rapidly beating pulse point.

I swallowed, but the moisture had fled my mouth. This was so alien to me, the idea of kissing a man and more, the very real truth that I *wanted* to kiss a man.

But who could resist someone like Adam? So handsome and talented and shockingly kind.

Someone who I'd admired so much that esteem had led to my own desire to be an actor, to wholly embody a character so seamlessly the way I watched Adam do on the screen time and time again.

Not me.

He watched me through lazily lowered lids, and I knew he wouldn't make it easy for me. I had to go to him with only the fuel of Savannah's desire at my back.

I stepped just a little bit closer, one foot between both of his so our thighs brushed together. His lips parted, tongue sweeping out to wet that lush mouth.

I placed my palm on his chest over his navy knit sweater, testing his firmness before sliding it up to his neck, warm and strong, and finally to his jaw. It was a square ridge of bone beneath my hand, so different from Savannah's delicately curved face.

"Today, please," Savannah ordered, but there was excitement there, an eagerness she couldn't hide.

But I was still a proud Italian man, so I didn't press into Adam's body as he leaned against the counter. Instead, I tightened my grip on the side of his face, fingers in his crisp hair, and hauled him toward me. His eyes flared wide in the split second before I covered his mouth with mine.

He tasted like spearmint toothpaste, and he smelled like bergamot and pepper. A small moan of surprised arousal moved up his throat and over his tongue onto mine. I ate it off and delved deeper, slanting his head and pressing my body more firmly along the line of his. He was hard everywhere, with no soft edges to press into, only the friction of two muscled bodies meeting.

It was strange to realize that I could stand in that kitchen kissing this man for hours and that much of that desire was separate from the excitement of Savannah wanting me to kiss her husband for her. So much of it existed just for Adam, the person—*man*—that he was.

"Enough," came her ragged voice.

I remembered myself, pulling away slightly, our warm breaths shivering over my damp mouth, but Adam hauled me back. Disobeying his wife or because he couldn't resist, I wasn't sure.

Either way, he sucked on my tongue in a way that had me imagining him sucking on other things before abruptly disengaging from me. My hand was still caught in his hair even as he resumed his casual lean, and for a moment, I was both embarrassed to be caught clinging and reluctant to let go.

"Well," Savannah said, a little primly even though her voice held a mild tremor. "That was certainly a lovely way to start my morning. And, I hope, a precursor to how I will end my night?"

I was still staring a little bewildered at Adam, but he smiled easily at his wife, almost blandly like he was completely unaffected. "Yes, darling, if you'd like. For now, we must be off."

He pressed a kiss to the side of his wife's head as he moved out of the room on brisk strides. I could hear him in the foyer, gathering his coat and belongings.

"Sebastian?" Savannah called lightly.

When I turned to her, one side of her smile was caught between her teeth. She pressed close to me, and something about her body against mine grounded me again. Her hands were cool when they reached up to tidy my hair and smooth down my button-up.

"You look very smart today," she praised. "Tonight, I'd like to continue what we just started. Would you like that?"

I settled into my old skin with a little shiver and grinned wolfishly at her as I cupped the back of her neck in my big palm. "Would you? I think we both know I'm willing to do filthy things to please my *duchessa*."

The noise she made was practically a purr. "Excellent. I'll see you for dinner then, and I fully intend for you to be the dessert."

I laughed at her, feeding the remnants of sound to her on a brief, deep kiss before I followed Adam's path into the foyer. He was waiting for me in a luxurious dark grey overcoat and loose Burberry scarf, his leather-gloved hands tapping away at his phone. A lock of wavy golden hair fell onto his forehead, and the gold of his Audemars Piguet was nearly the same shade as those silken waves. He looked every inch like the movie star and international sensation that he was, and it occurred to me how many people fantasized about being in exactly the position I found myself, perched on the precipice of being his lover.

He caught me looking and seemed almost surprised, eyes flaring wide slightly as he looked up from his phone. It surprised me in turn, because how could such a man, a movie star at that, be shocked at catching an admirer enjoying him?

His expression smoothed quickly into a small, self-satisfied smile, but not before I saw that glimmer of vulnerability. It made me like him even more, which was dangerous and strange.

Having a kind of… crush on a man.

A crush on Adam Meyers.

I snorted softly, me and most other women and men on the planet.

Chapter Eleven

Sebastian

"So," I said as I pulled my ancient leather jacket from the post by the door and swung into it with old familiarity. "What is so important that you're sweeping me out from under Savannah today?"

His chuckle was almost a cough. "And risk her wrath, you mean? Yes, my wife does have a foul temper. It's convenient then that she usually gets her way."

"I can't imagine saying no to her," I admitted as he opened the door for me, and I walked into the fresh, cool air of a London morning.

Adam hummed as we fell into step together across the cobblestones to the car parked to the left of the house. The sleek vintage hunter-green Aston Martin DB6 Volante suited Adam to a T.

The jangle of keys caught my attention, and I held out my hand for them, more than eager to drive such a gorgeous beast.

Only Adam laughed at my gesture and clucked his tongue as he opened the car with the remote and flipped the driver's door open. "No one drives this car but me, Sebastian."

"I'm the driver," I said redundantly. "Why else would you want me with you today?"

"The company?" he suggested blandly as he sank into the leather interior, and I crossed to the passenger side albeit reluctantly. When I entered the leather-scented interior, he looked at me, brow arched. "The visual appeal, perhaps."

My mouth curled into a smile unbidden. "Flattery won't get you far with me. I've been told I'm handsome all my life."

"I'll have to be more inventive, then," Adam declared as though I'd challenged him. "Has anyone ever told you that you have eyes the colour of sunlight caught in amber?"

I blinked.

But he didn't wait for a response, checking his mirror and pulling the car deftly out of the small courtyard and through the gates into the street.

I continued to stare at him as he easily navigated the car through the chaos of early morning London traffic. Questions bubbled up my throat and lodged like gravel at the back of my tongue. I wanted to ask why *me*? How did I get so lucky to catch the eye of one of the most famous actors in the world? What did he see in me that made him take the risk to bring me into his home and bed?

"You're being awfully loud over there," he said after an indeterminable period of time.

"I have some questions."

His laugh was low and smooth. He flipped open a pair of Gucci sunglasses and pushed them on to his face, obscuring those expressive green eyes I relied on to read him. "Well, we have about forty minutes before we reach our destination, and at my own behest, we're trapped in a car together so, feel free to ask."

"Anything?" My heart pounded harder behind my breastbone at the thought of limitless access.

I didn't know why I was like this, so hungry for invasion, so eager to dig deeper and deeper like a tick burrowing beneath the skin. But I wanted to know everything about the people who intrigued me, the ones I might one day love or love still. No detail was too minute or trivial for my interest.

And here was Adam Meyers, my boyhood idol, offering himself up on an Aston Martin platter.

He hummed. "I reserve the right to refuse to answer, but there's no harm in asking. Savannah said you signed the NDA when you began driving for her."

A little reminder I wasn't to share anything I learned.

"Okay, then." I settled comfortably into the supple leather seat, spreading my thighs wide and cracking my knuckles in a way that made Adam smile. "Let's start easy. Where are we going?"

"Pinewood Studios."

I waited, but he didn't elaborate so I said, "And that would be for what reason?"

A flash of a grin. "You said flattery wouldn't get me far with you, so really, I'd rather not say."

"Adam."

"Sebastian."

"Come on," I said with a laugh. "I take back what I said then; tell me why you've asked me to go to a production lot with you."

I could feel his gaze slide to me for a second behind the dark lenses of his glasses. "You know, I read your script."

My entire body froze at once, breath arrested mid-inhale in my lungs, thick as syrup, joints locked, molecules suspended. I'd known there was more in this "arrangement" for me than just the promise of passion, that Savannah wanted to launch me the way Helen had launched a thousand ships on Troy.

But the idea of Adam reading my script, a project I'd laboured over for the last three years, one built on the dreams and terrors and idols of a young man growing up under the oppressive gaze of the Mafia in impoverished Naples, made my spine seize.

It was so *vulnerable.*

A kind of… assault on my confidence and my soul I hadn't been braced for.

Vaguely, I recalled that he'd already told me about reading my script, but in the heat and bewilderment of that first confrontation at Finborough Theatre, I hadn't really grasped it.

When Savannah had forced me to leave the town car so she could read my words, I'd been in a state of shock, but also in a space without stakes. She wasn't in the industry and in my ignorance, I hadn't assumed she had any stock or say in it. So it'd been a pretty woman, a wonderful woman I lusted after voraciously, reading my script. Uncomfortable, yes, but not paralyzing.

Not like the idea of your actor idol reading your heart poured onto so many pages.

Suddenly, I was desperate to get out of the car, as feral as a trapped animal in a metal cage.

A strong hand gripping my knee jerked me back to reality and I flinched, pushing myself against the car door.

"Hey, hey," Adam murmured, coaxing me like a spooked stallion, only it didn't work. He was too handsome and otherworldly sitting in his Aston Martin driving to the biggest production studio in London. "Sebastian, look at me."

"I am," I gritted out, but didn't add *that's the problem.*

"No," he said, driving competently, not looking at me but tilting his chin to invite my study. "Look at me. Tell me what you see."

"You," I told him, too earnest, embarrassing myself by exposing how much that simple "you" enchanted me. "Adam Meyers."

"And who is Adam Meyers to you?"

There was something in his tone, a grim kind of warning, but I didn't know how to be anything but honest.

"The first time I saw you on screen was in *Joseph's Courage*. Your mama was crying in the foreground being comforted by your father and sister, but the camera was focused on you by the window. It was dark but the candlelight caught the side of your face and turned you to bronze, something lovely but cold and unfeeling. I'd never thought a man could be so beautiful until that moment. And then you turned, just a little, toward the camera, and a single tear track down your cheek made a mockery of the audience's first judgement of you."

I paused, remembering the scene so vividly I felt that same keen sadness now that I had then.

Inelegantly, I shrugged. "I followed your career after that. Everything you were ever in."

"And you have a favourite?"

Warmth worked its way into my cheeks, and I was grateful he couldn't see my blush beneath the olive of my skin. "*Antony.*"

"Ah, '*eternity was in our lips and in our eyes.*' Very romantic."

"It helped you were oiled and bare-chested, probably. Even though I'm only realizing that now," I admitted.

That wrought a real laugh from the actor. "Well, I'm happy to hear it, then. People usually say it's the *Jonathon Cross* trilogy or *Object of Desire*."

"It was a good action series," I agreed. "One of the best, for sure. And you were brilliant in *Object of Desire*, but it was too disturbing to be a favourite. I'll never forget that scene with the bodies hung in the trees and you standing beneath them in a bloody rain."

Adam's smile was a slice of red across his face, wound-like and very much like the expression he wore as Alistair Flare in the film. "It's one of the highest-rated films on IMDb, you know."

"I know." Again, I shrugged. "I liked you as Antony, Byron, Heathcliff, and Hamlet best. The classics. It's the films that leave you with a feeling of having your chest carved out and what remains of your insides rearranged that I love."

"And that's the kind of screenplay you've written," Adam said, a little smug at bringing the conversation back to his original point. "I read it in one sleepless night before I met you. Savannah didn't say a word when she handed the pages over. She just looked me in the eye with an excitement I've only seen a handful of times when she found projects that were as near perfection as they could get. Projects like *Object of Desire.* I missed an interview with Graham Norton reading *Blood Oath*, Sebastian, and an entire night of sleep."

He paused as he pulled off the road into a massive car park and swerved too fast into an empty spot near the studio.

When he turned to me, his face was solemn with gravitas. "When I finished, I felt I'd never breathe right again. It's that same feeling, isn't it?"

"Yes," I breathed because that same vulnerability I'd feared minutes ago was stripping me raw again. Only this time, Adam was there to soothe the raw nerves. It was to inexplicably show that he understood my screenplay, maybe even that he understood a little bit about me for having written it.

"I called Andrea that morning."

"Andrea…" My breath stuck in my throat for one dangerous second when I almost choked and died. "Andrea Felice?"

Adam's grin was a slight curling of one side of his full mouth. "The same. It had to be an Italian director, of course."

"Of course," I breathed, struck dumb.

"We can discuss the particulars with him now."

I watched mutely as Adam alighted from the car, his smart leather shoes clicking on the pavement as he rounded the Aston and opened my door for me. When I didn't move, still too busy processing the miracle that was currently *actually* happening to me, he reached down, gripped my forearm, and hauled me into the open air. One palm pressed to the center of my chest, pushing me to the side of the door as he closed it and then pinning me to the metal.

He examined me, not too close, and I knew it was so that if anyone were watching, we'd only look like two men engaged in an intense conversation and not two almost lovers taking another step down the path of intimacy.

"Why me?" I blurted, my heart beating too hard and too fast like it was going to escape the confines of my chest and knock straight into his hand. "Why are you doing all of this for me?"

Adam cocked his head slightly, and even though dark lenses obscured his gaze, I could feel the sharpness of that gaze on my skin like a razor's edge.

"Why me?" he echoed. "I suppose it's the same thing you experienced watching me on the screen. I liked the look of you the moment I saw you, costumed in a dirty soldier's garb with muck on your face and a spotlight turning those yellow eyes to pure gold. And then, when I read your words, I had a sense of you that hooked me through the ribs and tugged me toward you. All the best actors have an aura, this magnetic quality that speaks to the audience like a promise. You had that up there on that stage, and having read *Blood Oath*, I knew that promise had real potential."

He paused, dramatic as only an actor could be.

"Shall we see just how much?" he suggested, knocking his fist against my chest lightly as though testing it for durability.

I swallowed thickly, resisting the urge to grab that hand like an anchor, fighting the keen instinct welling up inside me to pour my astounded gratitude for him into a passionate, public kiss.

"You look terrified," Adam noted. "Don't be, we'll do it all together."

"I hate to repeat myself, but why? I just can't fathom why you'd spend time on me and this project like this."

"I've been acting for nearly a decade now, Sebastian. I have an eye for talent and scripts that have the potential to win awards. Count the golden statues on my mantel and tell me you don't believe that."

"I believe in you, obviously," I said with an eye roll. "It's me that I'm unsure about."

"Well, let me be sure enough for us both. And if that isn't enough, remember that my wife was the one to spot the merit in you first. Savannah may be many things, but *wrong* is rarely one of them." He shot me a wink and turned on his heel, overcoat flapping open behind him as he set off at a brisk pace into the maze of warehouse buildings.

"And in a moment, you'll have the opinion of the great Andrea Felice to add to that arsenal against your silly self-doubts, hmm?"

I shook myself as I pushed off the car and strode after him. Andrea Felice was one of the best Hollywood directors of his generation, right up there with Nolan, Scorsese, and Spielberg. The idea of meeting him, let alone working with him on a script I'd first started as a sixteen-year-old, was too mind-boggling to process.

"Is it true he doesn't let anyone use the bathroom while filming?" I asked because it was the easiest thing to focus on in this series of spectacular events.

Adam didn't pause in his quick pace, but he looked at me for a second before grinning widely, all those lovely white teeth on display. "It's true. There are bathroom breaks at eleven and six o'clock. He expects his actors to drink accordingly."

I laughed. "I can understand that a little. When I write, I do not like to be interrupted by anything, even my own bodily urges."

"Hmm," he practically purred as he shot me a sidelong look while leading us down a narrow corridor between buildings. "I'll have to see if I can test that one day."

"I'd rather you didn't," I muttered because I had no doubt he'd break my concentration in seconds.

But Adam didn't hear me; he was too busy greeting a man wearing a headset and holding a tablet before ushering us both into the wide mouth of a warehouse entryway.

Inside, everything was dim but for a collection of gear and people milling around a single corner of the cavernous space. I'd never filmed a movie before, but I recognized the accoutrement of a working set: the lights and rails for the steady cameras and the chaos at the fringes where assistants and makeup artists waited for instructions and touch-ups. The set itself was constructed to look like a bedroom at night, only illuminated by the glow of a bedside table and the artificial beams of moonlight spilling through an opened window. Two actors stood beside the bed, marking out the scene and speaking quietly. I couldn't recognize them from so far away, but if they were in an Andrea Felice film, I had no doubt they were A-list.

"This looks like a closed set, Adam," I murmured to him, clutching his shoulder to stop him from barrelling right into the shot.

"Hush." He brushed my hand off with a roll of his shoulder and stalked forward to a man sitting in a chair marked "Director" who was speaking tersely in Italian into a cell phone.

"Andrea," he greeted.

Che cavolo.

I was about to meet Andrea fucking Felice, and Adam fucking Meyers was going to be the one introducing me.

How did I get here?

Oh right, I'd tried to seduce a married woman.

So much for karma being a bitch. It seemed to me she was Lady Luck herself.

Andrea let out a booming laugh that echoed through the warehouse as he stood and jerked Adam into a hug before gripping his shoulders and exuberantly kissing each cheek.

"*Ragazzo*," he said in that big voice, shaking Adam by the shoulders. "It's good to see your miserable face."

"Yours too," Adam assured him with that genuine grin I'd also seen in the car park. "I've brought you another face to look at today, though this one is much handsomer than either of our old mugs."

On my cue, I walked forward to take my place beside Adam. Only years of acting allowed me to look at Andrea without my mouth hanging open in wonder.

"Signor Felice," I greeted in Italian. "I'm Sebastian Lombardi. It's a pleasure to meet you after admiring you for so long."

Andrea could have been an actor himself if he hadn't had the vision and talent of a natural-born director. He was handsome in the way of Italians from the south, short and muscular with wiry dark hair and eyes like gleaming cocoa beans beneath thick brows and lashes. His hawkish nose suited his large features and made him look somehow intellectual. He was only in his late thirties, but the creases beside his mouth and eyes gave him character.

Or maybe it was that I knew him to be one of the brightest minds in cinema.

"It is a pleasure to meet you, knowing there is a sharp mind behind such a beautiful face," he responded in Italian before shooting a roguish grin at Adam and switching to English. "You certainly know how to find them, Meyers."

Adam shrugged blithely. "One of my many talents."

"Savannah would argue it's her talent, I think, that found me," I quipped, just to deflate what I was coming to understand was false bravado, a very finely honed mask Adam wore even when he was offstage and out of sight from the cameras.

Andrea laughed and slapped me on the shoulder. "*Sì*, too right. You are lucky she isn't here to dress you down in front of an audience, Adamo."

Adam's only response was a rakishly raised eyebrow that made me visualize that exact scene in a much too intimate way.

The director just clucked his tongue and turned his attention back to me, pushing me down into his own chair so he could stand before me with his hands held wide, face glowing with excitement.

"We only have ten minutes for the toilet break but let me tell you how I envision this. Opening, the streets of New York in the early twenties, wide lens, filled with bustling bodies all in drab colours like the drabness of the dirty streets. It zooms in slowly, so slowly you cannot really mark the transition, onto a single man moving against the majority of the crowd, shoving into shoulders, ducking packages, but remaining strong and proud in posture. He is wearing a hat, one of those newsboy caps, so you can't see his face. When the gunshot rings out, everyone screams and scrambles, shocked and scared, but the man only looks up directly into the camera, completely unafraid. Cue the title in bold block letters." He mapped out the transitions with his hands in big gestures. "*Blood Oath*!"

Behind him, Adam clapped and was joined by the two actors on set who had wandered closer along with a handful of film crew.

"Sounds intriguing," the female actress who I recognized uneasily as the up-and-coming starlet Willa Trombley drawled. "Any roles for me in there, Andrea?"

He waved his hand dismissively her way, his eyes still fixed on mine. "Well, what do you think?"

"It sounds perfect," I admitted. "You've put a lot of thought into this already."

"*Assolutamente sì.* Adam and I have spoken about this almost every day for the past ten days." He nodded the entire time he spoke, hands still moving, and I realized he was so fantastic at capturing movement on film because he was hardly ever still himself. Unbidden, I remembered the young woman by the pool last night, Linnea Kai, and her quicksilver changes of position.

"Andrea and I even banded about casting ideas for certain roles and who might work well as the cinematography director."

"Music too is so important in an epic film like this," Andrea added seamlessly, like they'd had this exact conversation before. "Hans just retired, such a shame. But we can get Marguerite Fischer. She worked on *Thorn* and *Bluegrass Blues*. Both scores are…" He closed his eyes and hummed a few pretty notes.

"We think it could attract some serious attention with the right leads," Adam continued, his passion brightening his dark green eyes to shining emeralds. "Antonio Carozza would be an interesting idea for Roberto, and even though Ric Ashton is only of Italian heritage through a grandfather, he's an incredible actor who would do the job justice."

"Well," Andrea demanded, "what do you think of it all? As you can see, you have successfully lit a fire in our bellies."

"I'm honoured," I told him after a moment, and I was.

But I was also… annoyed?

If I was allowed to be annoyed that a world-famous actor and director were so interested in my script. It was just that this was *my* proverbial baby. Something I'd quite literally poured my blood, sweat, and tears into for the past three years. The sleepless nights, the agony and distress that trying to tell a story properly could wreck on the human body. I'd endured it all happily because I'd been possessed by this story and the character of Roberto D'Amato, the immigrant Italian who arrives in New York and is instantly press-ganged into joining one of the local Mafia families.

It was a story that was too close to my heart in many ways. Roberto's struggles mimicked my own as a boy with a gambling drunkard for a father, three beautiful sisters, and a struggling mother at home in need of my help and protection. There had been no one to protect me from the local Camorra's attentions, just like there was no one to help Roberto in New York.

Both our tales of survival were achieved by the skin of our very own teeth.

And maybe because of that, I wasn't willing to let even an inch of this story go to someone else's power and control.

Even Andrea Felice and Adam Meyers.

What did they know of Roberto and his struggles?

What did they know of *me*?

I'd been quiet too long. Andrea's face fell slightly, and he shared a look with Adam that started to clear the space before the former even said, "Leave us. Take an extra ten and come back with more energy than you gave me before."

Obediently, almost everyone who'd lingered on set for their break dispersed to the outer edges or elsewhere entirely. Those who remained made themselves busy enough to maintain an aura of privacy.

"What's wrong, Sebastian?" Adam asked, gently pushing Andrea out of the way with a bump of his shoulder so he could bend down to look in my eyes and grasp my shoulder. The feel of his hand on me was grounding.

I realized my grip on the wood chair handles was white-knuckled and slowly unpeeled my fingers. Andrea noticed and cocked a brow at the behaviour.

"It's not that I'm ungrateful for your enthusiasm…" I spoke slowly, enunciating so carefully I almost eradicated the last traces of my Italian accent. "But this script isn't just an idea I had one night that I thought could make good cinema. I wrote a part of my own soul, of my own history into that script. The ink might as well have been blood let from my own veins. As much as I love the idea of the great Andrea Felice and Adam Meyers spearheading this project, it just isn't possible for me to hand it over for a fee and wash my hands of Roberto D'Amato and his story."

I sucked in a deep breath through my teeth and looked up into Adam's face and then Andrea's behind him. "I'm sorry to disappoint you when I'm frankly shocked and overjoyed to have two men I've admired most of my life take an interest in my words, but I can't compromise on this project. It would be like compromising a part of my soul."

In the wake of my impassioned speech, both of them stared at me through a long silence. I fought the urge to squirm under the scrutiny and instead tipped my chin higher the way my sister Elena was apt to do in the face of adversity.

I could find another way to make my dreams come true, I assured myself as panic soured my stomach and made me want to puke.

"Well, he's got the dramatics of an actor, doesn't he?" Andrea said blandly, planting his hands on his hips and shifting his weight onto one foot.

Adam sighed. "You should know the combination of Italian genes and acting chops makes for an intense marriage."

I blinked at them. "Are you… *teasing* me?"

Adam's stern face broke into that wide grin I was becoming addicted to. "Why yes, Sebastian, I believe we are."

Andrea laughed and stepped closer to clap a hand on my shoulder and give me a bit of a shake. "We had to see the passion, uh? If you have the fire in the pit of your belly to see this thing through all the obstacles and chaos of filmmaking from beginning to end. You gave birth to this story, *sì,* and it is a beautiful one, of course. But before I made my offer, I wanted to see if you have the *forza* to bring Roberto to life."

"I have it," I told him, somewhat redundantly, but excitement flourished in my once rancid gut, and a kind of giddiness I'd rarely felt in my life was taking hold. It was the sensation, I thought, of being on the precipice of your dreams coming true. "You're serious? You want to work on *Blood Oath* with me?"

Even though I'm a no one, I thought but didn't say.

Andrea grinned, the same slightly maniacal grin echoed on Adam's face. "*Certamente*."

When I looked at Adam, he opened his palms in faux innocence. "I'd like a producer credit, if you don't mind, but otherwise, this is your baby, Sebastian. I only wanted to give you the tools to see it through. Though, if I may, I think it's obvious the only right person to play Roberto D'Amato is *you*."

The small seed of self-confidence I'd always kept zealously protected in the heart of my chest took root and burrowed deep into my gut.

"He's a complicated character," I said, but it was almost a question.

Adam shrugged, but there were stars in his eyes meant only for me. "Who better to play him, then, than a complicated man?"

I nodded slightly as I digested the turn of events and then let the giddiness in my belly show on my face. "Well then, Andrea, I think this calls for a celebratory drink in the two minutes you have left of the restroom break. You don't have any grappa on hand, do you?"

Andrea scoffed. "I'm an Italian." He pulled a flask out of the side pocket of his chair, prompting Adam and me to laugh at his efficacy.

"*Salute*!" Andrea toasted me and then took a swig before handing it to me.

I mimicked him but locked eyes with Adam as I took the burning liquid down my throat. Something hooked through my ribs and vibrated at the line stretched taut to its anchor beneath Adam's own breastbone. The space between us throbbed with its beat, like the heart in my chest and the cock between my thighs that twitched at the sight of Adam's own darkened gaze. When I handed the flask off to him, his fingers rubbed over my own, and he maintained our intense stare as he took a long, hard pull of the grappa.

"To you," he murmured instead of the Italian *cheers*. "To your future."

And at that moment, I might have fallen just a little bit in love with Adam Meyers.

Chapter Twelve

Adam

It was a good day.

No, not that.

A bloody *brilliant* day.

The best I'd had in a fucking age.

I felt… light, filled with something cool and clean like the moonlight turning the nightscape around the speeding car to silver.

We'd meant to spend an hour, tops, on set with Andrea, but somehow, time and enthusiasm had colluded to make us lose track of time.

Even when Andrea went back to shooting the final scenes for his upcoming drama, Sebastian's raw joy at being on a film set had rooted me in place. There were meetings to be at, people to hobnob with if I wanted to secure my BAFTA win in a few weeks, my agent blowing up my phone with new film offers now that the nominations had been released… Endless tasks to see done.

Yet I was transfixed by the Italian actor/writer/chauffeur who stood beside me with the kind of wide-eyed zeal I hadn't seen on a film set in years, if at all. I'd forgotten, looking at Sebastian, what it felt like to be new to the scene. To watch the mechanics of filmmaking, the multiple camera angles, and the drudgery of repeating your lines again and again to obtain the right nuances for the master shot, for the individual shots, how many people were needed on set for such a variety of reasons a civilian would have no hope of guessing their purpose.

And all of it, Sebastian ate with a proverbial spoon.

"È *meraviglioso*," he breathed as Willa Trombley cried repeatedly for the camera, each shot absolutely exquisite.

I didn't speak much Italian, though I took Latin at Eton long enough to parse his meaning.

"It is through your eyes," I agreed, unable to look away from the Italian enough to appreciate the harmony on set. "You seem to have the ability to find beauty in everything."

His grin was free, a boyish kind of contentment that he'd earned my praise. The expression made me want to lavish him with poetry in a way I'd never done before. It made me want to put him on his knees and teach him how to earn it from me.

"I learned young. My twin sister and I made it our motto, really. We became determined to find beauty in the darkness."

"Was your childhood so bad?" I couldn't help but give voice to my curiosity.

His tone was so casual for the words that came next. "There was a lot of darkness in our lives for a long time. It was either see the beauty in the shadows or give up and let that hungry blackness swallow you whole. It taught me to be grateful every day for the small joys." He shot me a cheeky grin. "And for the big ones like here, today."

I thought about my own sense of ennui, how my life seemed to blur day by day into a kind of stagnant, grey-toned reel of B footage. Nothing to punctuate it, nothing to make me sit up and take notice.

How embarrassing it seemed now, in the face of Sebastian's gratefulness and optimism, to be so jaded when I had untold privilege.

He caught my wince and pulled his attention from the scene to put a hand on my elbow, discreetly enough that no one would notice. Still, his touch was… nice. Savannah wasn't particularly affectionate outside the bedroom nor had my parents ever been anything close to the touchy-feely types.

But it seemed Sebastian was.

A hand on the elbow, a bump of shoulder into shoulder. Little things that somehow added up to something large enough to weigh pleasantly in my hollow chest.

"Did I say something to upset you?" he'd asked.

It wasn't his fault that his youthful earnestness made me feel eighty-two and at the end of my life instead of twenty-eight and at the height of it.

"No," I murmured, but I gave in to my own impulse to touch him and clasped him strongly on the shoulder. "Should we steal something from the craft services table and take it to a place I know?"

Sebastian's grin turned coy, making my gut clench. For someone who'd never been with a man before, he was shockingly good at flirting with one. "A *private* place you know?"

"Exactly," I agreed, already shoving him forward to the entrance.

Andrea was busy, so I didn't bother with goodbyes. However, I figured we would pop by later to see if he was still filming. In the meantime, I focused on the beauty in the grim blankness of my life that was one Sebastian Lombardi.

He chatted with me freely as we left the warehouse and moved to the craft services tent set up outside. His hands waved to and fro, talking just as eloquently as his words as he told me about his thoughts for *Blood Oath*. He only paused briefly to contemplate the loaded food tables with slack-jawed awe before grabbing a paper plate and loading it so high that the thin material buckled in his grip, and he had to carry it with two hands.

"Hey, Meyers, looking good," a friendly, familiar grip called to me as he walked by.

I jerked my chin up in his direction but didn't take my eyes from Seb as he contemplated his wobbly plate, plucked a breadstick from the masses of food, and stuck it between his lips like a cigarette as though that would help level the load.

"Ready?" he mumbled around the bread.

I cocked an eyebrow at him, but he only grinned. "I grew up poor, okay? If there's free food, I'm eating as much of it as I possibly can."

"How you keep that eight-pack is a real wonder," I grumbled as I took my own sparse plate of protein and some veg and led him away from the tent deeper into the maze of Pinewood Studios.

"I think it's my youthful metabolism," he quipped, easily falling into step with me on those long legs when most people struggled to keep up. "When did you lose that, do you reckon, *vecchietto*? A decade or so ago?"

I almost choked on my unexpected laughter. "You wanker, I'm twenty-eight, thank you very much."

He peered at me and then risked losing his plate of food to poke at my temple. "Bit of grey hair there, though."

"It's distinguished," I said haughtily.

"Sure." He crunched the breadstick and ate it carefully without the use of his hands.

It was quite entertaining.

The gardens at Pinewood Studios were a massive appeal of filming at the lot. They had the forest abutting the back of the property that had stood in for France, The Balkans, and mystical woods like the ones in *Harry Potter*. But I led Sebastian to Heatherden Hall, a magnificent manor home ringed in cultivated gardens with a small pond and pretty stone bridge crossing it.

We were both quiet as we stood on the bridge and looked out over the water, the sound of the fountain a quiet trickle in the background. The house itself rose from the pretty gardens in all its pale yellow and cream splendor.

"It's gorgeous," Sebastian said quietly, as if in reverence to the grandeur of the faux estate.

I grinned, but it felt a little wrong on my face as I settled on the steps facing the house, and Sebastian followed suit. "I grew up on an estate much like this."

"I could pretend to be surprised by that, but I did do some research before I agreed to be your live-in house boy," he admitted unashamedly, before ripping a mammoth bite out of his turkey sandwich.

"It wasn't quite as pastoral as this lot. Cornwall is all cliffs and vivid greenery and crashing ocean waves. It smells like salt, and the wind always bites, even on a balmy summer's day."

"It sounds like you love it there."

"Does it?" That surprised me. I hadn't been to my father's estate near Falmouth in over half a decade. "I didn't as a boy. That's certain."

Sebastian slid me a careful look as he chewed before saying, "I didn't grow up enjoying Naples very much, but I love it. The heat in midsummer, the stink of the ocean and the sear of the pavement through your thin-soled shoes. The food. Uh, English food is nothing in comparison." He made such a face of disgust I had to laugh. "I think loving and hating our hometown is the same kind of necessary tension we have with our parents. We love them because we have to, we *want* to, and we're wired and raised to. But we can hate them for all the ways they've wronged us."

He was silent then, looking out over the gardens, lost in his own reverie. Shockingly, I found myself wanting to join him there. Savannah and I had something of a silent agreement about our pasts: we didn't talk about them. As though they would cease to exist by not acknowledging them.

It was unlike me to even mention my childhood home, let alone indulge in conversation about it, but Sebastian seemed to stir up the murky banks at the bottom of my gut, revealing things I'd thought long since lost.

"Shall we share our sad little histories, then?" I suggested casually, as though my heart wasn't doing something funny in my chest. "Tit for tat."

He looked down at his plate, fingered the edge of a spring roll, and then put his plate to the side. "All right, then, if you want."

I wanted to talk about my own life like I wanted hemorrhoids, but I was too curious about his to be cautious.

"What do you want out of life?" I asked, casting a wide net, not because I wanted a generic answer but because I wanted *every* answer he had to give me.

Surprisingly, he ducked his head to smile secretively at his hands.

"What?" I pressed, hooked by his uncharacteristic bashfulness. "Don't think I'll shame you for saying fame and fortune, mate. It would be rather hypocritical of me."

His laugh was an exhale. "No, no. I mean, of course, I'd love to have the pick of films to star in. Funding for any screenplay I write. But truly? My dream will seem childish to you, and I may only be eighteen, but I don't want you to see me as naive."

"Well, you did willingly enter into a scandalous affair with a married couple, so I think the ship sailed on your naivety long ago," I quipped just to see him grin.

"*Va bene*," he murmured, tipping his head to the rare sight of the British sun bright in the sky. "I want *l'amor che move il sol e l'altre stelle*."

Before I could translate the beautiful phrase using my grade school Latin, he looked at me with those sun-gold eyes and repeated in English, "I want a love that moves the sun and the stars."

I blinked, struck physically by his confession.

Love?

The eighteen-year-old sitting before me with scads of talent and beauty on the cusp of recognition and acclaim wanted something so transient and intangible as *love*?

What happened to teenage boys wanting to shag anything in a skirt and eschew all sense of emotion and responsibility?

His chuckle was sad and a little bitter. "I can see you judging me, Adam."

"Processing," I corrected, but I felt off-balance and a little defensive.

If he wanted that kind of emotion, why was he with Savannah and me? He had to know there was no way we could ever give him… *that*.

I wasn't sure we could even give him enough emotion to move a bloody paper clip, let alone a fucking galaxy.

"Don't worry," he said, staring off over the gardens as if he was looking into a kind of future where that love awaited him. I tried not to feel irrationally and unfairly envious. "I know this isn't that."

I wanted to argue at the very same time that I wanted to bury this conversation six feet deep in an unmarked grave so we'd never stumble upon it again.

So, like the emotional coward I was, I tossed out, "You mentioned a twin sister."

"I did," he said, and everything melancholic in his demeanor evaporated in the heat of that bright smile. "Cosima. She's my best friend, but then, that's probably not surprising."

"Do you read each other's minds or anything?"

He laughed and I had the thought that if I died with that sound ringing in my ears, I'd be happy to go. "Not quite. But we know each other in a way that's hard to explain. Not telepathy exactly, but, hmm, I think it's like reading braille, maybe? I can *feel* her thoughts and emotions. Even now with her back in Milan, I can feel her sometimes. A kind of premonition if she's having a good or bad day." A frown flittered across his face. "I've had some bad feelings lately, but she's assured me everything is going swimmingly. And it seems to be, financially at least. I wish I could do more, but for now, she's our family's primary breadwinner."

"Well, if she looks a thing like you, I've no doubt she's in high demand in the model industry."

Sebastian rolled his eyes, but the quirk of his full mouth, shadowed by the beginning of an inky five-o'clock shadow I wanted to scrape with my teeth, gave him away. "I told you flattery wouldn't get you anywhere."

"I beg to differ." I opened my hands to indicate our setting, quite romantic, and our closeness, his knee knocking companionably into mine. "It got me in this lovely garden with an even lovelier man."

"Touché," he conceded gracefully. "You know, speaking of my sister, I think she'd like you. She always preferred British cinema and actors best. Our father is Irish, you know, so maybe it's in our blood."

"Irish and Italian?" I whistled. "That explains some things. Quite a volatile combination of cultures."

He punched me playfully, but that little grin broke open into a full-fledged smile, and honest to Christ, it made my breath stop in my throat.

"It's made me doubly passionate, maybe, and it definitely helped me learn English. Even though he was an Italophile, he made sure to educate us in all things British. Cosima and I took to it best, though."

"You have barely a trace of an accent most of the time. It's quite remarkable given you've only been here, what, a handful of months?"

"Half a year. I was fluent before moving, but I've picked up some Britishisms, I think."

"Well, you've certainly picked up one Brit," I teased, putting my finished plate aside to angle my knees into his, pressing between one of them so I caged a strong thigh between my own.

"Have I?" he asked, his gaze warm on my mouth.

I licked my lips just to watch that golden gaze darken to syrup. "Truthfully, I didn't expect to like you this much."

His lips twisted into a wry smile. "Don't tell me I'm the first man you've taken on a date."

I reeled back just a bit, struck by the realization that this did, in fact, seem like a date. It hadn't been my intention at all. The venture to Pinewood was meant to be about business. Sebastian had more than just talent on stage; his screenplay was truly magnificent, and I was excited to have a hand in getting it to the silver screen. Andrea was a natural fit, and he happened to be filming in the country.

But no, looking at this frankly stunning man sitting beside me, caged between my thighs like I couldn't be without his touch, I had to re-evaluate.

Of course, it had been more than business from the start.

Savannah and I had agreed to no more lovers for a while. Not after what happened with Oscar. Not with what was happening to our marriage, crumbling at the edges like an old painting.

But then, there he'd been, devastating Savannah's iron control and razing my own the moment I saw him embody a dead soldier in an indie production at Finborough Theatre.

Something in him called to me, beautiful and deadly as a siren's song.

I wanted to disregard my rules and throw myself boldly into his arms.

The worst part of it was I thought he would catch me.

Reputation be damned, the irreparable damage to his fledgling career would take a back seat to the desire I saw so blatantly in his gaze.

Social constructs and the petty injustices of our industry would not rein in this man of passion.

But he deserved more than that.

Just being our driver and live-in lover.

He deserved a golden statue the same shade as his eyes for acting and writing.

He deserved fame and acclaim and whatever his heart desired because he was a good man, and I had the awful feeling he'd been exceedingly unlucky in life thus far.

And here I was, ready and shockingly eager to change that.

So maybe this was a date.

Maybe I wanted to go on three dozen more, with him, with my wife, our marriage revived by his rawness and fire and honesty.

But for him, for her, for me… my career, I wouldn't.

We had all, in our own ways, worked too hard to give it all up now for something that had no guarantees, no money to live on or success to soothe our brittle insecurities.

"It's a business lunch," I corrected Sebastian, but softly, the words tempered by the hand I clasped on his knee, the squeeze I gave that firm thigh. "And we best be going."

"Okay," he said easily because I was discovering he was just like that, good-natured and easygoing except when he was riled. "Don't think I won't remember you owe me something about your history when I shared and you haven't. But… thank you, Adam, for doing this. I know you said my work merits it, but I don't think I'll ever be able to express how much your faith in me means. It's… well, it's everything."

He looked at me then a little differently than he had in the car on the way up from London. Not like I was Adam Meyers, the actor, but more like I was Adam Meyers, his friend. A little warm, a little possessive.

The sentiment was punctuated by the hand he lifted to squeeze my shoulder, closing the loop between us, a current running through my hand to his thigh and back up through his hand to me.

I wanted to kiss him more than I wanted my next breath.

But we were in public. Though the gardens seemed deserted, you could never trust a setting rife with film folk not to capture something interesting on their phones and sell it to the paps.

"It's my pleasure," I told him sincerely, and then, risking it a bit, I pushed my hand up his thigh to squeeze again near his groin. "Or it soon will be."

Sebastian had laughed, bright and happy, so he didn't see the way I looked at him and wondered what it might be like to prioritize this… friendship over all the fears I had that lay between us.

Chapter Thirteen

Adam

It was dark when I pulled the Aston through the gates into the car park before the house. I didn't immediately alight from the car and neither did Sebastian, as though we were both afraid the magic of the day, complete with an afternoon of walking the lots and then watching the last of Andrea's shoot before grabbing dinner together at his hotel, would dissipate the moment we opened the doors to the brisk London air.

"Thank you again for today," he said, turning to face me, his eyes animal yellow in the shadows. "No one has ever been so kind to me as you and Savannah. It's… well, I hope I'm worthy of it."

"I think the fact that you're even worried says you are. Most people in this industry become arrogant or entitled quicker than you can imagine."

"I won't be like that," he said, quiet but fierce, as if the idea offended his very core.

And I thought maybe it did.

I wondered what it must be like to be so pure.

"We won't be entering a happy home," I warned him, explaining some of my own reticence to go inside. "First, I took you off for myself, and then we missed dinner and kept Savannah waiting for dessert. She won't be pleased, to put it mildly."

"Hmm," he hummed, apparently unperturbed by the idea. "I'm sure we can find a way to earn her forgiveness."

My laughter was a sharp bark in the close interior. "Well, yes, I'm sure we can. Shall we, then?"

He nodded, eyes glittering darkly in the shadows, smile a wedge of moonlit white. "Please."

We walked in tandem across the pavers and up the stairs to the door. When I unlocked it and pulled the door open, the main floor was dark and cool, but light seeped down from the top of the staircase.

"Before we do this properly for the first time," I said quietly, gripping his forearm before he could move deeper into the house. "I'll have you pick a safe word, Sebastian. Something uncommon you can say to stop all play immediately if you're uncomfortable for any reason."

His grin was wicked. "Are you trying to scare me?"

"On the contrary, I'm trying to keep you safe."

I watched warmth suffuse his features and felt the echo of it in my chest.

"Oh, well…" He cleared his throat and swallowed roughly. "Lunatic, then."

I arched a brow at the bizarre choice and had the deep pleasure of watching him grin shyly.

"It means moonstruck," he explained. "Driven crazy under the influence of the moon."

I opened my mouth to agree that was a rather poetic and fitting safe word, when he stopped me by adding, "I think of you like that sometimes."

Like his moon.

I blinked, stunned speechless by this eighteen-year-old romantic once again.

"Who the hell are you, Sebastian Lombardi?" I asked without really meaning to.

His smile widened, and he winked at me before pulling away. "Hurry up and find out."

Silently, I hung up my coat beside his, and we put our shoes in the closet before padding softly up to the second floor and down the hall to the primary suite. The door was slightly ajar, the faint scent of lilac and murmur of music—"Prelude No. 4" by Chopin—a faintly ominous soundtrack to our homecoming.

When I pushed the door open, Savannah wasn't lying in bed asleep or pouting.

It wasn't her way.

Instead, she sat at her vanity as though we'd caught her getting ready for bed, antique glass perfume bottle opened, the stopper pressed to the delicate curve of her pale wrist. The window beyond the table looked over the front of the house, so she would have been watching for us to pull in, timing her erotic tableau perfectly for our entrance.

Her eyes raised in the mirror to watch us in the reflection, lashes still thick with make-up, mouth a perfect rosy red. Hair a pale cloud of brushed-out curls around her delicate face like an old-school Hollywood starlet, and her slim body clad in deep purple satin with black velvet trimmed lingerie, she had engineered herself to look as magnificent as possible.

It was a warning, though, as much as it was a promise.

If we didn't earn her forgiveness, all that beauty would be high on a pedestal out of reach.

But if we were willing to work for it, the goddess that she was could be ours.

The problem was, of course, that I bent the knee for no person. I had two kingdoms, one before a camera and one before my wife.

So when I crossed the Aubusson carpet, it wasn't on my knees, crawling to a woman who so clearly deserved such worship.

My act of adulation came in a different form.

I stopped directly beside Savannah and leaned against her vanity, arms crossed, legs crossed, gaze fixed not on her but on my gift.

"Sebastian," I ordered quietly. "Come here and apologize to my wife."

He only hesitated for a moment, and I had the sense, as his gaze flicked about the room, that it was more about entering our domain than it was the command itself. When he moved, though, it was with the sinuous grace such a tall, broad-shouldered man rarely possessed. I enjoyed watching him, just as I knew Savannah did in the mirror's reflection.

Struck by sudden inspiration, I held up a hand to stop him mid-step just a few feet behind Savannah's chair.

"I've often found apologies work best when I strip myself bare," I mused with a deliberately heated glance up and down his form.

His Adam's apple bobbed hard in the tanned column of his throat, but when he lifted his hands to unbutton his white dress shirt, they were steady, and his gaze was unclouded as it rested on me.

"Do it slowly," I suggested with an edge of malice.

Seb's hands stilled, then moved again, languidly pulling his unbuttoned shirt over one shoulder and the other, letting the linen slip down the rounded muscles of his deltoids and over his bronzed forearms. When the material pooled in his hands, he held it there for a moment, his carved torso framed by the soft fabric. His chest was covered in a light smattering of dark hair, nipples like caramel candies, abdominals perfectly stacked boxes above a dark, dangerous trail of black leading into the waistband of his denim.

If Savannah was a goddess, Sebastian was the beautiful virginal offering.

Savannah's breath hitched slightly, and I glanced down to watch her thighs press together. I fought my own urge to press the heel of my hand against my erection to ease the burgeoning ache.

The shirt fell to the ground soundlessly before Sebastian's large, long-fingered hands worked at his belt, flicking it open with a soft click that seemed to echo in the room. The air between the three of us felt thick and hot with tension. Savannah wanted to go to him, I could tell, her eagerness barely concealed. One hand on her shoulder kept her still and aching.

Normally, she was very controlled, but anyone would tremble in the face of such a specimen as Sebastian Lombardi.

The rasp of the zipper sounded like a rough gasp as he lowered it to reveal white boxer briefs. With his lower lip pinched between his teeth, he watched us both with lowered lids as he eased the denim over his ass and thick, steely thighs. Something about body hair on men made me salivate. I wanted to pull at that dark trail leading to his groin with my teeth and scrape my nails up those furred thighs until I reached the thick of it at the base of his cock.

He was confident now as he should've been. Even though I was the one giving the orders and Savannah was the one being revered, Sebastian had us both utterly entranced.

"So hard for us already," I said, as though I was disappointed at the thick, long swell of him behind the cotton. "I hope you can handle what I have in store for you, Sebastian."

His chin canted up in defiance even though he didn't say a word. Instead, he punctuated his nonverbal response by sliding a finger beneath the waistband of his boxer briefs and pushing them down so achingly slowly, I forgot to breathe.

"Do it," Savannah hissed, eyes flashing, hands curled into fists as she fought to restrain herself.

"Do it," I echoed, tone unyielding.

I wanted to see him. The brief tryst we'd had in the back of the car outside the Finborough Theatre was weeks ago, and I'd been yearning for the sight of that thick, curved cock since then.

Without changing his pace, Sebastian revealed it to us, his erection so hard it was flushed a deep rose, the veins prominent along the shaft and the head wet with precum.

I'd make Savannah suck it off in short order and then give me a taste with a kiss, I decided as some precum caught in his treasure trail when his cock thumped against his stomach as he released it from the fabric. The dense black hair around it and his heavy sack were trimmed and wildly attractive. I couldn't wait to press my nose to his groin and smell his musk.

"Very good," I told him and watched as he quite literally shivered at the praise.

With a sudden surety that made my wife gasp, I picked her up in her chair and swiveled them both to face the room and Sebastian himself.

"Come," I said, standing behind her. "Get on your knees and show Savannah how sorry we are for being late."

Sebastian strode forward instantly and dropped to his knees already reaching for her. His eagerness made a groan rise in my throat unbidden. The sight of his dark head between her pale thighs made my teeth ache and my dick throb.

Savannah almost choked on her gasp as he threw her legs over his shoulders, dropped his head, and dove into her sweet cunt. Even with the thin layer of satin between them, he had her hips juddering in moments.

To make matters deliciously worse, I tugged down the cups of her bra to plump up her sweet little tits and began a slow, wicked torture of her pink nipples, plucking and pulling and twisting until she keened with pleasure.

"Take off her pants," I ordered Seb, who obeyed with a quick, rough tug that tore the material at her hips. "You have five minutes to make her come on your tongue, or I'll be very disappointed."

He groaned into her wet folds, the flat of his tongue following her leaking juices from thigh to clit. "Yes, sir."

This time, I let myself moan too. The sound of that moniker in his rich voice nearly made me come like a boy in my trousers. Instead, I pulled my phone out of my pocket with one hand and set a five-minute timer. I was a fair Dominant who liked to set clear rules so that my lovers knew exactly how to please me and exactly how to deserve a punishment.

Something told me Sebastian was an overachiever.

And I was proved right three minutes later, his thick fingers pumping into her cunt with obscenely wet slaps, his lush mouth sealed around her clit, when Savannah dissolved to pieces on his tongue.

"Such a sweet slut for us," I bent to whisper in her ear, nipping at her lobe. "Show him what a good boy he is for fucking you with that pretty mouth."

She arched like a too tightly strung bow, producing a sharp, off-key note that was nonetheless gorgeous to my ears in the moment before she snapped and gave over to her climax.

Sebastian ate her languidly as she spiraled like a feather to the ground, her pants turned soft, her head lolling between her shoulders so it rested against my stomach, her fingers resting gently now in his thick hair.

"What a talented mouth you have," I said in a voice I barely recognized. Though we'd played with half a dozen partners over the five years of our marriage, I had never been so aroused as I was then, Savannah destroyed by both Sebastian's physical efforts and my mental gymnastics. She loved to feel both the lady and the whore, and having a man bow to her needs while the other lorded it over her was her ultimate fantasy.

One I'd always been happy to cater to because it so closely aligned with my own.

But this was somehow more than that.

It was specific not just to my wife but to *him.*

The big, beautiful black-haired man on his knees between Savannah's thighs, his mouth wet from her cunt, his fingers still inside her, propriety now like he owned her a little after earning her cum, but his eyes. Oh! His golden predator's eyes were on me and though his posture was submissive enough, those orbs blazed with glorious inner fire as they pinned me in my place.

You may control me for the moment, they dared, *but like a caged animal, I can turn on you in the span of a blink.*

I fought a hard shudder and rolled it off my back. There would be no battles for control in this, my domain. Sebastian was mine.

(Mine but I was not his.)

"On your knees on the bed, Savannah," I told her, wrapping my hand around the front of her throat to tip her head back from me. "I think the only way to absolve ourselves of our sins is to repent again and again until you cry out for mercy. What do you think?"

A throaty little purr was my response. Her lids fluttered shut as

I dipped as though to kiss her and instead bit at her bottom lip. She shivered.

I stepped back to give her room to stand and motioned for Sebastian to do the same. He rocked back onto his heels, still on his knees because I hadn't given him verbal leave to get up. Oh, but he was a sweet sub when he wanted to be, even if he didn't know it yet.

Savannah got gingerly to her feet and wobbled slightly in her high heels. Seb reached out to steady her with his hands at her hips, which was frankly inspiring.

"I think she may need help getting to the bed," I suggested with a raised brow.

Immediately, he pushed his shoulder into her belly and tossed her up over his shoulder. She let out a little squeal of indignation and hit him lightly on the back, but he ignored her, stalking across the space to the bed and depositing her gently, with utter control of his strength, onto the mattress.

They looked beautiful like that, his body bowed over hers, dark and masculine, hers a pale curve like a crescent moon against the night sky. I could have sat in the chair beside the bed and just watched them fuck all night, languidly fisting my own cock, edging myself as I made them edge each other, but I was too greedy.

I needed to be inside my wife.

I needed to be inside *him*.

It was too soon to introduce him to the delights of anal sex, but I could find other ways to show him how a man could fuck another man, and I was ludicrously eager to do so.

But when I moved to the edge of the bed and ran a proprietary hand down Sebastian's flank to the round, muscular swell of his pale arse and he arched shamelessly into my touch, it was Savannah who took umbrage.

"I believe," she said in something of a sultry hiss. "You are both apologizing to me for your bad behaviour, so the focus should be on *me*."

"Greedy girl," I admonished, but with one lingering caress of Sebastian's beautiful body, I stepped away and walked toward the head of the bed. "On your hands and knees then, Savannah. Show us how much you can take."

She shifted sinuously into position; Sebastian draped over her back as one large hand fiddled with her nipples. I undid my belt and unfastened my trousers but didn't take them off. I enjoyed the power of being fully clothed, the obscenity of my large cock protruding from the fabric as I got onto my knees on the mattress before Savannah.

I fisted my hand in that cloud of silken hair and angled her head back sharply so she gasped, pretty mouth falling open. I slotted my thumb onto her tongue and watched as she instinctively suckled on it.

"Would you like Sebastian to fuck your greedy wet pussy?" I asked her. "Would you like him to ride you and use you until he's begging me to let him come inside you?"

She moaned around my thumb, and Sebastian echoed her, his gaze hot on the two of us, his hands resting lightly on her rump like he waited for my permission to proceed.

"After he's tested, I'll even let his cum fill you up to the brim until it's leaking out of your hole, and then I'll fit myself between your thighs and lick you clean," I promised them both to a resounding chorus of more moans.

I couldn't stand my own game anymore. My cock throbbed so hard it bobbed and weaved beneath Savannah's face. I removed my thumb from her mouth and replaced it with my length, feeding it to her inch by inch, watching as the shaft stretched her lips wide. Her lipstick left raspberry-coloured smears on my skin.

Even though Sebastian was still behind her, I could feel his coiled desire waiting to spring. I looked up at him as I slotted the last inch of my dick deep inside Savannah's throat.

"Would you like to fuck my wife?"

He swallowed thickly as he nodded. "Yes… sir."

My hand tightened in Savannah's hair when she tried to pull off and breathe freely again. I wanted her to struggle slightly, to earn the right to be fucked at both ends.

I reached into my pocket for the condom I'd thoughtfully placed there earlier that day and tossed it to him. He caught it one-handed, eyes on me as he ripped the package open with his teeth and then rolled it on his dick. With one hand holding her still by the hip, he slotted his head at her opening, and though I couldn't see properly from my angle, I could tell by his movement that he was slowly burying himself inside her.

Savannah moaned and gurgled around my cock, as hot and tight as her pussy was around Sebastian's.

Fuck, but I loved this.

Sharing her, watching her cheeks turn pink and her eyes tear, the way her pupils blew wide, and all the carefully cultivated aspects of this woman just evaporated in the heat of her lust. I wanted to use her because I wanted to be used. There was a divide between us that had existed for so long, maybe it had been there from the very beginning, and it had just deepened over the years. Only like this, our kinks and secret fantasies spilled between us, did it feel like we could truly see each other and, more, *want* to be seen.

I pulled her off my cock as Sebastian mimicked my movement at her behind, both of us notched at her entrances, hands on her hips and her face. My gaze sought his over her back and locked. Without prompting, we began fucking into her in perfect tandem, filling and emptying her like metronomes in time with the classical music swelling around us.

"That's such a sweet slut," I praised her as we moved faster, her mouth wet and slack now, her tongue out over her lips and teeth so I could just slot myself in and out as fast as I pleased.

Her eyes were closed tightly in bliss, fingers curled into the bed sheets for leverage to rock back onto Sebastian's cock and forward onto mine. She was blissed out and lost to the moment.

It was the most honest she ever was, and there was a kind of beauty to it in my mind.

"Are you going to come for us?" I demanded when her moans became incessant and her lips tightened around my length.

I pulled out of her mouth so she could pant out a "Yes!"

"No," I told her. "I don't think that's how you ask politely."

I knew she was ready when she didn't frown or protest, when she tipped her chin up to look at me with wet eyes, tear tracks down her cheeks, eyes blown black and mouth swollen and pink to say, "Please, sir."

I hooked my thumb into the side of her mouth to hold it open and pressed my cock inside her again. She groaned hungrily, instantly working her mouth over me.

A moan rumbled through my chest. I looked up at Sebastian to find him sweat-dampened, a curl of black hair stuck to his forehead, his muscles straining with the force of his thrusts as his groin slapped again and again against Savannah's wet pussy.

"Do you want to come for me, too?" I asked mildly and watched as his tongue darted out to taste a bead of sweat on his upper lip. "You've been so good using her tight little pussy. Both of you have done so well. I think I'd enjoy seeing you come."

"Yes," he growled. "If you want me to."

"Good fucking boy," I praised, ignoring the way heat gathered at the base of my spine for my own climax, forcing myself past it to focus on my lovers. "Make her come, and then I'll let you spill all over her pretty pussy."

He groaned, one hand delving beneath Savannah to play at her clit.

"Slap her lightly," I ordered, staring him down when he hesitated. "Trust me, she loves it."

She groaned in agreement around my cock.

He did then, slapping wetly at her pussy, splitting his fingers no doubt around the bulk of his cock in her cunt. She jerked at the impact, once, twice…

"Come all over that thick cock for me, sweetheart," I told her. "Show him why I'm so addicted to you."

She complied with a growled scream, lips clamping down on my cock, teeth carefully sheathed. We anchored her at both ends as she shook apart, her sleek body undulating with pleasure between us.

"Magnificent," I praised softly as I pushed back her hair to watch her lips tremble around my cock. "Now drink me down like a good girl."

Sebastian startled me by plastering himself to her back, suddenly so much closer, his face within reach. His eyes were pinned on the connection of my cock in her mouth and the heat of it was enough to prompt my own orgasm. I fisted the base of my shaft and pulled out, Savannah's mouth still open for my cum because she knew and loved the taste of me. It was impossible not to close my eyes as my climax robbed me of sight, of sound for one blissful moment of full-body electrocution, but the sight of Savannah and Sebastian with their mouths open, gaze pinned on my cock was seared into my memory forever.

Because he wanted a taste too.

I could see it in his eyes, and it made me come so bloody hard I almost passed out.

Instead, I curled over myself, pumping long ropes of seed onto my wife's tongue and mouth, on her chin and cheeks so when I was finished, eyes opened once more, she was covered in me.

Her tongue darted out to lick up the traces on her lips, but I stopped her with my thumb pressed there.

"Don't be greedy now, sweetheart," I ordered softly. "Share with our guest."

Her eyes flashed with renewed hunger as I helped her roll onto her back. Sebastian arched over her with his knees and hands on the bed.

"Lick her clean," I told him, watching as he fought with himself, gaze flicking between me and Savannah's cum-soaked skin. "It's okay. I know you want to taste me."

I cupped the side of his face, trailing the same thumb I'd used on her salty tongue to trace over his lips. His tongue darted out to follow the path, and his eyes darkened.

"Come here," Savannah tempted, cupping the back of his head on the other side of my hand and bringing his face down to her.

She started off with a soft, open-mouthed kiss, sharing the residual taste of me with her tongue. They moaned into each other as he settled his weight fully on top of her. After a moment, I pulled him back with tight fingers in his hair.

"Lick her clean," I repeated intractably.

He shivered slightly, eyes wide on mine, mouth red from Savannah's kisses. When he bent his head, my spent cock kicked. He licked a trail of cum off her cheek and hummed lightly with approval.

"Fuck her until you come," I told him. "You earned it."

He sighed as he instantly fisted his shaft and sank back inside her heat, fucking her slow but hard, grinding into her clit as he continued to lick her clean and share the taste of me in languid kisses.

I watched them as I sat back against the headboard, the two of them churning just between my legs, fucking each other for me, pushing their boundaries because I asked them to. It was fucking heady. Nothing could compare except for the high I got on stage or on set. The feeling of having an audience in the palm of your hand.

"Pull out and come on her cunt."

Sebastian growled as he fucked her hard and then pulled back, resting on his heels to rip the condom off and spray his cum over her slick, used pussy.

Before he'd finished, I was down there, licking up his mess and hers. The combined taste of them on my tongue was salt-sweet and ambrosial. I hummed as I swallowed the warm cum and Savannah's juices, licking her until she came again, a shivery orgasm she sighed through, and then I licked her clean again.

When I looked up, Sebastian was slack-jawed, cheeks flushed, hair a mess. He was utterly debauched and the most gorgeous man I'd ever seen. Without thinking, I reeled him in with a hand on his neck and shared the remnants of cum on my tongue with him. He groaned into my mouth and clasped me even closer, licking behind my teeth in search of more.

"Enough," Savannah said sleepily, pulling at my hand from where she lay. "I'm exhausted."

Part of me wanted to tell her she could drift while I finally had some time to explore the man before me, but I knew she wouldn't like it. More, I knew I shouldn't want to do anything without my wife, even if she slept beside me. That was the agreement really. Together or nothing. I was lucky enough to have a partner who allowed me to indulge in my fantasies, and I was cognizant of being grateful and not pushing her too hard.

The truth was Savannah brought every man we'd played with to our marital bed, not me. Still, she'd done it for me because she knew I wanted it. Had coaxed the secret fantasies from me like she'd coaxed my dreams, whispers late at night drunk on martinis in the bar near my flat after I'd returned home from my stint in the RAF, disillusioned and alone. She'd promised a future for us both of success and happiness, the attainment of our wildest dreams. It made me smile to think about that unhappily married American girl and the boy I'd been then and to know, against all the odds, Savannah had been proven right.

I pulled away from Sebastian with a little grin, shaking my hand on his neck a little in affection. "*Bellisimo.*"

His laugh was a sharp, startled syllable. "*Grazie, signore.*"

"Sleep," Savannah insisted, pulling us both down by the hand on either side of her.

As soon as we flopped to the mattress, she arranged us to her liking, turning into Sebastian to rest her cheek on his chest, one leg thrown over his, her rump in the bowl of my hips, my arm tucked around her chest like a blanket.

She was out like a light the moment she settled.

"The remote for the music and the lights should be on the nightstand beside you," I whispered to Sebastian.

He reached carefully for it so as not to disturb Savannah and flicked both off. We plunged into darkness, only the light from a waxing moon falling through the open curtains.

"You're still wearing your clothes," Sebastian noted.

"I am."

"I haven't brushed my teeth."

I chuckled. "Nor have I. Relax for a while, drift off even. If you wake in the night, feel free to go back to the carriage house. But for now, sleep with us?"

I could feel his hesitation, and I thought I understood it. We didn't usually let the men sleep in our bed, but there was something about Sebastian. Warmth on a chilly evening, perhaps, warmth in our chilly marriage, that drew us both inexorably toward him.

In some kind of answer to the unspoken question of what the bloody hell was happening between us all, I reached above Savannah's head to find where I thought I remembered Sebastian's hand rested on the pillow. His fingers flinched at first contact and then slowly curled around my own.

"Sleep, Sebastian," I murmured, giving in to my suddenly leaden lids closing. "Only the moon is watching, and we can trust it to keep our secrets tonight."

Chapter Fourteen

Sebastian

The next month was absolute chaos.

Adam was preparing for the lead in a Patrick Sullivan movie about a British gangster in the 1970s. The first table read was at the end of the month, so he had me run lines with him almost every day. It was fascinating to watch him learn a character, to witness, as the days passed, the way he sank further and further into the role until the day before the read-through dawned, and he was suddenly Freddie Bannerman, the scarred and angry ex-con who unexpectedly found himself king of a drug empire in London.

While he was busy with preparations and promotion for his upcoming film release, *The Devil Cares*, I spent most of my time either with Savannah, driving her to and from appointments, stopping for lunches around town or going shopping, sometimes, entirely for me so she could dress me up like a real-life doll. She was surprisingly fun when she let her guard down, laughing at my quips and teasing me for my silliness. She seemed so much younger than her thirty-four years when she was with me.

Thirty-four years old. She'd coyly refused to tell me how old she was for so long that I'd finally capitulated and looked it up myself.

Adam was twenty-eight.

They were both so much older than me, successful and wealthy and wise in so many ways I was decidedly *not.* It should have felt too much like a power imbalance, like I was nothing compared to them, with nothing to offer.

But, shockingly, I seemed to offer them a lot.

I made Savannah laugh and relax when she was usually focused to a point that made her icy and rigid as frozen stone. I made Adam gentle, the powerful facade he erected for everyone softening a bit for me. They both sought me out when they had time and seemed almost… jealous when the other had more of me. It wasn't a poisonous sentiment but more of a childlike one. They both wanted my time individually and together.

Unfortunately, we didn't have much of the latter.

I wasn't sure how Savannah and Adam even had a functioning marriage, thanks to their schedules. They barely saw each other except for public outings and late at night, when the three of us would fall into bed together.

And that happened almost every night when they were both at home, but never if one was away. It wasn't said explicitly, but I soon learned the rules of the Meyers's household.

I could kiss either of them whenever the mood arose, but beyond that, except for that first night I'd moved in out in the garden, we weren't to take it any further without the third person to bear witness.

Yet there also seemed to be a kind of rigidity to our nights together. It was always about Savannah, and the tension made me wonder if it was by mutual design or because she refused to let the attention wander away from her for even a moment. I was growing to know Savvy well enough to surmise it was probably some of the latter. She liked to feel powerful, the mover and shaker. Even though she wasn't the one with the Oscar, she had flex and influence in the movie industry in Britain, and it was obvious she enjoyed when people came calling for a favour or opinion on their work. Even when Adam received praise, she smiled coyly, a little curl of her lips that spoke of pride and a hint of arrogance.

It's all because of me, that look seemed to say.

And I was learning that a lot of it was because of her.

But not all of it.

Just as not all of my attraction in this dynamic was toward Savannah alone.

I just hadn't had any opportunity to explore it otherwise.

Unsurprisingly, I also had to be available at all times.

Once, I was speaking with Cosima over the phone, so I hadn't noticed the incoming calls and texts for almost an hour. When I checked, Savvy had tried to reach me ten times, and when I finally called her back, she told me not to bother.

She didn't speak to me for three days.

I didn't take it too personally even though it hurt. These people operated differently than me. If I was fire, Savannah and Adam were ice. They punished with silence and distance, not shouting and tears the way my family did at home.

They also were not physically affectionate outside of our "playdates" as Adam called them. Adam was almost painfully careful not to stand too close or touch too obviously when we were in public, though truthfully, we spent most of our time together shut away from the world in their house or at Pinewood Studios or Andrea's house.

Even Savannah seemed to find casual affection distasteful when we were alone.

It was an odd house with odder people, but I was shocked by how much I loved living with them both.

I was used to a full house; growing up in a tiny home in Naples with three sisters, one of those a twin, and an Italian mother was often a chaotic, cacophonous experience. Living with the Meyerses was leagues different than that, and I might have felt lonely or even used if it weren't for those nighttime rendezvous and daily flashes of intimacy they unwittingly gave to me.

The moment Savannah admitted she missed proper American barbecue, I'd surprised her with a Styrofoam case of pulled pork and brisket from Prairie Fire, where the pit master was a direct transplant from Kansas. She'd smeared barbecue sauce on my mouth with her fingers and licked it off with a girlish giggle. I'd fed her messy pork with my fingers and then made her lick them off when we were done.

Another when she got a cold the night before a movie premiere and had to stay home instead of going out with Adam. She was mostly upset, she'd informed me, about not wearing the gorgeous Dior vintage gown hanging in her closet for the evening. So I'd stepped into one of the suits the Meyerses had bought for me—hand-tailored on Savile Row—and presented myself to Savannah, where she was curled up on the couch watching the red carpet. She'd looked so small and young, make-up free and melancholy, and younger still when she'd taken in my appearance and the dress I had carefully folded over one arm and started to smile.

We watched the rest of the coverage together in our fancy clothes on the carpet in front of the television while eating popcorn.

It was different with Adam. We were either playing with Savannah, where our focus was always almost wholly on her, or we were working together on his lines or on preparing *Blood Oath.* He wanted to fast-track everything, especially when he found out Cosima and I were paying not only for Mama and Elena in Naples, with hopes to move them to the United States soon, but also for Giselle's tuition at *L'École des Beaux-Arts* in Paris. While he worked on securing financing and studio backing, Andrea and I worked over the script. It was incredible to work with an Italian on my story about Italian characters, but it was even better to have someone who understood my language and culture. It made me homesick while simultaneously soothing the ache of missing stitched into my chest.

With Adam, he showed his true self in smaller but more frequent ways than his wife. He did it by putting his hand on my thigh while *he* drove us both, always, around in his Aston. When he woke me up each morning before Savannah, with a bite to my shoulder or a kiss to my neck, taking advantage of the private moments of the morning to touch me not like a lover but like a partner. As though he just wanted to touch me because he liked me. When he was home, we worked out together in their basement home gym, pushing each other and competing so that every exercise was a game. Seeing him half naked and slicked in sweat was a lesson in temptation I'd never expected to learn.

Even though he was often gone, he would text me articles he thought I'd find interesting about the industry or ask my thoughts on his next projects. He valued me for more than my beauty in ways that no one outside of my family ever had before.

I was quite honestly living on cloud nine for that entire month. My only anxieties came from wondering when Adam would finally get around to touching me beyond a naked caress as he used and ordered my body to please his wife. We hadn't gone past holding each other's cocks, and I was astonishingly eager to try more, but not without his coaching. It was starting to keep me up at night after my lovers had dropped into sleep, wondering when and how.

Otherwise, for the first time in my life, I was truly happy. Until one morning, a month after moving, when a stranger reminded me of my reality.

I'd dropped Adam off for his read-through, and I was heading to meet Andrea for coffee nearby when I quite literally ran into a slim, dark-haired man.

"Watch where you're going," he barked, shoving away from me a little harshly for something that was just an accident.

I arched an eyebrow at him, unconsciously channeling Adam. "I think you were the one to run into me, actually. But no harm, no foul. Have a good rest of the morning."

I made to move past when I felt a firm grip on my elbow. When I stopped and looked back with a glare, the man was frowning at me.

"You're Sebastian Lombardi."

I blinked, a little thrown off by the recognition. Oh, a few regulars at Finborough Theatre had recognized me during the play's run through the late summer and fall, but it wasn't anything like a regular occurrence.

"Yes, I am."

His face broke into a slight, mean smile, and he shifted his grip to my hand, shaking it aggressively. "Well, what a boon. It's my pleasure to meet you."

"Why exactly?" There was something about his demeanour that was vaguely threatening.

He was slightly built with pretty features and a sharp chin that, combined with his mean grin, made him look vulpine.

"Well, I've been curious about who Adam and Savannah replaced me with."

Cazzo.

The words rocked me back like a blow to the sternum, but I was practiced enough at acting to keep the way I reeled beneath my skin.

"That's curious. I thought their last chauffeur was an old man. You look remarkably well for your age."

He flinched slightly, and his smile grew even more malicious as his grip tightened painfully on my hand. "I was before Albert, and I think we both know I occupied a very different position than that."

"Given I don't even know your name, I don't think you should make assumptions about anything," I warned, squeezing his hand even more tightly in return. "And I wouldn't want to be caught spreading any gossip about the Meyerses. I think they won their last defamation suit fairly handily."

He laughed then, a sharp sound like nails on a chalkboard. "Oh, don't worry about your lovers' reputation, pretty boy. I signed all the same NDAs you did. I just wanted to warn you, man to man, former boy toy to current, that the Meyerses will drop you just when you're starting to feel comfortable. They'll make you such pretty promises and build you up until you think you might burst, and then they'll drop you from such a great height, you'll shatter at the impact. It took me six months to get myself together again. I'm only trying to save you the same aggravation. Adam's internalized homophobia is so bad, he can barely stand himself when he's with a man, and Savannah just wants to be worshipped. She doesn't care by whom."

"Who is calling who a pretty boy toy?" I asked, accent thickening with rage, his fingers creaking under my grip until he winced. "I may be young, but I'm no boy. I've seen more in my life than you have in any of your wildest dreams or nightmares. You worry about yourself; it seems you need to if being let go by your employers took such a toll on you. But me? I'll be just fine. Now, good day, stranger."

I pulled my hand from his sweaty grip and turned on my heel, filled with rage and aching with confusion as I stalked back toward the car.

"It's Oscar," he called after me, uncaring of the people filing in and out of the studio behind us. "Oscar Hampton. Ask them about me, and you'll see I was only trying to help you, poor sod."

I slammed the car door behind me and peeled out of the lot in the town car, cranking up the radio on an Italian station. Umberto Tozzi filled the car's interior as I sped through the streets toward my meeting with Andrea.

I didn't want to let Oscar's words sink into my psyche without first asking Adam or Savvy about them, but it was hard to close myself off from his remarks. They were too pointed to be all lies. It was obvious Oscar was close enough to them to know they liked to bring a third into their marital bed, but did that mean everything else he'd said was true?

I felt sick thinking about being kicked out of their bed and their home. Not because of what it might mean to *Blood Oath*—I thought Andrea was invested enough to continue with the project anyway—but because of what such a separation would do to me.

Drop me from such a great height I'd shatter at the bottom.

It was only now that the threat of our tryst's inevitable end seemed so tangible that I realized how happy the Meyerses made *me.*

The way Savannah made sure there was good grappa in the house and Italian staples like buffalo mozzarella and prosciutto in the fridge and double 00 flour in the pantry in case I had the taste for authentic homemade pasta. The way she bought me clothes—not because she was ashamed of me but because she loved to spoil me. Gift giving was obviously her love language as much as acts of service.

The way Adam bought me a fancy laptop with all of his favourite films loaded onto the movie player so we could discuss them together. The way he knew I loved football, so he made a point to invite the great Spanish player Iker Ferrera over one night as a surprise. The way he listened to every thought in my head as though he could learn something from me.

They always touched me in the dark cover of night, as if I were living art they wanted to worship with teeth and tongue and fingertips. They made themselves vulnerable to me in a way they never did outside the sanctuary of their bedroom.

I was falling in love with them both.

It was painfully obvious it had been happening almost from the first moment I'd met each of them, and I couldn't even be angry with myself for not trying harder to resist it.

She was just such a woman, and he such a man; how could I ever have hoped to resist their gravitational pull?

But Oscar had thrown into stark relief just how tenuous our situation was.

I was their temporary lover, a guest in their marriage who would inevitably wear out his welcome. There was no permanency, and I was a man who longed for such a thing because I'd never really had it.

It was a lose/lose situation at this point, though.

If I left on my terms, I'd be breaking my own heart, and when they eventually asked me to leave, they'd do the breaking instead.

Either way, I'd be shattered.

Maybe, if I'd been a different man, I would have accepted the unavoidable conclusion of either path.

But I'd been raised to fight.

To bare my teeth at the enemy no matter how much more powerful they were than me and stand my ground like I had a real shot of winning the battle.

It had worked with one of the most fearsome criminal organizations in the world, and it had helped me secure a spot at Finborough Theatre despite my inexperience and the obstacles stacked against me.

Maybe it had given me an overblown sense of courage in the face of adversity, but I had just enough gumption to think I could change the outcome.

Because what if there was a third option?

What if I could convince Adam and Savannah to fall in love with me, too?

What if none of this had to end at all?

THE STAGE WAS PERFECTLY SET WHEN the Meyerses arrived home that evening. I'd done the bulk of the work, but Chaucer had helped me procure a couple of extra things and choose a bottle from their cellar that they wouldn't mind drinking for a casual dinner at home. If Chaucer thought it was strange that the chauffeur had taken it upon himself to cook the lord and lady of the house dinner, she didn't mention it or even cast me a sidelong look. She was efficient in the extreme. After being Adam's personal assistant for the last half decade, I was sure she'd seen worse than an Italian man hankering to cook one of his regional dishes.

In fact, Adam and Savannah seemed entirely more shocked than she had, when they walked into the kitchen and saw me at the stove with a black apron tied around my waist, stirring a sizzling pan of sauce. Jazz played softly in the background because it was Adam's favourite genre, and we usually listened to Savannah's classical instead.

After Chaucer left, I'd lit candles all over the island and the cozy table by the corner of windows instead of in the formal dining room.

I'd never attempted to do something romantic like this in my life. Girls in London were usually happy to go for a pint at the pub and then back to my place for a casual romp before disappearing from my life. It wasn't that I only wanted casual sex, but I'd been so busy with the play and focused on my career that I hadn't made time for romance.

Now, I had plenty of toe-curling, insane orgasms and the kind of comradery with Savvy and Adam I'd always wanted, but I knew it wasn't enough. I'd become greedy for more, and I had the sinking feeling that nothing would be enough of them, short of absolutely everything.

So this was my first attempt at wooing someone—someone*s*—and I was uncharacteristically nervous. This is why I slipped into my old, confident persona like an old, beloved coat as soon as the Meyerses stepped into my domain. Because it may have been their house, but it was my stage today, and I planned to own it.

"*Buona sera, bellezze mie*," I greeted them with a wide grin, placing the spoon in the marble rest so I could pour the decanted wine into two goblet glasses.

They both stood arrested in the doorway as I walked toward them. I even had to wrap Savannah's hand around the stem of the glass before she took it.

I pressed a kiss to both of her silken cheeks and then took the liberty to steal one from her mouth. Only then did she soften, leaning forward to press her breasts into my chest. When I pulled away, her eyes were closed and her mouth was a softly unfurled rosebud.

I smiled at her, not the showboating grin I wielded so often, but a true one just for her.

And him.

I turned to give Adam his glass. He accepted it with a wariness that made my gut ache. My kindness had him on edge, waiting for something the way a beaten dog receiving gentle attention doesn't believe he won't be struck for taken liberties.

What had happened to him to make him so afraid of his own desires?

I tried to remember what I'd read of his history, about the lord and lady parents who lost their ancestral estate but still lived in luxury because of the success of their son somewhere in the Cornish countryside. I'd always assumed Britain was more liberal and accepting than my native Italy, but I wondered if I was terribly wrong and Adam had been castigated for his sexuality.

I shook off the thought and gave him his own cheek kisses. When I moved in to press my mouth to his, he held himself still as though he couldn't trust himself or me.

I took it as a dare, whether it was meant to be or not, that I could make him break his control.

My hand slid around the back of his neck, fingers digging into the short hairs at his nape as I changed my angle and sealed my mouth over his. My tongue slid between his lips without asking, plundering his warm mouth as though I had the right. A choked-off groan was my only response before I broke contact and stepped back.

"Welcome home," I greeted them both. "Sit down at the island and enjoy the wine while I finish things off. It shouldn't take long. I know you're both probably famished."

They both blinked at me, but Savannah was the one to move first. She was used to being catered to, my *duchessa*, so it was easy for her to take this in stride. I watched as she glided to a barstool and daintily perched on the edge, her wineglass dangling elegantly from her fingers.

"What are you making us, Sebastian?" she asked as though she always came home to an Italian in her kitchen.

I grinned. "*Spaghetti alla puttanesca*."

"Well, that sounds exotic," she demurred before lightly adding, "Adam, come sit with me."

He moved a little stiffly to the barstool beside her, but sat down and looked at his wife, avoiding the sight of me moving about his kitchen so familiarly.

I wondered if I'd miscalculated.

Oscar's words rang in my inner ear, *Adam's internalized homophobia.*

"I thought it was fitting for you lot," I teased Savvy as I stirred the fragrant *sugo* and then went to the fridge to grab the hand-rolled pasta I'd made earlier that afternoon. "It's pasta in the style of a whore."

I made sure to watch them both as I delivered my line and was rewarded with a shocked bark of laughter from Adam and a little grin from Savvy. My heart warmed watching them, seeing Adam's shoulders soften just a touch and Savannah settle more comfortably in the stool, kicking off her high heels.

"Very fitting," Adam allowed with a rakish look. "I might have to reward you in that style later tonight."

"I wish you would," I agreed, turning slightly as though I wasn't watching him while I dropped the pasta into the gently boiling water to cook. "In fact, I know we haven't really discussed it. But I was hoping we could take things a little further tonight."

Instantly, the newly relaxed atmosphere in the room stretched taut.

"Oh?" he asked mildly.

"What did you have in mind, Seb?" Savannah asked, only a trace amount of eagerness in her tone.

We'd fallen into a routine of fucking Savannah together, lavishing her again and again as both our queen and our pleasure slave, a contrary union that shouldn't have been able to exist but somehow flourished between us. We used our hands and lips on her, fucked her mouth and her cunt, but we hadn't done anything where Adam and I were particularly intimate ourselves. Even fucking Savannah together, one of us in both her sweet holes, stretching her wide and filling her. Adam talked about it when he spoke his delicious filth to us both in bed, but for whatever reason, we hadn't crossed that boundary.

I wanted to desperately, not just because I knew Savannah would love it, come apart at her seams around the full breach of us inside her, but because I wanted to feel Adam.

He had promised to introduce me to intimacy with a man, and even though my attraction to him had startled me at first, I was more than willing to delve further. If I was being honest, I was just as wildly attracted to him as I was to Savannah, and I grew increasingly dissatisfied with our lack of involvement.

I shrugged one shoulder in faux nonchalance. "I was thinking Savannah's grown bored of us servicing her mouth and pussy. Maybe she'd like one of us in her tight little ass. Maybe even while the other is fucking her pussy."

Adam and Savannah both loved dirty talk to the point they could get hard and wet after just a few minutes of spoken filth. It was something I loved about them, knowing I just had to verbalize exactly what I wanted from them both to get an explosive reaction.

And they didn't disappoint.

"Oh," Savannah said, that beautiful flush the colour of the wine in her cup spilling down her front.

Adam licked his lips and rubbed his hand over his square, stubbled chin as though he had to think about it. But I knew that tell. It was only to draw attention away from the way his lids lowered and his eyes went black.

"Well, well, look who's getting creative," he practically purred.

I swallowed thickly and shrugged again, turning away to stir the sauce and turn it down to a simmer. A moment later, I almost jumped out of my skin when Adam's hands bracketed me at the counter, his breath a hot line down my neck.

"You want to fuck her together?" he husked out, and even though he wasn't touching me, I felt his presence draped all the way down my back. "You want me to sit her on your thick cock and work my way inside her tight arse?"

I nodded a little helplessly, reaching down to adjust my erection in my jeans beneath the apron. Adam's hand caught mine in an iron grip before I could do so. He flattened my hand to the counter and reached down himself to grip my cock and adjust it more comfortably down one thigh.

Dio mio, it was the first time he'd touched my dick in days, and I wanted more.

"Is this why you're being so good to us? Cooking us dinner, greeting us with that smile of yours that could light an entire city? Because you want permission to split Savannah open on our cocks?"

I bit out a curse, and I could hear Savannah shift on her stool like she was rubbing her thighs together.

Why was it so fucking hot when Adam slid into the dominant role? It was one thing to want a man sexually and quite another to submit to him so easily as I found myself doing all the time, but I couldn't connect logic to it other than to say it was simply his effect on me.

I admired him enough, trusted him another, to take control and let me just… enjoy pleasure for once in my life.

"Yes," I admitted. "But also, because I like to do nice things for you."

I turned in the cage of his arms to catch his wary expression. Before he could pull away, I wrapped my hand around his throat, fingertips pressing into his pulse point so I could feel it race away from me.

"You deserve them," I admitted softly but loud enough for Savannah to hear. "Both of you deserve something warm and beautiful to come home to."

Adam swallowed thickly, tension in the tall, strong line of his body. But he didn't pull away, and I decided I'd put him through enough. I pressed forward to kiss him, a hard stamp of possession, before pushing him away and draining the pasta.

"Sit down at the table," I told them both, listening to the sounds of them obeying me as I prepared the pasta dish, grabbed the focaccia from a nearby Italian bakery from the oven, and the light green salad I'd prepared from the fridge.

Once everything was laid at the table, I took off the apron and sat down with them.

"Next time, I'd prefer to come home to you cooking just in that," Savannah requested, a slight twitch to her mouth.

Adam smiled a little, but I laughed as I served her first. "Noted, *duchessa.* I'd worry about flying oil splatter, but I'm willing to brave that and worse for you."

"How flattering," she said dryly as she allowed me to fill her plate and refill her wine. When I was finished, she put a hand on my wrist and leaned forward out of her chair to steal a lingering kiss. Her eyes were warmer than I'd ever seen, a lush blue. "Thank you, Sebastian."

"My pleasure," I assured her before turning to serve Adam.

"I'm capable of dressing my own plate," he protested, but he didn't stop me, and when I finished, he reached beneath the table to squeeze my thigh.

"Well then, *buon appetito*," I said, raising my glass and waiting for them both to look me in the eyes before we clinked them together. "To us."

There was a second of hesitation before they both echoed me.

"To us."

Chapter Fifteen

Sebastian

Dinner was a resounding success.

They both ate everything on their plates, even Savannah, who was always on some kind of diet, and we finished two bottles of Italian red, the second one fetched by Adam himself from the cellar. We laughed, especially when they both told me stories about Andrea, whom they'd been close with since Adam worked with him on one of his very first films.

Savannah admitted she'd thought about becoming an agent but that she enjoyed managing Adam's career and hopefully, soon, my own. I thought she would make a shark of an agent, but when I told her that, she only smiled into space at something I couldn't see.

Adam admitted that he'd needed a night to relax after the read-through. It had gone well, but he was playing a sociopathic kingpin, and it took his mind to dark places.

Even though they were both loathe to talk about their pasts, I tricked Adam into telling me about his childhood a bit by inquiring about his relationship with the princes of England, Arthur and Alasdair. Savannah admitted her favourite movie was *Steel Magnolias* because she'd watched it with her mum dozens of times while on her deathbed.

When I told them I'd like time off to visit Mama and Elena in Naples for Mama's birthday, they both pouted slightly, which I took as a win, and then graciously gave me two weeks of holiday.

The atmosphere between us all was warm and languid, safe. No one could see through the gates and walls of the home into this kitchen and the intimacy within. Adam forgot to be wary of me or what he might feel, and he started to touch me again. Those little brushes of his fingers against my wrists or squeezes around my neck or thigh made my skin tingle and spark. Savannah laughed so hard, tears pooled in her lower lids and ruined her makeup, but she didn't get up to fix it.

By the time I pulled the grappa out, we were all tipsy and smiling. Adam took the bottle from me and poured out the glasses, but before he handed them to us, he paused with a long, slow curve of his lips.

"Have you prepared dessert, Sebastian?"

"No, it's not really my specialty," I admitted. "There's some fruit in the fridge."

"Excellent," he said in that low, velvety tone I was now conditioned to find arousing. "Fetch some berries and meet us upstairs."

I looked at Savannah, but she was already pushing her chair back and unbuttoning the pearls on her silk blouse as she padded barefoot out of the kitchen. I watched as the silk fluttered like a dove in the air and floated to the ground behind her.

"*Madonna mia*, she's a goddess," I muttered.

Adam hummed his agreement, but when I looked at him, he was staring at me with the intensity of a predator. I got out of my chair, backing into the kitchen away from him on instinct and because I was beginning to love this game we played. He stalked me into the kitchen and shoved me into the side of the fridge with a hand splayed flat against my sternum. Eyes locked on mine, he slid it up to my throat and squeezed lightly.

"I hope you're ready for a long night of debauchery, Sebastian," he murmured as he drew his nose along the line of my jaw, pausing to smell the place I sprayed my cologne behind my ear as though the scent was drugging. "We're going to use Savannah until she's boneless."

"Yes," I hissed, tipping my head back to give him better access to my throat.

He bit into the junction of my neck and shoulder in a way that shot pleasure straight to my already hard cock.

"Tonight, we'll both fuck her tight arse, but soon, Sebastian, I'm going to fuck yours," he promised darkly into my ear, hot breath making me shiver. Hot words making the bottom drop out of my stomach. I was both aroused and terrified. "I'm going to spend an hour sucking your dick and fucking you with my fingers, opening you up nice and slow because I have a thick cock, and it's going to stretch you so fucking well even with all that prep. I'll have Savannah sit on your face to muffle your groans as I work myself to the hilt inside you. I want you drowning in her cum as I fuck you, harder and faster until you're practically sobbing into her pussy and you're begging me to touch your dick."

I was panting, knees numb, held upright against the fridge only by Adam's hand at my throat and his thigh pressing a little too hard into my erection and thigh. Just when I thought he'd finished teasing me, he leaned into my mouth, licking my bottom lip.

"I'll come inside your gorgeous arse," he warned. "Just to have the pleasure of knowing my cum is deep inside you where none has ever been before. Just to watch it leak out of your abused hole when I'm done with you. Only then will I take your cock to the back of my throat and let you blow like a broken hydrant."

"Jesus Christ," I swore in English, reaching between us to pinch my cock so I wouldn't come like a boy in my trousers. "Your mouth should come with a warning label."

"This is the warning," he quipped, squeezing my cock alongside my hand before he stepped back, grabbed the grappa, and sauntered casually out of the kitchen and up the stairs.

I leaned against the fridge, panting and aroused beyond belief, for a good long time while I caught my breath and convinced myself I wasn't seconds away from orgasming. Only then did I reach into the fridge, grab the covered fruit platter, and follow my lovers upstairs.

SAVANNAH WAS NAKED AND SPLAYED OUT on the stripped bed with two large towels beneath her and a row of sex toys lined up at her feet. Adam stood at the end of the bed wearing only his trousers, opened at the placket to reveal the dense trail of flaxen hair under his belly and the groomed thicket lower down. He wasn't wearing underwear, and the glimpse of his cock beneath the opened fabric was scintillating. I'd never given him head before, but *Dio mio*, I wanted to drop to my knees then and there and lave him with my tongue.

His mouth curled to one side as though he could read my thoughts, but he shook his head slightly and crooked a finger to beckon me closer.

"How do you like the look of your dessert?" he asked me,

gesturing to Savannah's naked, lithe body laid out for us.

She was slim and small, her curves only small handfuls, but there was an elegance to her beauty that was deeply erotic. With her halo of short blonde curls and that full pink mouth, she seemed like something fallen from heaven straight into Adam's den of iniquity.

"Delicious," I praised.

Eyes closed, probably by Adam's command, she smiled smugly.

"Even more delicious prepared properly," Adam corrected, taking the fruit and laying it out on the mattress beside the toys I was close enough to recognize as a medium-sized butt plug, a small vibrator, a bottle of lube, and a cock ring with something attached to the loop that might have been a vibrator.

Before I could turn to look at Adam again, he was pressed up to my front, deftly undoing my denim and sliding his hand into my boxers to grab my stiff cock.

He hummed his approval, playing his thumb over my wet head in a way that made my breath rattle through my lungs. "The cock ring is for you. We wouldn't want you coming before Savvy and I have had our fill of you, would we?"

"No," I agreed. "But I can control myself."

He arched a condescending brow, and I wondered how I could find his arrogance so fucking sexy. "After you almost came in your pants in the kitchen, I doubt it. I like to be careful with my toys, so you'll wear it for me, won't you?"

"Yes, sir," I agreed because he was dipping the tip of his thumb into the slit of my cock in a way that made shivery currents of electricity tingle over my skin.

"That's my boy," he praised, raising a cup of grappa between us to feed me a sip. After I took it, he plucked a blackberry from the platter and took a bite himself before smearing the bitten half over my lips and licking off the juice. "The fruit brings out the flavour of the chocolate, doesn't it?"

I opened my mouth for the berry, but he kissed me instead, feeding me his silken tongue. Clutching at his wrist, I brought the berry between our damp lips and took it into my mouth. With only juice left on my tongue, I kissed him again. "*Sì, è più deliziosa.*"

Yes, it's even more delicious, I told him.

He grinned before moving onto the mattress to sit by Savannah's hip. "Take off your clothes while I prepare your treat."

I disrobed as I watched him dribble grappa into the divot of her naval and the hollow of her throat.

"Hold very still for me, sweetheart," he ordered her as he then proceeded to paint the top of her bare mound in purple blackberry juice, adorning the peak of each nipple with a ripe raspberry, and lining up blueberries in the ridges of her collarbones.

Finally, he placed a strawberry in her mouth and demanded softly, "Hold this steady like a sweet slut for us."

Her sigh feathered out around the fruit even as she held carefully still so as not to disturb the grappa.

When we both finished our tasks, Adam held the grappa carefully over her sternum and dribbled a line between her breasts that trembled and rolled slowly toward her belly.

"Well," he told me imperiously, every inch the lord of this house. "Get to work, Sebastian."

I swallowed thickly as I took in Savannah all trussed up in fruit and sweet wine for me, cautiously climbing onto the bed between her thighs to work my way up her body. I slurped at the grappa in her belly button, swirling my tongue there until she quivered, and then I moved lower, licking the blackberry juice from the top of her mound. The scent of her arousal was heavy and spiced in the air, but I ignored her sex to move up her chest, laving the liquor-soaked skin up to her small breasts. I ate the raspberries off her nipples, turning my head to watch Adam watch me attend to his wife. He didn't even touch himself, his erection a stiff tent in his trousers. I admired his restraint because all I wanted to do was fall on Savvy like an animal and fuck straight into her wet pussy until I filled it overfull with cum. I wanted to mark her with more than just fruit and wine. I wanted her painted in my seed and inkblot bruises from my fingertips.

I wanted every inch of her to be stamped by every inch of me until the lone space left was free only for Adam to fill.

"Doesn't she taste sweet?" he asked me. "I know you're dying to lick between her pretty thighs. Do you think she can keep the strawberry between her teeth while you make her come for me?"

"No," I taunted her, nipping at the peak of her breast with my teeth in a way that made her moan sharply behind the berry.

"Nor do I." He chuckled darkly. "But why don't we let her prove us right? Get on your knees on the floor and drag her to the end of the bed."

I did as he asked immediately, dropping hard to the plush carpet and dragging her over the silken sheets until her legs were thrown over my shoulders. I ate that pretty pussy almost every day, and I still hungered for that sweet musk in my nose.

I dove in with relish, letting my control slip and giving myself over to the lust running molten through my veins. She had such a lovely cunt, pink with delicate folds I sucked into my mouth and a small, throbbing clit I loved to torture with long, hard pulls and lashes of my tongue. Savannah started squirming in minutes, her hips gyrating against my face, smearing her juice all over my mouth and chin.

I loved it, nearly drowning in the taste and texture and scent of this woman.

"Sebastian," she cried out, strawberry falling from her mouth as she arched off the bed on a cry.

The sound of my name from her mouth made precum leak from my cock and dribble down the shaft like a fucking fountain.

"Naughty girl," Adam chastened her for failing his test. "I'll have to replace that with something else."

I tipped my head up to watch as he shucked his trousers and climbed naked onto Savvy's chest, straddling her tits and feeding her panting mouth his cock. I could only see the tight muscles of his ass flex as he thrust in and out of her lips and hear the soft suck and moan of her mouth around his shaft, but it was enough to make me moan into the folds of Savvy's cunt.

Adam used her as she used me until she cried out around his shaft, and her honeyed cum drenched my tongue. I licked every drop from her cunt, from the crease of her thighs, and even her little asshole. She jerked when my tongue found the crinkled flesh and then let out a little whimper.

Adam chuckled hoarsely and I realized he'd joined me at the end of the bed, the butt plug in one hand and lube in the other.

"Have you ever plugged someone before?" he asked me.

I shook my head, so he gently shouldered me to the side between her splayed legs and pushed her right leg back to expose her—clit to asshole—to our gaze.

"Such a pretty little thing," Adam praised her, running his lubed fingers from her clit down through her swollen cunt to the tiny clutch of her ass.

He rubbed his fingertips there for a long minute, Savannah panting audibly as she propped herself on her elbows to watch us with a flush-stained face and sweaty brow. She was so gorgeous like this, raw and exposed for us. It felt like such a gift; my heart clutched hard like her small hand was wrapped around the very muscle itself.

"*Magnifica*," I murmured as Adam started to work the tip of the angled plug into her hole, twisting and pressing lightly to open her up without pain.

"She likes a bit of stretch and burn," he instructed as he pushed and turned that toy forward and back, her ass starting to clutch at the toy when it retreated.

My cock was coated in my own precum, and it took every ounce of restraint I possessed not to touch myself.

But Adam hadn't given me leave to, and somehow, Adam had woven an invisible collar around the throat of my lust, so it did only as he bid.

"So I don't finger her first," he continued conversationally, as though he wasn't now fucking a toy completely in and out of Savvy's arse. "She likes to feel the ache the next day, don't you, sweetheart?"

"Yes," she hissed, eyes flying open to lock onto me. "I love going to lunch with the ladies at The Ivy, feeling how hard I've been fucked the night or morning before. Knowing I'm utterly debauched but looking every inch the lady."

Unable to help myself, I begged Adam, "Can I touch her now?"

"Oh, yes," Adam purred. "You've been so good. Why don't you fuck her with the toy and slurp up all this wetness? There's only one last thing to do before I let you inside her."

Savvy's pussy was so swollen and pink, glistening with juices that ran down the crease of her thighs into the mattress. The perfume of her arousal made my head swim as I dipped my head to lick into her tight entrance, fucking her with my tongue to get at all that nectar.

Her hand wove into my hair and clutched me close.

So I didn't notice Adam move until I felt him press his chest into my back and reach around to wrap his big hand around my cock.

The full-body shudder of pleasure that rolled through me felt like an earthquake.

"Steady," he soothed, smoothing his other hand over my chest to tweak a nipple. "See, this is why I have to restrain this big dick because you're so young and eager to come everywhere, aren't you? All over Savvy's cunt, all over her pretty tits and her prettier face. You want to paint her in it, don't you?"

"Fuck," I grunted, punching my hips into his grip, chasing the pleasure. "Yes, sir."

"I know, I know," he soothed. "Soon. But first…"

The hand on my chest disappeared and I felt it a moment later, coated in cool lube, probe at my asshole.

I jerked away from the fingers straight into the clutch of his grip on my dick, moaning and instinctively thrusting back onto his fingers. It was confusing because the fingers rubbing at my hole didn't exactly feel *bad*, just kind of…strange.

But then with Savvy under my tongue writhing in pleasure, Adam's hand squeezing my cock, I lost sense of the mechanics of things. Everything in me had turned itself over to sensation, to the heat and grip and burn of it. By the time I realized Adam had a finger inside me, it already felt good. There was a kind of hot ache, a stretch that made me fit my teeth to Savannah's thigh for a second as he added another finger, and then cool relief as he added more lube. He did something inside me—*inside me!*—that sent a burst of sensation skittering through my ass, up my spine to the base of my brain and down to the base of my cock. I thought for one teeth-clenching second, I might do something wild like come all over the end of the bed with my face buried in Savvy's pussy and Adam's fingers around my cock and in my hole. It was hot and shameless and fucking brilliant.

Suddenly, his fingers were gone, the sensation both a relief and oddly upsetting, but before I could complain, he hooked the cock ring over my wet cock and slid it to the base. He grabbed the end attached to the loop to tug between my balls, and then something cool and smooth was pressed into my hole.

"That's it," Adam praised, and his voice wasn't unruffled and cultured the way it usually was when we played. It was a rough, rumbly growl like he'd gone from man to animal. He tapped at the base of the small, curved plug with his thumb, and the resulting vibration inside me made my vision white out for a long second.

"Fuck," Adam growled into my shoulder before biting a line up my throat. "You're an absolute dream."

His praise struck my heart like a church bell, sending waves of feeling that were almost holy throughout my entire body.

I wanted to be a dream.

His dream.

Their dream.

I wanted to be their dream so I had a fighting chance of translating into their reality one day.

"I can't wait to fuck you here," he told me, still *tap, tapping* at the plug so my teeth clenched. "Slide inside you and enjoy this tight hole, fill it up with my cum."

"*Cazzo si*, Adam," I hissed. "Are you trying to unman me?"

His chuckle was a dark note. "Exactly the opposite. I gave you this." He tapped the plug and reached around with his other hand to press his thumb into the slit of my cock almost cruelly. "To ensure you could fuck Savannah the way she needs. Long and hard. Now, hop to it."

He gave my ass a smack that made me shoot a glare at him over my shoulder, but he only grinned smugly at me as I winced, adjusting to the plug.

"Savannah, darling, on your knees like a good girl," he demanded, his tone cold and crisp again.

I watched Savvy shiver as she obeyed, her eyes lingering on my cock, made harder and thicker by the cock ring in a way that was honestly obscene.

"I can't wait to be filled up," she confessed on a breath as she raised her bottom in the air and exposed her dripping cunt.

"Lie down," Adam told me, maneuvering me with those big hands on my shoulders to the head of the bed, then pushing me down.

As soon as I was on my back, Adam lifted his wife under her armpits and positioned her over my cock. I held my dick upright with my lip pinched between my teeth, using the pain to ground myself as he slowly lowered her right onto my cock. We had all done our testing and the results were negative, so this was the first time I was inside my *duchessa* skin to skin.

It was *magnifico.*

"Fuck," Savannah and I both moaned, her head falling back between her shoulders.

Adam's hands went to her breasts, pulling and twisting at her nipples almost viciously until they glowed red and swollen. Her moans only escalated as she slowly rocked her hips, taking me so deep it made her wince and pant. I clamped a hand over her hip just to feel her undulate and then used the other to circle her pink clit.

We made her orgasm in moments.

Watching her above me, eyes squeezed shut, head tossed back, rosy mouth open on a cry to God like He had a hope in hell of saving her from the two libidinous men wringing every drop of pleasure from her, was as close to a living dream as I'd ever come.

And then, when Adam climbed behind her and pressed her limp torso down onto my own, her breasts plastered to me, my cock drenched in her cum, I almost lost my mind as his fingers circled our connection, one sliding briefly inside her cunt alongside my dick.

"One day, maybe we'll both fuck her here at the same time," he mused. "Would you like that, Savannah?"

Her reply was a wrecked little moan against my throat. I chuckled a little weakly and tipped her face up to kiss her languorously as I felt Adam gently pull the plug from her ass and replace it with his fingers, adding to the stretch. The sensation of his fingers through the thin wall separating her ass and pussy was unlike anything I'd ever felt, and I groaned at the sensation.

"Just you wait until it's my cock," Adam answered, as though I'd spoken aloud. "You're so gorgeous like this, Savannah. Look at you taking my fingers so well. Can you take a third? Yes, that's it. Let me open you up for my cock."

Savannah panted into my mouth and then whimpered. "I'm already so full, and he's not even inside me yet."

"You're being so good," I told her, smoothing back her hair and pressing light kisses to her cheeks and nose and chin. "I love seeing you like this. So raw and beautiful."

She ducked, hiding her face in my neck. I pulled her back with my hand in her hair and pressed a firm kiss to her mouth.

"You have never been more beautiful to me than in these moments when you're sharing yourself with us," I whispered against her lips.

She surged forward to kiss me back, slipping her sweet tongue into my mouth as I felt Adam push into the tight clench of her ass. The pressure of his cock was so intense it made my eyes water. I tried to think of anything but the fact that we were both inside this gorgeous woman, fucking her together finally, but I couldn't.

Because Adam wouldn't let me.

"So tight," he said, locking eyes with me, jaw clenched and

eyes burning. "So fucking beautiful. Both of you. Fuck her with me, Sebastian. Let's take her apart."

And we did.

Rocking slowly at first, back and forth, in and out, gritting our teeth through the pleasure so we could focus on her. I reached between our bodies to put gentle force on her sensitive clit and watched her mouth open in a silent scream as she writhed, trying to fuck back on us both simultaneously.

She was so tight around me, her messy pussy leaking all over my cock and down my balls. The tight band around my shaft and the firm touch of the plug curved into my prostate heightened everything to intoxicating levels. I almost couldn't breathe through the sweet pressure. Every muscle was tensed to control my impulse to fuck wildly into her heat.

"You're both doing so well for me," Adam praised us, pulling Savvy back so she was mostly upright, his arm banded between her breasts. "Look at how gorgeous she is, all filled up with our big dicks, Seb."

I panted, chasing breath I couldn't seem to find because the sight of him so big and golden behind her, pinning his dainty wife between us as we pistoned in and out of her holes, was the most beautiful sight I'd ever seen.

"*Siete cosi belli*," I told them in my native tongue because I knew how much they loved it even when they didn't understand what I said. "You are both so beautiful."

As if she'd been waiting for my validation, Savannah slammed down on my cock, grinding her clit into the rough hair at my base. She threw her head back on Adam's shoulder and shouted as she absolutely came apart.

Adam held her still, his teeth gritted and jaw jumping as we both felt her milk our cocks, coaxing us to lose ourselves inside her.

"Adam," I grunted, straining to control myself, toes curling until they cramped, my hands clamped too hard over Savvy's thighs.

"Come for me," he ordered gruffly, folding her body back over my torso so she could lay limply against my chest as we both used her ruthlessly to find our own climaxes.

I curled a hand into Savvy's hair as she pressed her lips to my throat and locked eyes with my other lover as we both thrust inside her in tandem, a perfect harmony that had pleasure searing deep into my bones.

"I'm going to come," I warned them both, bucking up so hard I almost dislodged Adam.

"Do it," she ordered me, clasping my earlobe between her teeth. "I want to be filled up and leaking with your cum."

A moment later, every molecule in my body seemed to implode. My vision whited out like it had been caught in the blinding flashes of the paparazzi. My pleasure so violent it seemed to rip my skin from my muscle and bones, annihilating every thought in my head but two names.

Savannah and Adam.

Vaguely, I heard Adam shout his own release and registered the faint thump of his own cock through the thin walls of Savvy's pussy as he filled her ass with his cum. Knowing we'd filled her to the brim, that we'd leave her gaping and leaking and deliciously used up was enough to extend my orgasm into something almost painful.

We stayed locked together in the comedown, our breaths a soft susurrus of sound in the otherwise quiet room. Adam had to be exhausted, but he stayed on his knees pressed into Savvy, one hand stroking her back and the other wrapped around my calf as if he couldn't bear to let us go. Savvy just lay between us, sometimes pressing a slack-mouthed kiss to my neck.

Adam waited until we both softened enough to slide out of Savvy before he pulled away, dropping back onto his heels to look at her swollen folds.

"So pretty all filled up with cum," he murmured softly, truly entranced by the sight.

Savvy shivered as he drew his finger down her pussy and then down to the plug, following the wet slick of our combined wetness where it leaked between my thighs.

"Maybe next time I'll have you fuck Savannah full of cum and then use it as lubrication to fuck you," he suggested lazily, looking up at me with heavy-lidded eyes as he gently eased the toy from me and slipped it off my softening dick.

I bit my lip to keep myself from groaning, but Savannah pulled back to look at my face and confirm I'd be into that.

Her smile was small but genuine even though a little frown was between her brows. I smoothed it with my thumb as Adam patted her ass and then went to the bathroom, no doubt to get something to clean us up with. It was part of his whole dominant routine, and it was surprising how much I enjoyed the little moment of intimate pampering.

"Do you think you'll like it?" Savannah whispered.

It was my turn to frown in question, and she clarified, "Having proper sex with Adam."

"I think so," I admitted, even if my stomach clenched at the thought.

I'd been born and raised by an Italian-loving Irishman who believed in machismo and a man's right to do whatever the hell he pleased, even if it hurt other people. It didn't mean I subscribed to his fucked-up brand of ethics, but the idea of letting another man inside my body was one I still struggled with a little even though I wanted it with mounting desperation on a purely physical level.

"I'm worried you'll like it more than sex with me," she whispered even softer, her mouth sullen.

I laughed, but not in mockery. "Savvy, I'm as addicted to your sweet pussy as a man can get. Ask me, and I'd crawl to you."

That flush I loved painted her pretty face, and I couldn't resist the temptation to cup it in my palm.

"I'm worried you might like him more than me," she mouthed as if sound would manifest the words.

"He's your husband," I said lightly, even though my heart twisted in my chest. "I'd have thought you would both like each other more than me."

She stared at me hard for a long moment, gaze scraping over my features like a scalpel working to peel back my layers. She had an almost childlike confusion and a frustration I didn't understand.

Adam returned to the room with two warm, damp cloths, unabashed in his gorgeous nudity, but before he reached the bed, Savvy quickly murmured, "I don't know anymore."

I pretended I didn't hear her, but the words haunted me all through the night, long after both of my lovers had fallen asleep beside me.

Chapter Sixteen

Sebastian

I was preoccupied with my meeting earlier that day with Andrea while I waited for Savannah outside of Sexy Fish restaurant a few weeks later.

Andrea and I had decided to make *Blood Oath* as an independent film. The studios wanted to glamorize it too much, strip it of the raw, earthy grit I'd always envisioned for Roberto and his harrowing journey through 1920s New York. Andrea and Adam had the connections to get enough funding to do the project on our own terms without studio funding, and it seemed like an impossible offer to pass up.

Adam thought the Sundance Film Festival would be the perfect vehicle to launch the film and get bids from various studios after it performed well. I envied his confidence in the script and worked hard to emulate it.

The problem was, the only people who had ever encouraged me were my sisters, and I knew they were wildly biased.

I wasn't afraid to admit that living with the Meyerses and watching the way they operated so confidently in life had rubbed off on me. Their secret was simple. They believed they deserved the best because they were willing to work hard to earn it and wouldn't settle for anything less. It was manifestation on a level I'd never considered for myself, but the magic, Savannah had assured me one night over dinner, made their dreams attainable.

And so, I chose to believe in myself.

How simple and terrifying a concept.

I was so lost in the complicated maze of my thoughts that I didn't notice the couple exiting the restaurant at first even though they were only a handful of yards from where I'd parked the car and was leaning against the driver's door. It was only when I heard the laughter, light and soft, transient as a wispy cloud dissolving in the sun that my attention was hooked.

When I turned my gaze to Savannah, she beamed at an older man with a thick head of steely grey hair wearing what I could now recognize as an extremely expensive navy pinstripe suit and a gold Rolex that flashed harshly in the entrance lights.

As I watched, he raised that bedazzled wrist to smooth a lock of Savannah's hair back into her bun and then let his hand linger against her cheek.

What was even more shocking was that Savannah let him. It was hard to tell from my angle with her facing away from me and toward her lunch date, but I thought she might have even been smiling for him.

That same soft, confused little smile of vulnerability I'd thought for certain she'd only given Adam and *me*.

Unease skittered with eight legs down my spine and nested uncomfortably at the base of my back.

I pushed off the car, ready to do what, I wasn't certain, when she rocked forward on the tips of her high-heeled shoes and pressed a single kiss to the side of the man's cheek.

He blushed like a man much younger than him might have, but I understood.

That was the power of Savannah Meyers' regard.

What I didn't understand was the level of intimacy I was witnessing.

She wasn't a naturally warm person, so the privilege of intimacy with her was infrequent and hard-won. When people lingered too long over any aspect of physical affection at parties or luncheons or dinners that I'd witnessed her at, she always deftly blocked or ended their advances.

I racked my memory going over Savannah's schedule for the day and only came up with the lunch meeting with an unnamed bigwig from a studio in California.

He didn't seem like a stranger to her, though.

They seemed closer than I ever wanted to imagine her being with someone other than her husband or me.

They parted slowly, tension pulling like taffy in the air between them as Savannah backed away and then turned to walk toward the sidewalk.

It was only then that she noticed me.

There was just a slight pause in her step, one pearlescent high heel raised delicately over the asphalt before she resumed her gliding stride toward me.

But it was enough to speak of something a little like guilt.

"Hello, darling," she greeted breezily as she approached, and I opened the car door for her automatically out of habit. "I hope I didn't keep you waiting long."

I didn't respond with my normal flirtatious banter because

something uncharacteristic stirred in my gut.

Jealousy.

After she slipped into the Rolls, I closed the door and peered over the roof at her lunch companion. A limousine pulled up in front of the restaurant, and the driver got out to open the door for him. The grey-haired man seemed to sense my gaze and caught my eye just before lowering himself into the vehicle.

I bristled at the small smile he shot my way, and it was utterly irrational.

I knew it.

But I was Italian, hot-blooded and probably too passionate for my own good.

So when I got into the town car to drive Savannah home, the words I spoke burned as they passed over my tongue.

"Who the hell was that *stronzo*?"

"Sebastian," she scolded coldly, checking her makeup in a little compact mirror. "Don't speak to me like that."

"Like what, a jealous lover?" I dared to retort, meeting her gaze briefly in the rearview mirror.

"This is hardly appropriate."

"Because I'm just your lowly driver?"

"Don't be so *young*. It's unbecoming."

"I'm eighteen, Savvy. I *am* young. Is that beginning to wear on you? Is that why you kissed that man?"

"Sebastian, you can hardly call a kiss on the cheek anything lewd. You're Italian for god's sake. You kiss everyone on the cheek in greeting or parting."

"*Sì*, so I know I do not kiss my mama like that."

I'd only seen Savannah roll her eyes once before, but she did it then in a manner that wasn't at all playful. Snapping her compact closed, she stuffed it just a little too aggressively in her purse.

"You can't just flip a switch on this thing between us when it's convenient for you," I said, my voice low and rough, dredged up from deep in my gut. "I'm not just your driver. I'm not just your… toy."

"Sebastian," she said again, this time on a sigh that softened her rigid posture and had her looking small against the black leather seats in all her neutral-toned finery. "I do not think of you as my toy."

"Oh? Then tell me, I have been inside you nearly every day since I moved into your house. I've wiped your smudged makeup from your tired eyes after a vigorous fuck. I've eaten the sound of my name out of your beautiful mouth and stroked your hair until you've fallen asleep in my arms. How do you think of me? Because this stopped being a simple agreement almost the moment it began."

"It's more than sex if that's what you're implying," she said stiffly, her entire posture defensive.

"Of course, it's more than sex," I said too loudly, my gloved fingers squeaking on the steering wheel with the force of my grip. "But you won't give me anything about your past or how you truly feel about me. You'll only give me honesty in the dark of your bedroom."

Silence descended in the car, the quality of it static and uncomfortable against the skin. I could tell by her expression she was irritated and confused, and I wondered if anyone other than Adam had dared to speak to her so bluntly.

A small corner of my heart ached at the thought that I had pushed too far, but I refused to give in to the fear. She may have been older and in a position more powerful than my own, but that didn't mean she inherently knew better than me.

When it came to matters of the heart, I was beginning to believe—despite my lack of experience and their years of it—I might actually know better than Savannah and Adam Meyers.

"His name is Tate Richardson," she said after an interminable period of time. "He's one of the biggest producers in Hollywood. It was just a business meeting."

I swallowed thickly past the mass of questions lodged in my throat. Jealousy urged me to pry. Who is he to you? Why are you so close? What does he mean for you and Adam? For you and me?

I wasn't blind.

It was obvious Savannah and Adam had problems in their marriage and had for longer than I'd been around to witness them. It wasn't that they quarreled, necessarily, but from the beginning, I'd sensed a distance between them. It wasn't natural, more than a dedicated barrier they'd erected from either side. As if they were afraid, even after years of marriage, to take the final plunge into intimacy together.

Even so, they seemed lighter now. They laughed together more often and seemed to delight in the time we spent as a threesome.

I thought Adam would say the same thing and felt momentarily shocked by the fury I felt on his behalf.

"Sebastian," Savvy called softly just as the automatic gates slid open on her Chelsea estate. "Please don't be cross with me. He's just an old friend."

I'd been raised by women and therefore taught to trust my intuition, and something about that encounter had just felt illicit. Savannah's brief hesitation after had only underscored my suspicion.

But who was I to be the jealous lover? I was just the help.

So I nodded curtly. "*Va bene*, if you say so."

When we pulled through the gates, I opened the car door for her, then briskly made my way around the house to the path that led to the carriage house. She didn't call after me, but I could feel her gaze like a hand grasping at the hem of my coat.

I just needed the space.

Seeing her like that had brought my insecurities to the surface.

Because I was aware enough to admit that I'd never be fully satisfied with this status quo. Unable to love her, to possess her in every way. The animal in me yearned to own her.

Maybe if she loved me back, it would be different.

Maybe if she told me I wasn't alone in feeling this way, I could silence the impotence and jealousy that reared its head. I knew it would continue to arise again and again for as long as this arrangement lasted.

Being a third in a marriage wasn't even the problem. I never felt "other" or extraneous when it was just the three of us together. Sometimes I even wondered if they both enjoyed me more than they enjoyed each other.

But I was a romantic man, and no amount of exposure to British culture could change the fundamentals of who I was.

I wanted an epic love.

The kind of passion that made you call in late to work and go out of your way to surprise and cherish each other. The kind that made you want to crack open your chest and offer up all of your insides on a silver platter.

And *porca miseria!*

I wanted that with her.

The door slammed against the opposite wall as I pushed into the little cottage I spent very little time in. I looked around the space, searching for something to ground me. Moving across the room, stopping only to flick on the record player so that Frank Sinatra's voice filled the space, I grabbed my notebook, shucked my jacket and driving gloves, and threw myself into a chair at the little kitchen table thrust up against the wall.

Through the mullioned window, I could see the garden bursting with blooms as spring rolled across London. Everything was green and white with little pops of colour that appeared like little rebels fighting to be seen against the almost austere British garden.

I wondered idly if I'd brought colour to the Meyers' lives and if it was warmly received or unwelcome. It seemed to me that I made them uncomfortable as much as I brought them joy.

Tapping the pen against my mouth, I let my gaze wander away from the heavy boughs of the blooming hydrangea bushes and tightly cropped box hedgerows to peer at things only I could see in my mind's eye.

The problem, I thought, was that Savannah was the dream, and I was the dreamer. Could I ever really know her point of view without imposing my desires on her thoughts and actions? Maybe if she would actually communicate with me, but she and Adam both seemed too reluctant to speak about anything involving their histories or feelings.

Ducking my head, I wrote the title of the screenplay that was taking shape in my mind.

The Dream & The Dreamer.

"Sebastian."

I jerked my head up, heart racing at the shock as I found Savannah lingering in the doorway to the cottage. She seemed hesitant to enter, and I wondered if it was because she didn't want to invade my space or because it was beneath her to enter the home of the help.

There must have been something cruel in my gaze because she visibly swallowed hard and took a delicate step over the threshold.

"You come in here, you won't like the Sebastian who greets you," I warned her, feeling the sneer on my lips, the primal restlessness in my limbs that made me want to stalk and hunt and roar. "I don't feel like tending to a *duchessa* at the moment."

She stared at me, hands held in front of her almost primly even though her chin jutted up slightly at the familiar haughty angle. "Maybe

I don't want to be treated like a duchess right now."

I scoffed slightly, writing over the title of the new screenplay until the words were indented, the paper nearly torn by the force.

"Maybe I want to be reminded of what it feels like to fuck in the grass like animals," she said, her voice quiet but unyielding. "Maybe I want to fuck like you hate me because… because I feel safe knowing you never would."

"Never could," I corrected, sliding her a dark look with my eyebrows raised. "You want to be honest with each other, finally? You want to address the elephant in the room with the three of us when we play your games?"

She sucked in a sharp breath but hesitated again.

I pushed back sharply from the chair as I stood, sending it screeching across the hardwood. When I stalked forward, she shivered but held her ground. She was so slight, and I towered over her even in those ridiculous heels.

I slammed my hand against the wall beside her head, caging her in beside the open doorway. Her pupils blew wide, eyes dark and yearning for all the aggression barely leashed inside me.

"I'm not in the mood to play your games," I warned her. "I'm in the mood to fuck you exactly the way *I* want. Hard and rough. I want to leave marks on all this pretty skin so when you walk out of here tomorrow in your Chanel or Dior, the bitemarks on your neck match your pretty lipstick." I reached for the hem of her skirt and dragged my short nails up the inside of her thigh until I could cup her cunt in my palm. "I'll leave you so sore and used, you'll teeter on those high heels you love to wear. And when people wonder what happened to make you so unusually dishevelled, you'll know it was *me*."

Her mouth dropped open on a little exhaled moan, and I took it as the acceptance it was meant to be.

I sealed my lips over hers and fucking *took*.

This wasn't about being a tool of her pleasure or Adam's extra hands or cock to tease her.

This was about taking the woman I'd lusted after for months and never fucked alone.

About taking the edge off the enormity of emotion that roiled around inside my skin looking for an outlet when she never gave me one.

It was about making her *mine*.

The kiss was messy, teeth clashing, tongues coiling. She was too short to keep it up for long, so I lifted her with one palm across her pert ass and pinned her against the wall.

The front door was still open, but the idea that we could be caught stoked the fire higher in both of us.

I'd never felt so fucking possessive in my life.

There'd been many girls before Savannah, one-night stands and casual flings, but no one had collided with my life like a meteorite, changing my future landscape forever.

"God, Sebastian," she breathed, trying to fumble with the buttons of my white shirt and then giving up when they were half-undone to push the fabric over my shoulders, bunching against my biceps so she could suck and bite at my shoulders. "I need you inside me."

"I'll fuck you when I'm ready," I said, almost coldly, the way Adam liked to talk when he started dominating both of us.

That's what I wanted in my space with *la duchessa*. I wanted to be the one in control, to unspool every inch of her until she was laid bare.

I shifted my hand to the side of her lace panties, curled them in the placket, and *tugged*. They snapped across her hips and dropped to the floor at our feet.

"Those are four-hundred-pound panties," she informed me, but the effect was lost because her cheeks were flushed, and she had to pant around the words.

"And this will be a four-hundred-pound worthy orgasm," I promised darkly, testing the wet entrance of her pussy before deftly unbuttoning and unzipping my trousers.

A second later, I was at her entrance and thrusting inside her glorious pussy.

"*Cazzo*," I cursed, nipping at her bottom lip as she dropped her head back against the wall on a gasp. "You were made to take my cock, weren't you?"

"Yes," she hissed, legs locked around my hips for leverage to grind back against me. "Made for you."

"Your pussy and your sweet mouth and your wicked mind," I listed, punctuating each with a hard thrust. "Every inch of you is perfect."

She closed her eyes and turned her head away from me, which was unacceptable. I wrapped my hand around her throat, her eyes springing open to land on mine in shock.

"Watch me while I fuck you," I ordered, squeezing just a little bit, her pulse pounding against my thumb. Her pussy spasmed around me, and I knew she liked being manhandled that way. "You're mine right now, and if I want to tell you about how beautiful you are and how much I love your tight cunt, you're going to listen to me."

When she only stared at me a little dazedly, panting hard, nails carving half-moons into my shoulders, I flexed my hand tighter just for a second and leaned in close to snarl softly, "Isn't that right, *bella fighetta*?"

"Yes," she whispered. "Please, God, Sebastian, I need to come."

"No, not yet," I reminded her. "You wait until I tell you to."

She whimpered, but the sound was fuel to my fire. Inspired, I pulled her off the wall and walked us to the kitchen table, knocking my notebook aside to lay her flat back against the wood. I held her legs at the ankles and drove deeper inside her snug pussy.

She gasped, hands reaching overhead to brace against the window.

"More," she begged.

I set a punishing pace, hair falling over my sweat-dampened forehead, pulse hammering in my cock, my throat, and my chest. I could see the hummingbird thrum of it in her pale neck as she tossed her head back on a loud moan.

She wore a thin turtleneck that obscured her sweet breasts from view, and I didn't have the patience to take it off, so…

"Sebastian," she gasped as I dropped her legs on either side of my hips and used both hands to tear the bottom of the shirt, rending it all the way up to her sternum, then tossing the ruined ends up to reveal those braless tits. Pink-tipped and small, each a handful that was so fucking pretty I wanted to ruin them with bruises and cum.

"Six. Hundred. Pounds," she panted on each thrust, but it wasn't a complaint.

The sound of her wet pussy leaking all over my dick was the loudest noise in the room.

"You wanna come for me, don't you?" I taunted, twisting her nipples the way I knew she loved. "You want to forget everything else in your head but the feel of my cock getting you off and the sound of my name as you scream for more."

"Sebastian!" she called out, face screwed up in a near grimace as her climax tore through her.

I gathered her shaking legs in one hand and drove harder inside her clutching heat so she spiralled higher and higher. She didn't realize it, I knew, but she chanted my name like a hymn.

Like she was moved to divine madness by the feelings moving

through her.

Feelings I'd given her.

I tossed my sweaty hair out of my face as I chased my own orgasm and noticed movement outside the window.

Adam stood on the stone path to the cottage amid the flowers and greenery in a bespoke suit he'd worn to a business meeting.

He looked like he'd been standing there for a while. Gaze glazed and fixed on his wife being fucked hard by the chauffeur.

"Your husband's watching you be my good slut," I told Savvy, trailing my palm from between her breasts to the top of her groin, thumb stroking light and quick over her swollen clit. "He's staring at us through the window."

She gave a keening cry, animalistic the way she'd wanted it all along. "My God."

"No, just *me* and your husband," I corrected, grinding into her as deeply as I could, pressing hard on her clit so she made that fucking gorgeous sound again. "Owning you together."

The next climax took her by surprise, wrenched from her with a guttural scream, hands smashing against the window frame like she wanted to be sure Adam knew I was making her come this way.

I lifted my gaze from the gorgeous woman stretched out before me, clenching on my cock like a wet vise, and found Adam palming the huge outline of his rigid dick.

The sight of the two of them enraptured by me tore through all my remaining restraints, and I came with a bestial shout that I knew Adam would hear through the walls. I poured myself into Savvy's greedy pussy, letting her milk me for all I was worth as fireworks and pinwheels of color burst behind my squeezed-shut lids. The pleasure was so intense I felt like my body would never unclench, locked forever in this intensity of feeling spurred by the gravitational pull of both my lovers.

Finally, I slumped forward over Savannah, kissing the side of her face before resting my nose in the hollow of her throat to drag in deep breaths of that freesia scent. After a moment's hesitation, she locked her heels behind my back and twined her arms around my neck, one hand delving into the short hairs on the back of my head.

"You make me feel…" She let out a little sigh. "You make me feel like everything I've ever wanted to be."

"Smart, successful, sexy as hell?"

Her short chuckle was hollow.

"I wish I was the kind of woman who deserved you," she whispered into my ear.

I frowned, pulling away slightly to question what she could possibly mean by that when someone cleared their throat in the doorway.

We both looked to the left to see Adam leaning casually against the wall, arms crossed and eyebrow cocked. He looked absurdly posh for the little cottage, and for a moment, I thought he wasn't real, just a mirage I'd conjured from one of his movies.

"Well, that was quite a performance," he drawled, adjusting the Patek Philippe watch on his wrist as if he hadn't a care in the world. "If you're quite done, though, I came home with the intention to take you *both* out tonight."

"Oh?" Savannah asked with polite mildness as if we weren't naked and caught in a cinch on the kitchen table.

One of the house rules was not to fool around seriously when one of the Meyerses wasn't in attendance, and while technically Adam had arrived to play voyeur at the end, it hadn't been intentional.

But he didn't seem angry.

Even though he was being almost absurdly indifferent, I caught a sparkle in those glass green eyes that told me he found the whole tableau amusing.

"Yes, dinner and the theatre. I thought Sebastian should see Cecilia Mycroft on stage before she retires. She's in that production of *The Glass Menagerie* in the West End."

"Oh yes," Savannah agreed, pushing me gently away to sit up and right her clothes. After a moment, I pushed her hands away and smoothed the ragged hem of her turtleneck down before buttoning up her blazer. "I've heard wonderful things even though I can't say I like the old bat."

"Savannah," Adam scolded with a cluck of his tongue. "She's an icon."

She sighed. "Yes, well, so is that child star, Jace Galantine, and you won't see me lining up to see him in his next rom-com."

"She's a snob, really," Adam told me conspiratorially.

I laughed, lifting Savannah off the table and back to her feet, then lingering with my hands on her hips as she found her balance on orgasm-weakened legs.

"Not when I'm fucking her against a wall or a kitchen table," I quipped because there was still something skittering nervously around my gut like I'd done something shameful.

Adam cocked his head slightly as he studied me and then sighed, stalking forward and stopping only when we were toe-to-toe. He was just slightly taller than me, so I had the pleasure of meeting those long-lashed eyes head-on.

I startled slightly at the feel of his hands on my shoulders, pulling my shirt up my biceps and rebuttoning it without taking his gaze from mine.

"I like to watch you fuck my wife," he said bluntly. "I like knowing she brings out the beast in you and you in her. That you couldn't wait a second longer to get inside her even though I wasn't here to play. You weren't leaving me out just because I wasn't physically in the room." He leaned close to whisper in my ear, his stubble scraping deliciously against mine. "I know I'm always at the back of your mind urging you on. I know you're getting hard again just thinking about how I plan to punish you both tonight after our outing."

"Punish?" I breathed, then cleared my throat of the embarrassing breathiness.

"Mmm, I have to punish you both. Of course. But I think a little edging would do you some good. Teach you some restraint. Some patience." His hand fell between us to grip my damp, half-hard shaft. "I think Savvy and I shall tie you up and have our way with you for a few hours."

He put my cock away, zipping up my trousers and buttoning the fly before giving me a little pat there like I was a good boy.

"Would you like that, sweetheart?"

"Very much," Savvy agreed with a coquettish grin. "But first, our date night."

Date night.

It occurred to my slightly dazed brain that Adam had arranged a *date night* not just for his wife but also for me. In fact, because he wanted to show me something he knew I'd love.

My heart swooped just a little looking at my lovers standing side by side.

"Is it safe?" I found myself asking even though I didn't want to ruin the mood.

Adam only grinned and clapped me on the shoulder. "Friends have been known to go for the occasional meal. Anyway, Andrea is meeting us for the play, too. Apparently, he thinks Cecelia would be good for Maria in *Blood Oath.*"

I tried not to feel disappointed that Andrea would be there when we'd become such good friends.

"I thought you wanted to be careful," I said because I couldn't just let myself have this apparently.

I guess it was because I always waited for the other shoe to drop. I was living a fantasy, and there were always expiration dates for fantasies.

"We're celebrating," Adam informed me with a shared smile with his wife before picking up a little black gift bag I hadn't noticed by the entryway.

Savannah plucked it from his fingers before he could hand it to me. "I want to hand it to him."

Adam rolled his eyes dramatically at me but let his wife have her way. As soon as she handed it off, he pulled her into his front and wrapped his arms around her to watch me.

"What are we celebrating?" I asked, a little bemused as I pushed the tissue paper aside and unearthed a red leather box.

"We have officially secured 15 million quid from Tore Deo Ltd," Adam announced with a massive movie star grin. "Congratulations, Sebastian Lombardi, your first film is officially on the road to production."

"*Madonna mia*," I breathed, forgetting the box in my hand as I lunged forward to wrap both Meyerses in a bear hug. "I cannot believe this is happening."

"Believe it," Adam said with a laugh, pounding a hand on my back like we were two mates and then shifting his grip to squeeze my neck so I'd pull back enough to look him in the eye. "This is the first of many accomplishments in your life."

I scoffed, but Savannah reached up to grab my chin and tilt it down so she could glare at me properly.

"Do not be dismissive of your talent, Sebastian. I wouldn't have been attracted to you otherwise," she sniffed.

Laughter ripped through me so forcefully I tipped my head to the ceiling and unleashed it like a howl at the moon.

When I was finished, tears in my eyes, they were both smiling these small, tender smiles I wanted to cast in bronze and keep forever.

"Open your present now," Savvy ordered, pulling at my hand still holding the box so it was between us.

I moved back just enough to have room to open it, Adam's hand on my shoulder, Savvy's arm around my waist. My breath caught as I pushed the lid up to reveal a Patek Philippe watch glittering in a bed of cream satin.

It was rose gold with a thin frame of rectangular diamonds around the face and a black face strewn with stars like a snapshot of the galaxy.

"For the man who wants to move the sun and the stars," Savannah explained.

My gaze jerked up to look at her, but her smile was merely proud and a little smug. When my gaze averted to Adam in question, he shuttered his lids and looked away.

Because he'd told Savannah about our conversation in the gardens of Pinewood Studio. About what I wanted from life.

But he hadn't told her the whole truth.

I didn't want to move the sun and the stars like some great influencing mover and shaker of Hollywood stars the way Savannah did, or to be the brightest planet in their orbit like Adam.

I wanted a *love* so powerful it moved the sun and stars.

Changed the course of my life forever.

Became my new gravity.

Savvy didn't get that because I wasn't sure she knew a love like that could exist, and I hadn't told her that was what I wanted.

I'd told Adam.

And he had bastardized it and then added insult to injury by giving me a watch that symbolized something I knew he would never give me.

Based on the conflicted look in his eyes, he knew it too.

"For the man who wants to rewrite the rules of the universe," Adam amended softly, half apology, half entreaty.

I swallowed the hurt that sprang metallic as blood on the back of my tongue and stared at the most expensive gift I'd ever received in my life, rubbing my thumb along the diamonds.

"It's beautiful," I murmured.

Savannah obviously mistook my melancholy for overwhelming gratitude and slid her other arm around me in an affectionate embrace.

But Adam just stared at me as I hugged her back, his eyes dark and troubled. When my face came close to his as I curled around Savannah, he ran a thumb over the edge of my jaw and pressed it to the center of my lips.

"I hope you succeed," he whispered.

Chapter Seventeen

Sebastian

"You'll cause an accident," I warned Savannah as I caught her gaze in the rearview mirror of the Rolls.

She pulled her gaze from the glowing screen of her phone to fix me with a haughty look that asked the question for her.

"I'm a mere mortal," I confessed, one hand pressed to my heart. "How can I focus on driving when such temptation sits in my back seat?"

A startled laugh pealed through the interior of the car, and I was helpless against the joy that unfurled in my chest. I loved to surprise Savannah into releasing that giggle when she was so clad in finery and that well-honed aura of snobbery. In a vintage Chanel gown that was more elegant than sexy, she still managed to stir arousal in my gut. There was something about all that class I wanted to rip apart with my teeth, workingman's hands, and cock.

Adam beside her shot me a grin. "Try to contain that charm, will you? It's hard enough leaving you behind tonight as it is."

Something twisted too tight in my chest, as if my heart was a wind-up toy ready to pop out of my chest straight into his hands.

Because it felt good to hear that they would miss me tonight. Silly, really, when they were going to the British Academy of Film and Television Awards. Of course, I couldn't join them. They would exit the town car as the public expected to see them, international superstar Adam Meyers and his pretty blonde wife like an angel pulled down from the heavens on his arm.

There was no place for a third. A teenaged Italian man with no accolades to his name.

It was so impossible a fantasy, I couldn't even envision it in my mind's eye, and I was a *writer.*

Still, it was nice to hear those words from Adam when I'd oddly been feeling left out all day.

Since the dinner I'd orchestrated for them that night three weeks ago, the three of us had spent more time together outside of the bedroom. The Meyerses tried to make room for at least one at-home dinner date each week in their schedules, and we had taken to watching Kings Cross United games on Saturday mornings when we could. It was hard to properly date a married couple when they were both well-known figures in London society. We had to make do with dates at home, but I'd always been creative, and I didn't mind taking the lead.

Especially when Adam and Savannah both seemed to flourish under the extra attention.

For a moment, I'd forgotten just how clandestine our relationship was until this evening. The casual ease of our chemistry and affection for each other seemed too natural to hide away in the shadows, yet there was no other option.

Even if I did succeed in making them fall in love with me, this was all we could ever have. This was all I would ever be, a footnote to their marriage written in invisible ink.

I liked to think I didn't have a massive ego, but it hurt nonetheless to think about always being in the shadows. My heart stuck in a cage, unable to roam freely.

"I won't mention that you're hot enough to raise the global heat index, then," I returned flippantly, catching sight of Adam's responding grin in the rearview as I inched forward in the crowded line of cars waiting to drop off celebs at the front of the red carpet.

He did look insanely dashing tonight in the custom Tom Ford ink-black tuxedo with velvet lapels, and the crisp white shirt beneath it opened at the collar to reveal the strong column of his throat. Something primal in me wanted to lunge forward and bite at that neck, mark it as mine in a way everyone on the crowded red carpet would see. I'd had a similar thought when Savannah came down the stairs earlier that evening in a creamy diaphanous gown that floated around her slim legs.

"Better not," he agreed. "But I had a thought. Something that might make you feel included somewhat in the evening."

"I don't need to be included," I said a little too quickly. "It's *your* night. You're up for a bloody Best Actor award, Adam."

"I am," he agreed easily, hand dropping onto his wife's knee beneath her simple silk gown in a pale pink like the inside of an oyster, like the inside of her pretty pussy.

He pushed Savannah's knees apart and slowly pulled the hem up, up over her thighs so that the fabric pooled in her lap and exposed her nude underwear.

"But I think both you and Savannah need a reminder that while the night may be about me, I am about both of you," Adam continued as he produced a little egg-shaped vibrator from his tuxedo pocket.

Savannah squirmed in her seat, a flush deepening the blush painted onto her cheeks. "It would certainly make the night more entertaining."

I laughed a little breathlessly. "I'll never say no to playing with Savannah."

"Even when she's in front of thousands?" Adam pushed.

"Who am I to deny them her beauty?" I quipped, winking at Savvy, who hid a smile behind her hand as if she was a demure lady when Adam had her legs splayed and a hand under her panties playing with her clit.

"What do you think, sweetheart?" he asked her, nosing at the side of her face before placing a surprisingly sweet kiss on the edge of her jaw. "Do you want to put your fate for the evening in Sebastian's hands? He might turn this little toy on when we're in the middle of an interview with *Entertainment Tonight.* He might make you come when we're being photographed for every major magazine and news outlet in the world. I know you pride yourself on your control, but do you really think you can handle this?"

The gauntlet he'd thrown landed right in Savannah's lap. Without hesitation, she leaned back in the seat to spread her legs even wider, her hand going to her mouth to wet two fingers before sinking them inside her pussy. Her pale-blue eyes locked on mine in the reflection of the rearview mirror as she fucked herself slowly.

"I can handle anything either of you wants to give me," she declared with that haughty tilt of her chin.

Heat slid through my veins as slow and devastating as lava flow. When Savvy saw me adjust my hardening length in my trousers, her lids lowered further, and she groaned softly. I watched as Adam finally replaced her fingers with the little pink toy and then lifted his own digits for her to lick clean.

Fuck, they were gorgeous.

Weeks of living with them and sleeping with them, and I was nowhere near done with them. I doubted I ever would be.

"Good?" Adam asked her, adjusting her underwear to cover her properly and then lightly tapping her groin like she was a good girl deserving of a pat on the head.

Savvy licked her lips as she gathered herself and nodded.

I drove the car forward again, grateful for the tinted windows enclosing us in privacy as we arrived as close to the start of the carpet as I could get us.

"Good luck tonight," I said as I twisted to smile at them both. "I hope the world is right, and you win tonight, Adam."

"I'm going home with my gorgeous wife to you, so I believe the night will end well either way," Adam promised, but he reached out to squeeze my shoulder and then handed me the remote to the vibrator. "Have fun with her for me."

I grinned. "I will."

We both hesitated for a moment, leaning toward each other, and I knew he wanted to kiss me by the way his green gaze settled on my mouth. I wanted it too, hungered for it like I hadn't eaten in weeks, but this was definitely not the time nor place, even with the blacked-out windows.

"Good evening, my handsome Sebastian," Savannah said, pushing Adam back to place a hand on my cheek in farewell. "Go easy on me."

"Never," I promised wickedly just to hear her laugh.

A moment later, Adam opened the door, and the cacophony of screaming and shouting fans and photographers spilled into the interior. Savannah waited for him to get out and round the car to open the door before she slid out, taking his hand. I watched as they moved amid the crowd of cars and bodies until I lost sight of them to the red carpet, and then, heart oddly lodged in my throat, I inched out of the drop-off line and into London traffic once more.

My fingers drummed against the wheel as I followed the route home on autopilot, more preoccupied with the angst seizing my chest than with driving. I told myself this evening was a good reminder of my reality, that I shouldn't pin my hopes on an impossible dream. Somehow, it didn't alleviate any of the hollow pain behind my breastbone.

So I was startled out of my mind when a pebble hit the windshield just as I waited for the automatic gates to open to the Meyers' house. It had started to rain, which wasn't surprising given it was England and springtime, but it seemed to have caught the girl currently drowning in the downpour off guard because she was only wearing drenched denim and a tiny cropped tee.

I opened the window to say, "Linnea? What the bloody hell are you doing out here in the rain?"

"Waiting for you!" she called back. "Can I come in?"

I jerked my chin up before I could think about it, inviting her into the car before I pulled down the drive. She jogged forward instantly, her wet masses of hair slapping against her back. When she opened the passenger door, the scent of rain and something fresh and somewhat briny like ocean water spilled into the car.

"Hey," she said, turning to face me once she was settled, raindrops rolling down her face into her broad smile. "What's up?"

I laughed, shaking my head as I pulled forward. "I just dropped the Meyerses off at the BAFTAs. What are *you* doing here?"

She shrugged one bony shoulder. "Miranda is there, too. I figured you'd be alone, and I liked hanging out with you that one time."

I blinked at her as I parked, a little thrown by her boldness. "So you thought you'd just show up?"

"Do you mind? I didn't have your number, and you're the closest person to my age I know in London. I'm sick of hanging out with

Miranda's old cronies."

I swallowed my laughter, thinking about how Savannah would react if she heard Linnea say something like that about her age cohort. It was strange to think that Linnea was closer in age to me than Savannah was when I felt so connected to the latter.

Linnea's fresh youthful attitude was endearing, but it made me feel… older in a way that ached. Savannah's maturity was a balm to me, steadfast and knowing like none of my secrets or shame would taint her because she already had a wealth of her own.

"Sure," I decided impulsively because my only plans for the evening had been to wallow at the carriage house and occasionally flip on the vibrator remote just to know Savannah was squirming across the city from me. "What did you want to do?"

She shrugged again, but the move wasn't as casual as she wanted it to be because she was wiggling too much in her seat like there was too much energy inside her bones. "I don't know. What do you usually do for fun around here?"

I play sex games with the married couple I work for.

Somehow, I doubted that was the answer she wanted to hear.

"Honestly, not much. I'm usually too busy working."

She frowned at me, fingers drumming on her soaked jean-clad thigh. "How long have you been in town?"

"Since August." A few weeks after my birthday when Cosima had left for Milan. Suddenly, I missed her with the acuteness of a bullet through my chest. She would have loved Linnea's vibrancy and matched it with her own. She would have made this dreary British night brighter just with her presence.

"If you're so busy with work, have you had time to do any of the really touristy things?" she demanded, brow cocked and arms crossed. "Because if you haven't been to the top of the London Eye or seen

Madame Tussauds, then you might actually be deported."

"Oh? And an American would be an authority on this, how?"

Her grin flattened into sharp edges. "My mother is English, so I have an advantage over you."

"Touché," I allowed because she was funny and a welcome respite from my internal suffering. "Fine. Why don't you come in while I change out of my uniform, and we find you something warmer to wear? While I dress, you can pick our adventure."

"Really?" The word was too surprised, half gleeful and suspicious at the same time, like no one had let her take the reins on something in much too long. Like no one cared what she wanted to do very much at all.

"Really," I promised before getting out of the car and making my way to her side.

She frowned a little as I pulled the door open and shrugged off my jacket to drape over her shoulders. Her mouth dropped into a little moue of shock even as she fingered the fabric. "The walk to your guest house is like… four metres."

I lifted a shoulder. "You look cold. *Andiamo.*"

She followed me down the path to the carriage house and through the front door, lingering in the small living area to peer at some photos I'd placed frameless on the mantel place. I left her to it and climbed the stairs to strip out of my suit and put on comfortable jeans, a tee, and a cashmere jumper in navy blue that Savannah had bought because it brought out the gold in my eyes.

Everything I owned would dwarf Linnea even though she was tall, so I picked another cashmere jumper in black I'd accidentally shrunk in the wash.

Linnea sat on the edge of the coffee table with the photos from the mantel held delicately in her fingers. There was an expression on her face that was almost wistful, and when I cleared my throat to alert her to my presence, she jumped as if I was an axe murderer.

"You scared the bejesus out of me!" she accused.

I arched a brow. "I wasn't exactly quiet, but you seem to be lurking my personal affects too much to notice your surroundings."

Unabashed, she sniffed at me and returned her gaze to one of the photos, which she held at an angle for me to see too. "You have a big family."

"I do," I agreed, walking forward to sit on the edge of the coffee table beside her and taking the photograph in my own grip. "This is the lot of us. My mother, Caprice, eldest sister, Elena, my twin, Cosima, and Giselle."

"And who was that?" she asked, poking at the scratched-out portion of the photo I'd attacked with the side of a coin.

"Seamus," I admitted. "My father, though he was a shite one."

She winced, bumping her shoulder into mine. "Sorry, that sucks."

I laughed a little at her candidness. After weeks of living with the Meyerses, who hid their emotions at the center of twisty-turvy mazes, Linnea was utterly refreshing.

"Yeah, it does."

"You know, Miranda was like that," Linnea admitted. "I hadn't seen her in ten years before she showed up after Christmas."

I blinked. "And now you're living with her here in a foreign country?"

Her glare was pointed into the distance at someone I couldn't see, but I had a feeling it was at Miranda.

"Yeah. I guess she had a guilty conscience, and she told my dad I should see out eleventh and twelfth year here at North London Collegiate getting a 'proper' education." She made a silly face. "Dad thought it was too good an opportunity to pass up. Turns out, Miranda was just playing the role of mom to please her new sugar daddy. His name is Wyndam, can you believe that?"

I snorted. "Yeah, the Brits have some seriously bizarre names. Are they…" I tried to think about how to ask the question without sounding like I was coddling her. "Are they nice to you?"

"Wyndam more than Miranda, honestly," Linnea said with a little shrug like she didn't care. "But we have more in common anyway. He's a banker, but he's always loved cinema, so we try to catch movies at The Garden Cinema when he has time."

I'd never understand why people had children when they weren't ready or willing to actually parent them. There had been brief flares of interest from Seamus throughout my youth, but mostly he only made time for Cosima, whom he clearly liked best. I didn't begrudge him that because it was an open secret that everyone in the family liked Cosima best, but it did make me extra protective of her. Our father had never been a good man, at least to my knowledge, though Mama said differently. The man she had fallen in love with was not the one we knew as children.

It didn't matter how he might have started. In the end, he was a horrible father who jeopardized our lives for years, and I was glad to be rid of him.

Honestly, in my darkest moments, alone sleeping in my bed in the carriage house missing home so much I couldn't breathe right, I hoped he was dead so he could never darken any of our doorways again.

"I've never been," I said, shaking off the introspection. "Should we catch a film there tonight, then?"

Up close, Linnea's eyes were a startling colour, a blue so rich and bright they seemed almost purple, the colour of the night sky clinging to the last vestiges of sunset. They were absolutely arresting. Almond-shaped and framed in a bounty of fine golden lashes she hadn't bothered to darken with makeup, they somehow made her look older than her years. Maybe it was the expression in her eyes, a knowingness like she understood where my mind had wandered and sympathized with me over our shared parental neglect.

"Your eyes are almost purple," I whispered, a little transfixed by them.

Her smile was a soft, almost shy thing. "Miranda always says they're my saving grace."

My brows slammed together at the force of my sudden anger with this silly woman who would say something so scarring to her own daughter. Without thinking, I pinched Linnea's chin gently in my fingers and gave her a little shake.

"No, no, *trottalina*. Do you know the painter Modigliani? He once said, 'When I know your soul, I will paint your eyes.' The eyes are the door to the heart of a person. If yours are so lovely, it is because *you* are lovely inside."

"You don't even know me," she whispered, but there was no timidity in that fierce violet gaze as it roamed my face.

"I will if you let me."

She hesitated, a physical pause she held in her body, and released on a small exhale, a tiny grin curling her wide mouth. "Okay, then. I'd like to know someone who quotes Modigliani."

I laughed, pulling away now that the moment had passed and, with it, the shadow in her gaze. "My older sister is an artist, remember?"

"And so are you," she rejoined. "Acting is an art form."

"So it is," I agreed, handing her the cashmere. "Get changed, and I'll look at what's playing at the cinema."

Linnea stood, her wet hair splattering water all over the ground. She bit her lip and looked up at me through her spiky lashes. "How long do you have?"

Something about her shy yearning tugged at my heart. I recognized the loneliness in the gesture as something I felt myself. Even living with Adam and Savannah, it was impossible to feel totally included, especially on a night like tonight.

"As long as you want me," I promised with a wink.

THAT TURNED OUT TO BE THE entire night.

First, we went to The Garden Cinema to watch a showing of *Roman Holiday*. It was a gorgeous art deco building with red velvet chairs and retro finishing. We ordered popcorn that Linnea drenched in honey packets she pulled from her purse, and we ate it with sticky fingers the whole film. Shockingly, she was well-versed on movie knowledge, even with a movie made before her time, and she had me laughing under my breath as she told me old gossip about Carey Grant and Katherine Hepburn.

"You know," she whispered at one point when the actors were riding through Rome on a Vespa. "It's an open secret that Carey Grant was also into men."

A shiver crawled slowly down my spine, rattling my shoulders. "Oh?"

She nodded, plucking one of the last honey-soaked kernels of popcorn from the container. "Yeah, but I mean, c'mon. It's Hollywood. I know only a few actors actually 'come out,' but sexuality is totally a spectrum, and the industry is filled with beautiful people and lots of partying. I'm sure practically everyone has dabbled here and there."

I swallowed my laughter at her guilelessness. "That doesn't seem to bother your sensibilities."

She scoffed. "Why would it? It's the twenty-first century, and I'm a modern woman." Her gaze slid sideways appraisingly. "I hope you're a modern man, Sebastian. We're millennials, you know? We should be above old prejudices."

One corner of my mouth escaped the lockdown I'd imposed on my grin. "*Certo*, I'm as modern as they come."

She nodded firmly, like she'd known all along, but the way she tipped her head to tap her cheek against my shoulder was its own kind of validation.

After the movie, we washed our hands of honey residue and went on Linnea's self-directed film tour of the city. She had one of those fancy watches that tracked our steps, and in the four hours we wandered between the Shard's observation deck, King's Cross Station, Millennial Bridge, and other iconic-shooting locations, we'd walked over eighteen thousand steps. We ducked into a curry shop for supper and dared each other to eat the spiciest things on the menu. *Madonna mia*, they had milk on the menu because we both drank about a gallon each to quench the fire.

Linnea ended up winning by a landslide, given that Italian food wasn't all that spicy. She laughed until she cried when sweat started to roll down my forehead and soak the collar of my sweater.

I had fun.

Fun like I hadn't had since I was back in Napoli with Cosima. It felt like Linnea and I had been friends for years, the kind of easy enjoyment that could only happen organically or not at all. She was funny in an irreverent, witty way that reminded me a bit of Elena's cutting sense of humour, but there was a dreaminess to her when she spoke about her love of fashion and cinema that reminded me of Giselle.

When it came time to go home to retrieve the car and collect Savannah and Adam from their after-party, I found I was a little reluctant to say goodbye. I walked her into Westminster from our last stop at Big Ben, listening to her talk about her mother's promises to get her an internship after graduation at the St Aubyn fashion house.

She had two loves, fashion and cinema, which was almost as good a pairing as writing and acting.

"Have you ever considered going into acting like your mother?" I asked as we walked down the dark, relatively empty streets of the posh neighborhood.

"I've thought about it," she admitted almost reluctantly and then shot me a little look as if she sensed my curiosity. "I don't particularly want to be anything like Miranda, if you haven't noticed how much I dislike her."

I cocked my head to the side. "I don't particularly like my father, who was an academic writer and professor. That doesn't mean I can't be a screenwriter, though."

She made an irritated noise in the back of her throat and threw up her expressive hands. "That's not really the same thing, and you know it. Miranda and her gang are all so… focused on the wrong things. On the money and the status and the *gossip*. I think I'd like to act, but the idea of being in the world's spotlight makes me want to throw up. Everyone having an opinion about you when they don't even know you… just sounds awful."

I thought about Adam just that morning in the gym racing me on the pair of treadmills while Savannah used the elliptical in the corner and watched *Entertainment Tonight.* The host had mentioned Adam being cast in *The Devil Cares* and expressed their opinion that he was too posh and stuck up to play the role of Freddie Bannerman.

It didn't seem to affect Savannah who only rolled her eyes in our direction, but Adam had missed a step on the treadmill and had to recalibrate his stride to catch up to my speed again.

It was such a little thing. A single comment. But over a lifetime of exposure, it could be death by a thousand cuts.

Adam especially seemed sensitive to criticism, not only of his acting but of any negativity in general. Which was strange, really, because Savannah seemed to thrive on it.

"It does," I agreed finally.

Linnea peered over at me, the bright moon overhead turning her hair to silver. "Yet you're signing up for it."

I'd told her about *Blood Oath*, about how Adam and Savannah were kind of mentors to me as well as employers.

I shrugged. "There's a double edge to everything. You have to decide if what you love is worth the price you have to pay for it."

"Spoken like a true writer."

I shoved my shoulder against hers in response, and she laughed lightly before stopping in front of a lovely white townhouse.

"This is it," she said, not *this is home.*

Because I knew home was a pretty little house with a wraparound porch in Maui where her father and three uncles lived.

Linnea shoved her hands in her pockets, the sleeves of my overlarge cashmere rucked up to her bony elbows, her hair having dried in a nimbus of golden waves. She was lovely, I thought, not for the first time, and she'd be so beautiful one day people would lose their breath to her.

"Well," she said, scuffing the toe of her shoe on the asphalt. "Thanks for keeping me company tonight."

"It was my pleasure," I told her honestly, dipping a little to catch her downcast gaze. "I had a great time. Though, I thought your tour skewed a little too much Harry Potter."

"They're classics," she insisted again.

I only smirked at her because we'd been having the same argument all night. I didn't go in for fantasy much, and Linnea thought magic was the best kind of topic.

"I'd like to hang out with you again," she told me, forcing herself to lift her stare to lock with mine.

It was her most disarming quality, I was coming to realize. That bravery after a moment of natural bashfulness.

"*Certo*," I agreed easily. "You promised you'd teach me to surf."

Her head tipped back with the force of her laughter, mouth moving at the moon. "I did! I can't believe I forgot about that. I can't wait to see that great big body fall again and again off the board."

"Hey," I argued. "Just because I'm a drama geek doesn't mean I can't hold my own in sports."

"Sure," she drawled, grinning beatifically at the idea of my embarrassment. "We'll see who's proven right."

"We will," I promised, moving forward to cup her elbows in my palms and place the customary kisses on her cheeks. "*A presto, trottolina*."

"*A presto*," she murmured back in a half-decent approximation of an Italian accent.

I tucked my own hands in my pockets as I pulled away and started walking backward away from her.

"Hey, Sebastian? What does *trottolina* mean?" she called just as I was about to turn away to walk properly back toward the metro.

"Little spinning top," I told her, deciding to relay the literal translation.

Her answering smile was as bright as a wedge of moonlight. Slowly, she spun in a graceful pirouette, and something inside the cage of my ribs did the same.

When I picked up Adam and Savannah at NoMad, I was still

thinking about the girl with the sunshine hair in a pool of moonlight spinning and spinning until I turned the corner and lost sight of her.

"Sebastian, darling," Savannah's sharp voice cut through my thoughts as I leaned against the car at the exit, waiting for them to emerge.

I jerked away from my lean against the Rolls and smiled at my *duchessa* as she moved gracefully toward me on sky-high heels. She had changed from her gown into a short, beaded number like something from *The Great Gatsby,* and Adam was in a similarly themed outfit of vest and dress shirt in different shades of green that made his eyes almost neon toned even in the dim light of the sodium lamps lining the street.

"*Siete sensazionali,*" I murmured because I'd lost some of my breath to those two golden-haired beauties walking toward *me.*

Savannah's narrowed glare softened at the reverence in my tone, and her hand was gentle as she placed it in mine so I could lead her the last few steps to the car and open the door for her.

"You were somewhere else," she accused lightly.

I helped her get settled and closed the door, taking the time to wonder how I should respond to that. When I walked to the other side, I passed Adam getting into the back seat. He gripped my forearm before I could move by and leaned in closer, breathing deeply.

"You smell of another woman," he noted, eyes flaring with surprise as he leaned back.

My pulse hopped straight into a sprint like a rabbit pursued by a predator through the brush.

I swallowed thickly and turned away from him to get into the driver's seat.

There was nothing wrong with spending the evening with Linnea. She was only sixteen, but even then, she was closer to my age than *both* of the Meyerses. It was only fair that I should be allowed to have friends outside of their marriage.

When I closed the door and buckled up, looking into the rearview mirror to pull out of the parking space safely, Adam and Savannah were both watching me.

"Well?" Savannah asked, acid dripping from the one word.

"Well what, *duchessa*?"

"Don't sweet-talk me, Sebastian. Were you with another woman tonight? Adam said you smell like perfume. And don't try to pass it off as mine. I certainly don't wear something as childish as *coconut*."

I rolled my eyes, but by the sound of Adam's low grumble in the back seat, that was not an acceptable response.

"I don't know why we're talking about my night when you two were the ones at the star-studded party. Tell me, was Clooney there?"

"Sebastian," Adam warned.

It was a command more than anything, and it affected me better than Savannah's peevishness.

I sighed. "You're both being very jealous. I spent the evening with a female friend. We went to the cinema and shared a curry."

The silence that followed my statement was sticky as a web cast between the front and back seats, ensnaring me in tacky fibres.

"I'm sorry, I wasn't aware it went against the rules for me to make friends," I said slowly, so dry the words scraped my throat coming out.

Savannah's energy was a palpable thing, a vibration that cranked high enough to set my teeth on edge.

"Of course, you can have friends," Adam soothed, but his tone was brittle. "We would never want to isolate you."

"Your current response says otherwise."

"I just encouraged you two days ago to catch that Kings United match with your old flatmates," Adam argued.

"Who are men," I quipped. "You know, I'm interested in you, right? Sexually. Yet you encouraged me to hang out with blokes, and you're… what? Jealous that I spent the evening with Linnea? If you're going to be possessive, at least be bipartisan about it."

"Linnea Hildebrand?" Savannah asked, shock clearing the furrow between her brows.

"Linnea Kai," I corrected.

"Miranda's daughter, though?" When I nodded, Savannah laughed, and the sound was airy with relief. "Oh, well, of course, you should spend time with the girl. Her mother was just telling me she doesn't quite fit in with the Eton class after growing up like a heathen surrounded by her father and truckload of uncles." She shivered delicately. "She's practically a boy herself, really. And she didn't inherit any of her mother's beauty."

"Savannah," I snapped, lungs compressed in my chest by the force of my anger. "Don't speak about her like that. I've just told you, she's my friend. Even if you can't respect her, have enough respect for me to be kind toward her."

Savannah blinked those huge, luminous eyes at me, suddenly looking younger than her years. An ingenue in a socialite's dressings. "Sebastian… she's just a girl."

"She's my friend," I declared resolutely. "And if you think I'll be flattered by your jealousy, you're both wrong. You have… *everything.* Our power dynamic is already unbalanced. If you start trying to control who I'm friends with and what I do in my time away from you both, this won't work."

Alarm trilled through the car, silent yet blaring, quiet with a heavy bass like thudding hearts.

"Don't be dramatic, darling," Savannah said softly, leaning forward to brush her fingers against my shoulder as I pulled onto our street.

"I'm… well, I'm sorry I was rude about your friend."

"I'm not sorry we were jealous, though," Adam added blandly, slouched insolently in his seat, eyes hot on mine in the mirror's reflection. "You've become ours, Sebastian, and if you say that wasn't by your doing, I'll call you a very poor liar. You knew what you were doing when you hooked us through the mouth and reeled us in. Now that you have us, you must suffer the consequences of our affection. Possessive and dramatic though it may be."

I rolled my lips between my teeth as I pulled through the gates into the driveway, waiting until after I parked the car to look at them in the rearview.

"Shouldn't you have matured past petty jealousy?" I asked, though it was mostly a tease, to show them that all was forgiven.

Savannah's spine softened back against the leather seats, and she looked truly relieved in a way that made my heart skip a beat.

She cares, she cares, my soul trilled.

"When you can't stop thinking about someone, they quickly become someone you're not willing to give up without a fight," Adam told me.

Each word hit my heart like a fucking gong.

He cares too, he cares too.

Something like relief and hope and joy tangled together into euphoria that echoed through every atom of my being. Before I could second-guess my instincts, I was unbuckling and crawling over the partition into the back with Adam and Savannah. They were both on the short side of the L-shaped seating, which gave me room to sink to my knees in front of them and wrap both hands around each of their necks to haul them in close.

I kissed Savannah first, plundering her mouth like I owned it.

Like it was due to me. My right to take it as her…

Lover?

It didn't matter. It was my right to take it because I was *hers* and she was *mine*.

I felt as if they'd drugged me with their proprietary affection. The slide of Savvy's tongue against mine had never felt sweeter, the grip of Adam's hand on the back of my neck never more claiming.

It was so easy to close my eyes and pretend all my dreams were reality just for this sliver of time in the back of the town car that had become the setting of so many pivotal moments in my life.

I slid my hand into the pocket of my jeans and flicked the switch on the vibrator remote I'd been toying with all night. The soft buzz of the toy filled the car's interior along with Savannah's soft gasp of pleasure.

"Did you change gowns because the other was ruined by the wetness seeping down your thighs all night?" I asked her, taking a more aggressive role with her than I ever had before.

Without ceremony, I pushed her thighs wide apart with my leather-gloved hands. I remembered wanting to touch her sweet pussy wearing the driving gloves the first time I laid eyes on her and marvelled briefly that I was able to do so now.

The only thing separating me from doing it right that moment was a thin wedge of cream lace hiding her from view.

I pulled her to the edge of the leather seat, ignoring her little squeak of alarm, and shuck off her panties in one pull. Leaving her thighs thrown over my shoulders so I was wedged between her legs, close to her pink folds, I used my thumbs to gently pull her open like the petals of a tightly furled rose.

My nostrils flared as the honey and musk scent of her assailed my senses, and I fixated on the pretty sight of her glistening pussy.

"She had to excuse herself twice during the party to clean up a bit in the toilet," Adam told me, his voice rubbed raw by desire.

I didn't look at him, but his gaze was sun hot against my cheek. "Good."

Rubbing my thumb along the inside seam of her thigh, I dipped it inside her to test the grasp of her greedy entrance and grinned when she moaned at the loss as soon as I moved away.

"You kept me waiting all night, but I've kept you wanting, so I guess it's a fair trade," I mused, dragging my supple leather fingers over the folds of her pussy, watching as moisture pooled at her entrance and started to leak down to her ass.

"Show me how much you missed me," she whispered, and the edge of desperation in her tone had me looking up to catch her expression.

It was… bruised. A tender, aching kind of softness that made her seem young and confused.

Good, I thought. I hoped that confusion was because she was falling in love with me despite everything between us.

I bent my head closer to her sex and blew lightly over her clit until she shivered. "Everything tastes like ash compared to the taste of you."

She gave a breathy little exhalation and moved both hands into the longer strands of hair at the top of my head as I bent to eat at her properly.

It was true.

She was fucking sublime on my tongue, sweet and tart and warm like fresh bread. I sucked at her labia, at her clit, and the sides of her tender-skinned inner thighs until she was pink everywhere and writhing.

Only then did I push two fingertips into her clutching pussy and prod at the little toy lodged inside her, vibrating away.

With my other hand, I handed the remote to Adam, who sat patiently beside us.

"Let's see how many times we can make her come before she's as limp as a rag doll," I suggested, hoping that he would continue to let me take the lead.

I knew it wasn't in his nature to follow second, but I needed the control tonight. Something about watching them exist in their public lives without a trace of me on them left me feeling primal and angsty. I'd only be satisfied if they *both* let me fuck them and mark them up as I saw fit.

If they both let me in enough to be vulnerable to my attentions with the barrier of their control between us.

Adam's face was flushed, lids low over darkly green eyes, but otherwise, he seemed almost unaffected sitting like a king on his throne in the back of a town car in a tuxedo that cost more than I'd ever paid in rent. When he tipped his chin just slightly to me, I felt every inch his proxy, filled with God-given power, except my only deity was *him*.

The rush of authority carbonated my blood and made my head swim.

"Turn it up," I ordered him. "See what she can handle. Are you going to be a good girl for us, Savvy? I want you so swollen, Adam will have to work extra hard to wedge that thick cock of his inside you, *capisci*?"

"Yes," she hissed as I bent once more to lave my tongue over her clit, my fingers nudging the toy as Adam cranked the intensity up so that it slid just a little in and out of her tight walls. "*Fuck*."

"I love it when you curse for us," I praised. "The lady becoming the whore just for her men."

"My men," she echoed, fingers tightening in my hair before one slid, almost hesitantly, over to palm Adam's rigid length behind his zipper.

This time, he hissed.

"Take him out and play with him. Just the tip," I warned. "He likes it when you tease the head and dip your fingertip into his leaking hole."

I watched as a full-body shudder wracked Adam's big frame. Savannah's small hand fished his dick out from behind his zipper. The sight of the thick erection, fleshy and flushed dark red at the tip like an overripe plum, made my mouth water.

After all these weeks of sex and games, I still hadn't taken that shaft in my mouth. Maybe I shouldn't have been shocked any longer by my desire for this man, but I was momentarily bowled over by it.

Reining in my impulses, I dipped my head and fastened my lips over Savvy's cunt again, slurping up the juices leaking fast from her entrance.

Her first orgasm hit with a sharp cry that pierced the interior of the car like a scream. Adam leaned over to muffle it with his mouth.

The second was muffled by his cock as he pulled her head down into his lap and slotted that fat shaft into her mouth and straight to the back of her throat. He pinned her there, hand on the back of her mussed hair while I pinned her quaking hips to the seat.

She was so wet that she slipped against the upholstery.

Which gave me an ingenious idea for keeping her still.

"Let's test both of your control," I suggested darkly and pulled away from Savannah, licking my lips as I drew the vibrating toy out of her and nodded to Adam to turn it off.

Her head lolled back against the seat as she blinked at me a little dazedly. With a wicked grin, I picked her up and lifted her over Adam's lap. He picked up the thread of my intent and held the base of his dick so I could slowly lower Savannah's swollen pussy over top of him.

She sank down with a trembly sigh, sinking onto it like she'd been aching for the stretch of a thick cock inside her.

I told her so, and she shivered.

Pinching her chin so she had to look down at me, I asked her for the words because I loved the sound of her dulcet tones speaking utter filth. "Do you love being stretched on your husband's big dick, Savvy?"

"I love it," she agreed. "I'm so swollen. It's almost too much."

"No, not yet. But let's see if we can get you there," I mused, then looked over her shoulder at Adam, whose jaw was ticking with the restraint of staying still. "Can you let her sit pretty on your lap while I make her come a few times all over you?"

He swallowed thickly and then nodded tersely.

"Adam," I coaxed, getting up on my knees to reach for his throat, cupping it in my hand to feel the rapid thrum of his pulse behind his placid facade. "If you keep her nice and still for me, I'll let you come inside her and then eat all that delicious fucking cum of yours right out of her stuffed cunt before I fuck her and add my own cum to that beautiful cunt."

"Jesus Christ," he growled, grinding Savvy a little on his lap so she groaned with him. "Just get on with it."

A mean little chuckle escaped my lips, and I felt like I understood how Adam must have felt dominating us in the bedroom like this. It was a power and privilege that made every atom of my body thrum in time with their heartbeats.

When I rested back on my heels to suck Savannah's swollen, deeply pink pussy again, it was stuffed with Adam's cock so naturally, I tended to both.

The second my tongue hit the silky skin over his shaft, he groaned so long and deep, it was almost a muted roar.

A lightning strike of arousal hit the base of my spine and burst through every inch of my body.

The little voice in the back of my head that still insisted I wasn't into men, that kissing and touching Adam while he was inside or touching Savannah didn't count, snuffed out in the bright heat of lust exploding behind my eyes.

I let myself drift away in it.

I let myself *love* it.

Sensing my desire, maybe, or encouraging me to explore more because he wanted it as badly as I did, Adam lifted Savannah slowly off his cock.

I licked up the juices that had leaked all over his shaft on the way up and then sucked and lashed at Savannah's clit on the way down.

Back and forth.

Salt and honey.

Him and her.

I was honestly *dizzy* with desire, losing myself to the rhythm of tasting them both.

Drugged, I barely noticed when Adam finally lifted her clear off his cock. Without thinking, I gripped his shaft before it could slap back against his belly and took it into my mouth.

He tasted like her.

The concoction of Savannah's wetness and Adam's precum made me moan so long, I couldn't breathe.

Vaguely, I was aware of Savannah's hands in my hair, tugging me back to her messy pussy as she sank back down on his cock.

Back and forth.

Tick-tock.

I lost sense of time and space, even my own raging erection was leaking copiously into my trousers.

Savannah came again on a rough, broken cry and went limp in Adam's lap.

It was my cue to give my sweet *duchessa* a break, so I leaned back on my heels and jerked my chin at Adam, whose eyes were blown to black with barely restrained lust.

"Fuck her hard," I told him. "She can take it, can't you, *bella mia*?"

Savannah tucked her head back against Adam's shoulder. "I can take anything either of you want to give me, and I'll love it."

Adam and I both groaned as he started to move. His grip was punishing around her hips as he lifted and lowered her, the beads on her dress clinking musically. I pulled down the bodice of the dress to play with her sensitive little breasts and then finally gave in to the pressure and freed my own cock. It throbbed just at the sensation of the warm arm against my shaft, and I knew when I finally buried myself in Savannah's used pussy, I'd fill her up far too quickly.

Just the thought of fucking into Adam's cum inside her had me a hair's breath away from shooting prematurely.

"I love having two gorgeous men like this," Savannah panted as she ground down on Adam's cock, clearly reinvigorated by his brutal thrusts. "I love being the center of your attention."

I laughed, the sound so husky I barely recognized it. My *duchessa* loved being prized, and I knew having us like this, lavishing her, using her, filled with no thoughts but ones of her was her ultimate aphrodisiac.

Just as she was mine.

Just as *this*, fucking this gorgeous married couple, was mine.

I'd never known to fantasize about such a thing, but now I wasn't sure I'd ever be complete without it.

"Fuck," Adam ground out, and a moment later, his hand was lashing forward to grip my shirt, tugging me forward.

I fell into them, catching myself with one hand on the seat by Adam's head. Instantly, Savannah turned her face into my neck, fixing her lips on my pulse point.

And Adam moved his big hand to my throat in a facsimile of how

I'd recently held him and used his grip to bring me in for a crushing kiss.

His tongue forced my lips open without courtesy, plundering my mouth almost viciously.

When he came, I ate the shout of pleasure out of his mouth and twisted Savvy's nipple so cruelly, she joined him seconds later.

Without hesitation, I pulled away from them both only enough to fist my own cock, pressing the head up against Savvy's entrance, still stuffed with Adam's cock. She gasped as I applied just a little pressure, snugging the head of my cock *just* at the mouth of her entrance right up against Adam's shaft.

The tight heat, the wet of her cum, and his cum against me was enough to blow the top off my control.

I came with a glorious shout like a marauder securing new territory for his own and splashed my hot seed all over them both. Inside her, against him, on both their spent, swollen sexes.

It was the most beautiful experience of my life.

And when I collapsed on the floor of the car, my head cushioned by Adam's furred thigh, my sight filled with the messy Pollock painting of cum I'd made of them, I let myself trail a finger in the cum leaking from Savannah and then stuffed it back inside her alongside his softening member.

"*Mozzafiato*," I murmured heedlessly, almost dreamily.

Savannah's hand softened in my hair, stroking against my scalp with her short, manicured nail. "*Breathtaking*," she echoed in English, remembering, no doubt, the first time I told her that.

Adam hummed his agreement, and I felt his hand join his wife's in my hair.

"Feeling better?" he murmured after a few long moments of companionable silence.

It was my turn to hum, my mind still drifting like I was in a waking dream. In Italian, we called it *svegliarsi nel mondo della luna*, waking in the land of the moon.

It occurred to me that we had so many expressions revolving around the moon in my language. Fitting, given that I'd often equated Adam and Savannah to celestial beings.

I whispered, "*Voglio la luna*."

Because it was as ironic as it was true.

"What does that mean?" Savannah asked, her voice still throaty with residual passion.

"I want to ask for the moon," I admitted in English. "I want to wish for things I know I can never have."

In tandem, their hands stilled in my hair.

"Who says you can't have what you want?" Savannah asked, a new edge worked into her tone.

I shrugged inelegantly. "Life, maybe? It's taught me this lesson before."

"How do you know if you don't ask?" she rebutted. "Your incredible film is in preproduction, and you're about to tell your mother and sister you have enough money to send them to the States. The world is yours for the taking and ours for the giving if it's in our power."

Adam was silent, a Greek statue looming enigmatically over us both.

And even though Savannah asked the question, it was Adam I knew I had to ask to grant my wishes. He was the moon in my sky, the one who quietly ruled me in elemental ways I'd never known existed.

"I want to be allowed to fall in love with you," I told them, twisting fully between Savannah's legs, my hands clasping her thighs like she was a life raft in a stormy sea. "I want to be allowed to tell you

I'm *in* love with you, and not saying the words is breaking my heart every day."

"Sebastian," Adam said. It was a warning and an entreaty all in one.

Love less, he demanded.

Love me more, he whispered.

"No, Adam," I said, clear and strong. Shaking off the nerves and the fear of rejection I knew was coming. Pretending for one crystal moment that they could be mine and want me to be theirs in a way that mattered.

In a way that could be forever.

"You don't need to be jealous of anyone else because I love you both more than I ever understood the human heart could love before meeting you. I know it doesn't make sense, and it goes against the rules of our arrangement, but I don't care. I don't want an arrangement, anymore. I want a *life*. A life where someone like me is allowed to love two people as celestial as you."

"Sebastian," Savannah murmured, cupping my jaw in one of her small, cool hands. "Why are you speaking like we've already broken your heart and cast you out on the streets?"

Because that's where this ends, I wanted to cry out in desperation, pound my chest and gnash my teeth in impotent rage. *Don't be foolish, bella amora mia, this was always how it would end.*

She seemed to read it in my face and made a soft, broken noise in the back of her throat before surging forward to kiss me, lips gentle and clinging. When she pulled away, her eyes were the palest blue, so translucent I could see through to the bottom of her soul.

"I love you, too," she whispered so quietly, the words were mostly mouthed. "I love you, and I don't know what that means except that you make me feel like the best version of myself. You make us feel complete."

The noise that rose from my chest was choked, hope cut off at the pass.

"Don't say it if you don't mean it," I warned. "I know I'm not—"

"Stop," she ordered fiercely, grabbing my face in both her hands. "I've never said something so honest in my life. I love you in all its terrifying and awe-inspiring glory."

My heart beat so strong and heavy in my chest it felt like a battering ram threatening to eradicate the walls.

"*La donna dei miei sogni,*" I murmured against her lips, cradling her face like the gift it was. "You are the woman of my dreams."

"And the man of mine," she agreed without hesitation, sealing her statement with the sweetest kiss I'd ever received.

The Patek Philippe watch was gorgeous, but it had nothing on that moment there with a woman I'd loved for weeks and never thought in my wildest hopes might love me too.

My gaze sought Adam over Savvy's shoulder to find him glaring at me with palpable frustration.

His jaw ticked as I waited.

And waited.

Not for a declaration of love like Savannah, but something…

A stray hope to cling to the way I clung to Savvy's face as she kissed me.

But the moon had always been elusive, and instead of participating in our joy, he watched, quiet and sullen as I brought Savannah even closer and kissed all the love right out of her sweet mouth.

Only, no matter how much I ate, there was a bottomless hunger in my heart I was worried would never be quenched.

Chapter Eighteen

Sebastian

Being home in Naples was both incredible and oddly dissatisfying. There was no denying I adored my mother, and I wasn't afraid to make it known. When she braved traffic to pick me up in Naples with Elena, I'd lifted her and spun her around like we hadn't seen each other in years instead of only a handful of months. The scent of semolina and rosemary that always perfumed her hair was the first sign I was *home*. She'd laughed in delight and patted my cheek before planting two smacking kisses on either one.

"*Ragazzo mio*," she spoke around her gorgeous smile. "You're home."

When I'd turned to Elena, she was watching us with bright eyes she immediately averted so I wouldn't catch her being sappy. My eldest sister prided herself on being above emotion, too intellectually minded to give into the dramatics of the rest of our family.

But what were little brothers for if not to embarrass their sisters?

I tackle-hugged her, gripping her around the middle and hauling her into the air. She slapped at my head as she protested, but there was a smile in her tone, and when I placed her on her feet, her gaze was reluctantly fond.

"*Patatino*," she said, referring to me by my childhood nickname of "little potato" because I'd been born with a misshapen head. "It's good to see you."

I rolled my eyes at her formality and kissed her temple, wrapping each arm around both of my girls as we walked out of the airport, my duffel slung over my back. The cacophony of Italian voices raised to call out to each other throughout the terminal settled something in my chest I hadn't even realized was restless. It was good to hear the language of my home and its people. England made me realize how many little cultural differences there were, especially now that I lived with the Meyerses. I loved learning about new customs, but it felt decidedly good not to be a foreigner for a little while.

I listened happily to Elena tell me about finishing her online undergraduate program and applications to law schools in the United States, to Mama moan about working under Eduardo in the restaurant she'd been sous chef at since we were young, and watched the landscape swirl by outside the window.

Our little house, old and too small for a family of five but too spacious somehow with only Mama and Elena living there, was exactly the same as I'd left it. The ancient piano Elena played more beautifully than anyone had the right to do on such an instrument. The bedroom I'd shared with my twin sister complete with our meager collection of books, mostly castoff textbooks from Seamus's university courses and my prized poster of *La Baia Di Napoli* signed by Sofia Loren herself, and the painting Giselle had done of *La Gaiola* beach we frequented almost every day of the summer as kids. My few friends in town had nothing new to report except a change in girlfriends. Everything else was the same, besides the absence of Giselle and Cosima.

I missed them.

Elena had never been the warmest or kindest of my sisters, her desire for *more* sometimes making her angry and bitter, but I spent as much time with her as she would allow.

"I'm not Cosima," she snapped at me when we were having espresso in the kitchen one morning and I put my arm around her for a sideways hug. "I don't need you suffocating me."

I arched an eyebrow at her, unconsciously channelling Adam.

She scowled at me and then into her coffee.

"What's up, Lady?" I asked patiently because she only lashed out when she was hurting.

The nickname was one I'd conjured years ago because Elena always acted like a lady, upper-class and haughty even when she was a child. It occurred to me that the two most aristocratic women I knew, Savannah and my eldest sister, had come from nothing.

I watched as she bit her lip, then jutted her chin out stubbornly before lifting flashing eyes at me. "You can't just come home and act like nothing has changed. You and Cosima just… *left* me here."

Anger curled like smoke in my gut. "You told Seamus and Cosima that deal to model in Milan was too good to pass up, even when Cosi said she didn't want to leave the family! We left you to make money to get you—all of you—out of here."

She scoffed. "You left to pursue your dreams of stardom. Don't sugarcoat it."

"I don't have to," I argued, dropping my espresso cup onto the saucer with a clatter. "Do you think Cosi and I wanted to be separated? Do you think I feel good knowing I've left my mother and sister in this hellhole with fucking mafiosi circling always just waiting for an in? Do you think I don't lie awake at night worrying if you're okay? Mama and Gigi and Cosima, too?"

She tossed her dark red hair over her shoulder and glared at the middle distance over my shoulder. For someone in her early twenties, my sister looked years older. Worn and tragic like an old oil painting left too long neglected in a dusty attic. "Don't act like living in London and getting a paycheck is such a bad thing."

"Elena," I snapped, furious with her for being so brittle and with myself for letting her get a rise out of me. Cosima was the one who always mediated our disputes and the one who reminded me that our eldest sister only ever lashed out when she struggled with her emotions. "I have a new job with better hours and better pay, but until recently, I worked seven days a week as a driver on top of starring in a production at Finborough. I shared a one-bedroom flat with five different blokes. If you think that's paradise, you're mistaken."

I hadn't planned to tell her about Savannah and Adam, anyway, but sitting across from her at that moment, I ached to have the kind of relationship where I could confide in her. But it felt impossible to imagine her doing anything other than judging me for being a live-in lover. She'd call me a sellout, a *puttano*, a morally corrupt stain on our family.

I'd heard her say similar things to Giselle, and our sister had only had the misfortune of being pretty enough to attract unwanted lascivious attention in town.

Elena crossed her arms defensively. "If you were working that hard, we'd be living in the United States already."

"Why are you being so ungrateful?" I asked her, frustration and disappointment curdling the affection I had for her in my gut. "I'm not saying you owe me anything, but I don't understand this hostility, Lena. I'm your brother, *porca miseria*. I'm trying to do what's best for all of us."

Her laugh was hollow as she pushed out of her chair with a loud scraping screech and stalked out of the room, throwing over her shoulder, "If that was true, I wouldn't still be here."

Later, when I'd asked Mama about it, she'd just sighed loudly and shrugged. "Elena is a complicated woman. It is not possible to know her when she refuses to know herself."

"We have enough money to get you both out of here," I told her as we worked side by side in the kitchen making *orecchiette* pasta, folding the little ears of dough with our thumbs before placing them to dry on the trays. "I wanted to take you to dinner and tell you, but Elena's bitterness stole my thunder."

"*Patatino*," she said with a cluck of her tongue that told me I was in for a mild scolding. "Be kind to Elena. She's been very down lately. I think she and Christopher are having a rough time."

Christopher was Elena's much older boyfriend, a man she'd met through our father because they worked together at the university. I'd never liked him, nor had Cosima or Mama, which might have explained why Elena stayed with him when he was so obviously not good enough for her.

My sister was whip smart, tall, and gorgeous, with a great sense of style even on a budget, and a secret tenderheartedness that showed itself infrequently but gorgeously like a green streak at sunset. She deserved the *world*, not some *stronzo*.

"Why does she stay with him then?" I muttered, watching our hands moving in tandem as we pressed pasta dough between our fingers. It soothed me, the routine of it, the custom of making pasta with Mama since I was just a tiny boy.

Mama sighed. "I'm not sure I set good examples for you all, hmm?"

I winced because there was no way to refute that. Seamus was the worst kind of father and husband, but she'd put up with him for years. I understood that he was the primary breadwinner—even if he gambled it all away too often to count—and that our culture encouraged marriage until the end, no matter what.

But the truth was, when Seamus disappeared without a trace soon after Cosima left for Milan, we'd all felt acutely relieved to have him gone.

"Do you miss him?" I dared to ask. We never spoke about him, now. Honestly, we'd barely spoken about him when he still lived with us.

Caprice Lombardi was gorgeous in the way of old-school Hollywood starlets like Sofia Loren and Marilyn Monroe, all steep curves and sultry femininity. The only reason she didn't have suitors knocking down the door now that Seamus had gone for good was because she had zero interest in men and a bad reputation for cutting them into very small pieces with her sharp tongue if they pressed too hard.

Elena had got that skill from her.

"I miss the man I fell in love with," she told me baldly. "He was this intensely handsome man with charisma and mystery. I fell in love with the idea of him more than the real him." She shrugged, opening her semolina-coated hands to the heavens. "I was just a girl."

"That doesn't invalidate your love," I said, maybe a little too quickly.

It was hard not to imagine what she might think of my affair with a married couple. Mama was surprisingly unjudgmental, but she would be disappointed in me for disrupting the sanctity of marriage. Even if I told her I was actually helping their marriage by sewing together their jagged edges like so many stitches.

"No," she agreed. "But I thought I was so worldly because I was dating a foreigner. I thought he loved me because he enjoyed my beauty and my authenticity. When they grew old, his attentions grew stale."

My thumb rent the little sphere of pasta in two.

Because Mama's words hit just a little too close to home.

What would happen when, inevitably, my novelty wore off?

I'd been living with the Meyerses for months now, but things were still fresh and exciting. There were so many ways to touch and be touched, so many questions to ask and answer to get to the hearts of two very different people. Both Adam and Savannah lived for work, and they were knee-deep in *Blood Oath* with me, excited to launch my career the way she had once launched his.

But…

What happened when I was launched?

What happened in another six months or two years?

They were already married, and based on Savannah's rhetoric, they didn't seem to want children.

So would I live in the carriage house forever? Their good mate who spent a little bit too much time with them?

The loneliness that grew like weeds in the fertile ground of my belly deepened its roots and reached its limbs up into my throat so I felt like I might choke.

Alone, but not alone, forever.

Like I was in this family of broken spirits held together by blood and hope.

"If you could go back in time and do things differently, would you?" I asked, an edge of desperation in the question.

The relief I felt when she immediately said, "No," was so acute, I had to grip the counter to regain my balance.

"No," she repeated, twisting to face me and cup my face in her hands. "Never, *patatino*. Regrets are inevitable in life. There will always be weeds in the garden, but not all of them are ugly. Without Seamus, I would not have my babies who give reason to my whole existence."

"But you could have married someone better and had children with them,'" I argued, for the sake of understanding how deeply this feeling went in her.

So I could know how deeply it may one day go in me.

Pain spasmed across her features, fingers tightening on my cheeks. "Maybe. But I do not spend my time on this kind of thinking. What I had with Seamus when I was young was beautiful. What he gave me in my children is even more beautiful. I can't regret any of it, and if I'm sad about the way it ended, well, then I focus on the future. And I hope that life has taught me to be a better version of myself, so if I have the opportunity to love again, I make a good choice for myself."

"Have you ever loved anyone else?" I'd never considered it, really. She was so young when she met my father, and he'd only been gone for half a year.

But she was the type of woman who inspired poetry, and she'd given that to her daughters. She'd taught her son to look for that kind of moving beauty within and without, which was why the combination of Savannah's intelligence and elegance hooked me right through the mouth.

"Yes," she whispered, dropping her hands from my face like I was on fire and turning back to the pasta with a kind of dramatized busyness that made me think she was lying about something. "A long time ago."

"What happened?"

Her hands hesitated over the drying pasta. "I-I wasn't brave enough to trust it."

"What happened to him?"

She turned from me, moving the pasta to the table and then going directly to the fridge, hiding her face behind the door. "I don't know."

It was a lie, but then, who was I to judge my mother for keeping things from me?

Mama's vagueness had always bothered me. When I was a boy trying to understand why she stayed with my father, who was a good-for-nothing son of a whore, when I was a young man trying to make decisions to protect my family and Mama didn't seem to share my desire to get us all out of Napoli, as a man now, trying to understand my sisters.

"A little mystery is a good thing," she always said, and it was a pretty turn of phrase, but as I grew older, it seemed more like an excuse to keep secrets than anything else.

And though I'd do anything for my family, and I knew in my bones they would do anything for me, there was no doubt we were a family of secret keepers.

Cosima didn't answer half of my phone calls anymore, Giselle hadn't visited home in the year and a half since she'd left for Paris, and Elena disappeared for hours at a time, coming home angry and sullen.

A small part of me wondered what would happen if I shared my own scandalous secret.

Would it start some kind of domino effect?

Truths rushing into the light after years of hiding in the shadows? And what then?

How was my scattered family supposed to withstand the brutality of such honesty when we weren't even together to work through it?

In the end, it didn't matter because I didn't have the balls to tell them, and even though they noticed me on the phone, smiling that private smile reserved for the Meyerses, neither of them had the balls to ask me about it either.

IT WAS A RELIEF TO RETURN to England, and not just because of the bad memories Napoli held for me or the inexplicable tension between Mama, Elena, and myself.

It was a relief simply to be back in the proximity of Savannah and Adam, who had become, in the short months I'd known them, akin to the sun and the moon lighting my life in their different ways. Without them, those two weeks in Italy were like a cloud-filled night, filling me with old feelings of being adrift and alone.

The moment I got out of the hired car in front of the gates to the Meyers' Chelsea home, I felt something settle in me. It was the way I should have felt going home, yet I felt it now walking across the flagstones to the black lacquered door and using my key to enter the sweet-smelling interior. It was quiet within, which wasn't surprising given it was hideously early on a Saturday morning, and even Savannah and Adam tended to take the weekend for a lie-in.

I dropped my things in the foyer, my keys on the round marble table between the tasteful chandelier and my shoes beside the closet, before I padded softly up the stairs. It was a bold move to climb the stairs to their bedroom when they weren't expecting me and could be sleeping or even fucking. The thought sent warmth tumbling through me. Two weeks without either of their hands on me when I'd grown accustomed to warming their bed almost every night was torturous. I was already half hard just thinking about them sleep-warm and scantily clothed in bed. Savannah always wore these little silk slips in feminine colours, and Adam slept in his boxer briefs, snug over his muscular thighs and ass.

It was a bold move but one I felt comfortable making because of the two months I'd spent living with my married lovers. I'd only spent a handful of nights in my own bed in the carriage house.

I had every hope they'd be just as eager for our reunion as I was.

Which was why I wasn't expecting the sight of Adam sitting alone on the edge of the unmade bed, hair rumpled, face creased with lack of sleep, and eyes vacant as they fixed on something disturbing in his mind's eye. He didn't notice me as I stood in the doorway, so I had a moment to take in the open door to the walk-in closet, the empty hangers on Savannah's side of the closet, and the clothes tossed haphazardly on the floor as if she'd packed in a hurry. The vase filled with flowers that usually rested on Savvy's marble-topped bedside table was currently shattered to pieces at the base of the wall beside the bathroom, water and bits of greenery clinging to the broken picture frame housing a lovely photo of them both on their wedding day. Even the air in the room was thick like a slowly dispersing mushroom cloud after an atomic detonation.

And Adam, a shell of a being, tossed on the edge of the mattress like so much debris.

The frightened, immature part of me wanted to break the terse silence with a joke, but I forced the impulse back down my throat and summoned the courage to move forward quietly to crouch at Adam's side. Only when I placed a hand on his strong thigh did he seem to come back to himself, swiveling his head to look at me a little blankly before he blinked and recognition settled in. His hand instantly covered my own, squeezing a little too hard.

"Sebastian," he said.

A sound of pure relief, a little desperate, a lot hopeful.

It made some last wall erected around my heart crumble into dust.

"Adam," I soothed. "What happened?"

He swallowed so hard, the movement looked painful. "We fought."

"That's not very like you," I noted, because they hadn't had so much as a tiff since I'd lived with them.

At least to my knowledge.

Adam's smile was a mockery of the term, crooked like the picture frame on the wall. "It's very like us. It's all we ever seem to do these days."

At my puzzled look, he let out a short chuckle that was more a barking scoff than true laughter. "Before you, it was all we could do to maintain a charade in public. With you, it's been, well, brilliant again. I thought we might regain some of what went missing over the years, but then you left, and… it all fell apart again."

"How, though?" But even as I asked, I could imagine it now that he'd brought their tension to my attention.

I'd often thought of them as my moon and sun, guiding me, acting on me in their different yet elemental ways. But I'd never thought about their relationship to one another. How did two opposing forces coexist in perfect harmony?

They didn't, not really. One took the spotlight at night and the other in the day. They had a symbiotic nature, of course, the moon reflecting the sun and one giving way to the other, but rarely did you see them together in the same sky.

And maybe for Adam and Savannah, I was that strange anomaly, the moon viewed during the day, two opposites held together in the same sky.

What an awesome and awful power.

What a wild responsibility.

Adam tipped his head back and closed his eyes, like even recounting the argument was exhausting. "She was angry with me for agreeing to talk to Sylvia Ramone about a theatre project in the West End after filming finishes for *The Devil Cares*. I want to stay in London for a while longer. I want to have some time to rest. Savannah doesn't believe in being idle."

I winced a little bit because I knew her well enough to acknowledge that truth.

Though she was always poised, Savvy was rarely still. Her datebook was busier even than Adam's most days, filled with meetings about ad campaigns, future projects, networking with studio executives and the wives of other influential actors and generally famous people. On the rare day when she didn't have much to do, she roped me into keeping her company on a variety of tasks she seemed to pick from thin air to pack her schedule with.

Success is never attained by the lazy, she liked to say.

While I thought she was right, it still puzzled me slightly that she was so focused on success, yet it was never directly for her; it was always a proxy. Adam, mostly, and now, myself.

Before Adam, I knew she had been with an influential American who moved to Britain with her and whose success Savannah took a large deal of accreditation from, but she never told me who it was.

"I told her I was tired," Adam admitted quietly as if he was confessing some great flaw and not something that was easily comprehensible.

The man had been making three to four movies every year for the past four years. When he wasn't filming, he was on a press tour or preparing for the next role. He was like some kind of savant machine, slipping in and out of characters so seamlessly I wondered secretly if he ever forgot who he truly was.

"It's okay to feel burnt out," I told him, squeezing his thigh and moving to my knees between his thighs.

I was tall enough that when he tipped his head back down, he wasn't much taller than me even seated on the bed. This close, I could see the dark circles beneath his verdant green eyes and the tension in the crow's feet beside them. He looked tired of body and of spirit. No, even more than tired, he looked defeated.

By his very own wife.

"Savannah should understand more than anyone how hard you work," I said carefully when he only searched my face intently, looking for validation I was eager to give him. "She's the one who manages you, after all."

"She does. I've often wondered if that might be the problem," he admitted softly, reaching for my shoulder as if to ground himself. "At some point, I became her puppet more than her husband."

"That's harsh," I objected because I couldn't believe Savannah was that cold, no matter how hard she tried to prove she was in business.

He shrugged expansively, an Italian expression that I thought he might have picked up from me. "The truth often is."

"So you told her you were tired, and she stormed out? That seems like an overreaction."

"I may be the actor in the family, but she doesn't lack drama," he quipped. "She was already angry with me for other things. Jealous, too, I think, that I've taken the lead on producing *Blood Oath*. She had a meeting with Tate Richardson from Hypnosis Studios the other day about financing without realizing we already decided to take an independent approach."

"*Che cavolo*, she would not like that."

"No," he agreed, gesturing to the thrown vase remnants. "It escalated from there. I am not a good client, and I am not a good husband, though that was only said as an afterthought."

"Where did she go?" I wondered.

"Bobbi's husband has an estate in Yorkshire. She went for the weekend to clear her head."

I pursed my lips, thoughts colliding into each other with such force, it made it difficult to keep them from spouting from my mouth.

Adam seemed to sense my tension and smiled slightly at me, moving his hand up to my neck to give it a squeeze. "What is it, Sebastian?"

"Do you love her?" I dared to ask because the truth was, *I* did.

I loved her so much that I often woke up in my small room in Italy with the smell of freesia in my nose and Bach stuck on a loop in my head. I loved the way she made me feel worthy of the success I'd yearned for since my youth. I loved the way she let just a little of the true Savvy, that teenage Southern girl in the grass longing for more, peek through when we were together. Loving her felt like a privilege, even if she never returned the sentiment, and I was unsure if I could give it up.

Even for the man I was falling in love with, too.

Adam's sigh was long and soft as an unspooling ribbon dropped at my knees. When he looked into my eyes, his were fierce and filled with fundamental certainty. "I do," he said. "But does that matter if the woman I love doesn't love me?"

I blinked, caught off guard by his honesty. "She loves you, Adam."

He only arched a brow in question.

"She does," I insisted. "Why would she be so intense about your career, about your success if she wasn't? Why would she bring me into the equation unless it was because she hoped it would help your marriage?"

Because she's selfish.

Adam didn't say the words, and I was reluctant even to think them, but they were a whisper at the back of my mind that was hard to ignore, a whistling wind through a crack in the door.

Adam didn't say the words, but he did say, "It's my birthday today, did you know?"

I rocked back to sit on my heels, staring at him a little slack-jawed. My hand would have slipped off his thigh if he wasn't holding it like an anchor. "Are you serious?"

"As death."

"Well…" I tried to find a way to rationalize Savannah's tantrum on her husband's birthday, but I honestly couldn't understand it.

In my family, no matter that we had no money, birthdays were a big deal. It was the day to do exactly what you wanted with exactly who you wanted. Just one little day in 365 of them each year. It wasn't a big ask, really.

Not diamonds or Aston Martins or castles in England.

It was just the simple belief that you deserved to be loved on your birthday just a little more than you were loved every other day of the year.

And Savannah had left him for a country house in the north because she was frustrated with his work ethic.

My jaw clenched with a spasm of anger I couldn't control.

I had to remind myself that this wasn't really *my* life or my relationship. Sure, I'd been invited in, something more than a guest but less than a permanent fixture, but it didn't mean I really got an opinion on their marriage.

So I rolled my lips between my teeth to keep my thoughts sealed and stood, clapping my hands together. "Well then, get up right now."

Adam stared at me with a knot between his brows, but I only shook my head and offered him my hand again to tug him to his feet. The length of his body pressed along the length of mine, hot and hard, sparking an electric current between us.

"It's your birthday," I repeated, a little soft, tipping my head to press my forehead against his so those tangled brown lashes and Granny Smith-apple-green eyes were all I could see. "And it's *illegal* to mope around on your birthday. So enough of this. We're going to spend the day having fun."

"I have a meeting at half past nine," Adam started to say, but I pressed my entire palm over his mouth and leaned back a bit to smile at him.

"Cancel it. You have a Lombardi living in your house, which means it's absolutely non-negotiable that your birthday is one of the best days of the year. Leave it to me, I've got this. Now, I'll give you twenty minutes to shower and get changed before I drag you out of this house."

I could feel his smile against my palm and moved it slightly so he could say, "And if I say no?"

"You won't," I said with my cocky grin.

"Confident, aren't you?"

"Supremely. Because if you agree to Sebastian's day of fun, I'll give you Adam's night of debauchery to do whatever you want to me."

I meant it to be fun and flirty, but the instant my words hit the air, they sparked the latent heat between us until every inch of my skin felt like it had caught fire.

"Anything?" Adam whispered thickly, his lids lowered, gaze caught on my mouth.

I licked my lips to tease him before stepping away, walking backward with my hands in my pockets to contain my temptations. "Anything. Twenty minutes before your birthday begins for real. Hurry up."

Chapter Nineteen

Adam

I couldn't remember the last time I celebrated a birthday.

Maybe when I was eleven years old, the year before my mother died in a car accident, and all semblance of warmth left my family for good. She'd taken me to the seaside for the day without my father. That morning was the first time I ever surfed, the lesson bought as a surprise by my mum. It would be our secret because Lord Peter Andrew Yardley, Marquis of Pemberton, would never allow his heir to do something as pedestrian as surf.

I'd fallen in love instantly, just as Mum had known I would.

The cold of the water despite my wetsuit, the symphony of waves lapping against the board and crashing into the shore, the bright adrenaline of finally catching a little wave and standing poised on the surfboard as it carried me in like the tide.

It was euphoric.

After, we bought sweets in a local treat shop on the boardwalk, then browsed the little storefronts before grabbing sandwiches at a local café and eating them with our feet dangling over the stone pier.

To this day, the sound of seagulls calling and the scent of ocean brine brought a smile to my face.

Ironically, Savannah didn't care for the sea or its accruements. The sand got in everything, and her fair skin went straight to hot pink under the sun's glare. It was one of the reasons she resisted moving to LA even though there were so many opportunities in Hollywood. She preferred the cool, cultured elegance of London.

"You're being very quiet and *cupo*," Sebastian said beside me as he drove us in the Rolls through the streets of London to some surprise location.

I propped my elbow on the window frame and looked over at him because he was so fucking gorgeous it eased some of the turmoil still sitting like rancid meat in my gut. A lock of wavy ink-dark hair had fallen onto his forehead, and my fingers literally itched to push it back and cup that stubble-darkened, strong jaw. I'd never seen anyone with eyes like his, twin gold coins like something found in pirate ships and at the end of rainbows. They were fantastical and covetable and every time he looked at me, I felt a surge of greed. I wanted to own him, possess him, and fucking hoard him, a dragon with its treasure.

"*Cupo*?" I questioned.

"Sullen," he supplied with a sidelong glance. "Remember, you had twenty minutes to get your shit together before we commenced our day of fun. No bad thoughts on your birthday, Adam."

"Easier said than done," I muttered, but it did make me feel better just sitting with him in the car.

The smell of leather and Sebastian's spicy cologne were a strange aphrodisiac after our first rendezvous in a car. Part of me was tempted to close my tired eyes and listen to his voice as a kind of lullaby to ease me into sweet dreams.

"Fine, let's utilize Strasberg's emotional recall to help you out," Seb announced, unperturbed by my cranky arse. "What's one of your happiest memories?"

I hesitated, and he clucked his tongue.

"Uh, uh, uh, you owe me stories about your past, remember? In the garden at Pinewood Studios, I shared, and you did not."

I loosed a long, dramatic sigh that only made him grin in triumph.

"I was just thinking of one, actually," I murmured, turning my gaze out the window so I didn't have to watch the play of emotions on his expressive face when I told him about her. "The last birthday I actually celebrated. It was with my mum the year before she passed away."

Passed away was a bloody idiotic term. As if it was a choice. As if she took a left instead of a right at a fork in the road and walked to her demise.

She was torn away, not passed away. Ripped bloodily from my literal hands.

I didn't realize I was sharing that until the silence pressed hard against my eardrums, and they popped with a jaw-aching pressure. Even then, though, I didn't stop.

I wasn't sure why.

Why I was telling Sebastian about Juliet Holland Yardley when I hadn't even spoken her name aloud in years.

"She was lovely," I admitted to him, the scenery blurring outside my window into a grey watercolour mass. "Warm and vivacious enough to fill our fifty-room house with sunshine every day."

"Ah, so that's who you got the charisma from," he said, softly like he was afraid to puncture the atmosphere and lose the sense of a confessional we'd established.

I laughed, but it was only an exhalation of scorn. "I'm merely a weak replica. She was the original. She used to captivate people at dinner parties with her stories. I think she made most of them up, but she didn't hide it, and people didn't care. They just loved that she made them laugh."

I rolled my head against the seat rest to look at the man beside me, the words bubbling up my throat before I could swallow them down. "You make us laugh like that."

"I'm honoured by the comparison," he said solemnly, and it made an indent in my soul because Sebastian was so rarely solemn.

He was bright and beautiful and filled with wonder, a young man who had tasted misfortune but decided to focus on the positive in life instead of wallowing in misery. He was so admirable, this eighteen-year-old who shouldn't have lived as much life as he had, who shouldn't be sitting there like a warm hearth for me to rest my weary self in front of.

"She was too good for my father," I whispered, but I wasn't sure if I really meant *you're too good for me.*

He seemed to catch something in my tone, chin sliding to face me for a moment to gauge my expression. One hand fell from the steering wheel to clasp over my knee and squeezed.

"I'm not sure you have to be worthy of love," he protested. "I'm no expert, but I think love just exists. Outside of worth and currency and measurements. It's not something that can be quantified based on a set list or characteristics."

"Maybe not, but it can be earned. And he didn't earn it."

And I don't know how to earn you.

How could I when all I had to offer him was a life of secrecy and shame?

Because no matter what, I would never share my private

predilections with the public. It would be pouring gasoline on my career and setting it on fire.

It would be roasting myself alive on the burning tongues of thousands of people's mockery and criticism and cruelty.

I couldn't survive something like that.

It was all I could think of when he and Savannah had confessed their feelings for each other before Sebastian left for his trip to Naples, and it was all I could think of the entire time he was gone.

It was one of the reasons we'd fought, Savvy and me.

"Why can't we keep him?" she'd yelled at me. "Why can't you love what's good for you for once in your miserable life?"

They were both good questions, fair enough.

But loving what was good for you didn't make you worthy of its goodness.

Loving him didn't mean I had anything of value to give him.

"Hey," Sebastian called, shifting his hand into mine and threading our fingers together so they were clasped on my thigh. "It's a happy day, *sì*? If you want to remember your mother today, let's remember her with laughter."

I sucked in a deep breath through my teeth, trying to cleanse the gunk in my soul with the scent of Sebastian.

"Okay, I'm in your hands," I told him, clapping my other hand on top of our joined ones. "Be good to me."

"Always," he promised, solemn again, as an oath this time, and my joking tone felt rude in contrast. "Always, Adam."

We drove for four hours.

I wasn't expecting such a long road trip, but I also wasn't worried about it as time stretched out behind us. For once, I was not in charge, and I was not expected to perform. I was merely a passenger, driven by a man I trusted more than I cared to admit, even to myself.

Still, I was shocked when we turned off the motorway and passed a quaint painted sign that heralded our arrival in Croyde.

My gaze snapped to Sebastian, suspicion warring with something like unfiltered joy.

"How did you know?" I demanded.

Sebastian remained calm in the face of my snapping energy. "There's a painting of Croyde Bay in your study beside a photograph of you and your mother on a beach. I don't need to be Sherlock to tie the two together."

Air leaked from my mouth like a tire puncture. "Oh."

"Oh," he agreed, slowing to turn down the lovely streets of the oceanfront town.

"I haven't been back here since I was eleven."

"Well, twenty-nine is a good time to come back," he declared with a smile as he pulled his sunglasses out of his pocket and opened them with his teeth before sliding them on.

It was ridiculous how sexy I found everything he did.

It was ridiculous that my heart was flapping about my chest like a fish out of water, unable to process how kind and thoughtful a gesture he'd made by taking me here. The site of a clearly cherished childhood memory.

"It's not the whole surprise, though," he warned me slyly. "I hope you're a strong swimmer."

"Please," I scoffed. "I grew up in Cornwall. I practically swam before I walked."

"Good," he declared. "Because I'd hate for you to drown on your birthday."

I laughed at him, shaking my head even though his irreverence was one of the qualities I loved most about him.

Loved.

Loved.

Like a best mate, I rationalized a little frantically as he searched for a spot in the car park along the Bay.

Like a man loves a man who is also a friend.

NO, my soul screamed, don't lie.

Don't lie like you always lie.

Not about him.

The purest man I'd ever known.

The absolute *best* man I'd ever known, truth be told.

I'd had other male lovers.

School at Eton with bumbling boys of a similar age, all hormones and horniness. College at Oxford where experimentation was a widely established rite of passage not spoken of in the bright light of mornings after. In those brief military years, when the fear of getting caught amplified everything to dizzying heights. Gay and lesbian citizens had been allowed to enlist in the British Armed Forces since 2000, but it was still something most soldiers kept hushed up to avoid the likelihood of bigotry.

Then, Savannah, who had suggested our first threesome after I disclosed my membership at a popular BDSM club in London. She'd been addicted from the first. Two men lavishing her with attention was her ultimate kink, and one I was only too happy to indulge her in.

But I'd never had anything like I did with Sebastian.

Not with Gregory in school and not with Bryce in the Royal Armed Forces.

They'd been my friends and Bryce could have been something… more.

But only Sebastian had ever stirred this insatiable need that went beyond lust.

I found myself just wanting to… be with him.

Breathe the same air.

Watch the same film with our bodies pressed in one long line, shoulders to knees.

Witness the way he'd conquer the industry with his wit and beauty and warmth.

I wanted the privilege of living beside him, and I didn't want it to end.

Ever.

The thought knocked me upside the head with a resounding crash and stole the breath from me.

I didn't want Sebastian to move out and move along in a few weeks or months or years.

I wanted selfishly and earnestly for him to be ours—no, honestly, *mine*—forever.

"Adam?" His voice was distant like the crashing waves through my cracked open window. "Adam!"

I jerked out of my horrifying revelation and blinked at him blankly. "There's no need to yell at me. I'm sitting right here."

"Your mind was gone," he argued, but he wasn't irritated. Only concern marred his brow. "Maybe up in Yorkshire with your wife?"

My heart gave a hollow pang at the thought of Savannah up north. I was angry about her histrionics, but mostly, I was fatigued by them. As soon as a problem erupted between us, she fled in a flurry of drama so we never had time to actually talk through our issues.

I knew she'd come back when she was ready, pull me into bed

with sweet words and kisses that were her versions of an apology she'd never verbalize properly, and then we'd just keep on living as we'd done before.

For an American, Savannah had always been startlingly good at being British.

"Maybe," I admitted because it was easier to admit to that than the truth of my pining for him. "I promise, though, I've done enough brooding today. I am at your mercy."

"Oh?" Sebastian practically purred, eyebrow raised. "I think I'd like that."

I was a grown man, and I didn't think I'd blushed in ages, but I came close there, imagining what he might do to me if given full access and control.

A shiver curled like smoke up my back.

He laughed, catching the telltale movement. "C'mon, *vecchietto*, it's time to have some fun."

Of course, a plum spot in the car park was available, and he pulled in smoothly, jumping out of the car almost before he'd even put it in park. I followed more leisurely, pretending I wasn't uncharacteristically giddy at the chance of spending the day at the beach with him.

I leaned against the side of the car as he rummaged in the boot, reappearing with two plush beach towels, an unfamiliar cooler, and a book he held between his teeth because he was out of hands. I reached over to pluck it from his mouth.

"*Grazie*." He beamed at me, knocking the cooler against my thigh to push me along. "Let's go, or we'll be late. The surf peters off late in the afternoon."

"You do know I haven't a clue how to surf, right? I was *eleven* the last time I stood on a board."

"Oh, I'm counting on it," he teased, eyes flashing bright in the late spring sunshine. "If I'm going to look like a fool, I'd rather be in good company."

I laughed. "You arsehole. You think my idea of fun on my birthday is to look like a bloody idiot?"

"Yes," he said firmly as we walked down the path to the beach, and he toed off his trainers, waiting for me to do the same. "I think spending the day doing something new, where you aren't expected to look your best or be the best will be refreshing. You aren't Oscar award-winning actor Adam Meyers today. You're just a bloke having a good time with a friend at the beach."

Why did that sound so fucking dreamy?

Just a bloke at the beach.

Only, in my dreamiest fantasies, Sebastian wouldn't just be a mate; he'd be something like a… boyfriend.

Lord, that sounded trite to say as a grown man.

But it also sent a secret thrill trilling through my heart.

"Sound good?" he prompted me as he walked up to a surf shack at the edge of the sand.

"Perfect," I agreed, unleashing the grin I'd been holding back so he could see just how much the whole idea meant to me.

"*Bene*," Sebastian said as we walked into the store. "Because I'm thoroughly looking forward to seeing you knocked on your ass."

I was still laughing when a tall, slender girl with a thicket of blonde hair bounded over to Sebastian the moment we entered the shop. She was all elbows and knees poking out of an oversized vintage Dior tee and rolled-up boxer shorts.

"Seb," she called even though she was currently throwing her arms around his neck to give him an exuberant hug. "It took you long enough."

He chuckled, ducking her under the chin in a brotherly way. "I had to get the old man out of bed. Be happy we made it here at all."

The girl turned her smile on me, and I was shocked by its vibrancy. She had eyes the colour of concord grapes surrounded by a thick golden fringe of lashes. Crinkled with mirth, I thought they might have been the prettiest eyes I'd ever seen, second only to Sebastian's. She was just a kid with a gangly body and a face with features she still had to grow into, but years in the industry had taught me that she'd be a great beauty one day.

"Hi," she said, bouncing lightly on her heels as she stuck out a long-fingered hand for me to shake. "We've kinda met before, but not really. I'm Linnea Kai."

Miranda Hildebrand's daughter, I thought, but didn't say.

My own experiences had taught me that not everyone enjoyed being linked to their parents.

"Pleasure to meet you," I said instead, gripping her warm palm. "I'm Adam."

Her wide grin stretched wider. "Hi, Adam. Are you ready to surf?"

I shot a disgruntled look at Sebastian. "Well, I was until Sebastian told me he'd be laughing his arse off every time I fell off my board."

Linnea threw her head back and laughed, a throaty, frothy sound that made me grin. "Oh, he's just deflecting. You were in the RAF, and I've seen you horseback ride in movies. I bet you'll take to it easily. It's this big oaf"—she jerked her thumb at Sebastian, who mock glowered at her—"who I predict will swallow his fair share of ocean water."

I couldn't be sure if it was her age, clearly younger even than Seb, or because I had a whole day in front of me without posturing or posing or responsibility, but I felt like a teenager myself again.

"Is that right? Maybe we should place a bet on it, hmm?" I suggested, arching my brows at Seb. "Best surfer as declared by Linnea at the end of the day wins."

"Wins what?" he countered immediately, crossing his arms in a way that made his biceps bulge, testing the limits of his grey tee.

"A favor."

His brows rose too, and he took a slight step forward, crowding me slightly. "A favor?"

There was only a slight insinuation in his tone, but I matched it with my own slightly throaty, "Yeah."

"An *anything* favor?" he pushed because that was who Sebastian was.

He pushed me to test my limits but never to exceed them. It was funny that he could be so like Savannah in that way yet so different. He respected my boundaries and the landmines that littered my history that were so easily triggered today. Instead of pushing me forcibly beyond them, he held my hand and led me through them.

So even though it scared me to think about handing over control to anyone, I sucked in a deep breath and looked down my nose at him as if he'd insulted me. "Of course."

"Deal," he said instantly, taking my hand in a fierce grip before pointing at Linnea who was watching us with catlike intensity. "You stand as our witness."

"And very willing judge," she added, clapping her hands together. "Now, let's get you boys outfitted properly and get out there while there's still daylight."

FUCK, IT WAS COLD.

Even with a wetsuit, the Atlantic was frigid, and my feet were numb as they dangled in the water. We'd been at it for two hours already and even though I was fitter than most men, exhaustion had settled into muscles I didn't even know I had. Surfing looked so bloody easy when a professional did it, but it was challenging.

I watched as Linnea picked up the next wave, her long, thin arms slicing neatly through the surf to maintain pace with the wave before it crested, and then, smooth as butter, she dropped into the trough of water just as it started to curl forward. Even though the waves were relatively small to accommodate Sebastian and me as beginners, Linnea carved it up like the seasoned surfer she was.

"*Magnifica*," Seb murmured from my left as we watched her finish out the wave with a spray of water, the sunlight hitting the molecules so it looked like she passed through a rainbow and out the other side.

"Truly," I agreed, a little dazed by her elegance as she slid into shore and then began an easy pace back out to us beyond the break. "She's a surprising girl, isn't she?"

Nothing like her mother, which I was grateful for.

Miranda, like Savannah, loved to talk shop. Industry gossip and knowledge. Only, she wasn't as smart as my wife, not as successful, and her desperation was uncomfortably palpable.

There was nothing desperate about Linnea Kai. For a teenage girl, she was oddly self-assured, full of life and laughter that seemed bursting beneath her skin. There was only an occasional glimmer of something melancholy I caught when she watched Sebastian and I banter. A kind of longing that said maybe she was lonely.

Was it strange that I wanted to comfort her by divulging that sometimes I was lonely too?

"I hope you don't mind her being here. She offered lessons to me, and at the last minute, she was the only one I could think of who was free to help out."

"Not at all. As I said, she's surprising… in a good way. Very charming really, if a little exuberant," I noted, amused by the way she spoke wildly with her hands and seemed never to be still.

"More graceful at sea than on land," Sebastian told me, paddling closer so he could lock his foot with mine beneath the water. The little gesture warmed my chest like I'd swallowed the sun. "Just like you're more comfortable on stage or before a camera than not."

"Oh, you think you know me so well, do you?" I taunted, splashing water up into his face.

He only blinked again, and I had to watch the water bead in his pretty lashes and roll down the hard, bronzed expanse of his chest.

"I do," he told me seriously. "And everything I know, I like very much."

"You're just trying to distract me from my prize," I joked because I didn't want to talk about how well he knew me and how good it felt to be known by him.

Fun, I told myself, *fun. Not longing and pining and wanting to wrench my own heart out of my chest and force it into his hands.*

Fun.

Seb's full mouth twitched. "Maybe, I am. I'm very motivated to win."

"What will you ask for if you do?" I asked.

"Are you sure you want to know? Anticipation can make things so much sweeter."

"If it involves any part of your naked body and mine, I don't think it can get any sweeter."

He blinked at me, a little shocked, apparently, that I could be sweet.

"Okay, lazy bones, who's going next? Right now, I'd say Sebastian is leading the boards, but maybe if Adam gets one or two great rides under his belt…who knows?" Linnea called as she closed the distance between us.

She sat up on her violet longboard and grinned as she pushed her braided hair over her shoulder. "Well? What do you think, Meyers, have you got it in you to beat the youngin'?"

I laughed. "Jesus, between the two of you, you'd think I was eighty, not yet thirty."

"Prove us wrong, then," she coaxed. "It looks like a big swell coming in."

"If you don't care, though, I'll take the win very happily," Sebastian baited me with a waggle of his black brows.

"Oh, sod off," I muttered, flattening my torso to the board so I could paddle into position. "This old man is going to make you eat your words."

Sebastian snorted, but Linnea let out a whoop of support as I got into place, looking over my shoulder to time my strokes to catch the wave.

This was the easy part, getting caught up in the ridge of water and powering myself forward by my arm strokes. Even getting up, balancing my feet just so on the board to balance it over the moving current was muscle memory at this point in the day. I hopped up and into my athletic stance as the wave curled under the board.

It was the ride that kept tripping me up. I lacked the patience to let it carry me and kept maneuvering out of the wave too quickly. This swell was deeper than I'd thought, my stomach lurching as I dropped into the bowl.

This time, Sebastian's goading voice in the back of my mind, I took a deep breath and just… enjoyed it.

The wind was a cold slap against my salt-tight skin, the rush of water all I could hear, and the corrugated water before me the only thing in my sightline. I felt, for one brief, brilliant moment, like I was part of the wave, a piece of an ocean that stretched across the equator, between multiple continents, and occupied nearly a quarter of the water's surface on the planet.

I had never felt less like Adam Meyers and conversely, more like myself.

Before I realized it, I was sliding into shore still balanced easily on the board, the water burbling into white froth below it.

I blinked at the beach, the handful of people out on the sunny April day to enjoy the rare sunshine.

When I turned back to look at Sebastian and Linnea, they were both clapping. As I watched, Seb turned his fist in the air and gave two barks of celebration, and Linnea cupped her hands over her mouth to yell, "*Hell yeah, Meyers!*"

A shocked laugh spilled out of my mouth, growing louder the longer I let it take me, riding it just like the wave.

"Take that, you wanker!" I called out to Sebastian triumphantly.

And he laughed and laughed all the way until I made it back to them both beyond the break. When I did, he leaned forward to clap me strongly on the shoulder and drag me closer enough to hug me.

"*Bravissimo*," he whispered into my ear, his wet cheek against my own, stubble as rough as sand. "You are magnificent."

A small part of me wanted to pull away instantly, uncomfortable with any display of affection, even platonic, in public.

But I wasn't Adam Meyers today.

I was just a bloke out with a good mate in the surf.

So I leaned forward and hugged him back, clapping a hand over his back and pressing my cheek just a little harder into his. "*Grazie, amore.*"

He stilled at my use of the Italian pet name and then grinned as I pulled away. He was a bloody vision sitting on that board, strong thighs splayed, all that Italian tanned skin pulled tight over well-honed muscle and the fall of wet black hair over his forehead.

He was the magnificent one.

"High five." Linnea cut into my thoughts with her demand, hand lifted for me.

I clapped it and grinned, boyish contentment curling through my chest. "I crushed it, I know."

She laughed. "You did! All it took was removing the stick up your bum."

"Hey!" I retorted as Sebastian burst out laughing.

Linnea ducked my hands as I made to playfully push her off her board, but I wouldn't be deterred. She was tall, but so light I could pluck her off her board and haul her over to mine. She flailed a little, and I took advantage by cupping my hands in the ocean in order to splash her full in the face with the water.

She sputtered indignantly, but before she could retaliate, Sebastian caught on and sent a huge wave of water over her body.

"You bastards!" she crowed, diving off my board into the depths.

Sebastian and I locked eyes over the splash she made and grinned wickedly in tandem.

When she emerged, we were right behind her, pursuing her with shark-like intensity into the shallows, where we proceeded to have an all-out splash war like we were twelve years old. Something about them, their sunshine energy sloughed all the years and miseries of my life off my back and made me feel reborn with fresh enthusiasm. I tackled Sebastian to the sandy bottom and laughed until my belly ached when Linnea tickled him until he begged for mercy.

It was more fun than I'd had in ages, and I owed it all to Sebastian.

Chapter Twenty

Adam

By the time we entered London proper again, I was sleepy and warm with contentment, half-dozing against the passenger side window as Sebastian drove us competently through the dark streets. Coldplay played quietly through the speakers, a pleasant soundtrack to my lazily meandering thoughts. I didn't allow myself to dwell on anything dark or unpleasant, instead focusing on the best birthday I'd had in years.

We'd ended our surf lesson with the splash fight and then collapsed on the beach against sun-warmed towels to dig into the cooler Sebastian had packed back at home. Our cook made thick sandwiches filled with turkey, cucumber, and sprouts, and freshly made shortbread dipped on one side in bright lemon glaze. There was enough for Linnea, too, who entertained us both with chatter about her elite London day school and life back in Maui. Her parents had been teens when they had her and were not very much in love, so it was her father who fought for her and was granted custody.

It sent a pang through my heart, listening to her talk about her mother as if she was nearly a stranger. It was how I'd felt my entire life about my father, and the sense had only deepened when my mother died. Even though I'd just met the girl, I found myself oddly grateful that she had her father and uncles to love her well.

Everyone deserved someone to love them unconditionally.

"You're very quiet. Did I kill you with too much activity, old man?" Sebastian mocked gently, reaching over to squeeze my knee.

Before he could move away, I gripped it with one of my own, tracing the ridge of calluses across his palm just because I enjoyed his hands. They were so strong and wide palmed, unlike any man I'd been with before.

I wondered with a little wince if I'd only pursued more effeminate men because of some kind of internalized homophobia. To be fair, Savannah had always been the Venus flytrap, catching suitable men for us to play with, but still. I resolved to do better.

I'd never be comfortable… coming out or anything of the like.

But I could do better for myself, at the very least.

Be a little more honest and a little more courageous.

"I had a brilliant time," I admitted baldly. "I think it might be the best birthday I ever had."

"And it's not over yet," Sebastian promised with a wink. "Though I am pretty salty that you ended up winning that favor. You don't have any need for one! We both know I'd do anything you'd ask. It's me who needed a little help."

"Anything I asked?" I echoed, my mind plummeting to dirty depths instantly. "Should we test that, do you think?"

"What did you have in mind?"

"Hmm," I hummed, tapping the slight divot in my chin as I pretended to think about it. "I do have a fondness for putting you on your knees. Usually it's for Savannah's pleasure, but I think it might be time I put you to use myself. I've wondered how that beautiful mouth would look wrapped around my cock. The last time, Savvy's pretty cunt was in the way of my viewing pleasure."

Sebastian's tongue flicked over his bottom lip, and his gaze darted to mine as he turned left. "It is surprising how much I liked the taste of you. The feel of you in my mouth."

My cock kicked in the confines of my trousers at the husky timbre of his voice saying those words to me.

"The idea of coming down your throat has me instantly hard," I admitted, palming my thickening erection for him. "But I'd hate to pass up playing with your tight arse again. Maybe even finally fucking you."

A small tremor rattled his broad shoulders.

"Would you like that?" I asked, voice hardening into that tone that came over me when I slid into my dominance.

"Yes," he admitted quietly. "I can't seem to stop thinking about it. I'm nervous, but I've gotten myself off in the shower to the fantasy one too many times."

I groaned. "Sometime I'll make you jerk off in the shower with me to the fantasy and then make you lick your cum off the tiles just because I can."

"*Che cazzo*, why is that so hot?" he asked, stopping in the driveway for the gates to open and leaning forward to nip playfully at my lower lip.

His enthusiasm was fuel to my fire, sparking even hotter fantasies. Fucking him in the shower, tying his wrists to his ankles so he'd be open for whatever the fuck I pleased, teasing him until he was a sweaty, trembling mess, fucking him while he fucked Savvy.

My vision almost whited out at the flurry of images in my mind's eye.

"Has anyone told you that you are a very dirty, very dangerous man?" Sebastian asked as he pulled forward into the courtyard and parked.

When he turned to face me, the lamp light from the fixtures over the garage caught his features in stark black-and-gold relief. Looking at him made it hard to breathe.

I'd worked with beautiful people for nearly a decade, and none had this effect on me.

Maybe because beneath the surface of his beauty lay a heart even more lovely than its packaging.

"You bring me to my knees," I admitted, possessed by some feeling that had seized my soul and urged me to take his chin in my fingers and bring him in for the kind of kiss I never gave any man.

I pressed my mouth to his, soft and open but without invading with my tongue. I tasted his lower lip, trailed my tongue over the top to feel its plush texture, and dragged it between my teeth to test its plumpness. Only when he moaned, hand reaching up to clutch at the back of my head, did I tilt his chin and slide my tongue into his mouth to tangle with his own. He tasted of the iced tea he'd bought from a petrol station and of sea salt still clinging to his skin. His scent swarmed my senses, sun-baked and salted musk and the remnants of the spicy cologne he always wore.

I wanted to bury myself inside him, beneath all that lovely skin. It seemed, at that moment, the only way I would ever find peace.

"In another universe," he pulled back just enough to whisper, the movement of his lips still pressed to mine as if he wanted to feed me the words. "We'd be together. I'd love you here in the shadows but also in the light. I'd walk down the beach holding your hand, and it would be the rightest thing in the world. I'd tell people *la luna è la mia amante*, the moon is my lover, and I'd be so proud."

"Sebastian," I muttered, gut-wrenched because wasn't that so bloody lovely?

Wasn't that exactly what I'd been wanting all day, to reach across the sand and take his rough-palmed hand in mine?

Wasn't that what I'd secretly yearned for all my life? The other yin to the yang of loving a woman. Both together, balanced and precious inside my soul?

Hadn't I been waiting for a declaration of affection since the moment he told my wife he loved her? Hadn't I yearned with a kind of desperation that made my chest ache and my breath come too short and too quick?

"Have I told you that?" he murmured, searching my eyes with a faintly amused smile on his lips. "You have this pull over me the way the moon does over the tides. It's elemental and terrifying, and I wouldn't change it for anything."

"I can't—" I started to say, the words cut into pieces by the blades stuck through my throat.

"In another universe," he agreed with a sweet, sad smile before kissing me again with both of his big hands framing my face.

I held both of his wrists as if I could anchor him to me forever. I wanted to protest even though it was true. Such fantasies were possible only at another time or another place, and maybe even then, only for other people.

"It's enough to love you," he admitted. "If you'll let me."

I swallowed around the stone in my throat so hard I winced. No matter how hard I tried, my voice wouldn't cooperate. So I nodded and hoped it would be enough.

Even though it wasn't.

Even though I'd never be able to give him even an ounce of what he deserved.

Yet the smile he gave me was absolutely beatific, bright as sunshine trapped between his lips.

"*Bene*," he whispered, almost to himself, a little giddy. "*Molto bene*."

"It's not much."

"I'll be the judge of that," he declared. "It may be your birthday, but you're the one giving me the best present. C'mon, let's get dressed. There's more to come that will hopefully tip the scales."

HE TOOK ME SOMEWHERE I'D NEVER been before, which was a surprise, given I thought I'd been everywhere worth going in the city.

Bernardi's was a tiny hole-in-the-wall Italian place in Shoreditch that Sebastian had discovered whilst living in the neighborhood with his *four* flatmates. The exterior was a plain, dirtied white stucco, but the interior felt as if it had been transported straight from Italy itself. Lifelike fake olive trees studded the interior, string lights, and terra cotta planters that perfumed the air with rosemary, oregano, and basil. It was busy, a mingling of languages and accents raised merrily over clinking glasses of big bowled red wine and traditional ceramics.

Sebastian beamed at me when I told him it was magical, and I felt the echo of that grin in my chest. I rubbed at my breastbone as I followed him to the table, a little concerned I was turning into some kind of sap.

Stoicism, practicality, and conservatism were hallmarks of my family, and while I'd shunned most of their principles when my father remarried, I'd still been raised with those ideals.

It was hard to shake the fact that I was out for dinner with a man even though I'd dined with countless men over the years. It felt different with Sebastian even though I knew no one was aware of our relationship. It just seemed so… unlikely that casual observers couldn't tell that I was head over arse in love with him.

I was so caught up in him, risking a look at his arse in those black trousers, that I didn't notice a woman was already sitting at the table.

Savannah watched me move toward her with an uncharacteristically guilty expression. Her short cloud of pale curls was caught up in a black velvet ribbon at her crown that matched the Audrey Hepburn style dress and pearls she wore. She'd always been a vision, even before she took to refinery and elegance—when wearing jeans she bought at Target instead of Walmart was the height of her fashion. Sometimes I missed that girl with the Southern drawl, who ate with her elbows on the table and sang along loudly and off-key whenever Dolly Parton came on the radio.

She'd always been a vision, and she always would be, through all her iterations, because Savannah was a woman who knew her worth and demanded others take note of it. It made her wonderfully compelling, and even after years of marriage, the cracks that had sprung up between us, I felt it still, staring at her in the low light of an Italian restaurant we'd never be caught dead in if not for the magnetism of Sebastian Lombardi.

The sight of her hurt as much as it healed.

She'd caused me more pain than I wanted to admit with her barbs late last night, but ironically, she was the only one who could make them all better.

I wanted her to hold me close and whisper promises into my ear.

I won't push you so hard.

You're more than your career.

I'd love you even if you retired tomorrow.

You are my priority.

I blinked hard to dispel the desire.

Even in a day as brilliant as this one, that was one fantasy too far.

The fact that she was even *here* was miracle enough.

She wasn't one for contriteness or apologies.

Obviously, Sebastian had worked his special brand of magic and brought her back.

"Adam," she said softly, so softly I couldn't even hear her over the cacophony of the restaurant, but I'd long ago memorised the shape of my name in her mouth.

She stood from the table as Sebastian and I paused beside it. We were tucked into a far corner behind carefully arranged olive trees and a wood-panelled screen, so we had a modicum of privacy.

"Another birthday present," Sebastian announced with a little encouraging smile in my direction. "One that couldn't be missed today."

"No," Savannah agreed quietly, but she stepped forward so that only a sliver of space existed between us, charged with all the words we never said. "Your wife should be with you on your birthday. That is… if you want me?"

The hesitation was new and, irritatingly, endearing. Why was it so easy to forgive her for her cruelty? Because I knew that she'd been brought up without love and didn't speak its language fluently? That I could relate to that and make exceptions for it because it was still better than I'd ever been loved before?

That was, until Sebastian.

Who'd shown up in our lives with an entirely new lexicon of love that he'd been teaching us slowly but surely the last five months.

And now, well, I wasn't sure what Savannah and I had between us was enough. If we could apply what Seb was teaching us to our tattered relationship or if we would both continue to focus on our newer, healthier one with him.

"I want you," I told her, surprised by the rawness of my words.

But it was the truth.

Healthy or not, I'd always want Savannah.

She was the one who took a brooding, restless soldier returned from war with too much baggage to ever unpack and focused his attentions on the one thing he'd ever felt passionate about.

Acting.

It was Savannah who found my first auditions, who sweet-talked the director of *Hamlet* into letting the unknown actor, but well-known aristocrat, star in his modern adaptation of the Shakespeare classic.

It was Savannah who recognized a need for male companionship and indulged me in threesomes that quenched both our thirsts.

Savannah had made a man with dreams into a man people dreamed *about.*

She had made me relevant on my own terms.

Not my father's or my family history's or my best mate, the Crown Prince of England, Arthur's.

My own.

So, of course, I loved her.

The way an artist loved his muse.

Or more, the way Pinocchio must have loved Geppetto, maybe.

I reached for her, sliding my hand into the hair at the back of her neck to bring her up onto her tiptoes for a kiss. My lips slid over the gloss there, vanilla scented, and my tongue found the familiar taste of her mouth.

The kiss was more than an apology. It felt like a promise between us both to do better.

When we broke apart, she smiled at me with a tenderness I hadn't seen in ages.

"Happy birthday, my darling," she breathed, reaching up to clean the remnants of lip gloss off my mouth with her thumb in a gesture she'd completed for me a million times in our lives.

The repetition made it more poignant.

I bit the pad of her thumb playfully. "Thank you for the gift of your presence, Savvy."

"*Eccelente*," Sebastian crowed, clapping his hands together before pulling out Savannah's chair for her and then moving swiftly around the table to do the same for me. My wife giggled at his enthusiasm, and I was grateful to him for breaking the serious note into a lighter cadence. "Now, we can feast."

Chapter Twenty-One

Sebastian

Dinner was *bellissima.*

Not only because the food was almost as good as Mama's and the restaurant always made me feel like I was coming home. But because both Savannah and Adam seemed lighter than air, floating in their seats, smiling freely and laughing openly throughout the entire meal.

It was as if, in the carnage of their epic argument, they had recouped something lost to them for a while. There was an *ease* between them that I realized hadn't existed before.

It was hard not to hope it was due to me.

But then, I was an actor and a writer. It was impossible for me not to make connections between the two, to romanticise my supporting role in the play of their lives.

After spending the entire day with Adam, seeing how happy and carefree the usually controlled, ludicrously busy Brit had been just playing in the surf and sand, chatting without intention about films we liked and places we'd visited, had been a revelation.

For me, sure, but more so, I thought, for *him*.

When was the last time he'd had a day of fun just because? I wondered.

Even when we'd gone that first time to Pinewood Studios, he'd insisted it was a business excursion and not a date.

When I'd finally told him, in a roundabout way, that I loved him, he'd told me immediately he couldn't.

Was there anything he really wanted outside of acting that Adam Meyers let himself have?

There was even a quality of reservation between the married couple.

A hesitancy to share their true selves with each other.

I thought with Adam, it was about not knowing how.

With Savannah, it was about fear.

Either way, that night felt like we'd entered a new stage.

From arrangement to relationship, one where I wasn't just the rented boy toy but a real partner. I knew I'd never stand beside them both on a red carpet, but what did that matter, really?

Public acknowledgment wasn't needed to validate the connection of human hearts.

Only acknowledgement between the three of us was enough.

And for the first time, I felt physically and emotionally linked to both of them and them to each other.

So it wasn't surprising that the moment we fell into the car together, clothes were coming off.

I had to drive us safely back to the house in Chelsea, but I still snuck glimpses at Savannah, a little wine drunk and slightly uncoordinated because of it, as she fumbled with the buttons of Adam's dress shirt. He had only a smattering of golden chest hair, his treasure trail sparkling in the low lights as Savvy pried open his belt and zipper to reveal the base of his thickening cock.

Adam crossed his hands behind his head, arm muscles bulging, abs rippling as they contracted. When I looked up at his reflection in the rearview mirror, he was grinning wolfishly at me, and I knew the show was for my benefit.

Savannah fell on him like a starving woman, licking every inch of his torso before dipping her head to swallow his cock straight down her throat.

"Beautiful," Adam praised even as he reached up her skirt, gripped her panties, and shimmied them down her hips. "Now, get on the ground between my thighs so Sebastian can see your pretty pussy start to drip down your thighs as you suck me down."

I swallowed thickly as we stopped at a light, and Savvy swiveled her hips to show me that pink slit, already glistening. Her bobbing head obscured the sight of his cock stretching her lips wide, but I turned down Chopin to hear the lewd sounds of her slurping and sucking on his shaft.

By the time we reached the house, Adam's hands were clenched tight in Savvy's hair as he fucked her mouth ruthlessly. A trail of wet had seeped down the inside of her thigh, and as soon as I turned the car off, I used my finger to clean it up and lick it up.

"Delicious," I praised her as Adam pulled her off his dick with a *pop* of released suction. When she turned to me, her lips were puffy and carnation red.

I leaned forward to taste Adam on her tongue and moaned at the flavor.

"Inside, kids," Adam ordered, already stuffing his hard length uncomfortably behind his trousers for the short jaunt inside.

Savvy giggled at the effort, but I shut my door on the sound so I could open hers. The giggle cut off with a squeal when I ducked inside and dragged her out into my arms, holding her like a princess.

Her eyes sparkled in the bright silver light of the full moon overhead. "Sebastian, you are a teenage romantic."

"And proud of it," I declared, bending down to nip at Savannah's mouth.

Adam chuckled, a smoky sound that curled around me like vapour, absolutely intoxicating. I followed him across the pavers and up into the house all the way to the bedroom.

As Adam turned on the lamps around the room, Savvy laughed when I placed her on the bed with a flourish and then dipped into a little bow.

"Very good service," she praised with a cheeky grin.

God, I loved to see her like that. Loose limbed and playful like she wasn't anywhere else.

"It's about to get much better," Adam promised. "Undress him."

Savannah bit her lip, eyes instantly darkening as she got up on her knees on the mattress to reach for my shirt buttons. As she slowly revealed my torso to her gaze, Adam adjusted the chair that usually sat in the corner to a position right in front of the bed. He sat in it like an emperor with God-given rights—strong thighs splayed, back leaned comfortably against the brocade silk back so the entire length of his torso was on display.

As Savvy undid the buttons of my shirt, he undid the buttons of his.

We were revealed at the same moment, eyes locked on each other.

He left the shirt open but pushed to the sides, a white frame for the golden skin of his carved chest and belly. His abs seemed deeply etched by the shadows cast by the low, honeyed lamp light, and his hair was cast in pure gold.

He looked otherworldly, something too powerful to be contained by the earth.

Savannah pushed the fabric of my shirt from my shoulders, but before it could fall, Adam drawled in that cool, posh accent, "Keep the shirt around your forearms, Sebastian. Don't let it fall."

"And if I do?" I countered, just to see the muscle flex in his square jaw, to watch the predatory gleam in his eye as he leaned forward on his forearms to fix me with his stare.

"Then I'll punish you," he said, enunciating each word so they had teeth. "I haven't done that yet because you've been so good for us. But I could… would you like that, Savannah?"

She pouted, her mouth painted poppy red. "Only if I can have my fun first."

He chuckled darkly. "Well then, you better be good so Savannah has a reason to touch you. Stand still and keep the shirt up, Sebastian."

"Yes, sir," I murmured, already losing myself to the fog of arousal that spilled through the room.

I liked this.

The submission to sensation.

It was hard to give up the final pieces of my insubordination, the same fiery obduracy that had kept me away from the Mafia in my youth. But once it was done, I felt relief like slipping into a cool, clean river. Washed clean of past horrors and current responsibilities.

I was just a body in the most beautiful way a physical form could be.

Filled with pleasure, accentuated by touch, used for love.

Savvy's silken hands traced over every inch of my torso, tested the flats of my nipples, and tugged slightly at the hair leading from my naval.

"It's my birthday," Adam said, as if it just occurred to him. "So why don't you unwrap my present?"

Our lover grinned, teeth cutting into the edge of her smile as she lowered her hands to my belt and made quick work of opening my trousers. With one hasty push, she shucked them and my boxer briefs down my thighs, where they pooled at my ankles.

My erection slapped against her face, smearing a trail of precum over her cheek.

She leaned back on her heels, finger tracing the line of slick so she could bring it to her mouth with a hum of approval. My cock kicked between us, and she gave a breathy laugh of satisfaction as she ran a fingernail down its length.

"So thick," she murmured. "I love being split open on this."

A rumble moved through my chest.

"I need a birthday card," Adam demanded, suddenly beside us, tossing a black tube to the linen cover beside his wife. "Write one on his skin."

Before he moved away, Adam ran his hand down my flank the way an owner might test his horseflesh. It was propriety and condescending somehow.

It shouldn't have made me moan, maybe, but I was beyond should nots and shame.

Savvy undid the top of the lipstick and reapplied it thickly to her lips, her resulting smile slicked as if with blood, glistening and primal. She reached up to score her nails down my chest as she set her lips to the pulse point in my neck.

"Your heart beats so fast when I have my hands on you," she murmured. "Does it excite you to have me like this?"

The bed squeaked as Adam got on his knees on the mattress behind Savannah, and he began to undress her with perfunctory motions.

She didn't lose focus.

Her red lips marked my throat and left a trail to each pec, a rosy rim around each nipple. Unsatisfied, she let Adam push her dress down her arms and then reached for the lipstick again, using it to trace vivid lines around my abdominals and then signing the work with a flourish of her own name.

"Mine," she whispered with a fevered intensity that matched the dark, glazed intent in her eyes.

"And mine," Adam reminded her with a sharp smack to her now bare ass. His legs were to either side of her kneeling form, one hand holding her hip as he gave her cheek another spanking. "This is *my* present tonight, Savannah. You're just preparing him for me."

Her hesitation was only slight, but it was there.

Adam spanked her again, harder, so she let out a little gasp, and her nails scored down the muscles arrowing to my groin.

"Don't be greedy," he scolded. "I'll sit you on his face to muffle his cries when I finally slide into that tight, hot arse. You'll love drowning him in your juices."

"Yes," she hissed, wiggling her bottom back to get more attention even as she used the lipstick to write "Adam's Gift" on the other side of her signature.

He spanked her again. "Get to work. I want his cock dripping like a broken faucet. Show him how well you take cock down your pretty throat, sweetheart."

She took my dick in both her hands, clearly marvelling at the heft and girth. It was the way a student of art might look at a sculpture or an astronomer the night sky. So much wonder and gratitude, and it was all for *me*.

"Suck it," I told her, my voice guttural with lust. "Mark me up with that lipstick like I've wanted you to do since the first time I picked you up in the town car."

Glee lit her expression. My *duchessa* loved to be praised and admired.

Mouth open lewdly wide, she slid the head of my cock over her tongue and straight to the back of her throat. When she hit the base of my shaft, she sealed her red lips around the skin, leaving a brilliant red mark.

And then she did it again and again, moving back each time just a little so that my shaft was covered from root to head in concentric circles like the rings of a tree in her mark.

"So gorgeous," she whispered to herself as she lapped at my leaking slit. "I could suck you all night long."

"You do it so beautifully," Adam praised as he played with her wet pussy.

Wet, because even though I couldn't see it, I could hear the play of his fingers stretching and pumping through her soaked channel.

"Do you want to prep him for me, sweetheart?" he asked her, running one hand down her spine even though his gaze was locked with me. "Do you want to stretch him on your little fingers to get him ready for my big cock?"

We both *shuddered.* I felt as if my bones might vibrate out of my body at the thought of queenly Savannah doing something so shocking to me.

"Yes," she whispered, her mouth obviously dry as she licked her smeared red mouth, eyes fixed on my cock but far away, imagining it. "Yes, please, sir."

"Excellent," Adam praised darkly, moving away from her to stand. "I want you to feel debased, Sebastian. I want to humiliate you a little because I know you'll enjoy it. Will you let me?"

"Yes," I agreed before he'd even finished talking. "Yes, sir."

The grin that captured his handsome face should have been illegal in every country, a weapon of mass destruction.

"Then get on your knees on the bed and brace on your forearms."

Warm shame pooled in my belly at the order because I'd be so… prone. It was how I most loved to fuck Savannah. There was something primal about the pose, something very willing to be taken presented on all fours with hips canted and thighs spread to accommodate another body between them.

But I did as he ordered me because there was something elemental between us. He was the moon, and I was the tide helpless against his magnetic pull. I'd do as he bade me for the rest of time if he let me.

My head hung between my shoulders as Savannah adjusted on the bed behind me, taking that spot left open between my thighs. The first touch of her hands over my ass made me flinch, but she hushed me like a spooked horse.

"You're beautiful," she admitted in a cracked voice. "Stunning like this."

She continued to smooth her hands over my ass and thighs, soothing me with light touches. After a moment, I felt myself relaxing, previously unaware of the tension I'd been carrying.

"I know something that will distract you." The voice came from my right, a husky, rich timbre that moved through me like warmth from a fire.

I turned my head to see Adam standing completely nude beside the bed. He was perfectly proportionate, tall and muscled without being bulky, covered in golden skin and golden hair. It was shocking, not only because his glory never grew stale but because he was so rarely fully naked when we played. He liked the power trip of remaining at least partially dressed.

But this was his birthday, and I could tell by his little grin that was exactly why he was in his birthday suit.

I grinned back, surprised by the laughter in my throat during such a vulnerable moment.

But this was one of the reasons I loved them.

Because even when I felt small, they found ways to make me feel seen and somehow all the more beautiful for it.

He stepped forward, and I realized there was a ring of red around the base of his cock from Savvy's mouth. His fist wrapped around the base so he could paint the wet tip of it over my parted mouth.

"You're going to play a game while Savannah plays with you," he told me. "Trying to erase Savvy's mark with your mouth."

I'd rarely had the opportunity to play with Adam's fat dick because Savvy was such a greedy lover. I found myself shockingly excited to try to take that shaft to the back of my throat. In fact, my mouth watered at the thought, and I opened my mouth instantly.

Adam sighed as he got on his knees in the bed so I wouldn't get a crick in my neck and then slowly fed me his cock. His other hand sank into the thick hair on my head and used it to slowly pull me forward on the long, long length of him.

"Swallow when you want to gag," he taught me imperiously, a lord teaching his serf to please him.

A full-body shiver rippled through me.

Savannah took advantage of the moment to press lube-slick fingers to my opening. She didn't penetrate, but I still startled a little, moaning around Adam.

"Hush, she's just going to open you up nice and easy for me," Adam soothed, but it wasn't soothing because his words were cold and heavy, a collar around my throat. "Focus on pleasing me. All I want you to think about is taking all of me into your throat. It's okay if you choke on it. I want you to."

In perfect unison, they pushed into my body. The weight of

Adam's dick on my tongue made me salivate, the stretch of my lips almost uncomfortable but somehow one of the sexiest sensations I'd ever had. Savannah's thin fingers felt strange as she pressed them into my rim, a sting followed by a low burn. It felt wrong for a moment, wildly so.

The discomfort would have thrown me completely out of my headspace if it wasn't for Adam's cock channeling even deeper at the entrance of my throat.

"Swallow," he reminded me and pressed farther.

I wanted to choke, eyes watering, breath cut off, but I trusted him enough to heed his order, and I swallowed. My throat opened up around him, and he slid down until my nose was pushed against the wiry curls at his base.

"Fuck," he groaned, elongating the words in three syllables. "This is exactly what I want for my birthday."

The praise settled over me and sunk beneath my skin. I could feel myself relaxing again, softening around Savvy's persistent fingers so that when she slowly started to thrust two in and out of me, they felt almost… good.

"That's it," Adam said, the cold Dom gone and, in his place, a warm, complimentary lover. His fingers roamed over my head, pulling at my hair, tracing my ears, dipping down to cup my hollowed cheeks and press his thumbs to meet his cock stuffing my mouth full.

It was like he couldn't get enough, deep enough, close enough.

Savannah pet my flank and muttered her own praise, but it was softer, like she was transfixed by the sight of her fingers inside me.

"Don't touch yourself, Savannah." Adam's words lashed across my back at his wife. "This is about what I want. And I want you *aching* for cock. We've spoiled you too much. Given in to your greedy ways, but tonight, you will wait."

I moaned as Savannah bent forward to press an opened mouth kiss to my ass just beside her fingers. "Yes, sir."

"Good girl," he praised. "I'm almost ready to replace your fingers with my cock. But let's make sure it's nice and wet, shall we, Seb?"

Without waiting for a response, he shifted his grip into my hair again and carefully began to fuck my mouth.

I didn't want careful.

I wanted a messy, hard fuck. I wanted to touch each other like we never touched Savannah, rough and desperate and animal.

I gripped Adam's ass in one hand, the other still propping me up, and squeezed so he'd fuck my face the way I wanted.

When his hands spasmed in my hair, I groaned in confirmation and then groaned again when he started to lose himself in my throat. He was a vocal lover, and I loved to hear him curse and moan and whisper filthy praise that rained like gold on my skin.

Savannah started to fuck me harder, too, her fingers curling into some place inside me that had little sparks of pleasure shooting straight up my spine.

By the time Adam pulled away with a rough "*Enough!*" and stood beside the bed, we were all panting.

All so close to coming, I knew it would only take seconds.

"Savannah, up here on your back with your legs spread. Sebastian is going to sink his nice big cock inside you, but he isn't going to fuck you until I'm seated deep inside him. And then we are going to fuck you together."

Even in her haste, Savvy was all elegance, sliding from the bed behind me with a hand trailing up my spine and then dropping as she took her place before me like an offering. It felt so strange, in a way I knew it always would, to be offered such a gift by such a man.

But then, tonight and every night, they reminded me I was both gift and giver as much as they were.

My cock was wet with precum and still red from Savannah's lipstick as I gripped it too tightly and notched it at her swollen entrance. She practically sucked me inside, reaching for me with needy hands, locking her legs around my own like vines so that I pressed along every inch of her slim, feminine form.

"*Cazzo*, you feel like heaven," I told her, burying my face in her scented hair to ground myself as pinwheels of pleasure spiralled through me.

She held me, anchored me, as Adam moved around the bed behind me and took up her previous post.

Adam was not so polite.

He slapped the inside of my thigh so I would spread my legs farther, and then, satisfied, he went straight for my slick entrance with more lubricant.

My entire body juddered like a failing engine as he smoothed his fingers around my rim, dipping just inside to test and stretch and play. I'd never known there were so many nerves there, but he was playing them all like a fucking conductor of his symphony.

Savannah pushed her hands through my hair soothingly. "You're so sexy. I don't think I've ever known someone so beautiful."

I groaned again when his fingers slid smoothly inside me–*Adam was inside me*—and twisted against that bundle of nerves Savvy had glanced by once or twice.

He lit me up from the inside out.

I gasped as he pressed into me, his chuckle dark and rough as he started to fuck me with one hand while the other tested the play of muscle in my glutes.

"So fucking sexy," he echoed. "I can't wait to sink into this heat and fuck you."

"Do it," I ground out. "Do it, now."

"No."

"Yes," I barked, bucking back against his fingers and then hissing as I pushed forward into the wet, sucking heat of Savvy's pussy. "*Vaffanculo*, Adam, I'll come like this."

"No," he commanded, slapping his hand down on my ass so sharply pain ricocheted through me. "Not until I give you permission."

But he took pity on me.

Maybe because I could feel his hand shake with need before he gripped my hip to elevate me slightly, and then the hot, wet press of his cock was suddenly at my entrance.

I squeezed my eyes shut, almost overdosing on sensation, a little terrified of what would come next.

Adam plastered himself along the line of my body, sandwiching me between my two lovers so he could whisper in my ear, "Now, you're really ours."

He slid into me straight to the hilt.

I howled, a wolf crying to the moon. But it wasn't a baleful sound.

No, it was one of glory.

Because as Adam filled me up and I filled Savannah, I felt connected to two living, beautiful souls in a way I never had before. In a way I never wanted to again with anyone else so long as I lived and breathed.

I'd found perfection.

The tight, aching stretch of Adam inside me was mind-blowingly erotic.

I felt my mind dissipating in the wave of pleasure.

"Fuck," I groaned at the same time as Adam when he pulled out slowly, only to spear me again with his cock.

The thrust ground me into Savannah, who keened and leaked all over me down onto the bedspread.

"Oh yeah," Adam almost crowed, sounding vaguely drugged, high off the pleasure of fucking me and fucking me into his wife. "You both may come whenever you need to. Such good, sweet sluts for me."

I sealed my panting mouth against Savannah's throat, tasting her rabbiting pulse with my tongue and then my teeth as her cunt spasmed around me with every thrust.

"God, I love to be fucked," Savannah cried out.

God, I thought dazedly, *so do I.*

"I'm going to fill you so full of cum you'll be dripping for days," I grunted in her ear, finding the last of my wherewithal to reach between us and palm her absolutely drenched cunt, framing the place where I was wedged inside her swollen folds. "Would you like that, *duchessa*? Stuffed full of cock and, even after, stuffed full of cum."

"God, yes," she called out as she climaxed, body arching into me like a bow, mouth opened on a silent scream, and cunt fucking milking me for everything I was worth.

I cursed between my teeth as fire erupted at the base of my spine where Adam was fucking me ruthlessly now, in a way I'd feel for weeks.

"Fill her up," he demanded, driving into me so hard I lost my breath.

My sanity.

"Fill her up before I fill you up just the same," he promised me.

And that was it.

I closed my eyes as terrifying pleasure collided with every molecule of my body, breaking me apart on an atomic level. Everything went white, then black then came back to life in brilliant, eye-searing colour as I spilled every drop of cum in my balls into Savvy's still grasping pussy.

Adam came seconds later with a roar of triumph, slamming into me one last time, hands with a steel viselike grip against my hips, breath in my ear as he filled me up with cum for the first time in my life.

We lay there shivering and shuddering with aftershocks of pleasure. I was pressed between them like flowers between the pages of a book—hot, sweaty, and bound to them in ways I would never want to change.

"*Vi amo*," I said because the moment demanded it.

It truly seemed that we were one soul divided into three different bodies.

And at least for that moment, they must have agreed because almost in unison, they both kissed either side of my mouth, their tongues sweeping each other's as they made to touch mine.

Each time we did this, I emerged a little bit different. A gradual process cut into segments with the same outcome as a caterpillar turning into some fire-drawn moth inside a cocoon.

And I wasn't just in love with them for showing me this new side of myself.

I was falling in love with myself for the first time in my life, as well.

Chapter Twenty-Two

Adam

It happened on a Monday, the perfect time to hit the news cycle.

TMZ was the first to report it, but it didn't matter much. The other outlets followed in seconds.

I loved a lot of things about Britain, but the tabloids were not one of them.

In the months since my birthday, things had been good.

Good in a way I didn't think it had ever been before.

Good in a way I should have known was too wonderful to last long.

I had just wrapped filming for *The Devil Cares* with a bone-deep feeling that it was the best performance of my life. Freddie Bannerman was one of the most complicated characters I'd ever had to embody. I relished the challenge, but I knew without Savvy and Sebastian at home waiting for me every late night or early morning, I would have ended the shoot run down and miserable. Instead, I got to recharge my batteries and remind myself who I was every time I sat down for a meal with them or fell into bed with them at the end of the night.

The carriage house was Sebastian's closet and occasional office, but for the most part, we'd all given up the pretense that he wouldn't spend every night with us. Our marital bed felt empty without his warm, big body pinning Savannah and me close.

Sebastian and Andrea were deep into preproduction for *Blood Oath*, having finalized the storyboard, shooting locations in New York and Italy, and finally, casting. He was barely our driver anymore, but neither Savannah nor I said a word. They were due to start filming in New York next month, and while we hadn't spoken about the logistics, I fully expected both Savannah and I to go with him for at least part of the scheduled shooting there. Consciously or not, we had left time carefully marked out on the calendar around those dates.

Whatever semblance of our original deal remained, it was that we'd promised Sebastian we would get his career off the ground, and it was a promise we both took as seriously as any work-obsessed industry people would.

It was our own version of a blood oath.

Neither of us would be happy, I knew, until Sebastian held his first Oscar aloft, the golden of the statue a perfect match for those beautiful eyes that seemed to see more of me every single day.

But it was Sebastian's birthday, his nineteenth, which made both Savannah and I feel ancient. So we all took the day off and went to a King's Cross United football match because they were Seb's favourite British team. In fact, Iker Ferrera and Sebastian had become fast friends after I'd introduced them a few months ago, and he'd become a frequent visitor at our Chelsea home. We were less careful around him, but only because I'd met him at the Dionysus Club, and he had a few kinky secrets himself.

We'd surprised our lover with tickets to our friend's private island off the coast of Spain for a full week when *Blood Oath* wrapped filming in January, and the smile he'd given us had been worth every single penny and minute of time we'd spent on him in the past year of our lives.

There was no way we would ever be able to repay him for the way he'd healed our marriage. For the way he'd brought compassion and communication and *love* to our lives.

For the first time ever, I had no idea what the fuck I was doing or where this was going.

I was just *living.*

Enjoying.

Allowing the hedonist at the heart of me to thrive and imbibe and fucking love while I could.

Because even though I quelled the little voice at the back of my head that said *this will end*, I didn't want to believe it.

That was why I stole Sebastian's watch from him a week ago. A difficult feat because he wore it every day and took ridiculous and adorable care of it.

I'd returned it to him while we watched the match, sliding the cool rose gold into one of his wide palms.

"I thought I'd lost it," he admitted with a slight blush. "I thought I was going to be sick."

"I hope it was worth it. I wanted to make an addition that I hope you'll like very much."

August in London could be absolute shite, but it was a gorgeous day as if the world knew Sebastian deserved nothing less than perfect sunshine on his birthday. The light struck his face full-on as he turned to look at me, his eyes translucent yellow gems against his inky lashes.

"You already got me a present," he reminded me. "A very

extravagant one. I'm still miffed about it, Adam. I only gave you a picnic and surfing lessons. Lord only knows what I'll get Savvy in September."

I shrugged. "I'm older and wealthier than you, Sebastian. Don't try to compete with me in the gift-giving arena. I'll always win."

He grinned at me. "I take that as a challenge."

I only arched a brow and jerked my chin at the watch still in his hand. "Flip it over."

His head bent as he did so, reading the words I had engraved on the case.

Our impossible universe.

I wasn't surprised by the hiss of breath he sucked through his teeth. In fact, I'd been hoping for it.

Because even after all these months, I still hadn't said the words.

I love you.

So simple to speak, just three little, itty-bitty words that meant so fucking much.

That meant the world.

Sebastian lived in this impossible universe where he believed that the force of love could eradicate the seemingly insurmountable obstacle of everyone else's hate. It wasn't the universe we existed in, but it was absolutely the one I found myself dreaming about.

Sebastian's impossible universe.

And every day I spent with him, I wanted it with a greater and greater ferocity that seemed to eat up my insides.

All I could think was *one day.*

When we were old and done with our careers.

When the three of us could retire to a house in the South of France or the wilds of the Scottish Highlands or fucking Timbuktu for all I cared. Somewhere far away from the paps and the gossips and prying judgemental eyes.

Where we could love each other quietly, but openly until the end of time.

It wasn't much of a promise. Much of a life to offer a nineteen-year-old soon-to-be superstar.

But it was all I had, and I wanted it with all my heart and soul and every bloody breath I breathed each day.

For that to be enough for him.

For me to be enough for him.

The promise of that impossible universe one day.

"Adam…" he said, twisting in his seat to face me because Savannah was taking a call at the back of our private box. "What are you saying?"

"Today, I'm saying I love you." God, but the words felt carved from my very soul with a jagged knife. I winced as they came out, cut up and still bleeding. "It's not much because we'll only have… *this* for so long. But one day, I want exactly what you want."

"Which is?" he whispered as the crowd got to their feet around us, cheering for the goal King's Cross United had just scored to tie the game.

I took the risk of taking the watch back to put it on his wrist myself. My hands lingered over his, and I tapped the face with my nail as I looked into his eyes and said, "One day, I want your impossible universe to be our universe. I want to hold your hand and Savvy's on a beach walk. I want to kiss you when we go to the supermarket. I want to love you in all the quiet and mundane ways of daily life that we can't have right now. That… that we can't have for a while."

"How long is a while?" he asked, and he was *eager*, not judgemental, not scornful like I'd secretly feared.

"Until we retire?" I said like it was a joke, but of course, it was the truth, and it fell flat and broken between us.

"But you love me," he reiterated, eyes so bright I had to blink away the sunspots. "You *love* me today and tomorrow and until then."

"Until the end of time," I admitted.

"Then *Madonna mia*, Adam," he said empathetically, grabbing both my hands in his. "Of course, that's enough. That's fucking everything."

"Not exactly a love to move the sun and the stars," I admitted, feeling so fucking small that I hated it and had to fight the urge to remain open with him.

"Let me be the judge of that," he argued with that movie star grin that made breath arrest in my chest. "Because from where I'm sitting, only a love like that could survive the wait."

Fear pierced me sharp and narrow like a needle through the bullseye of my heart, right at the centre of my insecurities.

Because it wasn't only Sebastian whom I doubted. That he would stay after a year or two years or five, satisfied with a secret relationship when he was such an open, honest man.

It was also *me*.

Even now, there was this risk of discovery that made my hair stand on end and my heart drum too hard and too fast.

I'd witnessed secrets just like mine bubble to the surface and ruin lives.

Even end them.

Could I live with the fear I'd been living with every day until I was old and grey that someone would discover us, and everything would disintegrate like castles in the sand?

I hoped so.

Sebastian was teaching me to be brave and bold for myself and not just my characters, so maybe, if I worked tirelessly and was very, very careful, we could have this.

This dream that seemed like such a far-flung reality.

"Let's just love each other," Sebastian suggested, sensing my disquiet as he always did. "Let's just let that be enough for now."

"I do, you know," I said, a little urgently, too forceful. "Very much."

"I knew before you ever told me," he said with a wink. "You aren't the kind of man to faff about with something you're not completely obsessed with."

I laughed, startled and relieved enough to laugh a little too hard and too long. When Savvy came back, she merely raised an eyebrow and told Sebastian to get up and switch seats so she could sit neatly between us.

She didn't know in so many words that I loved him, but she was clever, my wife.

She knew.

And though she didn't say it again after their confession in the car that night after the BAFTAs, I knew she loved him too.

We'd be okay.

Hours later, I was proven very wrong.

BEFORE THAT DAY, THERE WERE THREE "worst moments of my life" that defined me more than I would've liked them to.

The first: losing my mother in the car crash that had her pinned behind the wheel, dying rapidly but not fast enough beside me in the driver's seat. I'd held her bloody hand while she died, her last words a slurring rush of "IloveyouIloveyouIloveyou" that I could hear in the echo of my heartbeat anytime I felt panic. No one should watch their mum die, but the trauma was compounded by the way my father reacted.

Stiff upper-lip British stoicism.

Even though he was obviously eviscerated by her death, he insisted we move on briskly and efficiently.

Within a week, all her things were packed up and sold off or disposed of, the empty spaces in the house glaring to my eleven-year-old gaze.

We weren't allowed to talk about her. The name Juliet scrubbed from our vocabulary as if she had never existed.

And then, ten months from the day, my father remarried a woman whom he'd courted for the past four months.

Within the span of a year, the memory of my mother was eradicated except for the special space I kept for her in my own heart.

Happily, I was sent to Eton shortly after and then Oxford after that.

Though the family purse supported me until graduation, I never returned home to visit him and his new wife.

And when I enlisted in the Royal Air Force to be with Arthur Whitley-Fairfax, the future King of England, because he was my brother more than Andrew had ever been my father, our last correspondence was the letter he sent me threatening to disown me if I risked my life so foolishly.

I didn't mention I was enlisting with the bloody Crown Prince of Britain and that our station was probably the safest place on earth because of it. It wasn't worth the breath it would have taken to reassure him.

The second was just as devastating but perhaps harder to categorize.

Arthur and I had another best mate in grade school at Eton, a lad by the name of Gregory Madison. The three of us were thick as thieves until our third-year in uni when suddenly Gregory stopped coming round.

Arthur and I both pretended we didn't know why, but we did.

The last time we'd seen Gregory, he'd been bent over the couch in his apartment, taking it from behind by an older bloke I recognized vaguely from the graduate library.

I didn't know why I didn't ring him and say "Hi, mate, no need to feel embarrassed. I bugger the occasional bloke too. Looks like we have more in common than we thought."

But I didn't ring him.

And then it was too late.

Because Greg decided to take his own life two days before graduation after he told his parents he was gay, and they told him they never wanted to see him again.

Arthur and I found him when we dropped round to drag him out for a pint to celebrate the end of our courses.

Whenever I needed to summon tragedy for a role, it was Gregory I thought about. The way his beautiful body had looked naked and pale as paper in the bath surrounded by bloody water and the glint of razor blades. The way I'd dropped to my knees hard on the tile and dragged him from the cold water into my lap to begin CPR that was much too late. The way Arthur had stood there utterly ashen, looking as close to death himself as he could get while still breathing.

This was the boy who'd encouraged me to join the school theatre group. He'd rode his bike to my mother's house in Chelsea, where I stayed during holidays, nearly every day to keep me company in the big house. The first lad I'd ever thought to fancy with his big grey eyes and coltish limbs, who bit his lower lip when he was nervous, which was often because he was sweet but shy.

The boy who'd been my best mate for more than half my life.

Dead in my arms because of the shame others had forced upon him.

When I enlisted that summer, I knew it was Arthur's way of running from the incident but also from his truth.

Not one of us three had been straight as an arrow, and Gregory's death stalked us like some dark, knife-sharp shadow. If it caught us, I don't think either of us knew what would happen.

When I met Bryce in the Air Force, I wasn't ready to accept any part of my bisexuality, but he was hard to resist. Stolen moments in empty barracks, weekend leave spent in hotel rooms we never left.

At first, when he was killed in action, I thought it was inevitable.

Of course, he would die.

That was what happened in these kinds of situations.

"These kinds of situations."

Like being gay or bi or pan was situational and not natural, fundamental.

Unchangeable.

By the time I met Savannah, I'd spent a good few years burying my sexuality in a long line of women.

Because I was so fucking afraid.

It felt inevitable that I would lose those I cared about: my mum, Greg, Bryce.

And that the odds increased exponentially if I loved them, and it was in their nature to love me too.

So the night I'd read Sebastian's screenplay, I'd been fucking terrified.

Because my wife was already entranced by him, and it was bloody impossible to say no to her.

But more, because for the first time since Bryce, I wanted to know a man beneath his muscle and bone. I was captivated by the makings of him and not his packaging.

Then, the moment I saw him stand on that Finborough stage, I'd felt blood-curdling terror.

Because he was brilliant.

Brilliant enough to chase those knife-wielding shadows away and lull me into a false sense of security.

They say getting old makes you wiser.

But that clearly wasn't the case.

I'd really thought I could do it.

Have my cake and eat it, too.

Be straight seeming but have my male lover on the side.

What a bloody fool.

I knew it the second the first football fan stopped us on our way out of the stadium to shout, "*Faggot*."

I wasn't even standing beside Sebastian.

Savannah was under my arm as we walked together toward the car, and Sebastian was following not too close behind.

But I knew with gut-clenching certainty.

Something had happened.

"Hey!" the bloke yelled again, red-faced with drink as he slapped his chum on the shoulder and pointed at me. "That's the actor snogging the bloke on the beach."

My blood ran cold. In fact, it felt as if it froze in my veins.

"Adam," Savannah said, quiet but urgent, ushering me now by the arm a little faster toward the car. "Come on, darling."

There was static in my ears like the radio cranked too loud through a tunnel pass. I couldn't hear beyond it even though I recognized Savvy was still talking to me as we reached the Rolls.

Sebastian appeared in my vision, and I flinched away from the sight of him.

Faggot!

"Not now. Get in the car." I watched Savannah mouth to him before opening the door and shoving me inside.

I went willingly, cold and drifting like some spirit through the ether. I imagined the graves of Gregory, Bryce, and my mother cropping up in the car park, empty graves with markers reserved for Sebastian and Savannah and myself beside them.

When Savannah got in on the other side, I said woodenly, "What is it, then?"

She was already on her phone, tapping away madly. When she froze, eyes wide on the screen, I winced at her curse.

She wasn't a woman who swore.

"Bad?" I asked, but I couldn't hear my own question through the static.

I stared at my hands, touched my fingers together experimentally and found I could not feel them.

She was talking to Sebastian, voice clipped, and then raising her phone to her ear to call someone.

Probably my agent and publicist.

Something touched my knee.

Sebastian.

I didn't flinch this time because I seemed to have lost sensation in my limbs.

"Here," Sebastian mouthed and pushed his phone into my hands.

I looked down at the grenade thrown into my life.

A single photo.

The latest article of *The Daily Spread.*

Adam Meyers Caught Kissing A Bloke!

We weren't kissing.

But we were closer than you saw most mates on most days.

The shot had been taken at Croyde Beach months ago, the day of my birthday when Sebastian had taken us to meet Linnea for surf lessons. We were in the shallows, laughing so hard our faces were creased and contorted. I remembered the moment vividly.

I'd just tackled Sebastian to the sand, pinning him there with my whole body and using my one hand to secure his hands above his head so I could smear wet sand on his face and chest.

The photo caught us body to body in the froth-frilled edge of the ocean with my hand above his head, the other pressed flat to his naked chest, and our faces too close together, smiling those bright, wild smiles that spoke of fierce, unguarded happiness.

I'd never seen such an expression on my face outside of films.

And some fucking sleaze had captured it and sold it to this drivel to derail my entire life for a few hundred quid.

"*FUCK!*" I roared, hurling the phone into the half-raised partition, where it cracked harshly and fell soundlessly to the carpet.

"Adam—" Sebastian said quietly.

"Shut up," Savannah snapped. "Both of you. I'm handling this."

We both quieted.

For my part, not because I cared about whoever she was talking to on the phone—I doubted they could do much to rectify the damage.

But because I was having a full-blown panic attack.

Air squeezed out of my lungs faster than I could replace it. My eyes and throat were too tight and dry. I raked my nails over my neck as I tried to rip open the shirt I was wearing to get more air. Blood trickled down my chest, but I didn't notice. Spots popped across my vision, black and growing larger by the second.

All I could focus on was trying to breathe through the pressure of guilt and shame and devastation pressing the life out of me.

"Savannah!" I heard vaguely. "He's having a fucking panic attack. Get his head between his legs."

Something pushed my head between my legs, but instead of comfort, the movement made me nauseated.

Seconds later, I threw up on my shoes.

"Jesus Christ," Savannah cried out as I retched and retched, unable to stop even when nothing was left in my rancid gut but yellow bile.

"Get him some water," Sebastian ordered, but Savvy stayed pressed to the other side of the car away from my sick.

I didn't blame her.

My head rested on my thigh, damp forehead against the cool fabric of my denim. My vision swam so I squeezed my eyes closed and grabbed the seat beneath me, trying to right the vertigo.

This couldn't be happening.

How could life be so cruel to kick me in the teeth when I'd *finally* found the courage to express exactly what I wanted out of life?

It wasn't even a choice, not really.

I couldn't live with the truth coming out.

I'd seen what had happened to other actors, how it upset the trajectory of their careers, but I couldn't deny in the safe recess of my own mind that it was so much more than that.

I'd seen the way censure had obliterated Gregory's spirit.

I'd lived through losing him and my mother and Bryce.

I couldn't live through the slow erosion of my relationship with Sebastian and Savannah because of the hate and judgment and lies they'd spin about us like an ever-tightening net. The way they'd take a love so fucking pure it was like fresh oxygen delivered straight to my veins and make it some kind of poison, something toxic for strangers to poke at and ridicule in the comments.

Everyone would hate us, and how could we insulate ourselves

from that?

All that hate would just make us hate each other.

And then I'd be left with no wife, no Sebastian, and no career.

But maybe… if they could withstand the fire… if they wanted to face it together…

"Omari and Georgie are getting ahead of this," Savannah's cool, professional voice cut through my spiralling thoughts. "They'll both meet us at The Savoy in twenty minutes."

"Why not the house?" Sebastian asked.

"It'll be surrounded by now."

"It's a gossip rag," Sebastian said, trying to catch my eye as I straightened to rest my head back against the seat. "Surely this will pass over without much fanfare."

My laugh was hollow and led to another retched gag.

"Nothing is trivial if it gets media attention. It didn't start with *The Daily Spread.* It's been picked up by most major entertainment outlets," Savannah corrected, fingers flying over the keyboard on her phone, brow furrowed. "We have to make sure we handle this indirectly without seeming to handle it at all."

"Why not just let it blow over?" he pushed, curious but also scared.

Scared of what it meant for him.

I gagged again behind my hand and closed my eyes, trying to find peace where there was none to be had.

Because of course, this meant one thing for Sebastian.

For us.

He needed to *go go go* and not come back.

There could be no more photos of us at football matches or hanging out with Andrea at local wine bars. There could be no more intimacy behind closed doors because there would be no more privacy.

The British paparazzi were the worst in the world.

They'd scale walls and pay off garbage men. They'd flood the street of our house for days just hoping to confirm that the man in the salacious photo with Adam Meyers in fact lived on the same grounds as them.

They'd say Savannah was my beard, and Sebastian was my illicit lover.

It would tarnish *The Devil Cares* entire media cycle, destroying credibility for one of my career's best performances and films.

I'd been in negotiations to play Fitzwilliam Darcy in the remake of *Pride & Prejudice*, a role I'd been dying to get my hands on since I'd started acting, and that would go up in smoke *tomorrow* if this didn't go away quickly.

Mr. Darcy was a timeless romantic figure.

They wanted Adam Meyers, in love with his wife, handsome and straight-laced and *straight* to play the role.

"Adam, *breathe*."

I nearly jumped out of my skin because suddenly Sebastian was in the open door crouched beside me, lightly slapping my cheek to get my attention.

Contrary to his edict, I found I'd forgotten how to draw breath at all.

"Come on, *vecchietto*, don't give out on me now. *Breathe*, dammit. Like this." He took my numb hand and flattened it to his chest as he breathed in an exaggerated fashion. "Like this."

My vision flickered in and out. I hoped it would cut out completely and I could wake up in a different reality than this. My gaze snagged on the rose gold watch on his wrist, and without thinking, I reached out to grasp it. It was cool to the touch, Sebastian's skin warm. I could feel his pulse thrumming away madly, and it, more than anything, brought me slightly to my senses.

Because I knew with stomach-plummeting certainty that this would be the last time I held him.

"Adam," he whispered brokenly, eyes scouring my face. "Where have you gone?"

"Back to reality," I said, surprised by the sound of my voice.

"Come back to me," he said urgently, and I realized we had pulled into the back of the hotel where there was no access for the press. Savannah was outside the car speaking to the hotel manager while texting on her phone. "We can get through this."

I flinched at the *we* because of how funny it sounded now.

How childish.

I watched detached as Sebastian's eager, earnest expression dissolved molecule by molecule into something that made my heart ache as if it had been dipped in acid.

"Don't do this," he said, grip tightening on my frozen hands. "Don't you remember what you said only sixty minutes ago? Don't you remember promising me *one day*?"

"One day can't happen now," I said, but I was watching myself from high above our heads, as if the whole thing was happening to someone else.

Was this how Gregory felt when we walked in on him?

Exposed and turned inside out for everyone to leer at?

"Adam," Sebastian called harshly. "Look at me. This will go away."

"It won't if you don't. It won't because now there is speculation. Every time we are seen together, someone will dig up this photo, and rumors will swirl. This will stalk us our entire careers if we don't stop it now."

"You mean if Omari and Georgie don't get ahead of it?" he asked, but we both knew the answer.

It was written in the heartbreak dawning over his features, turning the gold of his eyes to wet sand, heavy and dark.

Shaking my head felt like moving ten tons of bricks, but I must have been successful because he winced, run through by the simple movement.

"I won't beg you," he warned, so proud even now, shoulders strong, chin tipped up at that haughty angle he'd adapted from my wife. "I shouldn't have to. You promised me one day we'd live in our impossible universe, but until then, we'd be together however the hell we could in *this* one. And at the first sign of trouble, you bail on it?"

I blinked at him, the words and emotions I'd felt so acutely when I'd seen the picture purged from my body when I'd vomited. Now, I was just a hollow aching shell.

"I will love you in *every* universe," he told me fiercely, a declaration of war as much as it was one of love. That he was willing to fight for me when I was not. That he was brave and filled with enough conviction to hone it into armor against all the judgements of the world.

For one crystalline second, it made me waver.

If he could bear the strain, couldn't I?

If he set the example, I could follow because it meant I wouldn't have to lose him to the fear and hatred around us.

But then Savannah appeared behind him and placed a hand on his shoulder.

"Let's go upstairs."

As was our habit, we followed her. There was sick on my shoes, but there was no one at the back entrance to notice, and the service elevator took us up to a floor that had obviously been cleared for us.

The click of the lock opening under the key card in Savannah's hand seemed to echo through the empty place.

None of us spoke.

Not even when we filtered into the gorgeous room and took up positions away from each other. But no matter how far apart we were, we remained three points of the same triangle.

"Adam wants me out," Sebastian told my wife combatively, daring her to agree. "He thinks it's the only way. Tell him how absurd that is."

I closed my eyes, turning my head away.

Because I *knew* what she would say.

Sebastian didn't because he'd always have rose-colored glasses on when it came to my wife. I'd watched her put them on him and kept quiet.

Because I wanted to look at her that way, too, despite evidence that illustrated her otherwise.

"It's probably for the best," she said softly, almost inaudibly.

I felt Sebastian's shock like a nuclear blast, rocking me back on my heels so I had to brace myself against the fireplace mantel.

"*Scusa*?" he breathed, reverting to Italian in his surprise.

"Just for a while," she amended. "You shouldn't be seen with him. But we can put you up somewhere, and you and I can still make time… it's just dangerous for this to continue with Adam. For… a while, at least."

"For a while," he repeated with a rough laugh that scored through me.

It didn't sound a thing like him.

"*Vaffanculo!* You Brits love your ambiguity," he insulted. "What the fuck does that mean? You put me up in some hotel like a cheap mistress until I can come home again?"

Home.

Through the glacial ice that had formed over my soul in the last half hour, I heard a great creaking *crack* in my ears, and a second of searing pain lashed through my chest.

He thought of us as home.

And we were taking that from him.

Nearly a full year of life together with him as ours, and we were ripping it all asunder.

For good reason, for the right reasons.

Even if he didn't understand now in his youthful ignorance, he would understand later.

In five years or ten.

It was best to avoid the inevitable bitterness and hatred that would settle between us over time.

A quick, violent end was better than a slow death by a thousand cuts.

"Don't be immature. Not now," Savannah scolded. "We can't have you two associated with each other this way when there is so much on the line."

"My heart is on the line!" he shouted, thumping himself viciously across the chest. "What more is there to care about?"

"The career we've worked so hard to launch?" she suggested icily. "The career Adam has worked at for years. His passion. *My* passion."

"Am I not your passion, too, then?" he asked, quivering with anger and hurt, a stuck bull caged in a space too small for everything roiling through him. "Am I so easily cast aside at the first sign of trouble?"

"I can still see you, my love," she said, the ice queen act cracking for a moment as she stepped forward, arms outstretched to him, hope stark across her face. "We'll have to be careful, but there won't be as many eyes on us as there would be on you and Adam."

It was cruel to all of us, what she was proposing.

For them to continue without me was worse than losing him altogether. The idea of catching his scent on her blouse, seeing the bruise of his mouth against her breasts… it would be a knife through the chest every time.

For us both, I thought.

But Savannah had never been good at giving up what she wanted, the consequences be damned.

Sebastian was already shaking his head, but he stepped forward too, taking her hands and dragging her roughly against his chest.

"Come with me, then," he coaxed. "Adam won't face the music to be together, but you could."

"Change the narrative… make him a cuckold instead of a homosexual?" Savannah actually mused.

He flinched, checking her face to make sure she wasn't joking.

She wasn't. I could have told him, but I didn't.

"I don't care about the narrative," he said slowly, bending down to look her in the eye. "I care about you. Both of you."

"Of course," she soothed. "But it's not a bad idea."

I'd had enough.

Enough of Savannah acting like my manager instead of my fucking wife.

Enough of seeing Sebastian fight for us when I knew he would only fail.

Savannah would never leave me for him, and he didn't understand that.

Even my star power was growing stale for her, and Sebastian was just on the cusp of success himself. She couldn't be satisfied with that even if she was satisfied by us in her heart and her body.

For her, it would always be about the mind.

And what Sebastian and I could give her.

"Get out."

They both looked at me, caught in their dramatic cinch, surprised to see me standing straight and tall.

"Get the fuck out," I told Sebastian coldly, allowing every frozen over particle to infuse my voice. "And you will not be taking my wife with you. This is over."

"Adam," Sebastian said, stepping away from my wife and toward me, every feature falling to such abject despair it was beautiful.

Beautiful because he *loved* me.

In every universe.

And it still wasn't enough.

I'd been a fool before to think such foolish thoughts as love conquered all.

The world wasn't built to run on such lies.

"Go to the house and collect your things. We expect you gone by this time tomorrow when we get home."

He stopped midway between Savannah and me, hands held up and open in benediction.

"Why are you doing this?" he asked coarsely. "You know we can get through this."

"This is only one moment in thousands," I corrected. "It will happen again and again, and the more we fight it, the more we confirm it. This has to end, and it will. Now."

"An hour ago, you loved me," he accused.

An hour from now I'll love you still, I thought.

"Not enough," I said.

Tears pooled in his eyes but didn't fall. He stared at me for so long, searching for secrets I refused to tell. He was so attuned to emotion that I wondered if he could see how gross my lies were, but after a minute, he seemed to buy them.

And a tiny portion of my soul I'd never recoup broke off and crumbled to dust.

Finally, he turned slightly to look at Savannah, who stood with her hands clasped before her hips. You had to look very closely to see the way they trembled.

"Savvy, *duchessa*," he said gently, holding his hand out for her. "Come with me."

She sucked in a small breath and rolled her lips between her teeth.

She wanted to go with him. Some small but profound part of her wanted to be swept away by our teenage romantic and forget about the foundation she'd built her life and sense of self on for so many years.

Maybe when she was younger, she would have gone.

Maybe some part of me wanted her to.

"No," she whispered.

Sebastian stepped back like he'd been shot, one hand pressing hard to his chest to stem the blood flow. His head dropped as if his spine had been cut off at the neck.

He stared at the floor for a long moment and then said, "Right. This was how it was always going to end."

"Yes," I said to make it easier for him. "Now, get out."

I hoped he'd hate me, that the teeth of that rage would break apart any love left in his heart and make it easier to digest and expel.

I hoped that he'd recover from this.

He was young and beautiful and full of love so I had to believe he would.

We wouldn't.

Savvy and me.

But he didn't need to know that.

And when he turned on his heel abruptly and stalked toward the door, tears streaking back along his cheeks, I knew he never would.

Savannah and I were masters of deception.

Maybe we'd even lie well enough to deceive ourselves.

It was certainly something to hope for.

The door slammed shut behind him.

A vase of flowers on the entryway trembled at the force. I walked forward instinctively to settle it, but the moment my hand touched the ceramic, I threw it across the room at the same door still vibrating in its frame.

"FUCK!" I roared.

I stared at the shattered pieces of clay and crushed petals until I heard the choked sound of muffled sobs behind me. When I faced her, Savannah had both hands cupped over her mouth, her eyes wide like she couldn't believe she was crying so hard.

I sighed, my body heavy as I moved across the floor to my wife.

When I wrapped my arms around her, she flung hers around my neck and stopped trying to muffle her cries.

It made it easier to give in to the tears myself.

Because even though we held each other like we'd never let go, I had the bone-deep feeling it wouldn't be long before we said goodbye to each other, too.

Epilogue

Sebastian

The moon was full in the sky, a brilliant glowing nimbus of white gold in an otherwise ink-dark sky. I stared out at the bedroom window at its silver face, trying to keep my thoughts empty and fixed on that one mark.

Otherwise, I'd fall to pieces.

And I'd only just gotten myself together to pack up all my things at the Meyers's Chelsea home.

I'd arrived there with a single duffel bag, and I was leaving with ten boxes stuffed to the gills.

Chaucer had been there waiting for me with packing tape and stacked cardboard. Her expression was wilted, a little sad and a little arrogant as if she'd told me so.

In a way she had.

Actors, she'd said, like she wouldn't touch them with a ten-foot pole.

In the future, if I ever found the heart to date again, I'd make that my rule, too.

"I'm sorry," she'd murmured after half an hour of working silently side by side to disassemble my life as I knew it. "It's not right, what they do."

I blinked at her. "Polyamory isn't wrong, Chaucer."

She rolled her eyes. "I'm not some backwoods hick. I meant, the way they take and take until there's nothing left."

"I had more left," I said automatically, feeling the mass of love I had for them in my chest like I was overstuffed with it and bursting at the seams of my skin. "I had two lifetimes worth left for them."

"So you really loved them, then?"

My laugh was a bitter little cough. "Does it matter anymore?"

She shrugged, sitting on the bed I rarely used in the carriage house folding my clothes. I liked her casualness. Being friends was easy because she made everything easy. No judgement, no games, just the offer of a friendly chat over tea when we had the chance or a stroll to the park when it was a rare lovely day. Even freshly torn in two with heartbreak, she acted like everything was okay, or at least, that it would be.

In an odd way, I appreciated that over sympathy.

I needed to get this done and get the hell out of there before I imploded in on the black hole Adam and Savannah had left in my gut.

"I don't think they ever loved any of the others. If that helps. It was also very businesslike and proper. They certainly never slept over in the big house." She bit her lip, smoothing the folds of one of the suits Savannah had bought me. "I've worked with Adam for five years, and I've never seen him so at ease with himself. I've worked with Savannah for five years, and I've never seen her act human with anyone, not even him until you. I think you made them *real,* and I think they'd forgotten how to do that."

I swallowed convulsively, trying to rid the stone lodged in my throat. "It doesn't matter now," I reiterated, trying to convince myself.

"You're a kid," she pointed out even though she was only a few years older than me. "You'll find love again."

"No," I whispered because I knew myself well enough to know the mechanics of my heart. It was the one constant in my life of inconstancy. "Even if you can't always see the moon and the stars in the night sky, they still exist."

"Poetic, but don't be so dramatic. You're nineteen. There will be others. People who actually have the emotional capacity to love you back."

My smile was a thin slice across my face, sharp and painful. She didn't understand like I did that the Meyerses *did* love me back. In fact, I knew in my bones they loved me just as desperately as I loved them.

The difference between us wasn't love.

It was courage.

Something the nineteen-year-old Italian had in spades that the much older, wiser, and famous duo seemed to be utterly lacking.

Even though rage flickered at the edge of my sorrow, a small part of me was convinced it was something more than that for Adam. The way he'd reacted had been too acute, a trigger for past trauma more than a fresh response to the scandal.

Something like this had happened before, maybe.

Something worse.

If he'd let me, I could have carried some of that weight for him. I could have helped him lay it all out on the floor to organize it properly and painfully piece by piece until it didn't hurt him so badly.

But he didn't trust me enough, or maybe himself enough, to do it.

And so here I was.

Packing up my shit only hours after he'd finally told me he loved me.

After he'd inscribed my watch like a fucking blood oath, promising me to be there at the end in all the ways we both wanted to be there for each other.

Pain sliced through me like a blade cutting through butter, top to toe.

I swayed, and Chaucer caught me by the elbow.

Her wide eyes were filled with concern in her freckled face as she stared up at me.

"Are you going to be okay?" she asked softly. "You don't look good."

Heartbreak didn't look good on anyone, I thought.

"Eventually," I said.

"Where will you go?"

As if on cue, which wouldn't have surprised me given who I knew waited outside for me, a honk sounded.

"Andrea's. He doesn't know the details, so I'm not sure he'll let me stay. If not, I'll get a hotel. The Meyerses did pay me to be their driver."

"You could stay with me," she offered hesitantly. "If you need to."

Warmth licked at the edges of my cold heart. "That would be very awkward for you."

She shrugged. "I've been thinking about a career change anyway."

My laugh was a mere exhale, but I was still grateful to her. "I won't put you in that position, but don't forget my phone number, *sí*? I'd like to stay friends. Have one person who knows what happened here."

"I'm happy to be the tombstone marking that grave," she said solemnly, with a twitch to her mouth. She shifted her arm to my waist and wrapped me in a tight hug. "I'll miss you around here. And not just because they'll be unbearable without you."

I squeezed her back, dipping to kiss the top of her red head. She reminded me a little of my sisters, and I took comfort from it. "*Grazie*, Chaucer. I'll text when I'm settled."

Moving away from her, I grabbed the folded note I'd left on the dresser and pressed it into her hand.

"Can you give that to Savannah when you get a chance?"

It wasn't cool of me to ask her, but I had to.

Because I wasn't willing to give up on her.

She might not have come with me that night in the thick of it, but she wasn't the type of woman to leave her husband in the middle of a crisis.

It didn't mean she wouldn't leave him at all.

I knew, looking at her gorgeous, brokenhearted face, that she'd *wanted* to say yes.

All I could hope for was that one day she would.

The note said: *Vivi la tua vita senza rimpianti, duchessa. Ti aspetto.*

Live your life without regrets, Duchess. I'll be waiting.

It was all I would do.

Both of them knew who I was and what I wanted.

A love that moved the sun and the stars.

And if they didn't feel that way…

Well then, I wouldn't see either of them ever again.

Tears burned the backs of my eyes, but I didn't let them fall as I collected the last two boxes and went down the stairs where the rest of them waited by the open door. Andrea had already started to move them to his car, and he was on a return trip when my feet hit the landing.

"Sebastian, *amico mio*, you look like hell," he stated plainly, fisting his hands on his hips as he studied me.

A broken laugh escaped my mouth, and I gave a little shrug. "I've seen better days."

"It's your birthday," he reminded me, and honestly, I'd forgotten since the day had been derailed, but it made sense in a way.

Last year, I'd said goodbye to Cosima on our birthday.

This year, I said goodbye to Savannah and Adam.

I swallowed thickly and shrugged again because it was all I had to offer.

Andrea's lips thinned. "*Bene, andiamo.* Get the last of the boxes, and we will leave."

I nodded, following him mutely as we efficiently packed the rest of my things into his Lamborghini Urus SUV. When we were done, I turned back to the cottage one last time and committed it to memory. Chaucer stood in the doorway hugging herself, but she lifted a hand when I opened the passenger door, and I reciprocated before closing it on my life as I'd known it for the past year.

Andrea didn't say a word. He put on a playlist through the speakers, snorting a little under his breath when *un anno d'amore* started playing. When he moved to change it, I knocked his hand away and settled comfortably against the window, staring out into the dark streets and up at that glowing face of the moon.

"I take it you'll be staying with me until we leave for New York," my friend said after some time when we were racing through the outskirts of London on our way to his hamlet in the countryside.

"If you'll have me. I know Adam is a friend, and we met through him. I'm not sure what this means for you now that our… friendship has ended. If you're still committed to *Blood Oath*—"

"Let me stop you right there, *ragazzo*," he insisted, holding up a hand. "If I stopped projects the moment someone had a falling out with someone else, I'd never film a movie. I am not trivializing what you have been through, but this happens in an industry where sex and ego are rampant, hmm? Do not worry about me. I fell in love with *Blood Oath* before I met you, and now, we are friends, *sì*? Neither have anything to do with Adam Meyers."

"He's a producer," I pointed out.

He shrugged in that same way I had, one shoulder quirked casually. "He's also an idiot. I doubt either will change because of some silly gossip."

My sigh exploded from my slack mouth. "You saw?"

"I am a film director. I heard because it is my business to have my fingers to the pulse."

I waited for him to say more, and when he didn't, I pressed, "Well, don't you want to ask me about it?"

"If you would like to," he offered flippantly. "But I do not care if Adam Meyers kissed a bloke nor do I care if that bloke was you. I care about the hearts and minds of my friends. So if you need to tell me about what happened, I will listen. However, I suggest we wait until we reach the house because I believe this calls for good wine or grappa. But if you want to never speak of this with me, then, that is okay, too, Sebastian."

He slanted me a look, mouth curling slightly at my shocked expression. "This is friendship," he said in Italian. "To me, this is what it means. Being here for you however you need me because your grief is yours alone until you want to share it."

"Thank you," I whispered, trying not to cry for the millionth time that night. At this point, my eyes were so dry from their effort that my lids felt like sandpaper. "I think for now, I don't want to speak of it. It's too… raw."

"*Bene*," he said as if the matter was closed. "We will thank our lucky stars that we met, no matter who introduced us, and we will focus our considerable efforts on creating the best movie the world has ever seen, shall we?"

Despite everything that had happened in the past few hours, I found myself grinning at him. Because I might have lost Adam and Savannah, but I hadn't lost everything.

I still had the friends I'd made, Chaucer, Linnea, and Andrea.

I still had my family, even if we were scattered across the world.

And I still had other dreams.

Ones *I* was in control of seeing come true.

Was there any other cure for heartbreak as healing as throwing yourself into work?

I was ready to find out.

And if I wondered secretly whether Savannah and Adam would see my meteoritic rise to fame and fortune and wonder forevermore if they'd made the worst mistake of their lives, well, that was a secret I'd keep just for me.

IN THE NEXT FEW WEEKS, THINGS moved quickly, even though my wounds healed at a glacial pace.

Andrea and I moved to New York City to film *Blood Oath.*

Elena and Mama came with us.

Using some of my savings and money Cosima sent from a particularly lucrative modelling contract, we put a down payment on a small brownstone in Little Italy for them. Andrea had an old friend who ran one of the best Italian kitchens in the city who gave Mama a job, and Elena was accepted in the law program at NYU.

They were safe and happy.

Knowing I'd played a part in that helped fill some of the bottomless pit the Meyerses had carved out of my soul as I worked tirelessly on the passion project they'd set into motion for me. I poured all the angst and turmoil and anger they'd left me with into my role as Roberto. It was healing only a little more than it was painful. Being on set of the film they'd both believed in so profoundly reopened my wounds every single day.

But it meant I gave the performance of a lifetime.

Or at least, that was what Andrea said every time we went over the dailies together.

Honestly, I had to agree with him.

We were just finishing filming in Naples four months after I'd left behind my life in England when the news broke.

Savannah Meyers had filed for divorce from her megastar husband, Adam Meyers.

My heart stopped clean in my chest for so long, I worried it wouldn't start again.

But when it did with a shuddering jolt, it beat harder and faster than it had in weeks.

Because I thought I knew what this meant.

She was coming for me.

My note had hit its mark, my love had left an indelible tattoo on her heart, and my *duchessa* was coming for me.

I waited for her to arrive every day for the rest of the week of filming in Naples, leaving orders with the crew to send her directly to my trailer.

When she didn't come, I figured she was waiting for me to wrap up filming. As a consummate professional, that would be important to her.

I returned to New York City and waited some more.

I woke up with her name in my mouth and went to sleep dreaming of her clothed only in moonlight approaching the side of my bed with open arms.

Six weeks passed, and she did not come.

Finally, I reached out to Chaucer to ask her if she knew anything.

My friend had, unsurprisingly, decided to stay working for Adam instead of Savannah after the split, but last she had heard, Savvy was moving to America.

My heart beat faster. I could taste the metallic surge of adrenaline on my tongue every time my phone rang or my email pinged.

Still, nothing.

And then, two weeks after that, I was out for dinner with Cosima who had recently moved to the city for good, when I noticed I caught a faint whiff of lilac and freesia.

Instantly, my heart moved into my throat, and I lifted my gaze from my sister to scan the restaurant.

"Are you looking for someone?" Cosi asked with a teasing lilt.

Her usually bright yellow eyes had been stale since she moved to the city, but they were crinkled now with mirth.

"I thought I smelled something," I said before I realized how that sounded and winced.

Her laughter soothed my nerves. "Ah, so you're looking for a woman. Of course. Well, one just walked behind you to that table over there."

She tipped her chin over my shoulder with a coy smile half-hidden behind a wine glass.

My breath crystalized with hope in my lungs as I turned slowly to face where she indicated.

And there she was.

Savannah Meyers in the middle of a posh New York City restaurant looking every inch *la duchessa.* Her short, pale blonde cloud of hair was curled into a soft halo around her delicate face, blue eyes bright even from halfway across the room. She was wearing her iconic white, a cashmere cream dress that accentuated her slight curves, and those red-soled boots I'd watched her buy one day in Harrods last year.

The sight of her punched a hole straight through my chest.

She was *here.*

And while she didn't appear to know I was in the restaurant, that didn't mean she wasn't in town to find me.

Finally.

"I should go say—" I started to excuse myself to my sister.

But then I noticed the man striding through the tables to meet her.

He was tall and thickly built like a retired linebacker but elegant in his three-piece suit with a head of thick silver hair.

Tate Richardson.

The man Savannah had lunch with and kissed too intimately on the cheek.

A kiss like a love note.

And here he was, stalking across the restaurant to claim her, which he did with a proprietary hand on her chin to tip her face for his kiss.

Savannah reached a hand up to hold her to him.

And a massive fucking diamond ring winked at me under the thousand lights of the chandeliers in the restaurant.

A ring that I knew was *not* her old engagement ring from Adam.

That ring had been understated and refined, not too big but absolutely beautiful.

This had to be five carats, an enormous rock that called attention to it like a beacon.

And it had mine completely.

I might have made a sound or maybe the reverberation of my shock could be felt across the entire restaurant because when Savannah pulled away from the kiss, her gaze snagged on mine.

I watched as expressions flipped like a stop-motion film across her features: shock, joy, hesitancy, fear, and obstinacy.

We stared at each other across a space cluttered with fashionable diners and clanking ceramics for much too long for propriety, but neither of us moved.

I didn't breathe and I wasn't sure I blinked.

Because there she was like an apparition from my dreams, but she wasn't there for me.

She wasn't even there for Adam.

She was with a new man.

Engaged to a new man.

Without a word, without an explanation, she had moved on from us both.

What was left of the hope I'd harboured those long months expelled from my body in a gusty sigh as she wrenched her gaze away from me and sat down in the chair her fiancé held out for her.

He sat down across from her, reached for her hand, and she gave it to him with a smile.

She didn't look at me again.

"Sebastian," Cosima called, reaching for my own numb hand. "What's happened?"

How was I supposed to share the dismantling of my entire universe with her?

How was I supposed to explain that I'd lost my dream and, in doing so, had lost the ability to be a dreamer myself?

I stared down at the watch I wore every single day that she and

Adam had given me and woodenly took it off my wrist.

"Excuse me," I said to a passing server. "Could you please give this to the woman sitting at the table near the back with her fiancé? She'll know what it means."

He looked unsurprised by my request, but I didn't watch him deliver it. Instead, I left a handful of bills on the table and left mid-meal to take my sister to a different restaurant for dessert.

She didn't complain.

But then, she had her own heartbreak in her eyes, so I thought she understood.

The End For Now.

Thanks Etc.

I've been waiting to write Sebastian's story since I was a teenager and first conceived of the Lombardi family. At first, it was an MF story set in New York about a down-on-her-luck woman and our Sebastian, a famous actor and director, who discovers her on the streets and puts her in his new film. While the kernel of this idea remains in the trilogy, it expanded into so much more without my consciously deciding to change the story. When I wrote the first few chapters of *The Moon & His Tides* as a short story titled *Intimo*, in 2018, Adam exploded onto the page and demanded his right to be with Sebastian, too. And, like Sebastian, I was helpless to resist his pull. To be honest, I didn't try very hard because MMF stories are some of my very favourite.

This love story is a complicated one and it does end on a dreaded cliffhanger. *The Sun & Her Burn* takes place ten years in the future, a favourite method of storytelling for me, and the circumstances of the love story change dramatically. I cannot wait to give you more of Sebastian, Adam, Savannah, and Linnea in book two coming soon!

Until then, I want to thank all the people who make my career and my life possible!

To Annette, my assistant and feisty fairy, who problem solves, organizes, and generally helps me live my life every day. Thank you for being so positive all the time, for loving me so well, and always supporting me with everything you are.

To Georgana Grinstead, my agent and publicist extraordinaire, who helps to make my wildest dreams of success come true. You are not only always in my corner advocating for me professionally, but also personally. I am so grateful to have you in my life in all ways and I'll always love you.

To Jess, thank you for joining Team Giana and making such a big difference to my work/life balance. I value your insight into my business just as I value you so much as a friend. I love to think about how long we've known each other and where we are at now. Thank God King and Zeus brought us together.

To Valentine, my Baby Darling and bestie. Sometimes you just meet someone and know instantly they are the absolute best kind of human and you want them permanently installed in your life. I knew after our Nashville trip that you were that person for me and I'm so grateful for your friendship. You always make me laugh, support me when I'm unsure, and just generally enrich my life with your amazingness.

To Najla and Nada at Qamber Designs, thank you for the gorgeous covers of this series and the teasers you made. You always know exactly how to bring my vision of my characters and their stories to life.

To Cat, my love, at TRC Designs who takes my abstract concepts for discreet covers and spins them into pure freaking gold! Thank you for creating these stunning ideas for The Impossible Universe series and for being such an amazing collaborator always.

To Jenny and Erica, my editors extraordinaire, thank you for always being so supportive, positive, and excited about my words. Working with you both is honestly a dream and I'm so grateful to have your skilled eyes on my works making them the best they can be.

To Sarah, thank you for proofing my stories and always promoting and loving my books.

Becca, my love, for being my best girl and always making me believe in myself even when I suddenly spiral. You're a rock for me and it means the world I have a steady place to rest my worries in you.

Sarah, @booksbatsandbrushes, my best Aussie girl, your friendship brightens my every day. Your artistry, the reels you send, the way you make me laugh, it all inspires me and makes each day easier to get through.

My Darlings, who are my safe space on the internet and a place I can go every time I need a smile or a reminder that people care about the stories I tell. Thank you for being so positive and supportive all the time. I'm so in debt to you all for making my dreams come true.

Poppies, thank you for being the best street team ever! You make a world of difference in my career and it means so much to me.

Em, who runs @fansofgianadarling on IG, thank you for being my fangirl and ride-or-die supporter!

Brittany, I love you and that's the beginning and end of it. I love going through the wild, crazy bookish world with you and knowing I can always count on you for life advice.

Kandi, for inspiring me every day with your creativity, work ethic, bright spirit, and beauty. Thank you for being such a wonderful friend.

To my girls—Fiona, Lauren, Madison, Armie, Bridget, Lisa—for inspiring me to write strong, sassy, hilarious, and cunning women who don't take any shit. Knowing and loving you has been a highlight of my life.

To my boys—Al, Devo, Kev, Sam, Chrissy, C-Pain, Jeffery—thank you for making me a part of this group. Twenty to fifteen years of friendship is no small feat and I'm grateful every day that life saw fit to give us to each other.

To my sister, Grace, who has always been a person I can count on to believe in my dreams and shout with joy when I find success. You are the best big sister ever.

And last but never least, my husband, the absolute love of my life and joy of my every day. Mr. Darling, sometimes I can't breathe for loving you and I'm constantly in awe that fate placed the kindest, handsomest, most loyal and lovely man I know in my path for me to find and love from now until forever.

Other Books by Giana Darling

The Evolution of Sin Trilogy

Giselle Moore is running away from her past in France for a new life in America, but before she moves to New York City, she takes a holiday on the beaches of Mexico and meets a sinful, enigmatic French businessman, Sinclair, who awakens submissive desires and changes her life forever.

The Affair
The Secret
The Consequence
The Evolution Of Sin Trilogy Boxset

The Fallen Men Series

The Fallen Men are a series of interconnected, standalone, erotic MC romances that each feature age gap love stories between dirty-talking, Alpha males and the strong, sassy women who win their hearts.

Lessons in Corruption
Welcome to the Dark Side
Good Gone Bad

After the Fall

Inked in Lies

Dead Man Walking

Caution to the Wind

Asking for Trouble

A Fallen Men Companion Book of Poetry:
King of Iron Hearts

The Enslaved Duet

The Enslaved Duet is a dark romance duology about an eighteen-year-old Italian fashion model, Cosima Lombardi, who is sold by her indebted father to a British Earl who's nefarious plans for her include more than just sexual slavery… Their epic tale spans across Italy, England, Scotland, and the USA across a five-year period that sees them endure murder, separation, and a web of infinite lies.

Enthralled (The Enslaved Duet #1)

Enamoured (The Enslaved Duet #2)

The Elite Seven Series

Sloth (The Elite Seven Series #7)

Standalones

Serpentine Valentine

About Giana Darling

Giana Darling is a *USA Today*, *Wall Street Journal*, Top 40 bestselling Canadian romance writer who specializes in the taboo and angsty side of love and romance. She currently lives in beautiful British Columbia where she spends time riding on the back of her man's bike, baking pies, and reading snuggled up with her cat, Persephone, and dog, Romeo.

Printed in Great Britain
by Amazon

57396195R00215